THE
# DUSK GATE CHRONICLES
BOOK SIX

# LEAVES
## OF REVOLUTION

## BREEANA PUTTROFF

FIRST EDITION
ISBN 13: 9781940481142

~~~~~~~~~~~

Cover Design: Mallory Rock

Formatting & Layout: Mallory Rock

~~~~~~~~~~~

Thirteen Pages Press
P.O. BOX 350944
DENVER, CO 80035

*Leaves of Revolution: The Dusk Gate Chronicles Book 6* is a work of fiction. Names, characters, places and incidents are products of the author's imagination, or the author has used them fictitiously.

*To my amazing Dusk Gate readers – you've made my dream of sharing stories come true.*

*Thank you so much for helping bring Quinn, William, Thomas, Linnea, Zander and the rest to life!*

# PREPARATIONS

"COME IN," ZANDER YELLED toward the door of his apartment as he walked out of his bedroom. "Oh, hi Mia."

"Hello, Sir Zander. I brought your clothes for the ceremony."

He managed to stifle his eye-roll before she saw — she was never going to stop calling him that. "Thank you," he said instead, reaching for the hanger she held toward him. "I would have thought you'd be too busy this morning with everyone else to be bothered with small jobs like this. I can take care of myself."

She raised an eyebrow. "You'd have shown up at the ceremony in what you're wearing."

"Is there something wrong with what I'm wearing?" He glanced down at his tan pants and the nicest top he'd acquired since coming here — a light blue wool sweater. He'd even ironed the pants with a strange metal contraption that had to be heated over the fireplace.

"Ordinarily, no. But you're an honored guest of the king and queen today. You'll need those." She nodded toward the hanger and then looked up at him, frowning at his damp hair. "I was going to send someone in to heat the bathwater for you, but I see you've taken care of it already. You don't have to do everything yourself, you know."

He shrugged. "What else do I have to do? I'm fine, Mia, but thank you."

"You're expected in the main hall in an hour."

"I'll be there."

"You'll ask if I can do anything else for you?"

"I'm not making any promises."

Shaking her head, she chuckled softly. "All right then, I'll see you downstairs."

Once she was gone, he carried the heavy wooden hanger into his room and laid the garment bag across his bed before untying the ribbon and pulling back the cover. He sighed. The white silk button-down shirt would have been one thing, but the green velvet tunic-thing to wear over it… He wasn't ready for that.

The black slacks, of course, were pressed far more neatly than he would ever be able to manage. Perhaps Mia was right – he should be grateful to live in a castle with servants who were happy to take care of things.

He made it downstairs less than forty-five minutes later, only to discover he was far from the first one there.

"Zander," Thomas said, walking over to meet him as he reached the bottom step, "I was just on my way up to find you."

"Why? I thought I was early."

"You are. I just thought maybe you would want the company."

"Oh." He still wasn't used to any of this – this place, these people, these *clothes*. Thomas' outfit was just as startling to him as his own. He wore the same kind of silk shirt and black pants as Zander, but there was a purple velvet cape over Thomas' shoulders, secured at the neck with a silver pin. "Thanks anyway. Is there anything I can help with?"

"We're just trying to keep the children from destroying too much while they finish readying the carriages."

Zander looked around. The youngest princes and princesses of Eirentheos were scattered about the hall, chattering and playing, though they were hardly destroying anything. Since the arrival of both royal families at the Philothean castle two days ago, Quinn and William had set the servants to work transforming the rooms and halls to a more child-friendly environment. Breakable vases and artwork had been moved to out-of-the-way places or stored and replaced with wooden and metal decorations.

The changes weren't only to accommodate the out-of-town guests; for the first time in decades, the castle would be home to a royal child of its own – Quinn and William's infant son, the future heir to the throne, who would officially receive his name today.

The tiny prince wouldn't be the lone child in the castle for long, either, Zander thought, seeing another figure approach them from across the room.

Linnea's dark purple dress clung perfectly to her still-flat stomach, hugging her waist before flaring out in rippling folds toward the floor, but he doubted she'd get many more chances to wear that dress before the early signs of her pregnancy gave way to more obvious ones.

She was beautiful, all dark curls and long eyelashes framing her bright gray eyes. Zander nearly couldn't breathe around the brick in his chest as he thought about the man who wouldn't be joining them today, the man who wouldn't be here to see Linnea grow round with his child.

The weight of his tunic, of the small round medal pinned to the front was suddenly much too heavy. He wasn't a hero; he hadn't fixed anything – least of all the one thing that mattered.

"Hey Zander," Linnea said.

He mentally shook himself – he couldn't allow his mind to go there right now. "Hi, Linnea."

"You clean up nice," she said.

A warm, shaky feeling settled in his stomach. He never knew how to respond to statements like that. Linnea spoke that way to everyone all the time, even in her grief. Part of him wanted to tell her she looked good, too, but it didn't seem right.

"And what am I?" Thomas teased, taking his sister's hand and twirling her around. "Just a hanger for you to display your loveliness on?"

Zander took a step back, glad for the save Thomas had provided him. He was about to escape and go find Josh or Daniel, the next-oldest Rose boys, when suddenly, one of the enormous main doors swung open, sending a blast of cold air into the room. Everyone quieted and turned toward the entrance.

Marcus Westbrook was standing there in the full green-and-gold regalia of the Philothean guard. The green silk sash draped over his tunic indicated his position as Queen Quinn's foremost advisor. Flanking him were several more members of the guard, also in dress uniform.

"Are you ready, love?" William asked, reaching down to straighten the chain of Quinn's necklace, placing her pendant just-so under the pin of her long fur cape.

"To face a few thousand people? Not really. This is not my favorite part of the job."

He smiled at her grimace. For as much as she claimed to hate it, when she actually had to stand up and speak, people listened – most of them anyway. "You'll do it beautifully."

She smiled, a warm glow lighting her cheeks. "Are *you* ready?"

"No. I wasn't much more prepared to be a king than you were to be a queen, you know. Nobody was supposed to care about my child's Naming Ceremony – they were supposed to have been bored with all of it by the time the fourth-born prince became a father."

Chuckling, she stretched up to kiss him lightly on the lips. "You've taught me more than you give yourself credit for. I don't think I could manage any of this without you, Will."

He kissed her tenderly before pulling back and studying her face, reaching down to pull a single curl loose from its jeweled clip, twisting it so that it bounced softly against her cheek, catching the light and casting the warm auburn glow he loved.

She gave him a wry look and opened her mouth to say something, but was interrupted by the knock on the door.

William hurried to open it, revealing an older woman with kind eyes. She smiled up at him. "Your Majesty?"

He resisted the urge to look around for his father. "Yes, Ruth?"

"They're loading the carriages now. Marcus will be up to escort you down in just a moment. Is there anything I can help you with?"

"No. We have everything we need. Did Lady Sophia make it down all right?"

"Well, she's downstairs and being helped into a carriage anyway, Your Majesty."

He sighed. "How upset is she?"

"I believe she expected to be allowed to carry the prince outside herself."

Closing his eyes, he pressed his fingers to his temples.

"I think your mother has her in hand, though. You and Her Majesty should concentrate on yourselves today. I'll do what I can as well." Ruth's smile was conspiratorial, and a swell of gratefulness filled William's chest.

"What are you doing?" Zander turned around at the annoyed sound in Linnea's voice.

He held his hand out toward the line of carriages along the brick driveway in front of the castle. "I'm just waiting to see where I should go."

"With us," she said, rolling her eyes and nodding toward the organized groups of people being helped into the vehicles by castle guards. "I apologize if it wasn't self-explanatory that we wouldn't send you out here to flounder on your own. Come on." She waved him toward the back of the line where the carriages were filling with William's family members and a few others he vaguely recognized as Quinn's Philothean relatives.

He started to follow hesitantly just as Thomas came up to meet them. "I'm not royalty," he said, in a last attempt to avoid that spotlight. "I don't belong with you."

"Yeah, that's what Quinn tried to say the first few times we dragged her with us to a formal event." Thomas grinned. "Keep opening your mouth like that and we'll find out you're her long-lost cousin or something."

He shuddered. "Definitely not. My family is crazy, but not like this."

"Come on, Zander."

Thomas and Linnea led him to one of the closest carriages to the back. There were only two more behind them – the one holding King Stephen and Queen Charlotte along with Simon and Evelyn and their son, and the one that carried Quinn's grandmother, Sophia, and her children.

Zander tried to make himself as invisible as possible by squeezing onto the seat between Thomas and the wall, after calculating which side most of the crowd would likely be on. Howard, Rebecca, and Maxwell were on the seat across from them.

Not one of them looked at him like he was out of place. Even the guard who helped them up and secured the door behind them bowed his head in respect.

"Oh, hey, I forgot to give these to you," Thomas said, reaching under his cape and pulling out something small and black. *Gloves,* Zander realized as he took them. They were made of soft black leather and wool, and they matched the ones Thomas and all of his brothers were wearing.

"Thank you." The gloves were warm against the biting chill that had crept back into the air in the last couple of days. It wasn't nearly as cold as winter weather at home – he might not even have worn a jacket in Bristlecone in weather like today's – but the cooling temperatures reminded him that he was missing spring there. That he might never see spring at home again.

"So…" Thomas waggled his eyebrows at him. "Do you have a bet on when Alvin will show up? Max says a few minutes before the ceremony, but I've got my coins on him just appearing after it starts."

"What? Why would Alvin do that? Isn't he performing the ceremony?" Zander honestly hadn't paid much attention to the preparations leading up to this, because it was all overwhelming and not that interesting, but he'd assumed, given the level of stress in the castle, that Quinn's grandmother had mapped out the tiniest details.

"Yes – at least as far as we know – but he is Alvin," Thomas said. "You can't plan for what he'll actually do."

Zander looked back up at the castle, at the banners and flowers and green bunting over everything, at the line of carriages and the rows of guards in full green-and-gold regalia, polished swords swinging from their belts. And he looked at the procession now starting at the top of the castle steps, Queen Quinn and King William – crowns and all – William carrying a green bundle. "I don't know. I think I'm going to have to guess he's already here."

"Ooh, a gambler," Max said, before he followed Zander's gaze. He narrowed his eyes. "That's cheating."

Zander shrugged and grinned. "So don't pay up, then. You were both still wrong." Alvin was up there on the steps too, standing next to Quinn as Marcus and several other high-ranking guards led them down the steps.

Quinn and William's whole path was lined with a dark green carpet that took them down the stairs and along the line of open carriages until they reached a much more opulent vehicle in the back. This one had a roof and large doors, and enormous curtained windows, though the windows had been removed for the occasion to give the onlookers a glimpse of the new prince.

Zander's rear-facing seat afforded him a perfect view of the whole spectacle. Marcus helped Quinn into the carriage, holding her hand as she stepped up and settled her long cape and dress inside. When she straightened for a moment before sitting down, she bumped her head on the roof of the carriage, knocking her green-jeweled crown askew.

For a moment, as her cheeks turned bright pink and wisps of hair fell out of place, Zander could see her – the Quinn he'd known just a few short months ago, the one who could laugh at simple things, who'd been the first girl he ever really loved, who'd said yes when he asked her to the Valentine dance.

But then William climbed into the compartment beside her, helping her sit, removing his gloves to return the crown to its place, tucking the disobedient strands back into their proper positions. Of course, everything had to be perfect for the display.

He didn't even kiss her as he sat down next to her, allowing Marcus to step up and arrange the bundle of blankets just-so on her lap.

Zander would have kissed her.

*No.* He mentally shook himself. He couldn't think like that anymore. She had made her choice – was married, had a *baby*, was a queen. And he was stuck here watching all of it, so he needed to keep control of his thoughts.

Alvin climbed into the carriage just in front of Quinn and William's. As he settled in next to King Stephen, he looked right at Zander and winked.

Zander looked away.

# THE NAMING CEREMONY

THOMAS SHIFTED UNCOMFORTABLY IN his seat between Zander and Linnea when Alvin winked at him. He wasn't sure what message Alvin was trying to send to him, but he had a few guesses, starting with the little silver bracelet that had weighted his pocket for the last few weeks.

Reaching into his pocket, he fingered the tiny silver bar with his name inscribed on one side, Mia's on the other. He hadn't seen Alvin since Ben's funeral. On that day, Alvin had given him a pretty intense talking-to about the way things had gone with Mia.

Alvin had been right – Alvin was always right – but Thomas hadn't been able to bring himself to heed his advice yet.

He and Mia had spent the last weeks on carefully guarded, polite terms. They'd spent time together – there was no avoiding that when they'd stopped together so many times on their journey to Philotheum from Eirentheos, and when she'd been so deeply involved in the care of his younger brothers and sisters and his nephews.

Even the last couple of days, as they'd begun to settle in the castle in Philotheum, Mia was a near-constant presence around the infant prince and in everyone's rooms – his, Linnea's, and Zander's in particular – while she attempted to learn her way around her new duties.

Of course, they were never alone at any of those times. Even on the rare occasion neither of them was working, Mia was busy soaking up her last moments with her parents, who would be returning to Eirentheos without her, and Thomas spent nearly all of his time with his own family.

It had taken until yesterday morning, when he'd found all of his clothes neatly put away in the armoire of his new room to realize that he was really doing this – that he'd be staying here when his parents and siblings returned home.

He wasn't giving up as much as Mia was, though, he knew. William and Linnea would be here with him, along with Quinn and his amazing new nephew who would earn his name and the birthright to his kingdom today.

No matter what stories he'd been telling himself, he didn't have a real excuse for not addressing this issue between him and Mia. Maybe today would be the day – a day everyone would be celebrating the baby prince and a promising future.

The carriages started moving. Thomas turned, intending to grin at Linnea, but she was staring intently in the other direction. Before he could call her name to get her attention, he saw her hand dart surreptitiously to her face, brushing her cheeks with the little white handkerchief concealed in her palm.

Fighting back the sudden lump in his throat, he dropped the tiny chain back to the bottom of his pocket and reached for his sister's other hand instead.

For once, she allowed him to take it, and even squeezed back, turning her face halfway toward him. "I'm fine," she whispered.

"I know."

"Are my eyes all red and puffy?"

"No. You're perfect."

"Thanks, Thomas."

He squeezed her hand again.

As the procession began moving forward, the small, warm bundle in Quinn's arms wiggled, and the baby inside opened his eyes.

"Well, hello," she said, lifting him close so she could kiss his forehead. He scrunched his little eyebrows and sneezed.

William chuckled beside her. "I thought maybe you'd sleep through your whole Naming Ceremony little one." He leaned in close as she settled the baby back into her lap, laying his hand over the gold-embroidered symbol on their son's long green velvet gown.

In response, the infant yawned so fiercely that his whole little body shuddered, making both of them laugh. When he finished he blinked up at them, his gray eyes wide, and the sides of his tiny mouth edging almost into a… "Is he smiling?" she whispered.

William nodded. "You are, aren't you, mister? You know what today is." He slipped one arm across her lap, reaching for the baby's fingers with his other hand. "Today's the day we celebrate you."

She shifted so she was even closer to William, relishing the warmth of both his body and his words, although she was mindful of the fact that as soon as their carriage drove through the castle gate and into the city, hundreds of eyes would be on her.

As they grew closer to the crowd, he kept his hand on her knee, gentle and reassuring in a way that made her feel strength flowing through his fingers and into her.

She heard them before she saw them, the throngs of people – her people – lining the streets of the city, cheering as the carriages came through, rising to a roar as Quinn and William appeared.

Despite her worst fears, the baby didn't cry at the noise, or even when a flower came through the partially open window, landing on her lap right by his face.

Instead, when she held him up near her cheek where the crowd could see him, he flashed the grin he'd just been practicing.

"Little Show-Off," she cooed. "Two moons old and already you're better at winning over your kingdom than I am."

William's thumb rubbed soft circles on her knee, but he didn't try to convince her differently. Becoming queen of Philotheum would have been a challenging task even if she wasn't the first woman to do it, even if she hadn't been young and pregnant for the first part of her reign and then left the kingdom for over two moons to have her child elsewhere, leaving an uncle in charge of the fledgling monarchy.

Even among the joyous crowd today, there were those who were quiet, watching the passing procession with suspicion in their eyes. She saw them, and tried her hardest not to acknowledge anything, instead smiling and waving, keeping the infant high and close.

Marcus, riding alongside the coach between Quinn and the crowd, flicked his gaze toward her protectively, confirming that she wasn't imagining all of it.

"So… Naming Ceremonies must be like the biggest deal ever in your world?" Zander said quietly to Thomas as they settled into the second row of pews after being formally announced and walking through a shower of rose petals.

Thomas shrugged, glancing around as Quinn's extended family was being announced and seated. "Well, they're normally pretty important, but I'll grant that this one is a little over the top."

"A little?" Zander looked at the elaborate decorations, the musicians lining the walls, the paintings and portraits and gifts lining nearly every inch of the dais at the front of the chapel. It was more impressive by far than anything he'd encountered, even in this world where he'd been staying in two different castles and traveling with armed guards on horseback. "I think we'd need a telescope to see down to the top from up here."

"Yeah," Thomas chuckled. "You're talking to the wrong person if you want to hear that this is too much for my nephew, though."

"Was it like this for both of your other nephews? Will it be like this for..." he glanced at Linnea who was chatting quietly with Rebecca as she held her sister's baby.

"Ryan's was a lot like this, yes. He'll be the heir to the throne of Eirentheos, just like Samuel will be for Philotheum. It maybe wasn't to *this* degree, but then things are a lot more settled in Eirentheos, politically speaking. This baby is very important to this kingdom. I think Sophia planned for this ceremony to be such a big thing to represent that."

Zander nodded. "Do you think Samuel is safe ... what with Tolliver still out there somewhere and..." he didn't know what the "and" was – he didn't completely understand the situation here, but he knew there had been a lot of concerned conversations lately.

The look Thomas shot him, though, made him wish he hadn't said anything. Perhaps today wasn't the best day to bring up the topic. "So, is it weird to you that two of your brothers and two of your nephews will be kings?" he asked instead, to change the subject.

Thomas shrugged. "I always knew Simon would be. It's a little strange that Will is, for sure. But I'm proud of him."

"Do you ever get jealous?"

"No. Not even a little bit. I don't envy either of my brothers that job." He sighed, looking thoughtful. When he answered, his voice was low. "I think it might bother Maxwell sometimes, though – that just because he's second born he'll never have that chance and most likely his children won't, either. Daniel's been kind of annoyed about that, too – though he's still kind of young to really understand it."

He was still contemplating his response to that when the music changed from a quietly joyful hum in the background to a thundering, victorious march. Everyone in the auditorium stood at the same time – it took Zander only a second to catch on. After a rousing crescendo, everything fell silent at once.

"Presenting Her Royal Majesty, Queen Quinn, His Majesty, King William, and His Royal Highness, the Infant Prince, Heir to the throne of Philotheum."

Guards in green and gold stood along the entire length of the main aisle. One by one, beginning with the ones in back, they knelt as William and Quinn walked together down the aisle, followed by Marcus.

Quinn held the baby facing outward from her chest, his long gown hiding her hands. He was alert; his eyes scanning the crowd.

When they finally reached the platform, William took the child from Quinn and placed him in a cradle in the middle of the dais. At this, he finally protested, his screech filling the whole chapel. Next to Zander, Thomas tapped his foot on the floor.

Up on the stage, Quinn looked absolutely composed, though Zander saw her eyes flick between William and the cradle.

William moved a step closer to the baby, but just as he did, Alvin appeared on the stage. Zander didn't know from where – he hadn't walked down the aisle with them, he hadn't been seated in the pews, but now he stood on the stage, calmly reaching into the cradle to retrieve the fussing prince.

"Well," Alvin said, cuddling the baby close and rocking him, "at least we know the future heir already has his loyalties in order." He grinned, kissing the infant's soft black hair and then handing him back to his mother – a move that clearly surprised more than a few people in the audience.

Quinn carried the baby with her as she and William were seated in two thrones on either side of the cradle.

"This day has been many cycles in coming," Alvin said, addressing the crowd again. "It's been a long time since I stood here before you to name another heir, Queen Quinn's father, Samuel. This day bears few similarities to that one, I suppose, other than the most important one. Today I have the privilege of restoring the most precious of gifts to your kingdom."

He paused, looking out over the crowd. "A gift, of course, is something that has to be accepted. Even the most beautiful gifts, those from the Maker himself, are only worthwhile to those who understand what they are, who value and protect them. Today, the Maker wishes to grant several gifts to the people of Philotheum. The first is the gift of tradition, of returning to your history, and your loyalty to the family chosen to hold your kingdom in safekeeping." He smiled at Quinn and William.

"The second gift is peace – peace amongst yourselves, and with your family in the kingdom of Eirentheos.

"The final gift, of course, is the sweetest gift of all; a beautiful infant heir who links your kingdom with Eirentheos, who represents a powerful political alliance built on respect and love, and who will someday be known to his people as King Samuel Owen Rose."

Alvin paused, giving the audience time to react, reminding Zander that nearly everyone really was hearing the baby's name for the first time. Quinn and William had only shared their choice with William's family – and with Zander and Owen, when Owen had still been here. There were many smiles in the crowd, many quiet murmurs of approval.

The name didn't draw a happy reaction from everyone, though. Notably, Quinn's grandmother, Sophia, looked as if she'd encountered spoiled milk.

"Prince Samuel will receive more than a name today. We have all gathered to bring our gifts to the future king. Many of you have come to offer your loyalty, your trust, and the keeping of your kingdom. Those related to the child have brought tokens of their affection, and will soon have an opportunity to come up and offer the prince their gifts."

"And the Maker has granted Samuel, through tradition and decree, two special gifts today. First is the gift of leadership. Samuel will wear the pendant of the firstborn and the gift of being a strong leader, firm in his judgments, gentle with his subjects, and convicted in the things he knows to be right."

At this point, Alvin walked over to Quinn and the baby, reaching into his robes and removing a tiny box, which he opened and took from it a small gold chain with a shiny circle dangling from the bottom. Zander recognized it as a necklace like the one Quinn now wore. Alvin carefully fastened the chain around the baby's neck.

"The second gift the Maker grants to Samuel today is the safekeeping of the people of Philotheum as the heir to the crown." He reached back inside his robes and withdrew another small object. Zander couldn't see what it was, only that the light glinted off of it as he held it toward the infant.

It was a crown, he realized, when Alvin reached over and placed it gently on Samuel's head. A very tiny crown, different from the one William was wearing – much simpler – but similar to the ones that both Simon and his son Ryan were wearing, only theirs were silver and Samuel's was gold like his parents'.

Once the crown was on the baby's head, Alvin took him in his arms again, holding him up for everyone to see. This time, the baby didn't fuss. "His Highness, Prince Samuel Owen Rose."

# AN UNWELCOME CONNECTION

"SO, WHAT IS IT you've been messing around with in your pocket for half the day?" Linnea asked, setting her empty glass down next to Thomas'. Most of the people they'd been sitting with for the meal had gone off to dance or socialize, or – in Zander's case – to hide out somewhere and pretend to be invisible, but Thomas and Linnea hadn't moved.

These days, someone was always baby-sitting her – if not Thomas, then Will or Rebecca, or even Quinn. But usually it was Thomas.

"Hmm?" He frowned, subtly dropping his hand back to his lap.

"Don't try that with me."

"It's nothing, Nay. I'm just…"

She reached over and pulled his cape back, digging into his pocket until she found the bracelet and pulled it out. Her eyes narrowed as she rubbed the thin silver bar between her fingers. "This is not nothing."

"Okay. It's a bracelet."

Mia's courtship bracelet, she should have guessed. She sighed, sitting back in her chair and throwing the little chain down on the table. His eyes followed her hand – he blinked when her own bracelet peeked out from under her sleeve for just a second. She met his gaze. "See? It means something."

He squeezed her shoulder, but she pulled back – she wasn't going to let him take the focus off himself *again*.

"This is not what Ben would have wanted," she said, watching him pick up the jewelry and return it to his pocket.

He looked at her.

"It's bad enough that he died." She heard her voice shake a little on the word, but she steadied her jaw and continued. "But this thing where it's affecting everyone else… where you're too wrapped up in taking care of me to fix what's going on with you and Mia – where Quinn and Will are afraid to even touch each other where I can see… It's not okay."

"Linnea…"

"No, I know, Thomas. You're all worried about me, and nobody knows what to do, and you're all grieving, too. But it's not like seeing William and Quinn kiss would suddenly remind me about Ben and make me sad again. I'm already there. And seeing you struggle like this with Mia makes it worse, not better. It makes me feel like his death killed your relationship, too."

"…" He opened and closed his mouth several times.

Linnea reached over and took his hand. The ever-present warm moisture coated her eyelashes, but this time no tears fell.

Finally, Thomas swallowed. "We were a mess before… *before*, you know. She didn't even tell me she was moving to Philotheum."

"You didn't tell her, either."

"Exactly. We were a mess. Ben dying didn't cause that."

"But it's keeping you from fixing it. Or at least you feeling like you have to take care of me is." She hated that more than anything.

"No." He shook his head. "It's not that simple. First of all, I don't feel like I have to take care of you. I *want* to, but I know you don't need me to do that at the expense of everything."

She shot him the dirtiest look she could manage. "You're using me as an excuse for not dealing with her, aren't you?"

At least he looked appropriately abashed. "I guess I kind of am. Sorry."

"You're lucky I love you, T." She shook her head.

"Well who doesn't know that?" He reached for her empty glass on the table. "Let me get you some more."

Standing up, she grabbed the glass back from him. "If you're going to change the subject to avoid having a real conversation anyway, let's actually get up from the table and pretend we're at a party for our nephew."

"After you." He grinned as he rose and extended his hand to help her up.

She rolled her eyes, but decided to let it drop, again.

Halfway to the buffet table, Thomas stopped short, nearly causing Linnea to bump into him. "What is he doing here?" he hissed.

"Who?" Linnea followed his gaze, over to where Quinn's uncle, Charles, was talking to several people, but, outside of family members, she didn't recognize any of them. Quinn, William, and Marcus were part of the group, too, though they were focused on Stephen, who was smiling and playing with baby Samuel.

Thomas didn't answer her question, turning to her instead with a fierce look in his eyes. "Get out of here now, Nay. Ask James or Dorian to escort you to Quinn's council room."

She wouldn't normally have allowed Thomas to be so abrupt with her, especially without telling her what was going on – but something in his expression made her turn and search the room immediately. James Blackwelder was furthest from the group Thomas seemed so worried about, so she went to him and asked him to take her to the council room.

The guard led her out immediately staying right at her elbow as they exited through a side hallway. Only once they were inside the meeting room, with the door closed, did he speak. "Is everything all right, Lady Linnea?"

"I don't know. Thomas … I think he saw someone he didn't expect to see, I don't know who. He just told me to ask either you or your father to bring me here right away."

"All right." James nodded as if she'd just told him something normal instead of bizarre. "Why don't you have a seat, and I'll start a fire?" He led her to an area in the far corner, away from the long table where Quinn now presided over meetings. Here there were several comfortable chairs and couches gathered in front of the large fire grate.

She was just settling into one of the leather chairs when James ducked behind a couch and emerged with a wool blanket. "You should be keeping warm, milady. It will be cold in here until the fire is going."

"Thank you. I suppose the news of my condition has spread to everyone by now?"

He shrugged. "I tend to fall behind on castle gossip, sorry. I just thought you should be comfortable."

The blanket was soft and warm; she wrapped herself in it as James knelt in front of the hearth, spreading kindling from the bucket on the floor.

"It's true," she said. "I'm with child."

He didn't stand, but he turned his whole body to face her. "I hadn't heard that. It's not any of my concern, but if you'll forgive my indiscretion, I would like to tell you how pleased I am to hear it."

"Thank you." She watched him turn back to the grate, so formal and solemn. "James?"

"Yes, milady?"

"I'm going to be living here in Philotheum – you don't need to be quite so afraid of me. Surely you've at least heard that I'm not the sort of princess who disdains interactions with guards."

He turned to her again, still mostly serious, but this time she could see a tiny spark of amusement in his eyes. "Even if I did partake of gossip, milady, I'd have assumed Ben was a special case. Certainly he was a rare man worthy of the honor."

She swallowed back the feelings that always snuck up on her whenever she talked about Ben with anyone. "He always spoke highly of you."

James' gaze fell to the floor. "I only knew him for a short while, but even in that time, he became one of my dearest friends. The fact that he didn't return … my life will never be the same. It may be presumptuous to say this, but I had hoped, when he returned with you, that I might be blessed with the friendship of the lady who occupied his every thought."

She smiled around the thick feeling in her throat. "Even under these circumstances, James, we can still be friends."

To her surprise, he gave her a little smile, betraying a hint of a less-serious young man underneath. Unless she was mistaken, James wasn't any older than William. She doubted he'd seen his nineteenth birthday. "I would like that, milady. Thank you for sharing your news with me. It gives me peace to know that his legacy will be carried by his child. Please know I will do whatever I can to serve the both of you."

Just as he was turning back to the grate, the door at the other end of the room burst open. James was on his feet in one swift movement, blocking Linnea, his hand on his hilt. She quickly brushed away the few escaped tears.

But it was Marcus who'd opened the door. He, too, rushed to Linnea's side, followed by Thomas, Quinn, William, Stephen, Dorian Blackwelder, and Luke Willoughby. Once everyone was inside, Luke closed the door and secured it with a heavy wooden bar.

Quinn looked first at Linnea. "Is everything all right?"

"Yes, I'm fine. Thomas just told me to come here. Nothing's wrong," she repeated, noting her sister's concerned look didn't quite go away. She stood and walked over to the table to prove her point. "At least not with me. What's going on, Thomas? Who did you see?"

"That man," Thomas said, looking at Quinn, "the one who was talking to Charles. What is he doing here?"

Quinn frowned, glancing at William. "I think that was Callum Haddon – if I'm thinking of the same man. Is he wearing a red shirt?"

"Yes." Thomas nodded. "Long brown hair, going a little gray, pulled back."

"That's Callum."

"Why is he here?"

"He's the head councilman in Brandleby. We invited councilmen from every town and village in the kingdom. Not all of them came, clearly."

"Is Brandleby close to the Rhinewald estate by any chance?"

"It *was*, before we dismantled the Rhinewald estate and sold off the pieces," Marcus said, his voice dark.

Quinn had gone pale, though, undoubtedly having the same thoughts that were making Linnea's hands clench into tight fists. There was only one way Thomas could recognize the man – one reason he was so distraught over seeing him.

William walked away from the group, toward the fire, bouncing and rocking Samuel in his arms.

"Okay." Quinn's shoulders rose and fell several times as she tried to compose herself. "How bad are we talking about, Thomas? Is Callum guilty only of withholding information about your kidnapping, or is it worse?"

"*Only?* Isn't just knowing about it and not doing anything bad enough?" The shaking had crept from Linnea's hands to her voice.

"Nay." Quinn's quiet warning came at the same instant Linnea felt her father's gentle, but firm, hand on her shoulder.

"I don't know how involved he was," Thomas said, looking at the floor. "He was at Harbin Rhinewald's estate already when I was brought in, though. And I saw him a few times after that."

Thomas was… Linnea had *never* seen him this upset. No, upset didn't even begin to describe him. His voice was small, in a way that suggested if he raised his volume at all, he would explode loud enough for the whole castle to hear. His shoulders were curled forward, his whole body wound tighter than a spring. She reached for his hand to squeeze it, but he yanked it from her grasp and took a step away from her. Her father pulled her a bit closer.

"Okay," Quinn said again, pacing back and forth. She looked up at Marcus. "We have several separate problems here."

Marcus nodded. "He needs to be questioned."

"We need to *arrest* him," she said. "But doing it now would be a disaster – people are here for a party, and we have no idea who's here with him."

"Which brings up the security issue." Marcus' gaze shifted between Linnea, Thomas, and William who still held the baby. "There's a strong chance Callum still has ties to Tolliver."

Quinn took another deep breath. "All of the guests' names were recorded?"

"Yes, Your Majesty. And checked against the invite list – but clearly we don't know everything about the people who were invited."

"It would be a bold move to attempt something during the heir's Naming Ceremony."

"Yes. Bold and unwise. It's difficult to sway public opinion to your side if you commit a crime in front of enough people," Marcus said. "Although that's the same reason you can't arrest a man with his level of influence in the middle of the party, either."

"Perhaps you can have someone follow him?" Stephen asked. "A small guard detail, to see if we can discover his associations?"

Marcus looked at Quinn. "I can arrange that, if you'd like, Your Majesty."

"Yes. Thank you, Marcus."

"In the meantime, we have to address the clear safety concerns. This man presents a potential danger to Linnea, Thomas, the other Rose children… and to Samuel, in particular."

Quinn's entire body twitched, though she retained her composed demeanor. "Yes. So what can we do, Marcus? Can I remove them from the party without causing a scene?"

"I think it's probably been a long day for the children already," Stephen said. "The babies all need to be fed and put down to rest and the other children surely can't be expected to maintain their composure for much longer."

Over in the corner, Samuel gave out a sudden squeak – his warning signal that he needed to eat soon.

"See?" Stephen smiled, though it didn't reach his eyes. "The future king over there is in agreement. I can start having the oldest children quietly escort the younger ones upstairs."

"I'll gather some Eirenthean guards to keep constant watch." Luke said, already heading for the door.

"I'll stay with you and Samuel," Marcus said to Quinn. "James, Dorian, help me out with these two, and also William, Thomas, and Linnea?"

"William and I will have to return to the party," Quinn said. "We can't just disappear."

Marcus nodded. "After you feed the baby, you return for a short time before we announce a formal exit. Samuel should stay here under guard, though."

"That's going to cause a problem. Sophia will come unglued if I don't take Samuel back with me. Do you really think we're in danger – in our own castle, at a party?" Quinn frowned. "I might want to rip Callum's throat out myself, but he's managed to keep his ties from Tolliver separate for this long. Perhaps he's turned against him?"

Linnea's hands started shaking again.

"Your Majesty." Marcus' voice was quiet, but dark. "With all due respect… We've made the mistake of underestimating the potential for danger twice now."

Quinn's gaze fell to the floor.

"I, too, would prefer if we could trust everyone in Philotheum, but we can't. As we've discussed, the situation is far more complicated than I think anyone realized, and we don't know everyone involved, or how far the deception goes. The biggest target in this castle is your son – followed very closely by you. Or perhaps I even have that wrong. I have no idea what Tolliver, and those who support him, are after. We must protect both of you."

# SOPHIA AND CHARLOTTE

AS QUINN HAD EXPECTED, there was fallout from the decision not to bring Samuel back to the party.

She was alone in her apartment, rocking an almost-asleep Samuel when the pounding on the door started, startling him awake. Instinctively, Quinn stood, moving behind the rocker.

"He should be in bed already," Sophia snapped as soon as she was inside the room. "If you put him to bed properly, he wouldn't be too tired to attend functions."

"He's only two months old!" Quinn said, taking a step back to keep him away from her grandmother's outstretched arms.

"Two *what* old? You can't be teaching him those ridiculous words. He'll never be fit to rule a kingdom if you don't train him properly. A prince has a duty to stay at an event until he says a formal farewell. Now give him to me. He needs to be put to bed. In his cradle, like a proper prince."

"He still needs to be burped." Quinn took another step back. He didn't need to, not really, but the rocking and patting motion might help hide the furious shaking of her hands.

"Let me do it."

When the door opened just as Sophia was reaching for the baby again, Quinn nearly fell over in relief.

Charlotte followed William into the room. She looked calm and composed, but a glint in her eye told Quinn that Charlotte had already assessed the situation. "I thought I'd come in to say goodnight," she said. "That was a beautiful ceremony today, Sophia. Your planning was just perfect."

"Thank you, Charlotte. I would have thought you'd be tending your younger children now."

"They're in bed, so I thought I'd step in here for a few minutes to spend some of the little time I have left here with William and Quinn. I'll miss them when we return to Eirentheos the day after tomorrow."

"I'm glad to hear your children are asleep. I was just attempting to impress upon Quinn the importance of a proper bedtime for a royal child."

"Yes, I'm sure she'll be putting him down here in a moment. I'm glad I had the chance to see you again this evening. I was just telling Ellen I hoped I would be able to tell you how beautiful those centerpieces were. She was wondering where you had disappeared to."

Sophia sighed. "I suppose I'd better go and find her, then."

"Perhaps we'll have more time to visit tomorrow. I've heard so much about your collection of paintings. I'd love to see them."

"I'm sure that can be arranged."

"Wonderful. I'll talk to you in the morning then."

Quinn had to use her finger to return her jaw to the right place once Sophia had disappeared into the hall.

"Are the children really asleep?" she asked as she handed Samuel over to Charlotte.

"I didn't say anything about asleep. They're in bed – or beds, more precisely. I believe Emma and Alex are trying to determine which mattress is bounciest. Alice might be reading in hers."

"No. Sarah distracted her," William said, chuckling. "Now they're building a hideout with all the quilts they can find. Father was helping, but he somehow wound up with three babies in his lap, so now he's giving directions."

"Oh, I wish you weren't leaving," Quinn said to Charlotte. "I am *never* going to be able to handle my grandmother the way you just did. She was about to rip Samuel out of my arms and put him in the crib so I could listen to him scream. And then she could tell me how he's only screaming because I'm doing something wrong."

"She means well," William said, looking at his mother. "She's just overly protective of Samuel – and upset that she didn't get to see him sooner."

"I know she is. I'm trying to get along with her..." Quinn sighed. She wanted to have a relationship with her grandmother, wished that things could be as easy with her as they were with William's family.

But Charlotte had narrowed her eyes at her son. "Did you even ask Quinn what Sophia said when she was in here?"

William looked at Quinn guiltily. "No. What did she say?"

"I don't know. The same kind of stuff as usual. Telling me I need to put him to bed. It doesn't sound bad when I say it."

"Of course not," Charlotte said. "When you repeat it, everyone just tells you she sounds like a concerned, well-meaning grandmother."

"You don't think she means well?" William asked, surprise in his voice. "You think she means to upset Quinn?"

"I don't know whether what she means is good or not, William. I haven't asked her, and I'm guessing you haven't either. I *hope* she means well. It's always helpful to assume that someone means well. The *problem*, as it concerns you, is that it doesn't matter what she *means*. Look at your wife."

He did. Quinn could feel the difference when he really looked, when his steady hand stretched toward her still-shaky one.

"Now," Charlotte said, lowering her voice as Samuel was getting drowsy in her arms, "at the risk of exposing my own neck as a grandmother, both of you need to understand that being polite to Sophia and trying to get along with her isn't the same as letting her run over you – over Quinn, especially. If she has good intentions, that's lovely. It's still none of her business when or where Samuel sleeps. Or what he eats, or whether he has socks on his feet, or even whether he remains at an event long enough to suit her. She's not his mother."

"She is the former queen. She knows more about this than I do. I've never been a queen before. Or a mother."

"So ask for her advice, Quinn. Twenty seconds before she starts in on you, if you can learn to time it. But remember you're the queen now. And you're Samuel's mother. The advice may be hers to give, but the decisions are yours to make." She kissed the now-sleeping baby on the forehead.

"We do have a guard outside the door," William said. "We could just ask James not to let her in."

Quinn chortled. "That would cause more problems than it would solve."

"Would it?" Charlotte asked. "I've no doubt it would upset her, but then she manages to upset both of you nearly every time she comes in here. Do you intrude on Sophia in her rooms?"

"I've never even seen the inside of her apartment."

Charlotte raised her eyebrow knowingly. "You're allowed to have rules like that, too, Quinn. Don't confuse being polite and respectful with allowing someone to do whatever they want to you. Some things can't be solved by giving in." She looked at Will. "And when Sophia is crossing a line, Quinn needs help standing up to her, not excuses for Sophia's behavior."

William nodded.

"You can't make people be who you wish they were. Sophia may come around, or she may never be quite the grandmother you imagine. In the meantime, William, Quinn needs your ear and your support more than she needs a grandmother. Standing up to Sophia isn't going to be easy. It would be nice if she had more family, but it's even more important for the family she has to cover for her."

Charlotte placed the sleeping infant carefully in William's arms before turning back to Quinn. "I wish this wasn't so challenging for you, and I wish I could be closer to help you navigate it. But my first advice is to listen to your feelings. If you feel like she's overstepping, she is. Be nice, but have rules." She hugged Quinn tightly. "And if you ever need me to send a message to my son to remind him whose side to take…"

Quinn giggled, glancing toward the bedroom where William had carried their son. "He's a fast learner. I think we'll be okay."

When William came out of the bedroom, Quinn was standing by the window, looking out at the dark night.

"I'm sorry if I've been making excuses for Sophia instead of standing up for you," he said, walking up behind her.

She turned to face him. "I don't blame you, Will. This is new for both of us. It's not like you *listened* to her." She smiled and nodded toward their bedroom, where Samuel was sleeping in a small cot right next to their bed, rather than in the elaborate cradle in the nursery. "Just because your mother has good advice for making things better doesn't mean I don't appreciate how you've tried."

"I love you, Quinn." He wrapped his arms around her waist, pulling her close. "Sometimes I look at you and I think I'm the luckiest man in two worlds, but then I talk to you, and I *know* I am."

Stretching up on her toes, she kissed him, long and slow. He held her tight, running his fingers through her hair and then down her back until he found the top button of her dress. When he started to unbutton it, though, she pulled back a little and shook her head.

"I'm still waiting for Marcus to report back to me about having Callum Haddon followed."

"Ah." He dropped his hand.

"Ready to re-think how lucky you actually are?"

"Definitely not." He took her hand instead, leading her over toward one of the couches. "So you and Marcus decided to have him followed?"

"For now." She nodded. "I want to arrest him, but I think this is safer until we understand more about what's going on. I hope it is, anyway."

"Does Marcus agree?"

"I think he feels the same way I do. We'd both happily lock him up forever for whatever role he played in Thomas' kidnapping, but if he still has any connection to Tolliver, this could be the break we've been waiting for in finding him."

"What about Charles? What are his thoughts?" William knew Quinn's uncle had been included in a meeting earlier.

A shadow passed over Quinn's expression. "Charles wasn't exactly unsupportive, but he thinks I should concentrate more on winning over popular opinion in places like Brandleby than on pursuing justice for things that happened before I was queen."

William felt a little sick to his stomach. "He thinks you should just let Callum get away with being an accomplice to Thomas being tortured?"

"He thinks that perhaps my emotional involvement is preventing me from seeing things in the most politically advantageous light – yeah, I had to take a few deep breaths at that, too."

"Do you think he's right?"

"I don't know. I think there are a lot of reasons he's right in that we shouldn't arrest Callum right now. I want him held accountable for his crimes, though. Sooner than later, regardless of politics."

"Do you still trust Charles?"

She sighed. "Yes. I trust that he wants what's best for the kingdom and for my reign. I'm not sure he and I agree completely on what that is… But the fact is, as much as I loved spending all that time with your family – being gone for almost three moons and having our son born in Eirentheos has made things more complicated here. It's not about whether I trust Charles. It's about whether anyone trusts me."

He rubbed her shoulder, but he didn't argue. She wasn't wrong. "We'll get there, love. Today was good."

"Yes. Today was pretty great. Samuel is exhausted. Maybe he'll actually sleep."

A knock at the door interrupted them.

"That'll be Marcus." William stood.

"I might be in meetings for a while."

"I'll wait up for you."

"You don't have to. It's been a long day."

He shrugged. "I'll catch some snuggles with Samuel maybe. But there's a certain topic I think I'd like to finish … um … *discussing* with you later."

# PURPOSE

THE DAY AFTER THE Naming Ceremony was the last full day William's family would be in town before returning to Eirentheos. Zander was hopeful this would mean a day he'd be left mostly to his own devices as everyone tried to make the most of their last minutes all together, so he was more than a little surprised when Stephen followed him to his room after breakfast.

"May I have a word with you, Zander?"

Zander fidgeted, but nodded, wondering if he was in trouble for something.

"You don't have to look so nervous," Stephen said once they were inside his room. "I'm only very lightly armed."

"You're armed inside the castle with your family?"

"It was supposed to be a joke. I'm really not intending to frighten you. Am I that intimidating?"

"Where I come from, a *king* asking to speak privately with me is about as intimidating as it gets."

Stephen's eyes crinkled in amusement. "I can concede that point. However, where you live now I expect it will be a commonplace event."

"I don't think I'll ever get used to that."

"People can get used to most anything, if they try. Adjusting to living in a castle with some friends with fancy titles doesn't rate impossibly high on the difficulty scale."

"Even if that castle is in an alternate universe you can't escape from, and you might never see your family again, and the king you'll be seeing every day is married to the first girl you ever loved?" He stopped talking and took several steps backward, putting a couch between himself and Stephen. He hadn't meant to say all of that.

"If you weren't so scared of me Zander, I'd want to give you a hug. You have certainly had your share of disruption and difficulty lately, particularly being ripped away from your family. I didn't come in here to speak to you as a king. I came to visit with you because I hoped maybe you wouldn't mind some conversation with a father."

Zander stared at him.

"I'm not *your* father, I know. And I could never make up for how much you must be missing him, but I did think that perhaps you could use someone looking after you like one, at least a little."

"I don't think you'd be very good at being my father. *My* father wouldn't be wasting this opportunity to tell me what I have to do with my life. Just before I came here, he'd informed me that I had no choice but to go into business with him. I don't see you saying that to William or Thomas."

Stephen raised an eyebrow. "You might reassess my abilities if you talked to my oldest son. He was informed of his life's work at his Naming Ceremony – I didn't wait until he was eighteen."

"Oh." Zander had never thought about that. "He doesn't seem to mind."

"Simon? No. So far as I know he's always been comfortable with the role he was born into. I suppose I can thank the Maker that my firstborn child is more like his mother than like me."

"*You* didn't want to be king?"

"When I was very young, I never thought much about it. I was the heir; I was going to be the king. In my mind, it wasn't a question – until it was. Until I realized that my brothers and sisters all had choices about what they wanted to do and how they wanted to live, but I didn't. I watched my father and saw how much responsibility he had – and I saw how much freedom my siblings would have."

"What would happen if you refused to become king? Can you even do that?"

"The crown would have passed to the son of my father's oldest brother – yes, there was a time I really thought about it. Especially after Samuel and Nathaniel came to live with us and then discovered the gate. In some ways I envied Samuel his circumstances – the thoughts of a teenage boy, I suppose – but the way things had gone in his kingdom gave him the chance to escape and have the kind of adventures I would never be able to have. And Nathaniel was free in every way. I visited them in your world a few times. At one point I even thought about following them there and not returning."

"*Whoa.* What changed your mind?"

Stephen sighed, perching on the arm of a couch. "A combination of things, I think. The first was my father. I had a huge fight with him one day – or I meant to, anyway. I told him that he couldn't force me to be the king and that I was going go live in the other world and do what I wanted with my life."

Zander let out a low whistle. "I bet that went over well."

"The reaction you're imagining is the one I expected – anger, yelling, demanding that I let go of my crazy ideas… That's not what he did, though."

"No?"

"No. He was calm – almost scary calm – and he told me it was my life, or it would be, once I was of age. He told me he loved me, and that I had until he died to change my mind, but that he had no intention of leaving his kingdom in the hands of someone who didn't really want it, anyway. Then he wished me luck at finding the path I wanted to take."

"And that set you straight?"

"It didn't *set* me anything. It didn't change my mind – mostly I was relieved that my father wasn't furious with me. But it made me think. I spent a lot more time with Samuel and Nathaniel for a while. I learned, slowly, that everyone's choices in life are limited – either by their circumstances, or by what they value, and usually by both. Making one choice always closes the door on other possibilities. Nobody has freedom from the consequences of their choices. In the end, we have to choose what's really important to us."

"And being the king was important to you."

"Being the king? No, actually. But there were other things I was choosing along with accepting my birthright. I chose my kingdom, to continue the legacy of my father and grandfather. I realized that giving up any of it would be giving up all of it. I would gain one kind of freedom, but lose another. Of course, it didn't hurt that I met Charlotte and then my priorities changed. It wasn't just about me then, but about her and our family and our future children. Girls change everything."

Zander chuckled. He paced back and forth in front of the fireplace as he considered Stephen's words. "So you think my father was right. I should have just taken the opportunity he was offering me – he'd pay for college and then I'd join him in his business."

"No. That isn't what I mean at all. My choice was only the right one for me. My friend Samuel made a different one, you know. He met a girl and chose to stay in your world to be with her and protect her and their child rather than fighting for his crown. His circumstances were different. I didn't come in here today to talk to you about your father, Zander. I came in here to talk to you about how *your* circumstances are different now."

"You mean because I might never see my father again anyway." He stared into the fire, not looking at Stephen.

"Yes. That's exactly what I mean."

Zander looked up in surprise.

"I'm not going to shy away from the topic, son. You have enough people around here to do that for you. I'm leaving tomorrow to go back to Eirentheos, so I came today to spend a few minutes discussing the issue nobody wants to discuss with you."

"What difference does it make whether we discuss it or not? I'm still stuck here. It's not like I have a choice."

Stephen stood and took a few steps toward him, although he still kept his distance, not encroaching on the protective space Zander had established for himself. "You don't have the choice of returning to your world right now, no. You don't have the choices you thought you were facing at home. Much has been taken from you, and I realize how challenging that is for you. I would love if I knew how to make it easier for you. But you still have choices."

"Like what? Looking for another gate to get back home?"

"That's one." Stephen's voice was quiet and calm, even in response to Zander's increasingly hostile tone. "We do know that it's likely other gates exist. You could choose to spend your time here searching for one. Perhaps the fact that you come from the other world will give you a unique perspective when it comes to finding one. You may be able to do it."

There was an undertone to Stephen's words. "But you don't think I should."

"I don't think you *shouldn't*. There are, of course, many questions surrounding whether or not finding another gate would be beneficial to our world, but my feelings about both you and Quinn tend to override my worries about the danger of finding a gate – I can't blame you for wanting to find a way back to your families."

Stephen took another step toward him, making eye contact and dropping his voice even lower. "I do hope that finding a gate and focusing on returning to your world doesn't become an obsession for you, though, Zander."

"What do you mean?"

"I mean… Can I be very honest with you for just a moment?"

Zander shrugged, but took one step backward.

"I know you're going through a difficult time. I can't imagine what it's like for you to lose your entire world and a good friend all in one night. You sacrificed everything for what must feel like nothing in return. You were left nearly alone in a world where the only person you really know is a girl you loved who chose another man. There's a very soft part of me that wants to treat you the way everyone else is – to give you your space, to appreciate what you gave up for us, and ask you for nothing else. We don't have any right to ask you for anything. But…" he looked at Zander, a silent warning that he wasn't finished speaking, "there's a bigger part of me that is a father. I see you the same way I see my own sons."

He paused, looking at Zander again. The expression in his gray eyes was warm, but firm. He *looked* like a father – almost as much as he looked like a king. Zander couldn't bring himself to speak.

"My greatest wish for all of my own children has always been that they would find purpose in their lives – that they would learn to give themselves over to others and to the world around them. Having purpose – and fulfilling that purpose – is the only real way to find happiness. In your world, I believe you would have found it. Perhaps you would have learned to eventually find purpose in working with your father, or maybe you would have found it somewhere else. I don't want to see you lose that, too. You live here now, and I want you to have purpose here – not just be floundering and hoping to be ignored for the indefinite future."

Zander sank down onto the arm of a chair. "I don't think I can just ride to the market and pick up some purpose."

Stephen chuckled. "I like you, Zander. More than you probably think I do. Enough that you're already another reason I wish I wasn't going to be so far away. You're right in that it's not so easy to find purpose. You can't buy it, and I can't give it to you, either. All I can offer you is a start – something productive to do with your time while you search."

"Like what?"

"I would like you to consider training to be a guard."

There were words, there had to be, but he couldn't find them.

"It wouldn't have to be a permanent decision, but it would be something. It would give you a chance to gain some new skills and meet some new people as well. I think it might be good for you to make some attachments here outside of Quinn's inner circle."

"Can I just do that? Just become a guard?"

"Yes. It's normally a long process but you're a special case – already a decorated hero. You'd start out in training – Dorian Blackwelder has agreed to take you on as an apprentice, if you're willing. Truthfully, Zander – Quinn could use another guard she can trust implicitly."

"Does Quinn know you're asking me this?"

"Yes. Although I will admit this was my idea. While she agrees that you might enjoy it and that she would be honored to have you among her guards, she was very wary of asking you. She doesn't want you to feel as though she expects it, or that you're not welcome here without taking on such a role. As I said when I came in here, this entire conversation is me overstepping and acting as a father. I'm suggesting this because I want you to find a way to be happy here. Maybe even meet a girl."

He raised an eyebrow. "I don't think meeting a girl is a great idea when I'm lying about who I am and where I came from, and I might leave and go back to another world someday."

"*That*, right there is exactly what I'm worried about," Stephen said, sighing. "I'm worried that you're going to put your entire life – your entire self – on hold while you wait for a possibility that may never come. You're here, and you need to live like you're here. If you have the chance to return to your world someday, and that's what you choose, you can deal with the consequences then. As far as the lying, when you meet the right girl, you won't have to. You'll know she's the right girl because you'll be able to tell her everything about your real self."

"I'm sure that will go over well. You can't tell me you'd allow one of your daughters to marry someone claiming to be from another world."

"I'll let you think about that statement for a moment, son. But I will tell you that I never demanded William and Quinn live here in this world to be together. If Quinn hadn't decided to pursue her throne, I'm nearly certain William would have stayed in the other world with her. I would have hated it, but I would have given them my blessing."

"Oh, right." Zander stood and walked over to the fire again, staring into the flames for a long moment. Finally, he turned to look at Stephen. "You know, the one thing I was supposed to get out of this whole mess was *not* having to worry about listening to a father."

Stephen laughed out loud. "Life rarely gives us the things we think we're supposed to have. More often, we have to learn how to use what we get."

"I'm learning that."

"You really are a wonderful young man, Zander. I do hope I get to know you better over time. Now… for more fun topics. We were planning on celebrating our last day all together with a game of crumple in the gymnasium, and would love for you to join us."

# CRUMPLE

"SEE, SAMUEL, THERE'S YOUR mother," Thomas said, propping the infant against his chest, facing out. "She's about to get the ball away from your father. He never sees her coming. Or maybe he just doesn't look. There! She's got it. Go Mama! Go!" He waved Samuel's little fist as Quinn ran toward the goal, and lifted him into the air as she moved the ball past Max and scored.

Quinn caught Thomas' eye and grinned, waving at him and Samuel.

"Be careful with him," a voice admonished.

Thomas settled the baby back in his lap and looked up. "Hello Sophia. I was hoping you would come out to join us. I'm glad you decided to."

"I still haven't had much of a chance to see my great-grandson. I wanted to see him asleep in his cradle this morning, but apparently the new security measures mean that even the queen's grandmother needs special consent to enter her chambers, and she wouldn't answer the door. I don't even know what all this ridiculousness is about."

It was harder this time, but he forced a warm smile. "Well, he's wide awake and happy now. Would you like to hold him?"

"Yes, thank you. You're the first one who's actually offered."

Ignoring the fact that he knew she'd held the baby this morning after an offer from William, he adjusted Samuel's hat and secured the warm knitted blankets before passing him carefully over to Sophia. "He's beautiful, isn't he?"

"Yes. He reminds me a little of Nathaniel when he was a baby. Of course, I was hoping he'd get Quinn's hair, but this color is nice, too." She pulled the hat down further, almost to Samuel's eyes, to which the baby objected with a squawk. "Do you think he's cold? It's a little chilly in here."

Thomas reached over and ran his finger up the baby's cheek, surreptitiously pushing the edge of the hat back up, and then dug inside the blankets to feel Samuel's hands. The infant quieted immediately at his uncle's touch. "He feels nice and warm. I think he's okay."

For a couple of minutes, everything was peaceful as Sophia held Samuel on her lap and smiled and cooed at him. Her whole face softened, and her eyes sparkled as she looked at the baby.

Then she lifted him up close to her chest, holding his head against her shoulder. Samuel immediately began to screech.

"He doesn't really like to be held that way," Thomas said gently.

"Nonsense. All babies like to be held close. It makes them feel secure. Quinn should be holding him like this all the time." She stood up with him, wrapping her arms more securely as she – almost imperceptibly – swayed on her heels.

Samuel cried harder.

"Maybe he's hungry," she said. "I could take him to the kitchens."

"He's too little for food." Thomas was having a hard time keeping his hands from reaching out and snatching Samuel away from her.

"I know that. But when my babies were this little, we spoon-fed them a mixture of milk and meal grain. It made them sleep better and grow more. He wouldn't be so fussy. Will you tell Quinn I took him to the kitchens? I'm sure he hasn't had his diaper changed all morning, either."

Thomas looked desperately across the room. Most of his family was deeply involved in a tense moment of the game, except for the very youngest children who were playing nearby, oblivious. Rebecca was there, but she was busy feeding her son, and Mia was distracted by Hannah who was also fussing. He couldn't exactly call over for help. Sophia was already heading toward the door. He didn't think the guards there would stop her. They didn't have instructions about this.

He finally caught William's gaze as Sophia reached the halfway point. He tilted his head furiously toward her.

"Break, please!" William yelled, running toward the sidelines. Thomas followed him. "Sophia! Is everything all right with the baby?"

"Yes, of course. He's fine," she said, though by this point he was screaming and his little face was red.

Quinn had been farther away, but Thomas could see her approaching now.

"Thank you for taking care of him for us," William said to Sophia, reaching toward Samuel. "Quinn was just saying she needed to take a break from playing to feed him."

"It's no problem for me to take care of him for a little while so you can finish your game." Sophia deftly took a step back from William. "I would love the chance to get to know him better."

"That's very gracious of you," William said. "We would much appreciate your help sometime, but right now I think Quinn needs to feed him." This time, he was more assertive than polite, taking two quick steps to close in on her while taking hold of his son in the same motion.

Thomas' hands were still shaking when William turned back around to face him just as Quinn reached them. The rest of his family was paying attention now, but – probably wisely – holding back.

Samuel's screams subsided quickly, though he was still breathing in hiccupping sobs when William handed him to Quinn. He didn't settle down completely until they all sat in a quiet corner so he could nurse.

"Let's all break for drinks," Stephen said, leading the rest of them toward the chairs on the sidelines of the large gymnasium.

Zander listened to William's younger brothers first groan and then engage in a debate over whether to play something else during the indefinite intermission, but then a servant brought in a large tray of cookies and fruit, effectively ending the discussion.

He wasn't sure exactly what had happened, but judging from the way William, Linnea, and Thomas were huddled around Quinn and the baby over in the corner, it had something to do with them.

The gym in this castle was much larger and nicer than the one he'd spent time in back in Eirentheos. One side even had a wood floor – which must have been a nightmare to keep clean next to the packed-dirt playing area – but this area was filled with comfortable, cushioned chairs.

Along the back wall were several long tables covered with green tablecloths – this was where the snacks were being laid out. Zander glanced over toward Quinn's little group. None of them budged.

Nobody was paying any attention to him. He was more than a little tempted to escape, to return to his room and ... well, something. Maybe re-arrange his few clothes in the wardrobe again. But then he remembered his conversation with Stephen earlier – about actually living here instead of just avoiding everything. He wasn't ready to even think about Stephen's guard suggestion, but this much he could make himself do.

Sighing, he headed back to the table and loaded up a plate with a stack of cookies, several apples, and some glasberries.

"Hey, Zander," Thomas said when he approached them, immediately standing to pull two more chairs over to them. He took the tray from Zander and set it down on one of the chairs.

"You don't have to do that," Zander said. "I just thought I'd bring these over to you."

Linnea narrowed her eyes at him. "Sit. Have a snack with us."

"Well if you're going to be *that* way about it…" He grinned as he reached theatrically for the largest cookie, taking a bite before he sank into the empty chair.

"Sure, make the pregnant lady get her own."

He coughed. "Twenty minutes ago, when you wanted to take Thomas' place in the game you were *'pregnant, not an invalid.'*"

William reached for two cookies, handing one to Quinn and one to Linnea before taking one for himself. "Arguing with a pregnant lady is way more dangerous than Max's tackling arm."

"I'll remember my protective gear next time," Zander said, earning him chuckles from Thomas and William. Linnea stuck her tongue out at him.

He looked over at Quinn, who was quiet as she fed the baby. "So, dare I ask what's going on?"

"Nothing." William shot him a pointed look, shaking his head. "Samuel needed to eat, and we decided everyone could use a break."

"Oh. You mean your team was so far behind you hoped we'd forget some of the points Quinn scored for us if there was enough sugar involved."

"Something like that." William smiled.

At times like this, Zander wasn't sure why he fought so hard against getting involved with them.

It was true that it was still hard to watch Quinn with William. There wasn't any real way to wrap his mind around the fact that the girl he'd been dating only … well, however long ago it was – a couple of months, tops … was now married and had a child.

Aside from that, though, he liked everyone. They always made every effort to include him and make him feel welcome – almost as if he belonged, although he so clearly didn't.

Even William, who could have treated him as a threat or competition, never did. He was unfailingly kind and considerate – enough that sometimes Zander wished he could hate him for it.

Maybe Stephen was right. Maybe he could actually find a way to have a life here.

William's siblings were already drifting back out onto the playing floor when Quinn finally finished feeding Samuel and handed him over to William who pulled a fresh diaper out of the cloth bag they always carried with them.

Zander was considering asking who was ready to join them when he looked up and saw Marcus standing a few feet away from them, a look on his face so dark that it made Zander's heart jump into his throat.

Quinn was already on her feet by the time Zander glanced over at her. She waved Marcus closer.

"I need to speak with you immediately, Your Majesty."

"Yes, of course." Her eyes flashed to William.

The rest of them were already standing.

"Does this have to do with Callum Haddon?" Thomas asked in a near-whisper.

Marcus nodded.

"I want to hear."

"So do I," Linnea said.

He wasn't entirely sure how it happened, but a few minutes later, Zander found himself in Quinn's private chambers with Quinn, William, Thomas, Linnea, and Marcus.

William held the baby as he paced and listened in on the conversation. Samuel was nearly always in the arms of family members the last couple of days. Although William and Quinn said it was because they were trying to allow Mia to spend her last few days with the younger Rose children, Zander sensed there was more to it – they were too protective, keeping him in sight.

"Callum has disappeared," Marcus said. Zander didn't know what he was talking about, but the tone in Marcus' voice made the hair on the back of his neck stand up.

"What do you mean *disappeared?*" Quinn's brow scrunched until her eyebrows nearly touched.

"The security detail responsible for tracking him hasn't been able to locate him for several hours."

"Did they lose him after he left the inn?"

"No. We know he was planning on staying at the inn last night rather than traveling all the way to his home. He checked in, he was there last night, but he doesn't appear to be there now."

"What about his horse and carriage?"

"They're still there."

"Then how do you know he left?" Zander wondered. "Maybe he's still in his room sleeping or something."

Quinn shook her head. "The guards watching him wouldn't have alerted Marcus yet if that were a possibility."

"Correct," Marcus said.

"Did they question the innkeeper?" Zander asked.

Now everyone was looking at him.

"Nobody is supposed to know we're keeping track of him," Quinn said. "Questioning innkeepers would open up all kinds of new complications."

"Then why are you having him followed?" He realized, after the words were out, that he should probably be keeping his mouth shut. Everyone here obviously understood something that he didn't, and he was probably only impeding the conversation. In a second, someone was going to ask him to leave.

But nobody did. To his surprise, Quinn answered him. "I don't know. I should have had him arrested yesterday, middle of the party or no. We believe he's connected to Tolliver – well, we know he *was*, and there's a chance that he still is."

*Tolliver.* Just the name set Zander's teeth on edge. "Do you think he might know where Tolliver is?"

"If he's disappeared, we may never find out."

He shrugged. "It isn't like he would have just told you even if you had arrested him yesterday."

They all stared at him again.

"I realize I'm new here, but I've had enough experience with Tolliver to pay attention to the stories about him." He met Quinn's gaze. "It's never safe to talk in front of someone on the assumption they're not paying attention or they couldn't possibly understand what you're talking about."

She didn't flinch; his comment wasn't even rewarded with a hint of a blush. She merely studied him, reminding him yet again that she wasn't quite the same girl he'd known in Bristlecone. Of course, the large oil painting of her in her crown on the wall over the heavy wooden desk shouted that fact as well.

"I haven't been dealing in secrets, Zander. I trust you. If I didn't, you wouldn't be standing here hearing this now."

There were the burning cheeks – his.

If she noticed, she didn't react. "I wasn't sure if you cared to hear any of it, but I have purposely included you because I think you've earned it. Since it seems you have actually been listening, I would like to hear your thoughts on the situation."

He swallowed hard, wondering for a second if she was humoring him – but she wasn't. Everyone, even Marcus, was looking at him with interest. "I just don't think – as far as Tolliver goes, anyway – that it makes much difference whether you arrested this guy yesterday or not. Arresting *Tolliver* didn't help. I sincerely doubt arresting some maybe crony of his would have helped you find him. It sucks that it sounds like he might have escaped now, too, but that doesn't mean you made the wrong call."

She sighed. "I appreciate that, Zander, but I'm pretty sure I've made about a million wrong calls on all of this."

"Well, that's what they want you to think, isn't it?"

"Excuse me?" This time it was Marcus who spoke.

"Look, feel free to tell me to stop talking, because I don't know the whole story here, but from what I can see, that's what Tolliver does – tries to do things that tie your hands so that whatever you do can be portrayed as the wrong choice. I mean – how many people in Eirentheos still hold Stephen at least a little bit responsible for children being poisoned by their schoolbooks?"

Thomas' eyebrows dug deep into his brow. "How much have you been thinking about this?"

Zander looked up at the ceiling for several seconds, debating how to answer. "I'm not sure I think about much else," he finally admitted. "I know you don't think I'm listening when you talk about Tolliver and what's gone on in the past, but just hearing his name... I can't help but... I don't participate in the conversations because I don't trust myself to speak." Even now, his hands were balled into tight fists at his sides, and he was sure his voice was shaking.

Everyone was quiet for a long moment.

"Is it terrible that I wish I'd killed him, too?" he whispered.

Thomas chuckled, though it wasn't a joyful sound. "Not in this room it isn't."

"Anyway..." Zander looked at Quinn. "I think that's what he does – puts people in impossible positions so that every choice is the wrong one – everything puts his enemies in discord that they have to deal with and be distracted by. Even his escape from prison makes it look like you made the wrong choice not executing him, but if you had..."

"Then I'd be the new queen who murdered my half-uncle."

"Well, I'm sure he didn't plan on being arrested in the first place," William said.

"You don't think arrest was a possibility he considered when kidnapping a princess? It was sort of win-win for him, don't you think? And lose-lose for you."

"I'm not sure Tolliver is smart enough to pull something like that off," Thomas said.

Quinn leaned her hands against the back of a couch, staring down at the cushions. Even without looking at her face, he could see that she'd caught on to his line of thinking. "Not to do all that himself, maybe. But he had Hector and Rahas. And clearly others as well. Who knows who else he's working with. I don't think even Rahas could get him out of prison all by himself."

Zander nodded. "I hope I'm wrong. I want to be completely wrong here. But there's just something… not right. I don't know. But I think you need to be careful. And not about whether innkeepers know you're investigating Tolliver's allies."

"If he really has disappeared," Thomas said, "the innkeeper likely knows something anyway."

As he twisted his hands in the bottom of his shirt, Zander wished the pants he was wearing had pockets. "If he's gone and left his horse and carriage at an *inn*, then someone probably tipped him off."

Quinn and Marcus exchanged a look that contained an entire conversation nobody else could hear. Finally, Marcus' chin tipped down in an almost imperceptible nod. "I'll send a detail to question the innkeeper and search the inn."

"Will you ask Dorian to lead?" she asked.

"Of course, Your Majesty. I assume you'd like James to stay here? He followed us and is outside the door now."

"I know. And yes, I would like him to stay with us, please. We need to speak with Stephen and his guards as well about protecting their family."

"Yes, Your Majesty. I will also compile a list of all the guards who were involved in following Callum along with anyone who might have heard about the mission."

"Thank you Marcus."

Rather than heading to the door immediately, which is what he expected, Marcus turned to face Zander. "Thank you for your willingness to be open and share your thoughts."

"I don't think I said anything you wouldn't have figured out."

"Perhaps not, but having more perspectives always helps in making a complete picture. And sometimes it takes a person saying the difficult things that nobody else wants to think out loud." He glanced at Quinn and then back to Zander. "If you decide to take Her Majesty up on the offer King Stephen spoke to you about, I would be honored to train you myself, Sir Zander." Without waiting for a response, he turned and disappeared through the door.

For a full minute, he couldn't even look up at the four pairs of eyes he knew were trained on him. Heat flashed through his whole body and trickles of sweat formed at his brow and under the collar of his crumple shirt.

"Nothing like putting you on the spot, huh?" Quinn said softly.

"What offer?" Linnea asked.

Thomas and William both shot her looks that should have been able to bring a train to a halt, but which Zander knew were powerless against a determined Linnea. He couldn't even be irritated by it. Instead, he found himself stifling a grin as he answered her question. "An offer to train as a guard."

Quinn took a step toward him. "Sudden pressure notwithstanding – it's an offer, not an obligation."

"I don't know. I'm starting to get the impression that you need me more than I need a job."

"Who could have guessed you'd be as good at reading situations like this as you are at trig?"

That hit him like an arrow in the gut, but he took a deep breath and met her half-smile. "I'm way better at this than I am at trig – you were just bad enough at it that you didn't know the difference."

"I might need to count on that."

"If I agree to be your guard."

"The fake hesitation has outlived cute now, Zander." Linnea said, rolling her eyes.

"Fine," he sighed. "Does it at least mean I get to carry a sword?"

Quinn smirked and held up one finger before crossing the room to the area behind the desk. At first, he didn't understand what she was doing as she ran her fingers down the line between two of the polished wooden wall panels, but then she pulled a panel back, revealing a dark cupboard. Reaching inside, she retrieved a long, heavy-looking object wrapped in green velvet.

He knew what it was before she reached him with it, but he still wasn't expecting what he saw when she laid it on the back of the couch and opened the cloth.

The sword was brand new; the shiny steel glinted in the light of the fire when he pulled it from its sheath. There wasn't a scratch on it.

Everyone stayed back as he lifted it to look; it was sharp enough that he could have sliced through the couch cushions without making a noise – but it was also perfectly balanced and exactly the right length.

"I wasn't just being measured for clothes, was I?"

Quinn smiled. "What fun would that be?"

"You were this sure I'd say yes?" The sword was the same as those carried by Quinn's highest guards – Marcus, Dorian, James … the same sword Ben had carried. The hilt was overlaid with swirls of gold surrounding the Philothean crest, and underneath that was an inscription. *Sir Zander Cunningham.*

"No. When I said the offer wasn't an obligation, Zander, I meant it. I…" She looked at William. "We commissioned this shortly after Ben's death, even before we returned to Philotheum."

There was something in his throat that was making it hard to speak – hard to breathe, really – so he just nodded.

"I wouldn't *practice* with that one, unless you aren't especially attached to your fingers," Thomas said, breaking the tension.

Zander slid the sword back into its sheath. "I'll keep that in mind." He looked back and forth between Quinn and William. "Thank you… I don't really know what else to say."

"I know," Quinn said. "But you deserve it. Thomas is right, of course, that you still need some more training before carrying it everywhere, but we're all learning on the job in this castle."

"Yeah." He ran his fingers along the leather carrying strap of the sheath, feeling the smooth, oiled texture.

Just then, the baby started squeaking in William's arms – though he'd been sound asleep only moments before.

"All right," Quinn said, sighing. "We have one more day with our family here, and we're missing it. Whatever is going on with Callum Haddon can wait until we either have news, or until they're gone. Tolliver's taken enough without taking our time with them, too."

In spite of the obvious tensions in the castle, and the constant interruptions Quinn had to deal with surrounding the missing Callum Haddon – the last full day of being with his family was a good one for Thomas.

Bedtime stretched late into the evening, as William, Thomas, Quinn, and Linnea took long turns with each of the younger children while Charlotte and Stephen snuggled and played with Samuel for hours.

Not until nearly midnight did Alice fall asleep – she'd fought it the longest, not wanting to separate from Will.

Finally, William and Quinn retrieved their child from Stephen and Charlotte, and – after many more hugs – retreated to their room with him just as the guard shift changed outside their door.

"You're both still sure about this?" Charlotte asked, handing fresh mugs of tea to Thomas and Linnea. "There will be plenty of room in the carriages tomorrow to take you back with us."

"About leaving the two of you – and the rest of them?" Thomas shook his head. "No. But about being here in Philotheum with Will and Quinn and starting a life here…"

"I know," Charlotte said. "I know." She sank down on the couch across from them. Stephen held her cup out to her before sitting down beside her. "And you, sweetheart?"

Linnea nodded in a way that wasn't convincing, but that also wasn't going to change.

Stephen held his hand out to the side and Linnea crossed to him, curling up under his arm as if she were still a small child. He stroked her hair.

"One of us will try to make it out in six moons or so," Charlotte said. "Even if we can't both be here."

"I'll take care of her," Thomas promised.

"I expect you'll need her care just as much." Charlotte reached across the short space between them to tap his knee. "You listen to her, especially when it comes to whatever is going on between you and Mia."

"Yes, Mother."

"I don't think I could do this if you two weren't going to be together," Stephen said. "I thought it was hard just leaving William here. This…"

Charlotte took his free hand.

"This is what you get for being too wonderful at parenting," Thomas said. "Maybe you should think about scaling it back for the little ones."

Stephen chuckled. "Oh, we've got that one taken care of. Just ask Emma – we give her far too many math assignments."

When the teacups were finally empty and stacked on the table, Charlotte sighed. "Are you sure you want to go all the way back to your own rooms?"

"Well," Thomas said, "it would be a shame to let these nice couches go to waste."

# DINNER IN THE COMMON ROOM

IF ZANDER HAD ONCE thought that life in the Philothean castle would be less busy after Stephen and Charlotte left with ten of their children plus assorted spouses and grandchildren, he realized now that he'd been mistaken.

It was quieter, perhaps, and there were fewer people to talk to — especially people he *wanted* to talk to, like William's brothers — but he'd never been busier in his life.

Guard training was intense. After three weeks of solidly continuing the sword training and horseback riding lessons he'd begun in Eirentheos, Marcus added a nearly full-time apprenticeship to his schedule.

At the end of his third day of working for ten hours alongside Dorian Blackwelder, and then another hour of sword training, he was practically crawling up the stairs, wanting nothing more than to collapse in his bed. He wasn't even sure he had the energy to ask a servant to draw a bath for him.

"Hey Zander." Linnea stood at the top of the stairs holding Samuel.

"Hi." He tried to smile at her, but wasn't sure if he was successful.

"You must be starving."

*Was he?* Maybe. He *should* have been, anyway. "Yeah, kinda."

"Ruth is bringing up dinner to the common room in a few minutes. You should join us. William, Thomas, and Nathaniel will be on their way up, and Quinn and Marcus are finishing up something and then coming too."

He raised an eyebrow. "Is Sophia gone, then?"

"Yes. She left for several days to visit a friend of hers somewhere. Jonathan is escorting her, but he'll be back tomorrow morning." The look on her face was a little too gleeful to be polite.

Not that Zander blamed her. "Nice to have her gone?"

Linnea grimaced. "There was a big fight this afternoon before she left because she wanted to take Samuel with her."

His eyes bugged. "For several days?"

"Uh-huh."

"So he could starve to death?"

"Oh, no, no. That was part of her argument. Samuel needs to get used to a wet nurse. Her friend has one, but Quinn really needs to spend some time while she's gone looking for one to hire. Sophia left a list of suggested ones, of course."

"Yeah, this just went into territory above my pay grade."

Linnea giggled – he hadn't seen her this happy in a while. "Anyway, she's gone, the fight is over, and Samuel is right here. We're celebrating. Join us."

"All right."

Most every evening, Sophia insisted on a formal, four-course dinner in the dining room. Two nights ago, he'd had to stand guard in full uniform while everyone ate at the long table attended by servants who cleared the dishes between every course.

He'd attended some of the meals himself, as well, but he usually tried to avoid them. Conversation around the table was stiff, polite, and boring – though with Sophia boring was often preferable to *interesting*.

Dinners back in Eirentheos had been the opposite. William's family rarely used the formal dining room outside of special occasions and entertaining guests. Although they shared a number of meals together at a table in a smaller dining room, the evening meal was almost always upstairs in the family's private common room, with everyone in comfortable chairs, children running in and out, several games going, and raucous, teasing laughter ringing from every couch.

When he'd first come here, he'd found those dinners overwhelming. He'd often taken a plate of food back to his room so he could eat in peace. It surprised him now to realize he missed it. Exhausted as he was, he didn't want to miss the Philothean version of one tonight.

He followed Linnea to the common room near Quinn and William's rooms.

James Blackwelder had recently begun his shift watching the infant prince and whoever was caring for him. He maintained a respectful distance behind them, but when they reached the common room, Linnea invited him inside as well.

Although he wanted nothing more than to collapse on one of the couches and close his eyes for a minute, the presence of the guard stopped him. James was around the same age as Zander, but he'd completed his apprenticeship over a cycle ago – what would have been ten years in Bristlecone. He knew James often completed a ten hour shift only to turn around and take on an extra one after only a few hours' rest.

So, instead of sitting, he asked Linnea if he could hold the baby for a few minutes, to give her arms a rest.

"Sure," she said, handing him over. "He needs a diaper change, too."

"Where's Mia?" he asked, only half joking.

Linnea's eyes narrowed. "She's joining us for dinner as well. She ended up spending half the afternoon packing trunks for Sophia, so I sent her to take a break and get a bath if she wanted. The diapers are in that bag over on the chair."

He didn't actually mind spending time with the baby, though at times it was hard because being around small children made him miss his own little sisters at home. It hurt too much to consider the possibility – the likelihood – that he would never see Ashley or *his* Sophia again.

Purposefully keeping his mind from going there, he carried Samuel over to one of the couches on the far side of the room, pulling a blanket off the back to lay him on before opening the diaper bag.

This common room itself was a brand-new addition to the castle, built in an impressive day and a half of work by Stephen and his sons when they'd dismantled one of the empty apartments in this wing, knocking out the walls between the sitting room and the bedrooms to create a big, open space.

There was no kitchen area like the common room in Eirentheos, but it was cozy, filled with an eclectic assortment of chairs, couches, and low tables dragged from all different corners of the castle. Charlotte had even managed to find several tall bookcases and a number of paintings and rugs to make it warm and homey.

Over on the other side of the room, Linnea was smiling at something James was saying, although Zander never got to find out what it was. Just as he was slipping Samuel's pants back over the clean diaper, William, Thomas, and Nathaniel appeared in the doorway.

They, too, were smiling and relaxed – apparently feeling accomplished over whatever they'd managed to get done in the space they were renovating into a clinic. William's grin grew even wider when he saw Samuel, and he darted across the room to the baby.

"Wow," he said, picking up his son. "Did Zander just give you a nice, fresh diaper?"

"Yep, although you're pretty lucky you were only wet, Samuel, or I might have made you wait for your daddy."

William chuckled, tucking Samuel's legs into the crook of his elbow so the baby could sit up face-out the way he preferred. The infant joined in his father's laughter. "Thank you, Zander. It's much appreciated."

"No problem."

"How was training today?"

"Not bad. I can *almost* lift my arms over my head again after all the throwing of weighted balls last week."

"You must be exhausted." William's eyebrows forked into a concerned shape as his gaze swept over Zander. "Have you even had a chance to sit down for a minute? You're still in your boots."

"It's all right."

"No it's not. You'll have to forgive my sister. She doesn't stop to remember that not everyone can keep going after ten hours of manual labor." As soon as the words were out, though, William visibly paused, his eyes flicking away from Zander and down toward the ground.

They both knew why Linnea didn't consider that a guard might be tired after a single shift. She was too used to a man who could probably have worked three shifts without hesitation.

"Anyway…" William didn't quite manage to meet Zander's eyes again. "If you want to take a minute to go get changed and comfortable before dinner, we won't start without you."

Of course he didn't. He did find a chair – the firmest one in the room – and he perched in the middle of it rather than leaning back, too afraid that if he did, his will would lose out to his fatigue.

The room grew busy quickly. Mia came in just as Zander was sitting down. She *had* gone and had a bath, it seemed, since it was one of the rare instances he saw her in regular clothes, with her hair down. She still went immediately to check on the baby, but William shooed her away.

At times like this, Zander realized what a pretty girl she was. She had the blackest hair he'd ever seen, which contrasted beautifully with her pale skin and bright green eyes. There was clearly something going on between her and Thomas, though he wasn't sure what the status of that was. The two of them were overly polite to each other, every great once in a while slipping into a more comfortable familiarity. Either they were thinking about dating – or courting, as he'd heard it called here – or they *had* courted at some point in the past and were negotiating their way through an awkwardly half-hearted breakup.

Back in Bristlecone, he'd thought gossip was stupid, but here he sort of wished he had friendships comfortable enough to at least clue him in on background information.

He was staring absently at the door when Quinn and Marcus arrived. The look on Quinn's face while she was still in the hallway woke him right up, though by the time she entered, she'd stifled it and was smiling instead.

William went to her immediately, greeting her with a delighted smile. He didn't kiss her – Zander had learned by now that he almost never did if there were other people around.

At first, Zander had considered that a failing on William's part – that he could have a wife like Quinn and not want to kiss her at every opportunity.

But now when he watched them he saw the other things. He saw the way William directed his entire attention to her, how as soon as he saw her, there was nothing in the room – nothing in the kingdom, probably – that was more important than simply saying hello to her.

He now saw how William consciously touched her, placing his palm right on the small of her back as they walked together, and that when he did it was like flipping a switch, one that lit up something in both of them.

They were fascinating to watch, actually, even outside of the feelings he still fought over Quinn. Honestly, he couldn't really see her that way anymore. If he struggled with jealousy, it was no longer over the simple fact that she was with William instead of him. He was jealous over what they had *together*.

They weren't two parts of a whole, the way he'd always imagined marriage to be – the way he'd had secret thoughts of being with Quinn back in Bristlecone – not two broken pieces that needed to be together to be complete. Instead, they were two complete pieces that when they were together became something more. They became a whole that was much larger than the sum of its parts – much more than a public display of affection.

He knew now that she'd made the right choice. Zander would have given her a kiss. William gave her – herself.

"Plate, Zander?" Marcus was standing in front of him, holding out a steaming plate of roasted lamb and dark purple root vegetables – he still couldn't remember what they were called, but he'd finally learned to eat them.

"Oh." He blinked several times. "Yes, thank you. I didn't even see Ruth bring in the food."

Marcus smiled as he sat down in a chair to the side and reached for another plate on the table in front of them. Someone had already set two large metal mugs of milk on the table, too. Zander had missed the whole thing.

"It's this hard for *everyone* at first," Marcus said. "I know it doesn't seem like that's true, but it is. You're doing better than you think you are. When Ben had his first moon of official training, I don't think he made it through dinner even once – he ate three breakfasts. And he'd been training with horses and swords since he was a toddler."

Zander blinked at him, not knowing how to respond.

"It's okay to talk about him, Zander. It helps to remember he was real – and also that he wasn't a perfect, mythical creature. He was a young man much like you. You remind me a lot of him, actually."

"Is it all right if I take that as a compliment without really believing it?"

Marcus chuckled. "Eat your dinner, son. Before you fall asleep and drop it."

The difference in the castle, this relaxed dinner in the common room was palpable. Laughter flowed as freely as the second helpings. Somewhere in the middle of it, as Zander scooped more of the purple vegetables onto his plate, he realized he'd grown to like them, rather than simply tolerating them because he was hungry.

Not everything was as happy as it seemed, though. Underneath all of the casual pleasantries, Quinn and Marcus were both stressed about something. Several times, Zander caught them glancing at each other, silently communicating with a mouthed word or a furtive shake of the head.

At first, he wasn't sure if he was the only one who noticed. William, Thomas, and Linnea joked with abandon, making silly faces to see if they could get Samuel to giggle. But when the dinner dishes had finally been cleared – replaced by a large bowl of thick, creamy pudding – it was Thomas who cleared his throat. "So what's going on, Quinn?"

Marcus' eyes swept the room with practiced precision, and Zander followed suit, noting both that someone had closed the door and that James had disappeared, likely to the other side of it. For a moment, he was afraid Marcus might ask him to leave, but he didn't. After a quick glance at Quinn, he answered Thomas.

"We had a visit today from a guard who normally works at the border crossing in Manderdale. He's almost certain he saw Callum Haddon crossing the border nearly three weeks ago."

"Three weeks ago?" Linnea spluttered. "So straight there from here?"

"Yes. We tried to keep all of this quiet for too long," Quinn said. "We only finally sent the order to the border guards to notify us last week. This guard wanted to bring the information directly to us, rather than sending it through channels where it might be compromised."

Zander was more concerned about the word *border*. "Have you let Stephen know Callum might be in his kingdom?"

Quinn shook her head. "Not Eirentheos, Zander. Manderdale is on the border between Philotheum and Dovelnia."

He frowned. "That's the kingdom Tolliver's father was from, right?"

"Yes," Marcus answered. "Hector first came here to Philotheum as the ambassador from Dovelnia."

"Okay. Do we have an ambassador from Dovelnia now?" He hadn't met one.

Quinn shook her head. "No. Dovelnia withdrew all of their support from Philotheum after Hector's death. Or it may have been when we made the announcement that Samuel's *daughter* would be ascending the throne, rather than someone's son."

"Nice. Why would it matter so much to them? It's not their throne."

Nathaniel spoke this time. "The throne of Dovelnia has always prided itself on being very *traditional* – *that's* their word, of course. It doesn't matter to them that our traditions are just as strong, but different. In their kingdom, the throne can pass to any son in the royal line; their king actually chooses the succession order of his children. If he doesn't think his firstborn is up to the task, he can list another son as his heir."

"Yes," Marcus said. "As it happens, King Ivan's oldest child is a girl, though his next two children are sons, but he has named his younger son as his successor."

"What if a king doesn't have any sons?" Zander wondered.

Marcus shrugged. "They have a lot of disputes between members of the extended royal family. At any rate, our relations with Dovelnia have been strained since Hector died. Now we have evidence that they're harboring at least one of our enemies."

"Has anyone seen *Tolliver* at the border crossing?"

"He hasn't been reported at one, no."

"But then it's possible we were lucky this time to hear from a border guard who is loyal to me," Quinn said, looking down at her hands. "We don't know that all of them are."

"Many are," Marcus said. "There are ways to get to Dovelnia without going through any border checkpoints, and the control is light at many of them, especially away from the larger cities. Let's not assume the worst. There are guards in every position throughout the kingdom who are very loyal Friends of Philip. Their loyalties are to your family *and* to you."

"So…" Zander looked between Marcus and Quinn. "Is that the only way if you know you can trust a guard or not? If they're in the Friends of Philip and have that tattoo?"

Everyone was quiet for a long moment before Quinn finally spoke. "No, not exactly. There were some who never even knew about the resistance during Hector's reign as Prince Regent. Others probably disagreed with Hector and Tolliver but were afraid of the consequences of actually tattooing their disloyalty on their bodies. Some of them are loyal to me now."

"But you can trust the Friends of Philip more."

"Overall, yes. But just because a guard is *not* a Friend of Philip doesn't mean I can't trust them. *You're* not and you're here in this meeting. And I can't require my guards to join because that would just defeat the purpose. I can't even show favoritism to guards who are Friends – or I have to be very careful if I do."

"*Should* I join the Friends of Philip?"

"No, Zander. See? That's the problem right there. It has to mean something, it has to be a personal choice, and joining by itself doesn't make you trustworthy – nor does not being a part of it make you dangerous. Besides, it's mostly symbolic now anyway. The resistance succeeded. We won – the throne was returned to the 'rightful heir' and all that. So, no, it's not necessary to join."

"What if I wanted to?"

Nathaniel cleared his throat. "Do you want to?"

"I don't know. I'm just asking a what-if."

"The 'what-if' is not whether you can or should join – the whole question is whether you want to. So, no, if you can't honestly answer that you want to, that you're willing to make that commitment, then joining is not the right thing for you."

"There's nothing wrong with that," William added. "You're not in that place emotionally, and why would you be? I wouldn't have joined a resistance against anything in Bristlecone."

"Not even if you were stuck there and it was important?"

"After being stuck there less than two moons? No. Besides, if you joined right now, you'd end up missing several days of training. There's no swinging a sword right after getting *this* tattoo." He put his hand over the upper left side of his chest.

"It can't be that bad, can it?"

"Join," Linnea said, with a tone in her voice he was becoming entirely too familiar with. "Find out."

"Can I go back to my world now and write a few more college application essays? Maybe take a Calculus test?"

"Sure, just find a gate," William said. "Or build a transporter or something."

"I'll get right on that. Anyway, so Tolliver may be getting help from the king in Dovelnia?"

"Yes," Marcus said. "At this point, I would say it's very likely he is. We've known for a while that he has to be getting support from somewhere, and we've suspected Dovelnia before – from the beginning, really."

"So what does that mean?"

Marcus looked at Quinn again.

She swallowed hard as William slipped his hand behind her back again. "Our best guess is that they have some kind of plan that will allow Tolliver to take back the throne."

Zander's mouth was suddenly dry. Judging by the expressions on the other faces in the room, he wasn't the only one.

"What kind of plan?" Thomas asked.

"If we *knew*, we could defend against it." Marcus was staring at his hands. "Right now, all we know is that Callum Haddon is definitely involved – and he was here, in the castle talking to a large number of guards and other people. We also know that someone with intimate knowledge of our investigation alerted him, so we're clearly compromised."

"Why is this just happening now?" Thomas asked. "Quinn's been on the throne for a long time."

Marcus shrugged. "Tolliver was in prison most of that time. Also, we don't know exactly what they have planned. Up until now, we've assumed the biggest targets were Quinn and Samuel – that Tolliver would eliminate both of them and then take what he wanted."

Though Zander knew Marcus only used it because he couldn't bring himself to utter the real term, the casual sound of the word "eliminate" sent chills up his spine. He suddenly felt naked without his sword. "And now you don't think so?"

"I don't know. But that idea fails to take a very important factor into consideration. The Dovelnian king is very religious. Their oracles are highly regarded as sources of absolute truth. While we never took the prophecies completely seriously – they did. Hector and Tolliver did as well. They may not want Quinn on the throne, but Samuel…"

Quinn had obviously heard all this before, but she started to breathe faster, and she reached then for the baby, pulling him from William's lap into hers. William reached all the way around her back, scooting her so close to him that they practically became one person.

"Okay," Thomas said, clearly seeing the same thing Zander was. "The question is, *what do we do?*"

"Well, our first priority, obviously, is keeping everyone safe. We're increasing the guard coverage here, especially over Quinn, William, and Samuel. All three of you – and actually Thomas and Linnea as well, will need to be accompanied constantly by a guard we trust, unless you're in this wing which will be closed and guarded.

"We'll keep the Blackwelders with Quinn and Samuel as much as possible, and utilize other Friends of Philip guards when we have to. Also, all guards who work with the family or in the castle itself will be investigated thoroughly, including their associations. We expect some massive backlash, but any guards we have any questions about will be reassigned to positions away from the castle."

"Sophia may murder me herself for that one." Quinn cradled the baby closer. "Jonathan should be returning in the morning, and we'll make some more decisions then. Charles went home for the evening, with two guards he knows well – he's nervous enough that he's considering sending Thea and the children somewhere he feels is safer. If something *did* happen, then Gianna would be at risk, too." She looked at Nathaniel. "We also think you should hold off on bringing Cammie and the children here until we know exactly what we're dealing with."

"Of course."

Quinn paused, studying Nathaniel for a moment. "She wasn't planning on coming anytime soon anyway, was she?"

It wasn't any of his business, but Zander had been wondering about the absence of Nathaniel's fiancée himself. He'd sort of expected to see her and her children at the Naming Ceremony.

"No, Quinn. Not until Tolliver has been dealt with. He frightens her."

Quinn swallowed but nodded – two of Cammie's children had been affected by the shadeweed poisoning incident. "I sent a message to Stephen a few hours ago as well, but he likely won't receive it until morning." For a moment her eyes fell on the couch where Thomas and Linnea were sitting together; Zander had a feeling she was about to say something else, but then Marcus cleared his throat.

"There are also riders going out to all of the Dolvenian border crossings tonight alerting them to a lockdown. All traffic in or out will be registered and reported directly to us."

Thomas let out a low whistle. "That could start a war."

"Better to be prepared to defend ourselves than to be caught by surprise," Quinn said. "If we haven't already put ourselves in that position. Anyway, we're more likely to run into problems when word reaches King Ivan that I've ordered all of my troops to defensive alert. If we're right about how much information is leaking across the border to him, he may know by tomorrow."

# BEDTIME

WHEN THEY LEFT THE common room to head to their own apartments, Linnea made it to her door, but then paused and turned back around, heading the other way down the hall. A second later, Thomas appeared at her elbow.

"I can't get rid of you, can I?"

"I would be failing in my big-brotherly duties if you could. Besides, I want to know the answer, too."

James was in front of Quinn and William's door – literally blocking it with his body. He shook his head when Linnea and Thomas approached. "Their Majesties are not to be disturbed in their room if it isn't an emergency."

For a moment, Linnea hesitated. She was proud of Quinn for setting a boundary and enforcing it.

Thomas was apparently even more impatient for an answer than she was, though. "They only just went in there, James. Will you at least ask them if we could meet with them for a moment?"

James frowned. Sensing his indecision, Linnea added her own, "Please?"

"Stand over there – both of you." He pointed to a spot far enough down the hall that they wouldn't be able to see the inside of Quinn and William's room if they opened the door.

William did open it, and after a brief conversation with James she couldn't hear, he waved them in.

"I do like the security," Thomas said once they were in the sitting room.

"Yeah, us too," Quinn said from her spot on the couch where she was feeding Samuel. "What's going on?"

There was no reason to avoid getting to the point. "Are you thinking about sending me and Thomas back to Eirentheos?"

William's mouth popped open at her question, but Quinn looked at the floor.

"No," Linnea said. "That's not an option."

"It was only one possibility Marcus and I discussed. If things get too dangerous, it's something we should consider, Linnea."

"And what? Leave you here to deal with the danger by yourselves? Absolutely not."

"It's my danger. It's my kingdom. I'm the one who needs to deal with this. It's bad enough I'm dragging William into it."

"Dragging me?" William cleared his throat. "Last I checked, Quinn, I made my own decision to be here – my own *commitment.*"

"So did I," Thomas said.

"Me too. Queen or not Quinn, you don't get to pick what the rest of us are willing to fight for."

"You're pregnant, Nay."

"Yes, with a child whose father died in service to this kingdom, whose entire family has been dedicated to the protection of *your throne* for generations. This is what I chose when I married Ben – this is the legacy I intend for our child to inherit. Don't ask me to dishonor that."

Thomas sat down on the table in front of her. "That prophecy, Quinn? It might not have been real in some ways, but it was in the way that counts – you and William and Samuel – you united our kingdoms. When you did that, you got us too, and there's nothing you can do about it. It's not *your* fight, it's *ours,* together."

Quinn was silent for several moments, looking at all of them and then down at the sleeping infant in her arms. "Fine. Stay. Fight. But the next time you try to make me cry at this hour of the night, there will be consequences."

"It's not that late you know," Thomas said, grinning as he stood and leaned over to kiss the top of her head. "There's at least an hour left where it's permissible for us to make you feel loved. I've got more."

"Go. We'll see you both in the morning."

When they were far enough down the hall to be out of earshot of James, Linnea turned to her brother. "It goes for you, too. Don't ask me, don't even make a suggestion. Not now and not ever."

Zander sat bolt upright from a dead slumber. His heart was galloping faster than the horse he'd been dreaming about riding. The room was still pitch black, although he hadn't even managed to get his curtains closed before passing out a few hours before.

It wasn't the dream that had woken him, though. It was the thought he'd had just as it ended, in that space between consciousness and sleep.

He didn't bother to light any lamps, instead feeling his way to the chair where he'd thrown his clothes last night before his bath, and running his fingers quickly through his hair to straighten it, unsure whether it was damp now from being washed or from sweat.

Not that it mattered. As soon as he'd pulled his boots on, he hurried to the door and started jogging down the dark hallway toward William and Quinn's room.

He only made it a few feet before a subtle noise behind him made him stop in his tracks and spin around, cursing himself for not having his sword, or even the small knife he normally wore strapped around his calf. *Oh well.* "Who's there?" he called.

"That depends. Who are *you*?"

He sighed, not sure whether to be relieved or livid. "It's Zander, Prince Jonathan. I didn't think you were returning until the morning."

"I wasn't originally, but I need to speak with Her Majesty urgently."

"So do I."

"About what?" Though he'd recognized the voice of Quinn's uncle immediately, he noticed now that it was thick and rough, making Zander wonder if he'd been running. Whatever the reason, it was making Zander's panic more intense.

"If it's all the same to you, I'd prefer to discuss it with Qu— with Her Majesty."

"And if it's not all the same to me? You've intrigued me now, Sir Zander. Tell me what you've figured out."

Zander didn't know Jonathan well at all. He didn't know whether Quinn's youngest uncle was trustworthy or not, and right now, with the revelation he'd just had, he wasn't feeling trusting toward *anyone*. He wasn't entirely sure it mattered … Jonathan's hand hovered dangerously near his hilt, and Zander was sure he wouldn't have been a match for the man even if he *had* been armed.

Besides, Jonathan was here, in the castle, wanting to talk to Quinn, instead of several hours away with Sophia – a fact which only made Zander more confident about his suspicions.

He swallowed hard but took a chance. "I realized that this is a very … *interesting* time for Sophia to be so far away from the castle."

"And now I see why Her Majesty was so quick to circumvent the normal process for assigning a guard in training to such a high position within the castle. Let's go, Sir Zander. We haven't got much time." He said the last part with his back already to Zander as he hurried down the hall.

"It's an emergency, James," he called when they were still several yards from the door. "Wake both Quinn and William, please. Is your father asleep?"

"Yes."

"You'll need to wake him."

"I'll wait and see what Their Majesties have to say."

"Yes, all right. Just wake them."

William answered the door so quickly that Zander was fairly certain he hadn't been sleeping. When he followed Jonathan into their sitting room, he saw why: Quinn stood in the doorway to the bedroom holding a bright-eyed baby.

"What's going on?" she asked.

"Quinn…" Jonathan's voice was still rough – from more than just exercise, Zander realized. "I don't have time to explain everything – we have hardly any time at all. You – all of you – are in danger, and we need to get you out of the castle *now*."

"What do you mean? What kind of danger?"

"An attack on the castle – before dawn."

Quinn closed her eyes. "Tolliver?"

"Yes."

"Can we mount a counter-attack?" Zander asked. "Kill him now?"

"He won't actually be here. I don't know where he is, but they don't plan on sending him until the castle is secure. Dovelnia has dedicated several hundred troops – they've been in the kingdom for weeks. Some of them for moons. It's incredibly organized, Quinn. I can't believe we didn't see any of it."

"It's three in the morning now," William said.

"Yes. Get dressed."

Quinn took several steps toward Jonathan, handing the baby to William as she walked. She looked into his eyes, scrutinizing his face before asking the question Zander was so desperate to know the answer to. "Can I trust you, Jonathan?"

He steepled his fingers, placing them against his lips. "I can't make that decision for you, Your Majesty. My only answer is that right now, tonight, even in this castle, there are very few people you *should* trust, but if you don't count me as one of them, you're unlikely to survive until tomorrow, at least not outside of a cell."

She nodded, looking at James. "Can you please get Thomas and Linnea, Nathaniel, and Mia, Marcus, and your father? Who else can I trust, Jonathan?"

He shook his head. "There are several you can, Quinn. It was wise to assign those you knew were Friends of Philip to the most sensitive tasks. I think we can trust the guards in the stables and at the entrances tonight – at least the entrance I used. But we need to get out of here while drawing as little attention as possible, even amongst those you trust. If we travel with too large a group tonight…"

"I can't leave them here! Many of them are Friends of Philip! It won't be safe."

"They'll manage, Your Majesty," James said, stepping back through the door. "This is what we've dealt with – the kind of situation we're prepared for. We can get a message back to them once you and the prince are safe."

# FLIGHT

LESS THAN AN HOUR later, Quinn was standing in the stables. She had the baby tucked inside a cloth that wrapped around her body, securing him close to her chest. She rocked and bounced to keep him calm as Marcus helped her slip into a long, thick leather cloak to keep both of them warm, though she was as far from calm as possible.

Jonathan led them over to a large carriage she'd never seen before, already hitched to horses. Black and plain, similar to the kind she saw throughout the city, it carried no markings of the Philothean crown. "I borrowed it," he said. "Sort of, anyway. I thought we'd need something less identifiable."

Behind the lead horses, she was relieved to see her own horse, Dusk, hitched next to William's mare, Skittles. Behind them were Thomas' and Linnea's horses, Storm and Snow. None of their horses were overly fond of hauling vehicles, but they'd be all right with such a large team, and she preferred they have their own mounts.

Though she rarely prayed, Quinn sent up silent hope that she was truly making the right decision – that she wasn't trusting her uncle to take them right into the kind of trap he claimed they were avoiding. Her gut said he wasn't lying, though. Something wasn't quite right, but it wasn't because of a lie.

Samuel moved against her, settling his head against her chest, renewing her resolve to get him to safety.

She hoped especially that she could trust the four guards surrounding the carriage now, who were working to load the few things they'd carried down with them. She knew all of them – they were all Friends of Philip, which made her feel better, but she was nervous about everything right then.

Thomas was already helping Linnea climb inside.

"Where do you want me?" Zander asked. "I can ride if that works better." Like everyone tonight, Zander was dressed in plain clothes rather than his new uniform, though his cloak concealed his sword.

"No. We need as many swords as we can get inside the carriage."

"Thomas is still better with his sword than I am with mine. You just don't think I'm good enough on horseback yet." His tone was teasing – he was trying to inject some levity into the situation, which she might have appreciated at another time.

"Please, Zander."

"Okay. I'm sorry. What can I help with?"

She looked around. "Where is William?"

"Um… he and Nathaniel said something about getting some things out of the clinic. I haven't seen them come in here yet."

This time her silent exclamation probably wouldn't have been considered a prayer. "What?"

"Your Majesty, we need you in the carriage. I don't know how much time we have," Jonathan said. "We're not in a position to defend ourselves here in the stables."

Inside her coat, Samuel began to fuss – he always reacted instantly whenever she was too stressed. "Shh, baby, it's okay," she whispered, kissing his head. She took several deep breaths and rocked him.

"I'll find them," Zander said, heading for the door.

"Quinn!" Jonathan had dropped the formalities – clearly he was getting upset, but his tone struck a nerve in her.

"Enough. I'm not leaving here without everyone. I don't know where William and Nathaniel are. And we might be in danger here, but if I'm trusting you to protect me as the queen, then you had best treat me like one. Do *not* order me around."

To her surprise he looked at her with interest, raising an eyebrow. "Interesting time to finally start acting like a queen, *Your Majesty*."

She didn't know what he meant by that, but right now, so long as he wasn't hissing at her, she didn't care. "Zander just went to the clinic to find William and Nathaniel."

"If I send another guard to go and retrieve them right now, will you get yourself and the baby into the carriage with Marcus?"

"Send James or Dorian."

"I'll go," James said – she hadn't even noticed how close he was.

Samuel was in a full-on cry by the time she headed for the carriage, although it was reassuring to see Marcus standing there right by the steps at the end. He took her hand and helped her up.

The carriage was different than the kind she normally rode in. This one was long, with the entrance at the end, and long benches along the sides under the windows. The trunks they'd packed in such a hurry were stowed under the benches already. She looked around, calculating. Each bench could easily seat four people; five would be a little tight.

Well, that was good – because it might be a little tight. Thomas, Linnea and Mia were already huddled together on one of the benches.

Mia looked up and pointed at the baby with a questioning look.

She shook her head – she needed to be holding him right now, needed his solid little weight against her, even if he was fussing.

"Thank you, though," she mouthed before turning back to Marcus. "Zander and James aren't back yet?"

"It's been less than two minutes."

"How many minutes do we have? We're already on borrowed time. I'm going to murder them."

"Are you sure about this, Quinn?" Marcus' voice was low and close to her ear – he, too, had dispensed with all formalities, although she was certain his reasons for doing so were different. His tone was fatherly.

"Do you think I have any reason to mistrust Jonathan?" she whispered.

"No. Too much of it fits with the other information that has come to light."

She took a deep breath – there hadn't been time to talk this decision through, to even think about anything except moving quickly. "Do we have the ability to safely defend the castle?"

"Safely? Almost certainly not. There would probably be loss of life. If we were ultimately unsuccessful, you most likely either wouldn't survive, or would be imprisoned, depending on what their plan is – the same goes for everyone here in this carriage."

"And what are our chances of being successful?"

"I don't know. Not zero, not one hundred percent."

She looked over at the seats where Linnea and Mia were huddled together, watching Thomas start a fire in the small grate, then back to Marcus, her eyes landing on the medal he'd earned in the surprise battle that had claimed his son.

Outside of the carriage there was a sudden commotion – Jonathan shouting, "Did anyone see you? Any guards? Anyone?" followed by the most reassuring sound in the world, William's voice. "No. We didn't even use lanterns."

"The guard who should have been patrolling the south yard wasn't," Nathaniel's voice added. "James checked for him but nobody was there."

Jonathan uttered a dark expletive. "Do you know who was supposed to be there? Never mind. It doesn't matter right now. We have to get out of here. Get in the carriage."

Just as William, Nathaniel, and Zander appeared in the open doorway, all three of them straining under the weight of huge crates filled with medical supplies, Quinn nodded to Marcus.

After he'd figured out how to store the crates mostly under the seats, William faced her. "I know. I'm sorry," he whispered, taking her hands.

She squeezed his hands tightly, with maybe just a little too much involvement of her fingernails.

"I'm really sorry." He pressed his forehead gently to hers for a few seconds before leaning in closer to kiss the baby's head. Samuel's writhing and fussing was slowly calming.

Behind them, Jonathan closed the door.

"He's not riding in here with us?" Zander asked, suspicion coloring every syllable. Quinn shrugged, squinting through the window to watch as Jonathan and James extinguished the few lanterns lighting the stable. At almost the same time, Marcus twisted the dial on the one in the carriage, plunging them into darkness.

Samuel whined again as her heart picked up pace, threatening to burst its way out of her chest.

William grabbed her around the waist just as the carriage started moving, guiding her down on the bench next to Mia.

Nobody breathed as the carriage left the confines of the large barn. In the moonlight outside, Quinn could see Jonathan riding alongside the guards. William kept one arm around her back, the other on Samuel, rubbing the infant's back. At least the baby seemed to like the motion.

The horses moved slowly, as silently as possible, creeping toward a far back gatehouse.

Though he didn't make any noise, William's lips were moving as they grew closer to the exit, as they waited to either be caught or make it out safely. Except for Quinn and William, who curled tighter and tighter around the prince, every person in the carriage had one hand on the handle of a weapon.

"Did anyone ever think to keep a *gun?*" Zander muttered under his breath.

For once, Quinn had trouble disagreeing with the idea.

For all the stress, when they reached the gate, nobody was there; the two guards who had been on duty there tonight were now in their traveling party. She watched out the window as they dismounted their horses and went inside the guardhouse to release the latch that would allow them to lift the heavy metal grate. Once the carriage was safely through, they closed it again though there was no choice but to leave it unlocked. Not that it probably mattered.

Still, nobody spoke. Breaths were shallow and fingers held tight to knives and swords until long after the silhouette of the castle had disappeared from the horizon.

Finally, somewhere far outside the city, on a bumpy dirt road in the middle of a forest, the horses came to a stop.

By the time Jonathan opened the door and Marcus extended a hand to help him in, Quinn was sure the same question was burning in everyone's mind. "Where are we going?"

Even in the dim moonlight streaming through the windows, she could see Jonathan's frown. "How am I supposed to know? That's what I was coming in here to ask you."

"Excuse me?"

"I came in here to ask you what direction we should be traveling, now that we're clear of the castle and hopefully away from the paths of any incoming troops."

"I don't know! I thought you had some kind of plan!"

"I did. I got you out of the castle before you were arrested or killed. I expected, *Your Majesty*, that once that goal was accomplished, you would have made some decisions about what we should do from here."

Her head was actually going to explode – for real, bone fragments flying everywhere. She pinched the bridge of her nose, careful not to bump Samuel who had finally fallen asleep. "How are the horses?"

Jonathan sighed. "They're good. We've been quiet more than fast, but they will need water soon. There is a stream nearby."

"Can you have some water brought up for them, please?"

"Of course."

The carriage was silent for several seconds after Jonathan exited.

"Well, at least he's probably not kidnapping us," Zander said.

Quinn, who'd finally had some time to think, – although not about where they should be going – shook her head. "Probably not. Unless he's trying to see where we'd lead him."

"Which is where, exactly?" Zander asked. "Back to Eirentheos?"

"No," she said, even though at the moment that was the only place she wanted to go – besides Bristlecone, maybe. "I don't know where this situation is heading politically, but I'm pretty sure that running away from the kingdom is the worst decision I could make."

"It's also where they'll be expecting you to go," Marcus said. "I wouldn't be surprised if Tolliver or whoever this is already has spies at the Eirenthean border crossings."

Zander coughed. "You wouldn't be *surprised*? What tipped you off? Hector and Tolliver using the gate? Or the two incidents of *biological warfare*?"

Quinn's head snapped toward him.

"Poisoning children through their school books, intentionally infecting animals with rabies... I think it's safe to say that Eirentheos has a little bit more of a problem than a few spies at border crossings. I don't know who all is involved, but they've clearly been targeting Stephen and his kingdom for a long time."

She frowned. "Do you think it's the same people?"

"You'd better *hope* it's the same people. Does Eirentheos have any other enemies?"

"No," Nathaniel said. "Eirentheos is very isolated geographically. It borders only Philotheum. The next closest kingdom is across the Southern Channel, but there's always been peace and respect between them."

"Well, then you – we – likely have the same people interfering with both Eirentheos and Quinn's throne. Probably for the same reasons – they want to weaken the link between the two kingdoms, distracting Eirentheos and reduce their ability to interfere with their agenda in Philotheum."

Marcus cleared his throat. "That's quite an astute observation, Zander. Especially for a newcomer."

She couldn't fully see the expression on Zander's face in the dim light, but she could *hear* it in his response.

"I know nobody's asked – but in case anyone is silently wondering, it feels *fantastic* when you underestimate my ability to understand what's going on."

Marcus was the only one in the carriage who didn't even try to stifle his chuckle. "Fair enough, Zander. I apologize. You've shown an incredible ability to assess situations quickly and accurately. You might consider being more careful in the demonstration of that ability if you don't want us to come to rely on your input."

"Well, I sort of question whether you'll actually ask for it when I tell you what I *don't* understand."

Quinn was intrigued. So far he seemed to be nailing everything – including pieces she hadn't completely put together. "What don't you understand?"

He looked down at his feet, his next words – strong and defiant as they were – slightly muffled in the thick wool of his cloak. "I don't understand why I'm the first one voicing these conclusions. Is everyone really so naïve that they don't see the consistent, undermining attacks that have been going on – or are those conversations happening somewhere else, and you're all just smiling and nodding while you let Quinn play princess but keep her from really ruling?"

She knew they were only words – that Zander was speaking from his gut, that his instincts might not even be right – but the question was like a physical assault, making her gasp. Samuel stirred against her, letting out a low fussing noise. She stood to rock him, swaying back and forth on her feet, though she wasn't sure which of them she was really attempting to calm. What disturbed her even more was the long, poignant silence after Zander finished.

Marcus stood, too, and Quinn found herself unconsciously taking a step back. The dark shape of Marcus' shoulders sank, as did the bottom of her stomach.

Behind her, William shifted; she could feel he was going to rise as well, but she held her hand back in a signal asking him not to. He settled back.

"There is a third possibility, Zander," Marcus said quietly, although he faced Quinn. "Your observations are remarkably accurate, but your interpretations of them are, perhaps, colored by the knowledge and experience you gained growing up in a different world."

"Colored *how?*" Quinn asked. "Is he wrong, Marcus?"

"It's true, Your Majesty, that we've had concerns for some time that Dovelnia was possibly involved in the poisonings in Eirentheos and the fact the gate was compromised. We don't have solid evidence to connect Tolliver or King Ivan to the rabies situation, but it's certainly suspicious, especially with Tolliver then appearing at the gate, and his apparent ability to move between the kingdoms without detection. None of this information has been hidden from you."

"It just hasn't all been explicitly shared with me, and moreover some of your concerns about the implications of the information have been withheld."

"Yes." Marcus' chest rose and fell.

"Do you believe I'm incapable of ruling the kingdom as queen?"

"No." His answer was immediate enough to allow her to breathe again. "I do, however, believe that you are young – the youngest ruler ever crowned in either Philotheum or Eirentheos.

That would be a challenge even without your … *complicated* background."

"And then there's the fact that I'm a girl."

He hesitated – but only for a second. "That probably influences decisions about what concerns to bring to you more than it should. I try not to allow it to affect me personally, but I'm far from perfect. I'm learning on this part of the job as well, Quinn."

His candor relaxed her a little. Whatever was going on wasn't quite as sinister as Zander's conclusions had implied. Still… "So you're trying to protect me."

"All things considered, protecting you is my job."

"You know what I mean."

"Yes, but I'm not sure you understand what I mean – how I – how everyone perceives serving you. Many decisions are made with consideration of an entire future with you – your *family* – ruling the kingdom. You're not some interchangeable stand-in, here for a little while, and so we have to humor you and deal with you. You're the rightful queen, appointed by the Maker at the time of your birth, the mother of the future king, and the grandmother of the ruler after him." He paused, his head tipping toward the floor before he looked back up at her.

"And you're young and inexperienced in every possible way. You have no parents, at least in any meaningful sense, and you're both a new bride and a new mother – to the future king, no less. So, yes, I have to admit to a certain level of protecting you. Or attempting to, anyway."

"Who else is in on this?" Zander demanded.

Quinn sighed. Part of her wished that Zander would cool it, but another part was grateful for his willingness to push for answers. She looked at him. "I would guess that it's primarily Marcus and Stephen. Nathaniel has likely been involved in it as well … and Charles."

Marcus didn't argue, and Nathaniel remained silent. "It's not some kind of conspiracy, you know," Marcus said, more to Zander than to her. "We're not deliberately withholding critical information — it's more a series of judgment calls over what issues are important enough to push you to deal with. Clearly, with the new information that has come to light today, some of those judgment calls have been in error."

"Did you ever plan to share your concerns with me?"

"Yes. I mistook — rather gravely, it seems, how much time we had to deal with the possible threat coming from Dovelnia."

She took a long, deep breath through her nose, thinking as she patted the baby's back to the rhythm of her heartbeat. "Are you keeping anything from me now? Information *or* concerns?"

"I quite dislike that tonight's incident happened with Lady Sophia out of the castle."

"Oh, I think we're all on that page. I have a number of questions for Jonathan as soon as we're somewhere safe… Do you think we're safe out here with Jonathan, Marcus?"

"As safe as we are anywhere."

"Well, that's not a ringing endorsement, but I guess I'll take it."

They both chuckled quietly. From behind her, William reached up to gently brush the side of her hand.

"I do have an idea about where we could go," Marcus said, glancing around the carriage, his gaze landing on Nathaniel.

Nathaniel nodded.

"I'm listening," Quinn said.

"Nathaniel and I have some friends — they're Friends of Philip."

"We've known them for a very long time," Nathaniel said. "I've been in contact with them about starting a clinic in their village. Staying hidden will be difficult, but we're going to run into that everywhere."

"Will they take us, do you think?" Quinn asked.

"I can go and talk to them privately at first. If they refuse us… they're near a forest."

She inhaled deeply before slowly letting out a breath. "Well, carriage camping in the forest is better than nothing, I guess. At least there will be wood for the fire. Shall we tell Jonathan?" She sank back down onto the bench, finally allowing William to put his arm around her shoulders.

Zander stayed on his feet. "Can we really trust Jonathan with this kind of information?" he asked as Marcus headed toward the door.

Quinn wasn't entirely sure about that herself, but she shrugged. "If he's isn't really on my side, I'm sort of screwed either way, don't you think? At this point, we need to get through tonight. It will be dawn soon."

Zander didn't sit down, even when Jonathan climbed into the wagon with Marcus. Jonathan raised an eyebrow and chuckled under his breath when he saw him. "Have you come up with a plan?" he asked Quinn.

"I think so. Marcus thinks we should…"

"No, Your Majesty. That is not information I want to have right now. Your horses are watered and doing well, the carriage is in good shape, and Neil is bringing in some more firewood for you all for the remainder of your journey tonight. Then he will accompany me away from here. Dorian, James, and the others will remain here with you. Please, please, stay far away from any main thoroughfares until you're much farther from the castle than we are now."

"Where are you going?"

"That isn't something you should worry about. It's best for each of us to have as little information about the other's whereabouts as possible right now. I will do what I can to get in touch with Charles and see that he and his family are safe. For the present time, please be careful not to try to contact *anyone* in any way that might allow your location to be traced."

Quinn was too stunned to do much besides nod a couple of times and then stare as Jonathan exited the carriage and mounted his horse.

After Jonathan and the guard, Neil, were gone, Nathaniel cleared his throat. "Now that it's just us, I have another idea."

# TOBIAS

THE SOUND OF THE carriage door opening woke Zander from an exhausted, dreamy half-sleep. When he finally managed to pry his eyes all the way open, he saw Marcus standing in the opening, blocking a stream of vivid yellow sunshine. He looked around for a moment, trying to orient himself and clear his thoughts enough to understand what was going on.

Linnea was the only one asleep – besides Samuel, who was splayed out in dramatic fashion on William's chest. Everyone else had either awakened at Marcus' return or had never been asleep to begin with. Even after traveling all night and for several hours this morning, they were all too on edge to truly rest.

"What's the news?" Quinn asked. Zander didn't think she'd slept at all.

"The birds have returned. We have a place to stay," Marcus said. "Although we'll have to leave the carriage here. It's not possible to travel with it all the way to where we're going, and I don't want to take any chances of someone finding it and getting closer to you." His voice was dark, tired, and filled with worry. "News of trouble at the castle has made it this far already."

A sharp thrill of fear raced down Zander's throat all the way down his body, slicing him in half.

Quinn was having a similar reaction. "How is that possible?"

"The Friends of Philip are used to quickly communicating important events. There is already considerable worry about your welfare. We need to get you hidden quickly. James and Dorian are saddling the horses now."

"I'll help," Zander said, standing and brushing himself off, mostly in an effort to return sensation to his extremities.

Marcus gave him a sideways glance, the fatherly kind that *almost* asked whether he was up to this, if he'd had enough sleep to even contemplate riding a horse, but then he sighed and held his hand out toward the door. There wasn't another choice anyway.


The ride through the forest and along dirt trails was tense. All of the guards formed a tight circle around Quinn, William, Thomas, Linnea, and Nathaniel as Marcus led them to wherever they were going. Every noise was cause for alarm. Zander brought the whole group to a halt once when he heard a rustling sound in the nearby trees which turned out to be a capiya – not that the discovery of one of *those* creatures made him feel better.

Zander was impressed – although Quinn hadn't done much riding for several months, and he'd had intense training lately in the skill, she was still much more at ease on Dusk's back than he thought he could ever be on a horse. And she had Samuel tied to her chest.

Exhausted as he was, he was alert – they all were. A shift in the wind brought with it a cold breeze that warned them they needed to make it to shelter before dark.

Two long hours after leaving the carriage, they emerged from the thick woods at the top of a hill. Down below them, in the only clearing he'd seen since they left the carriage, was what looked like a farm. A low, but large and rambling house surrounded by outbuildings, including an enormous barn. The roofs of all the buildings were made of thick, weathered wood shingles. An inviting ribbon of smoke curled up from the stone chimney at the northern end of the house.

Not for the first time since coming to this world, Zander had visions of the fairy tales he'd read as a child. Today he was almost waiting for a wicked witch or a giant to appear at the edge of the woods on the other side of the clearing – or soldiers, he reminded himself.

Marcus led them down the hill, stopping in front of a tall iron gate. Up close, the stone wall that surrounded the property was higher than it had seemed as they'd approached. He was straightening to dismount when a man appeared on the other side. He was older, his hair a silvery gray and his hands wrinkled and worn.

"Sir Marcus, Prince Nathaniel," the man said, lifting the iron latch inside the gate and pulling it open. Despite the appearance of his hands, they were strong and moved the heavy bar easily. "Come in."

When Quinn rode through the gate, the man dropped to one knee. "Your Majesty, it is an honor."

She shook her head. "The honor is mine, Sir…"

"I'm Tobias Sheppard. Most simply call me Tobias. Welcome to my home. Come on inside. Quickly. There is plenty of room in the stables for your horses."

Even in the short time he'd been in this world, Zander had learned that lengthy, overly polite introductions were the norm, so when the man ushered them into a large living room and immediately began discussing business, he knew things were bad.

"Is everyone in your party all right, Your Majesty?"

"I think so. Prince Jonathan and one of my guards left us early this morning. I'm not sure exactly where they were headed."

Tobias leaned his hands on the back of a large chair. "Did he know you were coming this way?"

"No."

"Were you seen by anyone as you were headed in this direction?"

Quinn started to shake her head, but Marcus responded, "Earlier this morning, when we still had the carriage, we passed by a small village, close enough to be in view of some of the houses. I don't think we were seen, but I can't be certain."

"Okay." Tobias nodded.

"What news have you heard?" Quinn asked.

"Not enough to be very helpful. Reports of troops traveling through the capital city, and of smoke coming from the castle this morning."

"Smoke?" Zander asked.

Nobody else looked surprised, though. When Quinn responded to him, her expression was upset, but resigned. "That would be an effective way of rooting us out if we were hiding somewhere in the castle."

"So it could be a good sign, then? They don't know if or when we got out safely."

"Sure," she agreed. "It could be good news. Depending, of course, on who else they murdered in the process."

He gulped and took a step backward, even though she wasn't actually angry – just sad. She needed to be angrier.

His ill-chosen observation had drawn Tobias' attention, though. "I'm afraid I don't know everyone in your party, Your Majesty."

"Of course, I'm sorry," she said. "This is Prince Thomas and Princess Linnea of Eirentheos." She pointed to each of them.

"Yes, I know all of the royals and Sir Marcus. I also recognized James and Dorian Blackwelder when I saw them, and the other guards outside helping them with the horses are, I believe, Kian Mondragon and Ethan Power?"

"That's correct." Quinn sounded as impressed – and curious – as Zander was.

"I don't know your maid."

"Mia Willoughby, Sir," Mia said quickly, bobbing her head at him.

Tobias' eyebrows went up. "Any relation to Luke?"

"Yes. He's my father."

"Very nice," he clicked his tongue. "You are surrounded quite well, Your Majesty. Which brings me to my last question." His eyes fell on Zander.

William cleared his throat. "This is Zander Cunningham, our newest personal guard."

"In training," Zander muttered under his breath.

"An apprentice? Interesting. In King Stephen's castle, you would be considered quite old to begin training for a position with the family. You've also only just arrived in Philotheum, and yet you seem quite well acquainted with Queen Quinn – rather impertinent for an apprentice, actually."

Uncomfortable warmth spread through Zander's chest and arms as Tobias looked him over. He didn't know how to respond to the man's observations – but he didn't get a chance to, anyway. "You're not from here, are you?"

Now he couldn't tell whether the sensation was fire or ice, but it was hard to breathe around whatever it was. He coughed. "From Philotheum? No."

"You're not from Eirentheos, either."

"What are you implying, Tobias?" Quinn asked in a tone Zander hadn't known she possessed.

"I'm implying that perhaps you brought Mister Cunningham with you from the other world."

Around him, even the air grew tense – at least the air surrounding William, Thomas, and Linnea. Nathaniel and Marcus didn't look as shocked as he would have expected. Quinn must have noticed that as well, because she didn't react with shock, instead she squared her shoulders. "Actually, it's Sir Zander Cunningham."

"Ah. So this is the man who killed Rahas, then."

Zander took a deep breath, the way he always had to when the … *incident* … was mentioned. A second later, he was surprised to feel Linnea's hand on his elbow.

"Yes," Quinn said. "We owe much to him that the outcome of that battle wasn't much, much worse."

"By worse you mean Tolliver gaining access to a portal that would allow him to travel to another world, yes?"

"I think we've shared enough about ourselves for the moment, Mister Sheppard. I would like to hear about you."

"Was I wrong in assuming that everyone in your party here knows that you were born in a different world than this one?"

Quinn looked around. "The guards outside don't know."

"I didn't speak of it in front of them." The way he frowned made Zander wonder what else the man knew that they didn't. "Surely all of King Stephen's children are aware, and I know Marcus and Nathaniel both are."

"I'm more interested in how *you* know."

"Your uncle has done well at keeping his relationship with me secret," he said, nodding at Nathaniel. "I hope that's a sign you'll be safe with me, the way he and your father were many cycles ago."

"You knew my father?"

Given the man's obvious age, Zander wasn't surprised that he'd at least known *of* the crown prince of Philotheum, but it sounded as if he was implying more than a passing acquaintance.

"Yes." The man's eyes went again to Nathaniel, the two of them exchanging a silent conversation. "Samuel was my nephew."

A deep crease appeared in Quinn's forehead. "How is that even possible? My grandfather didn't have any siblings."

"That's true."

Zander understood just a second before she did – she took a big step backward, right into William's chest. Not that he blamed her.

"You're Sophia's brother."

"Yes."

"Why have I never met you before, then?"

"My sister and I had a falling out many cycles ago. I've not been welcome around her since."

"When she married Hector?" Quinn guessed.

Tobias chuckled. "It would have happened then, I'm sure, but our problems began a long time prior to that – when she first began courting your grandfather, actually."

"What was your fight with Sophia about, then?" Zander appreciated how suspicious Quinn sounded.

He glanced behind her at Nathaniel and gave a small shake of his head. "Your Majesty, my problems with my sister were not of a political nature. Suffice it to say that she was afraid her connection to me might damage her chances of marrying Jonathan in the first place."

Inside the cloth wrap around her chest, the baby began squirming and fussing. William reached for him as Quinn studied Tobias. "*Would* her connection to you have upset my grandfather?"

"I don't know. Your father didn't seem to think it would have. It didn't bother him or Nathaniel."

"I trust Tobias more than I trust most people," Nathaniel said. "If it hadn't been for my fear that we might someday need his help like this again, I would have introduced you to him before this. None of my other siblings know of his existence. Marcus is the only person in the castle besides me who knows Tobias."

Quinn nodded, her features relaxing a little. "My main concern, of course, is that this is the first place Sophia will come looking for us. Or that our position will be compromised here."

He frowned. "You think you're in danger from *Sophia* finding you?"

"We have enough reason to suspect that's the case, yes," Nathaniel said.

"Hmm… Well, you certainly have no reason to fear me contacting her. We haven't spoken in so long, I don't know if she even believes I'm still alive."

"You don't think the queen of a kingdom could find out whether her *brother* died or not?" Quinn asked, her voice rising into that tone again.

Tobias looked at Nathaniel again then back at Quinn. "She didn't know her *sons* were still alive, Your Majesty."

"Yeah, there's a little too much of that, don't you think? If she's smart, she'd realize that she may have missed a lot of things. This might be one of the first places she looks."

"Even if she's not smart, Tolliver obviously has more knowledge than we gave him credit for – or someone close to him does." William said. "I think it's a stretch to assume we'll be safe here."

Tobias sighed quietly, pressing his lips into a thin line. "Do you have somewhere safer to go? There's a storm moving in; do you really want that baby sleeping in the woods?"

William closed his eyes, patting Samuel on the back. His non-response was enough of an answer for everyone.

"Besides, I think you underestimate Sophia's capacity for denial. I changed my surname to match my beloved's many cycles ago after I promised Sophia I would stay away from her and her future family. Nobody knows who I am or where I came from – not anymore, anyway. I became a widower three cycles ago."

"I'm sorry to hear of your loss," Quinn said.

"Thank you. We had a long and fulfilling life together, enough happiness to last me. Not everyone is lucky enough to have what we did for as long as we did. But I appreciate your kindness. Anyway, the point of my story is more that everyone who knows my secret is in this room, except for Sophia, and she is more afraid of me finding her than I am of her finding me."

"You're that scary?"

To Zander's surprise, Tobias smiled. "You may want to reserve your judgment on that until you see the condition of my guest rooms. They haven't been tended to in ages, I'm afraid."

"I'm sure I can help with that," Mia said, shrugging out of her cloak and smoothing the skirt of her dress. "If you can point me to the rooms and to any supplies you might have."

That seemed to settle the discussion for then. Zander wasn't sure what to think of Tobias or his secluded farmhouse, but it appeared they'd be staying here, at least for now. There really weren't any better options. By the time he stepped outside to help the other guards finish bringing everything inside, the sky had already grown dark with thick, heavy clouds, and the wind had changed from cold to biting.

# THE FRIENDS OF PHILIP

"CAN I HELP YOU with that?"

Mia looked up over the cream-colored sheet she was shaking out over a bed in one of Tobias' guest rooms. "You really don't..." She stopped, squeezing her eyes shut for a second, and then nodded. "Sure."

Thomas reached for the edge of the sheet, pulling it flat against the mattress and leaning down to tuck the edges in. It was softer than he expected, made of a nicer material than he'd guessed it would be. The mattress was thicker, too. "So Quinn and William will be in here, then?" he asked, nodding toward the diaper bag sitting on one of the armchairs by the fireplace. He knew it was a stupid question, but it was better than silence.

"Yes." She followed his gaze. "I need to get some water on to boil for those diapers – we'll be out by tomorrow and they'll need time to dry since I'm not going to be able to put them outside."

Through the window, he could see big, fluffy snowflakes falling from the moonlit sky.

"I'll go and get some water going on the kitchen hearth. You have enough with the rooms – let me do the diapers."

She tilted her head and huffed out a sigh. "It's not your job, Thomas. I'm Samuel's nurse – and I haven't even been especially useful at that yet."

"Quinn will need you plenty sooner than you think. As soon as that baby's old enough to be awake more and hard to carry everywhere."

"She will if we survive this, anyway." Mia said without looking at him as she reached for a heavy quilt folded on a chair.

"Mia…" he closed most of the distance between them.

"What, Thomas? Are you going to tell me it's not that bad? We wouldn't have fled the castle in the middle of the night if that wasn't exactly how bad this is."

He pressed his lips together. "We still can't think that way. We did get out of the castle, and for tonight we're safe."

She kept the quilt in front of her, looking down at it as she nodded. "I know."

"Do you regret your decision to come to Philotheum?"

"No." Stepping away from him, she took the side of the quilt and began to shake it out over the bed.

He put his hand over hers, stopping her, and put one finger under her chin, gently turning her face toward him. "You don't?"

"No." She took a small step back from him, but didn't look away this time. "I'm scared that this is happening, but I knew … after Ben … that Tolliver was likely to cause problems. I feel like I'm supposed to be here, doing what I can for Quinn and William and Samuel. I might not be able to fight for them like Ben did, but I'm honored to be able to serve the true queen and the heir."

Thomas nodded – he understood the sentiment as well. As strange and frightening as the situation was, this was where he wanted to be, with his brother and sisters and his nephew. More than anything, he wanted to win this fight with Tolliver once and for all.

"So, then, this…" he motioned with his finger to the space between them, "is all about me, isn't it?"

She cocked one eyebrow. "Are we going to talk about that now?"

"Well…" He picked at a hangnail on his thumb. "We kind of need to at some point."

"Do we? Because we've been doing… *whatever* it is we're doing now every day for long enough now that I think we could keep it up forever."

"Is that what you want, Mia? For us to just continue like we've been?"

"I wasn't the one who wanted that in the first place Thomas."

He took a deep breath in through his nose, willing himself to not be irritated with her, to really be able to talk about this, but it wasn't easy. "You're the one who wanted to go to Philotheum without telling me."

Her fingers wrapped around the edge of the quilt again, her knuckles turning white in a way that sent a painful pulse rippling through his stomach.

"You're right. I was. But was I the only one? Is it all my fault if neither of us can talk about what we're thinking?"

"No," he whispered. Now he was the one not looking at her.

There was silence for several seconds as he stared at his hands and she began shaking out the quilt again.

"This isn't the time, Thomas," she finally said once the bed was made. "I have a million things to do, and we're all emotional… Let's just do what we need to do for now."

He started to nod, started to take the easy way out, yet again, but then his hand slipped and brushed against his pocket, jingling the bracelet inside – making it clink against the small coin his father had given to him before returning to Eirentheos.

"All right. But… later, after things have settled for the evening, can I make you a cup of tea?"

She was quiet again, for almost too long, before she finally said, "Okay."

When he reached the kitchen, only Tobias and Zander were in there. The older man stood at a tall counter in the middle of the room, chopping onions and peppers, while Zander sat on a stool, watching and drinking steaming tea from a metal mug. Thomas frowned at Zander.

"Leave him be," Tobias said. "He offered plenty of help, but I can tell he's not so used to the rigors of this world yet. We made a deal. I'll cook if he teaches me a recipe from his world."

Not for the first time since encountering Tobias earlier today, Thomas nearly choked on his spit.

"Are you all right?" Tobias asked, looking up from his giant pile of vegetables for only a moment.

"I'm fine. Could you use any of *my* help? It looks like you must have a very impressive indoor garden somewhere."

"I do – and usually not nearly enough company to cook for and share it with. The chickens are well fed, though."

"Well, that one *was*," Zander said, nodding toward the counter next to the large pump-fed sink, where strips from a freshly plucked and gutted chicken were soaking in some kind of oily sauce in a large ceramic bowl.

"So… What are we having?"

"Fajitas," Zander said.

"Fa- what?"

Zander grinned. "You're always feeding me unfamiliar food. I thought it was my turn to introduce you to something completely different. "So we're having fajitas. Well, sort of. He doesn't have exactly the right peppers – or steak."

"It's hard to justify butchering a cow just for myself," Tobias said, shrugging. "The recipe sounds interesting anyway. But, no, Thomas, I don't need your help, either. You look like you might be busy yourself. Is there something I can help *you* with?"

"Uh, yes, actually." He held up the bag of soiled diapers. "I was wondering if you had a washing tub I could borrow?"

"Ah, yes, Thomas. Just through that door over there, you'll find a laundry sink. It's not anything fancy, and it'll be cold in there, but you should find what you need." Tobias' attitude was dismissive of his house, but in truth the property was quite nice for a rural farm. Clearly he had added onto it over the cycles, and upgraded many rooms. The buildings were in need of some maintenance here and there, perhaps, in areas that were probably becoming more difficult to keep up with as he aged, but even so it was a beautiful and cozy home.

"Thank you. We may be imposing on you a bit more for washing clothing. I'm afraid we all packed in a rush and aren't as well prepared as we'd like to be."

"You're welcome to anything, truly. I wasn't sure I'd ever get the opportunity to meet my great-niece in person. I intend to care for her while she's here – and the rest of you as well – however short the time may be."

Thomas didn't understand Tobias at all. If he'd wanted to meet Quinn before this, he would only have needed to send a message to the castle introducing himself.

"Well, we all appreciate it. Quinn is always interested in meeting the family she never knew she had."

Tobias smiled at him quickly before turning his attention back to another onion. "Feel free to boil some water over the cooking fire for those diapers. I imagine the queen and king will be finishing their discussion with Marcus any time now and will join us."

There was an implied dismissal in Tobias' words, but Thomas couldn't help his curiosity about the man. Some of his interest came from wanting to know just *how* safe they were here at this farm, and whether anyone else might discover them here – but if he were being honest, most of it was simple fascination with the intriguing man. After he'd set the offending bag down out of the way in the laundry room, he went back into the kitchen and searched for a pot to boil water in.

"Do you have any children?" he asked Tobias as he chose the largest cast-iron pot he could find on the wooden shelves that lined one wall of the kitchen.

"No. We were never blessed with the honor. We did enjoy a close relationship with the son of some dear friends, but his marriage took him to a village several days from here, and I only get messages from him in between visits at feast-times."

"And no other family?"

"Nobody is going to drop in on me unexpectedly, Thomas. A few well-placed Friends of Philip know how to reach me – and I have some friends in the village who check in on me from time to time, but only because I'm a doddering old man. They'd be easy to hide from long before I offered an invitation up to the house. Your concern is understandable, though. I don't mind the questions. You have no reason to trust that you'll be safe here. I know you're only here because you have nowhere else to go tonight – but that's fair enough. I've no doubt I'd feel the same as all of you if I were in the same position."

"If the floor is open for questions," said a voice behind Thomas, "I'd like to know how you know about the other world."

"Hello again, Your Majesty." Tobias set down his knife and wiped his hands on a white towel he had draped over his shoulder. "There's a fresh pot of tea if you'd like a cup."

"I would like answers, Tobias."

"Yes, I know you would. I'm not avoiding giving them to you – I think you're actually going to be rather disappointed in how little I know that you don't already. But there's no reason to stand there and be uncomfortable while we talk. I'll make you a cup of tea and you can have a seat by the fire. You too, of course, King William. I see you have your hands full with that beautiful baby. Please, sit down."

Quinn's posture relaxed a little as she walked over to one of the comfortable chairs just to the side of the fireplace. Thomas guessed that Tobias must spend most of his time in this room; there was a little table between the chairs stacked with several books. There was even a little stack of clay tiles; Tobias set out two of them and placed hot mugs of tea on top for both Quinn and William.

"He truly is marvelous," Tobias said, pausing for a moment to stare at Samuel. "If he wasn't sleeping so peacefully, I'd ask if I could hold him."

"He'll wake again soon," William said. "I'm sure you'll have the chance before the meal is over."

Tobias smiled. "That would be wonderful. I'm not at all fond of the circumstances, but I must say I'm not disappointed to get a chance to see him up close – and while he's tiny, too."

There was a catch in his voice that Quinn must have caught, too. "Up close?" she asked? "Have you seen him from far away?"

"I did make it to the city for his Naming Ceremony. It was all amazing, of course, but I like seeing him snuggled with his father in front of my fire much more."

"You think Sophia thinks you're dead, but you would risk going to an event where she'll be?"

"It's not as if I went to the *castle*, Your Majesty. I merely attended the ceremony, in the back with the commoners. Nobody knew I was there. I didn't even tell Nathaniel this time."

She looked over at Nathaniel, who was on the other side of the kitchen with Marcus, retrieving more mugs from a high cabinet. He was clearly familiar with this house.

"Do you and Nathaniel speak regularly?" she asked.

"Yes." Tobias didn't hesitate. "We exchange messages at least once a moon; more often since he's returned to Philotheum. And he was kind enough to visit me several times each cycle for a long time, although that stopped once he became known more publicly. It's good to have him here again."

"We need to start at the beginning, I think," Nathaniel said, coming up behind Tobias and patting him on the shoulder.

Tobias nodded, retreating back to his vegetables as Nathaniel set his mug down on another of the tiles and pulled a stool over from the kitchen counter.

Marcus turned his attention to the chicken on the counter – Thomas noticed the old man didn't object to *his* help. Apparently Marcus already knew everything.

He pulled up a stool of his own so he could hear the whole conversation. Zander passed him a hot mug as he scooted closer, too.

"Tobias is right," Nathaniel said, "in that it's really not much more than you already know. I've told you nearly the whole story before this, but for various reasons, I've left Tobias out."

"Because of Sophia?" she asked.

"She's one part of it. Another part is that Tobias has been a safe refuge for me for a long time, and he was the same for your father before that. I didn't want to jeopardize him *or* us – and while I've never liked hiding things from you, Quinn, right now I'm very glad I kept this secret."

"So how did my father find Tobias if he's so well hidden and nobody knows about him?"

"He didn't. Tobias found him. Shortly after Samuel found out that he was going to be sent to Dovelnia, one of the guards in the castle slipped him a note, suggesting that he consider finding a way to escape the castle and learn about what Hector was really up to, and offering him a safe place to stay. The note was from Tobias."

"And my father just believed the note from someone he'd never heard of?"

"No," Tobias said from behind them. "But he had enough of his own suspicions, and once Hector came into his bedroom and threatened him, he was willing to take a chance."

Nathaniel nodded. "He also trusted the guard who brought him the note… Benjamin Westbrook."

Thomas' heart gave a little jump at the too-familiar name. Instinctively, he looked for Linnea before remembering that she had gone to take a nap. His eyes fell on Marcus instead. "Your father?" he asked.

"Yes. He died before Ben was born, but I like to think they had more in common than just their names."

"He was a good man," Nathaniel said. "One of the few people Samuel implicitly trusted. He was also the one who helped him escape from the castle that night and reach Tobias safely. We're all probably lucky he lived past that day. I know I was."

"Without his vote of confidence, Samuel probably wouldn't have taken a chance on me," Tobias said, moving from his cutting board to the stove and pouring oil from a glass bottle into a cast-iron pan. "He wasn't an especially trusting man by the time he'd lived with Hector for several cycles. Not that I fault him."

The baby was stirring now, beginning to grunt and shove his fists in his mouth. William's focus didn't shift from the conversation as he passed Samuel to Quinn. "So Benjamin knew who you really were as well?"

"He knew me as Tobias Sheppard – as many people do. He did not know my birth name or my history. That was a fact I shared only with Samuel, and later with Nathaniel. Even Marcus didn't know that truth until much more recently."

Thomas cleared his throat. "So what does *Tobias Sheppard* know about the Friends of Philip?"

Tobias didn't answer immediately; he took his time scraping the sliced pieces of chicken into the pan, filling the room with popping and sizzling. Then he set the cutting board and knife into the sink and wiped his hands on the towel over his shoulder as he turned around. "I know everything about them – down to the last member. I created them."

"Wait. What?" Marcus asked, standing from his stool and walking toward Tobias.

"That's a secret guarded at least as well as my real identity. I debated even sharing as much with you all here – but so many things have been kept from Her Majesty up until now, I think it's best I trust her with all of my truth. Besides, Quinn, you and that baby are the only reason left that the Friends of Philip were created at all."

Quinn closed her eyes for several seconds, and her foot tapped on the floor fast enough to make the baby's blanket flutter. Samuel didn't seem the least bit bothered by the motion, but Thomas knew Quinn was reaching her limit.

William must have seen it too, because he stood up and walked around behind her, resting his hands on her shoulders and bending to kiss the top of her head. "Do you need any help with that dinner, Tobias?" he asked when he straightened. "I think we're all starving and we could hear the rest of this later."

# STORM

"OKAY, I NEED TO know exactly what you let me sleep through earlier," Linnea said, following Quinn and William into their room after dinner. Thomas was right behind her. "You're supposed to wake me up for that kind of thing."

"No, I'm supposed to look after the well-being of my little niece," Quinn said, setting her hand over the tiny bump under Linnea's shirt.

"I'm fine," Linnea said, setting her hand over Quinn's. "I promise."

It made Quinn feel a little better – a very little. By the time they'd arrived at Tobias' house today, Linnea herself hadn't looked great at all. Quinn suspected she'd been sick again without telling anyone. The stress of the journey and the situation were wearing on everyone.

"We'll fill you in, Nay, don't worry," Thomas said. "Are you…"

He was interrupted by a quiet knock on the still-open door. "Your Majesties?" Mia asked, stepping inside and over to where William had laid the baby on the bed. "Do you need my help with anything?"

"Thank you so much Mia, but he's calm and I think I'm going to try to get him to sleep," Quinn said.

"You're welcome. If you're looking for any of his things, they should be in the top two drawers in that chest over there. I'll just go and finish taking care of the diapers that are soaking in the washtub."

Thomas watched Mia as she slipped quietly from the room. When he turned back to them, Quinn noticed that his cheeks were a little flushed. She felt like laying into him – telling him to go and sort out whatever was going on with Mia right now, but she didn't have it in her right then. Instead, she headed over to the chest of drawers to retrieve pajamas for Samuel.

A strong gust of wind rattled the panes in the small windows. William walked over and pulled back the curtain to look out. He let out a low whistle, causing Linnea to rush to the window, too.

"*That* is a storm," Linnea said. "There must be three inches of snow already, and it wasn't even snowing before dinner."

"I thought you said the weather wasn't usually this bad this time of the cycle," Quinn said, scooping the baby from the bed and joining them.

"It's not," William answered. "But that doesn't mean it *can't* be. We have had storms like this during carperos before – didn't you get blizzards in late fall in Bristlecone every few years?"

"Yeah." She shook her head, looking out again at the blowing snow. "It's usually not a good omen for the rest of the season. Tolliver – or Ivan or whoever – sure picked a fantastic cycle to take over my kingdom."

"That may have been part of the purpose." The unexpected voice startled Quinn, and she whirled around to face Tobias.

"What do you mean?" she asked.

"This harvest season and the fallow season have been predicted to be the roughest in many cycles. The crop farmers have been talking about it for many moons; even in the planting season, nearly everyone sowed extra and kept more young animals to raise."

She sighed. "I'm the queen. I should know this."

"Yes." Tobias' voice was matter-of-fact. "A queen should know and be overseeing these issues."

"Is this something else that has been kept from me?"

"I expect so, yes. I can understand why Charles may not have felt it was an important enough issue to trouble you with when there were so many other things going on, especially if he hadn't considered it from a political angle."

Quinn pinched the bridge of her nose, trying to sort out the thousands of conflicting thoughts racing through her brain. "Do you think it's as simple as that, Tobias? That he just didn't consider the implications?"

Tobias raised an eyebrow. "I realize that Charles isn't here, and that everything is uncertain, but from what I understand he did a quite respectable job running the kingdom in your absence, and he probably deserves more of your trust than you asking that question of someone you just met today."

She swallowed guiltily – he was right. "And yet, you continue to earn more of my confidence by the minute, Tobias. I appreciate your honesty, even when it's at my expense."

"I will continue to work to earn it, Your Majesty. As far as Charles is concerned, I don't know if he's given you any reason not to trust him, but you might do well to remember that he is also quite limited in knowing how to lead a kingdom. He wasn't raised in that role either. From everything I've heard, he did the best job he could while you were away, but it wouldn't be fair to expect perfection from him any more than anyone expects it from you."

"Oh, I think nearly everyone expects it from *me*, Tobias. Except perhaps for those who are counting on being able to take advantage of my weaknesses."

He shook his head. "It's a challenging way to come into your birthright – but not an insurmountable one, I don't think. We'll get your castle back."

"The castle is not my biggest worry, Tobias, but I do appreciate your support."

"Yes, well … Enough discussion of that for this evening. I think we could all use a break from thinking about something that can't be dealt with tonight. I came to speak with you because I realized I hadn't answered the question I promised I would."

"How you know about the other world."

Nodding, he reached into the front pocket of his long white sweater and pulled out a worn-looking leather book. He held it between his hands as he spoke. "There have always been stories about another world. Some believe the world first began there, others just believe that people have long traveled back and forth between the worlds. Most people, of course, believe that the stories are just that – stories. No different than the stories we tell children about talking animals and magic people."

"But my father believed in Earth?"

"As rulers of the kingdom, it is only prudent for the royal family to keep an open mind about what people believe – especially concerning a portal that could present an unknown threat."

"And you?"

"*I* have always had a special affinity for books – stories, history, philosophy, science, – the older the better. You've no idea how often I got in trouble for bringing home an enormous crate of books after visiting someone, or helping a family clean up a home after an elderly relative died."

Quinn smiled. "You'll get along well with my husband."

"Mmm-hmm… I'm sure I'm the only one in this room suddenly interested in Tobias' library," William muttered close to her ear. She knew without looking that his eyes were bright with curiosity. But he was right – a mirror would have revealed the same interest on her face.

"My library is in the basement, or I should say, my basement *is* the library, despite the fact that it's supposed to be a safe house,"

Tobias said. "Any of you are more than welcome to use it as much as you wish, for as long as you're here."

"We may take you up on that," Quinn said. "We've found the royal library to be somewhat lacking on the topic of the other world."

"Yes, your father and Nathaniel discovered that as well – that any works even mentioning the possibility of gates or another world were conspicuously absent from the castle."

"Do you think that was intentional?" Thomas asked.

"It's hard to imagine that it isn't, considering the relatively large number of texts that make mention of the other world, even if the writer doesn't believe there's any truth to the idea."

William nodded. "There are many books at the castle in Eirentheos that talk about the other world – just very few of them have useful information about finding gates or the differences between the worlds. None of them would have led us to the gate. Mostly, they're stories."

"Perhaps not, but then you, William, would have been reading those books with a level of background knowledge that may have led you to overlook information that might have a different meaning to someone who had never seen a real gate or traveled to the other world."

"I suppose that's true."

"What do you mean?" Quinn wasn't sure she followed.

William put his hand on her shoulder. "He means that sometimes knowing too much already makes it harder to see the subtle things in front of you – like maybe the way someone who doesn't know that it's highly unlikely for a large number of children to be exposed to shadeweed would have an easier time seeing that they have been."

"Right," Tobias said, chuckling. "I mean that someone who doesn't think they already know what information is right and wrong about the gates might not overlook a small piece of information that turned out to be critical – that might be the one piece that helped find a real gate."

"So the question is – who took all the small pieces of information?" Linnea said, turning away from the snowy window. She'd been staring out at the night the whole time they'd been talking – it would have been easy to believe she hadn't been paying attention to the conversation, but Quinn knew better.

Thomas pulled the curtains closed as Linnea walked over to Quinn and held out her hands for Samuel. The baby fussed for a second, but calmed quickly when Linnea swayed gently back and forth.

"I think we can guess who," William said. "It's obvious that Hector knew how to find a gate, and a long time ago, too. What we don't know is who else he might have shared that information with, besides Rahas and Tolliver."

"Yes. And we don't know if any of the books they had gave them information about another gate." Tobias rubbed the leather cover of the book with his thumbs before handing it to Quinn. "I've had this journal for many cycles, since I was a young man. I don't know who wrote it; but it's very old. I found it at market on Blue Sand Island, of all places. It was your father who deciphered the chart in here that gave us a rough idea of what days during each quarter the portals might open. It still took some trial and error once he located the gate in Eirentheos."

Quinn flipped through the worn yellow pages, careful not to rip or crumble anything. There were words and drawings on every page, but they seemed random and most of them didn't make sense to her – until she reached a place near the middle where the journal stayed open easily.

"That's the clearing where the bridge is," she said. "There's no bridge, but I recognize that bend in the river – that's where we dug for the magnet."

"You're right," William said, tracing the drawing softly with his finger.

"But what are these numbers?"

He frowned, leaning closer. She turned and reached into the pocket of his wool jacket, retrieving the case that held his glasses.

Chuckling softly, he whispered, "Thanks." He put the glasses on and studied the page again. "They look like map coordinates… but I don't think they're correct for that location."

"They're not," Tobias said. "At least not according to the maps we use in Eirentheos or Dovelnia. Nathaniel has said they look like coordinates that might exist if we had a larger-scale map of Deusterros. Or they might be written in code."

"Maybe…" William said, taking hold of the book. "Can I?"

Quinn let go of the journal, leaning into William's shoulder instead, watching as he leaned close to study the numbers, muttering softly under his breath. He turned the page, revealing yet another sketch of trees and river, but this one was unfamiliar – and only half-formed, as the next page was ripped out, leaving a small jagged edge of paper in the margin. She bent the ripped piece both ways, but none of the markings on it were decipherable.

"Are those more coordinates?" she asked, pointing to the bottom of the intact page.

William nodded. "Half a set. Where's the other page?" he asked Tobias.

"It was gone when I first got the journal. I've never had any idea where it might be. There are a couple of other missing pages as well, but nobody can even guess what was on them."

"Can we figure out what *these* numbers mean based on the other ones for the gate we know?" Quinn wondered.

"Nathaniel thinks so. He spent many moons studying it and he thinks he can decipher what this coordinate means," Tobias said.

William nodded. "But with only half the pair, that's not very useful. We could pin it down to a line that spans half the globe."

"The line does run through Philotheum," Tobias said. "If Nathaniel's calculations are correct. But William is right – it's still not useful on a practical level. We need more."

"Not that it matters much anyway." Quinn stepped away from William and the journal and sat down on the edge of the four-poster bed. "It's all very interesting, but figuring out the location of a gate is just too dangerous, especially right now. We can't use it and expose this world to that kind of possible damage."

Everyone was silent for a moment, and when Quinn looked at Tobias, he was looking at her with a strange smile. "What?" she asked.

"So you do intend to fight, then?"

She frowned. "Of course I do. What kind of question is that?"

"An honest one, Your Majesty. This situation hasn't been easy for you; you're in over your head, people who should be supporting you are threatening your life and the life of your child… And now it appears there may have been a coup. A reasonable person with another world – another family – to safely escape to would be finding that gate as quickly as possible."

William sat down next to her, resting his hand on her back, the journal still open on his lap.

Quinn took a deep breath before clearing her throat. "I'm not sure where you got the impression that I'm a reasonable person, Tobias. I may not have the first clue what I'm doing here, but that is my throne and my castle. Philotheum is *my* kingdom – not Tolliver's, and certainly not Ivan's. I'd like to believe it won't come to a fight – especially because I have no idea how to win one with three guards, one of whom who is not even trained properly – but I'm not going anywhere."

In Linnea's arms, Samuel began fussing. Tobias glanced at them as Linnea carried him to the other side of the bed and Thomas brought her a clean diaper. "I don't like the circumstances that caused it, Your Majesty, but I am honored to have my niece under my roof through this storm."

# DROPPINGS

WHEN HE'D FINALLY CRAWLED into bed the night before, Zander had been so exhausted that he'd been afraid he might not wake again until dinnertime. But early the next morning, when James Blackwelder pulled on his boots, the quiet noise roused Zander immediately. The weeks of intense guard training were paying off; although no light entered the room when James pulled back the curtain, Zander was alert.

"Is it still snowing?" he asked, slipping his feet into his own boots and shrugging into his warmest sweater. When he'd first realized he would be stuck in this world, he'd thought he'd miss his truck the most, or maybe his cell phone, but no – living without central heat was much worse. He crossed the room to put another log on the fire.

"Yes," James said. "And there's already more on the ground than I've seen in a long time. We should go and check on the horses."

When Zander and James reached the kitchen, Dorian was already there, removing a steaming kettle from the hook over the fire.

A warm, tempting smell drifted from a covered Dutch oven on top of the stove.

"Did you do all this?" he asked Dorian. A glance out the window told him little about the time. He thought he might be seeing the first hints of sunrise, but the light was obscured by the thick layer of clouds and the heavy snow swirling in the harsh wind. The amount of snow on the ground was surprising even to Zander, who'd lived through more mountain blizzards than he cared to remember. "How long have you been up?"

Dorian shook his head. "Only a few minutes. I put the kettle over the fire and pulled that out of the oven, but it was already here, with a note from Tobias. He went back to bed."

"Wow." Grabbing a thick towel, he lifted the heavy cast-iron lid of the pan, careful not to burn himself. Immediately, he wished he hadn't done that – the smell of the thick concoction of eggs, potatoes, cheese, and some kind of meat was overwhelming; now he was too hungry to wait.

"Go ahead and dish us up some," Dorian said. "We're going to need the warmth before we try to walk through that snow."

"Shouldn't we wait for everyone?" If there was anything he'd learned living in the castle with Quinn and William, it was that even the smallest things – like eating and heating water for bathing – were undertaken with consideration for the king and queen. Not because either of them actually cared – Zander knew that fact bothered Quinn on more than one level – but because that deference mattered to everyone else.

"There's a second pan; Tobias' note said to put it in when we pulled this one out. Perhaps Their Majesties will get the rest they need this morning. We certainly won't be going anywhere today."

"Tobias is very accommodating," Zander said.

"Indeed."

"Is it improper for me to say that this isn't what I would have expected from Lady Sophia's brother?"

"Very improper," James said, but his tone was amused. "Of course, you're not wrong."

"Tobias is a good man." Dorian handed each of them a plate from the shelf. "I've been lucky enough to meet him several times, but I never knew where he lived – and I didn't know he was related to Lady Sophia. I didn't know anything about his background. It's an honor to be invited into his home."

"When did you meet him?" Zander asked.

"The first time was when I decided to join the Friends of Philip. After a few others decided I could be trusted, they brought me to meet Tobias. He inked my tattoo. I've seen him a few times since then – the ones I remember are when James joined, and a few days after Queen Quinn released us from prison."

"So if you'd met him before – wouldn't you have known who he was when he did things like coming to Prince Samuel's Naming Ceremony?"

Dorian cleared his throat. "Zander, I've answered your questions thus far because Queen Quinn trusts you, and you already know whatever Tobias has told you. I will leave it to him to choose to share anything else."

The rebuff was kind, but Zander felt it to his core, knew that it was absolute. Whatever secrets Dorian knew about Tobias would remain hidden. Before that moment, he had known that belonging to the Friends of Philip was important to those who were part of it, but he hadn't realized how deep it ran, how many secrets were buried beneath purpose and loyalty.

Risking Dorian shutting him down completely, he asked a different question as they sat down to eat. "How did you decide to join the Friends of Philip? Was your father a member as well?"

"No." Dorian took a bite of the savory casserole. For a moment, Zander was afraid the single word would end the conversation, but a moment later, he continued. "My father is still alive; he has a bakery in a small town close to the Dovelnian border.

He didn't much approve of my deciding to become a guard when I was a young man, and he certainly has no idea that I was part of the resistance. The last time I spoke to him, he was disappointed that I'd ruined my son by raising him to be a soldier, too."

"I thought being a castle guard was kind of an honor."

"It is, to many people. James and I have only been castle guards since Queen Quinn's coronation. Before that, we worked on patrols in the region of Brandleby, but I still don't think my father is impressed. He would have preferred I stay far from politics and in the kitchen with him."

"He's not happy the crown was restored to Quinn?"

"Not especially. He wouldn't care one way or the other, I don't think, if it didn't have any effect on him personally. His bakery did well under Hector's reign, and there was no fighting anywhere near Brandleby until Queen Quinn came to power and arrested Harbin Rhinewald and several others who helped him – including some men who were friends of my father's. That area is struggling economically now because so many of the queen's supporters fled, and Hector's supporters were stripped of the power they had. I think that if my father knew of my involvement in *that* situation, he would have turned me in himself."

"Wow. What about your mother?"

"My mother died when I was very young, giving birth to my sister – who didn't survive, either."

"I'm sorry to hear that." He wasn't sure he liked thinking about *that* difference between this world and his, either.

"It was a long time ago. My father remarried when I was fifteen – and I applied for guard training at sixteen. He has two sons with my stepmother, and both of them now work in his bakery. He has someone to leave it to. In a way, everyone got what they wanted in the end."

Zander thought about that as he took a bite of the breakfast concoction – it tasted even better than it smelled. This conversation with Dorian was fascinating to him. As different from Earth as he sometimes felt this world was, the similarities were so much more powerful.

"What made you join the Friends of Philip?" It seemed like a risky thing to do without a strong reason.

"My father might not have had strong political opinions, Zander, but I did. I joined the guard to protect and serve King Jonathan – not an imposter from Dovelnia. After Jonathan died, I looked forward to the day Prince Samuel would take the crown. During that time, I heard whispers and rumors about the resistance, but I didn't really understand why it was necessary. But when Samuel died, I knew something was wrong. I still didn't join the Friends of Philip for a number of cycles, but once it became clear that Hector intended to circumvent tradition and allow Tolliver to make a bid for the throne, I sought out the resistance for myself."

"Even though you knew you might be risking your life?"

"I did risk my life, Zander. Both James and I were nearly executed for our participation in the Friends of Philip – but I don't regret it."

"Nor do I," James said from across the counter. "I would do the same thing again without question, even if I knew the outcome would be different."

"Everyone in this house right now has made *that* commitment, I think." The new voice startled Zander; he hadn't seen the other guards come into the kitchen.

"Let's hope it doesn't come to that, Kian," Marcus said. "But Her Majesty acknowledges your sacrifices in being here and is honored by them. I'm sure she'll tell you that herself as well."

"Actually, I think we'd all feel a little less guilty if you could ask her to *stop* expressing her gratitude every time she speaks to us," Ethan said, grinning as he piled food onto three plates.

After breakfast, the five guards gathered in the small room behind the kitchen next to the door leading outside. Zander fastened his heavy cloak as tight as he could, and pulled the hood over his head before wrapping his green scarf around to conceal as much of his face as possible.

As he dressed, he noticed a large coil of rope hanging from a long peg beside the door.

"We'll need that," Dorian said, following his gaze.

When Dorian opened the door, a blast of cold air assaulted them, making Zander wish again for central heating and covered transportation. Snow swirled so thick in the wind that it was difficult to see the dark outline of the barn, even though it couldn't have been more than thirty yards away.

As soon as they stepped out in it, Dorian tied one end of the rope to a wooden post staked next to the door, and spread out the coil, offering a hold to each of the other guards. At first, Zander was confused, but when a sudden strong gust of wind blew enough icy crystals into the air to completely obscure the barn, he understood. The rope would keep them from wandering out into the blizzard and getting lost. Hopefully.

Well, at least they would be safe from soldiers today.

By the time they reached the barn, he was sort of wishing for the soldiers. Dorian tied the other end of the rope to a stake just outside the barn door, and they hurried inside, trying to keep the snow out.

The barn offered respite from the furious, icy wind, but not from the cold. He could see his breath in the air as he walked over to the adjoining stalls which held the two most important horses in the barn; Quinn's mare, Dusk, and William's tawny mare named Skittles.

A thin layer of ice covered the water in their troughs.

"Break that up," James said. "We can pour a little warm water over the top before we leave." He nodded toward the far corner of the massive barn where Dorian was kneeling in front of a woodstove. "We'll have to come out a little more often to check on them while it's storming like this."

Since coming to this world, Zander had learned more about horses than he ever would have wished to at home, but he still felt like a novice around the other guards. While learning to care for his mount was an important part of his training, it hadn't been a priority back at the castle where there were stable hands to do most of the physical work in the stalls.

For a few minutes he tried to help with Dusk and Skittles, but he was slow and inefficient next to James, Dorian, Ethan, and Kian. Eventually, he decided he'd better use the time to do the work with his own horse, or everyone would be waiting on him to finish.

"Hello Ember," he said quietly as he pulled up the latch of the heavy stall gate. The tall bay stallion bent his head toward Zander's shoulder in greeting. He patted Ember's silky neck, and the horse nudged his cheek.

He had to admit that his truck had never been this happy to see him.

Of course, he thought, as his eyes fell on a steaming pile at the back of the stall, his truck had never done *that* either.

"Come on, boy," he said, leading Ember out of the stall and into the wide main aisle of the barn with the other horses. The horse followed him without hesitation.

Zander still wasn't sure whether Stephen's gift of this horse to him was intended as a joking commentary on his lack of experience, or just an extraordinary kindness – surely this patient, unassuming animal would have been a more fitting mount for one of the children – Alice, maybe.

Not that he was complaining. Ember was an amazing animal. Gentle – and enormous – as he was, he could keep pace on even the longest, most strenuous ride. Although Zander wasn't skilled enough to experience it for himself, he knew Ember was an incredible jumper, too. Even Linnea had asked to take a few turns on the course with him, despite the fact that her horse, Snow, was renowned for her perfect jumps.

He stroked Ember's long neck a few times before tying his lead rope to a post and heading over to the hooks along the wall to retrieve a pitchfork.

Just as he reached the door to Ember's stall again, something hit the side of his head. For a second, he was too startled to understand what had happened, but when he reached to rub the spot on his temple, a warm, gooey sensation made him pull his hand back immediately. "Ugh."

Across the aisle, Kian started laughing and pointing up toward the ceiling.

Zander took a step back before he looked up – a wise move, because another thick white glop dropped in the spot where he'd been standing.

"What in the…"

At least a dozen large birds were perched in the rafters of the barn. There could have been many more, but the hayloft obscured his view of half the building.

He recognized the offender immediately – Raeyan, Quinn's light gray seeker was directly over his head. The white patches on the bird's chest were unmistakable.

Although the birds were a variety of colors, they were clearly all seekers, sheltering in the relative warmth of Tobias' barn. It took him a minute, but he finally spotted William's bird, Aelwyn. No doubt Aelwyn's mate, Sirian was here somewhere, too. There were more birds in the rafters than he could match to owners, though. One, a smoky charcoal-colored bird, was watching him with interest. Zander wasn't sure if the creature was amused or sympathetic.

"How did they get in?"

Kian chuckled as he shrugged. "Maybe they followed you – just so they could do that."

"Yeah. Thanks, Raeyan," he muttered toward the ceiling.

Despite his best efforts to clean himself off with icy water from the pump in the barn, by the time they stumbled back out of the snow and into Tobias' kitchen, the mess in Zander's hair had frozen solid.

It might not have been so bad if Quinn, William, Thomas, Linnea, Marcus, and Tobias hadn't *all* been sitting at the table eating when he walked in.

"You've got a little bird problem in your barn," he said to Tobias.

Tobias chuckled under his breath. "Yes. I should have warned you. I have a hat I always wear when I go in there."

"Always? Quinn's bird did this to me, not yours."

He'd done it again – referred to Quinn informally in front of the other guards. They reacted as if all the air had been sucked out of the room.

Quinn, however, was barely managing to conceal laughter. William and Thomas seemed to be having the same problem. He didn't make eye contact with anyone else – his neck was getting hot enough already.

"Oh, I'm sure we have some extra guests right now," Tobias said. "I had no idea how much company we'd end up with when I built that window for mine to get in and out, but the others always seem to find it."

"Do you have more than one of your own?" Owning one of the birds – or, rather, having a seeker accept a person as a companion – was somewhat rare. None of the guards had one, with the exception of Marcus, who was technically Quinn's advisor, not a guard, and those who had them most definitely only had one.

"I don't know if I'd call them my own, but a good number of them like to roost in the barn. Half a dozen or so will occasionally consent to being made useful."

Quinn stared at him like he'd grown a third eye. "You have several seekers you can use?"

"Yes." Tobias' response was indifferent, delivered as he took another bite of potatoes.

"Well, that could be useful."

"Indeed. They're rather handy companions. You're welcome to ask for their services in whatever way you need, Your Majesty, although I wouldn't try it today. All of the ones I know are picky about storms like this."

The look on Quinn's face might have made Zander laugh out loud if he wasn't so... something. Embarrassed? Freezing? Confused?

He didn't even bother to mumble an excuse as he made a hasty exit from the kitchen.

# COMMITMENT

ZANDER WAS HALFWAY DOWN the hall when he realized that someone was following him. For a second, he couldn't decide whether to turn around and see who it was or just hope they'd go away. After deliberation, he decided he'd rather know if it was one of the other guards – so he could find a place to hide other than the room he was sharing with them.

What he saw when he glanced back made him stop in his tracks.

"Finished with breakfast already?"

Linnea shrugged. "I'm not all that hungry this morning."

"You should be; you've got..." The look on her face stopped him again. "You've got to be sick of people telling you what you should be doing," he said instead.

"And here you thought you were slow on the uptake on things in this world."

"Not everything is so different here."

"I wouldn't know. I never got the chance to compare."

He paused, studying her furrowed brow and the faraway look in her gray eyes. "That bothers you, doesn't it?"

"If you had known about the gate before you came here – that there was a way to travel to a whole different world, and your older brothers were allowed to visit it, but you never were, would it bother you?"

"I don't have older brothers."

The look she shot him was more than worth it.

"So you just figured out how to be a jerk all on your own?"

"What can I say? It's a talent."

"I guess one talent is better than none."

"I've gotta take what I can get, Nay." He chuckled. "In all seriousness, though, yes, that would bother me. I would have probably snuck off and done it anyway."

"That might be a little easier to do on your side than on mine."

"Maybe," he allowed. "Of course, if I knew I might get permanently *stuck*, I don't know if I'd have taken the risk."

"It would be worse to be stuck on the other side."

"How do you figure *that*?" He reached up and wiped away another drip from the melting mess in his hair – melting slowly at that, since it wasn't exactly warm in this hallway.

"Well, for starters, losing ninety percent of my lifespan, missing all of those days with people I care about…"

She had a point – he'd never given much thought to that aspect before. "Of course, you people over here only live ten times as long if you don't get attacked by a rabid animal, or poisoned by some plant, or murdered by your stepfather."

"Samuel was murdered in your world, you know."

"Still, in my world there are no armed guards who consider beheading me for not saying 'Your Majesty' when I talk to Quinn Robbins."

Linnea grew quiet, giving him a plaintive look that he liked much, much less than her murderous one. "Is that what you're so upset about?"

He narrowed his eyes. "Who said I was upset?"

Her eyebrow arched into an impossibly perfect *v.* "Who said I was stupid?"

"Well, if you think I'm so upset, did you consider that it might be because I have an enormous clump of bird poop on my head?"

His harsh tone didn't faze her. "No. If you were in a regular mood, you might be annoyed, but you'd see how it was funny, too."

"Is that why you followed me? So you could laugh at me about it?"

Even the accusation of following him didn't make her flinch. "No. I came to see if you might want some help – or at least some company."

He didn't understand the sudden tightness in his throat; he coughed to cover it up. "You want to help me clean bird poop out of my hair?"

"Okay. Keep you company."

Five minutes ago, he'd wanted nothing in the world more than he wanted to escape from all human contact. Now... he wasn't so sure. He started walking down the hall. "Are you going to stop trying to make me talk about my feelings?"

She followed. "Are you kidding? You think I'm going to pass up an opportunity to focus on someone else's problems?"

"Go back to the kitchen, Linnea."

"Are you sure? Because *I'm* not sharing a room with anyone, and none of the guards are going to pop in there and give you a hard time. They'll at least knock first."

He whirled around to face her. "You'd let me clean up in there?"

"Sure. If you're nice enough to me, I might even let you heat up some water over the fire and leave for a while so you could have a bath. There's a washroom between my room and the one Quinn and William are in."

"*I* can be nice."

"Go and grab your clothes. And a comb. *That* I won't share today."

"So, are you doing okay?" Linnea asked when Zander showed up in her room with his stuff.

Without looking at her, he set his clean clothes down on a chair and headed toward the fireplace. A large pot already hung from the hook over the fire.

"Did you do that?"

"Yes."

"Linnea! You shouldn't be carrying that kind of stuff, should you?"

"Oh, calm down. Someone else left the water in here. I just put it over the fire."

"Still…"

"Zander, nobody has time for me to be helpless. There's cold water in that bucket right there. You can carry that into the washroom if it's so important to you." To punctuate her assertion, she sneezed loudly.

He couldn't muster quite the same dirty look as she could, but he tried his best. "Bless you. And you're asking me if *I'm* okay?"

"Yeah, I am. Surely you have a more interesting answer than I do. I'm a ridiculous mess who might not ever be completely okay again – the least you could do is provide a distraction."

He stared at the flickering flames of the fire, debating exactly how warm he needed the water to be. "I'm as fine as anyone else – except I don't know what I'm doing with, well, anything, and I know the other guards wonder exactly what the heck I'm doing here, and everyone in the house is in the Friends of Philip except for me, and I don't have any useful advice for anyone, and there is bird poop in my hair."

Keeping his eyes trained on the fire, he braced himself for her laughter, but it didn't come. After a long moment, he turned to face her.

Her expression was soft, serious. "Was that so difficult?"

He stood and picked up the bucket of cold water to carry it to the promised washroom. "I don't know if it was difficult, just useless.

What does it matter if I'm upset? Nothing changes." Walking away from her, he went into the adjoining room and took his time dumping the bucket into the small tub. For good measure, he grabbed a washcloth and soaked it before heading back to the room.

She was still there, sitting on the edge of the bed, watching him calmly as he started trying to scrub his hair. "Do you want to join the Friends of Philip?"

"Linnea, I've been in this world for exactly five minutes. I barely even know what that means. It's some kind of crazy commitment of your life to a cause on a planet I have nothing to do with!"

She frowned. "You could only commit your life anymore to this 'cause' if you donated limbs or were actually killed, you know." She sneezed again.

He wished he had a handkerchief or something to offer to her, but he didn't, and she beat him to it anyway, pulling a white cloth from her pocket. "Limbs might be easier."

"Exactly. You know, it's a step that you moved to Philotheum, and that you agreed to do guard training, and you've been a little more pleasant with everyone – most of the time – but when are you going to start acting like you really belong here?"

"How about when I actually *do*?"

She tilted her head and narrowed her eyes. "So, in your mind, then, never."

"Yeah, probably. I *don't* belong here. I'm not from here."

This time she buried her face in her hands. "This? Really? *This* has to be the similarity between you and William? It took me forever to figure out what drew Quinn to both of you, and, well, I'm disappointed."

"What are you talking about?"

"*You*, and this whole not-belonging here because you weren't born here nonsense."

He raised an eyebrow.

"Do you know why people – the guards – are treating you like you don't belong here?"

"Because I slip up nineteen times a day and don't call Quinn 'Her Majesty'?"

"Well, yeah, that's part of it, but it's more your reaction to it than anything else. You're a hero who earned your place here as much – or more than – any of the other guards. And you have a legitimate reason to be used to just calling Quinn by her name."

"It's not legitimate to *them*."

"It's not anything to them. It's none of their business. It's between you and Quinn, and if she doesn't call you out on it, it's not their problem."

"She should call me out on it."

"She should. And you should quit doing it, at least in front of them, but that has nothing to do with you belonging here or not."

He sucked air in through his nose. "So how do I belong here, Linnea? When I'm not even supposed to be here?"

She was quiet for a second, pensive. Then she looked at him. "Supposed to isn't real, you know, Zander."

"What?"

"This world you have in your head, this other place you're 'supposed' to be – it's not real. Don't look at me like that. I know the other world *exists*, but the image you have in your head of yourself being there right now – that's not real. Trust me. I have a world like that in my head, too… a whole world of what's 'supposed to be' with Ben and decorating a nursery in the castle."

He swallowed.

"But it's all just imaginary. That's not how it happened. Ben's not in this world, and you're *not* in that one. Maybe it'll change in the future, but today is never going to be different. Where you are, right now, is how it is. This is where you belong. Nobody belongs any more or any less than you. And if you would just accept that, you would start to feel it."

The spot he'd been scrubbing on the side of his head was starting to get sore.

"Yeah, it's clean now, Zander," Linnea said.

He dropped his hand. "So what are you saying I should do, join the Friends of Philip?"

She shrugged. "I'm saying you've already *joined*, only without the tattoo. Whether you get it or not is up to you, but don't walk around thinking you shouldn't be able to or you're not entitled to. Like it or not, you're one of us now."

The water over the fire was bubbling; Zander grabbed the hook and swung out the little metal arm to bring the bucket out of the heat, and picked up the thick oven mitt. Before he slid it on, though, he looked back at Linnea. "Is getting the tattoo really as painful as the stories about it?"

"It would get you out of barn duty for a day or so."

He chuckled softly. "All right. I'm going to take a bath. It will be nice to actually be clean."

She stood up and nodded toward the washroom door. "Good. There's someone else who needs a good testing of the presumption that talking to me won't *change* anything."

# COMMUNICATION

THOMAS PAUSED IN THE hallway, taking several deep breaths and trying to decide what to say first. No good ideas came to mind, but he knew he needed to do it anyway. Linnea was right. Now that they were out of the castle and things were so dangerous, he couldn't afford to keep letting the situation with Mia disintegrate.

He either needed to fix things with her, or end them so they could both move forward. And he knew which one he wanted.

After a final fortifying breath, he knocked on the door of William and Quinn's room.

Mia opened it almost instantly, cradling Samuel in one arm.

"Oh, Thomas. They're not in here right now. Quinn is meeting with Marcus about something, and William and Nathaniel are talking with Tobias. Or at least they were."

He took it as a good sign that she was being informal. When she really wanted to distance herself from him, she was careful to use titles and formal speech. "Actually, Mia, I came here to talk to you."

She gestured for him to come in the room, but she took several steps back and held Samuel close to her chest. "I don't want to fight, Thomas," she said quietly as he closed the door.

When he turned around to face her again, her expression had changed; he could see the strength she was trying to exude, the mask that had taken over to show him that he couldn't hurt her.

He reached for the coin in his pocket, clenching it so tightly in his hand he was sure it would leave an indentation – maybe that was what he needed, an outline of a rose in his palm.

"I know," he said. "I don't want to fight with you, either. I don't want to hurt you. I know I have."

Her rigid mask faltered for a second; he caught a glimpse of softness in her green eyes, but then the solid shield dropped over her face again. The pain he knew it was hiding sliced something deep inside him, nearly making him gasp.

Linnea's words rang in his mind. It didn't matter how any of this had started or whose "fault" it was. If they kept playing emotional chicken, nobody was going to win, and he knew he had everything to lose.

So he took a deep breath. "Mia, I'm sorry. I know I've been distant, and expecting you to take chances I wasn't willing to take." He pressed harder on the coin. "I don't know how you still feel about me, but I want you to know that I care for you, maybe more now than ever. I love you. I don't know if you'll have me back, but I don't want things to be like this between us anymore. Even if you've totally given up on me, I want to still be here for you, and to stop hurting you."

Now the mask was gone, shattered in a million transparent pieces as she closed her eyes and her hands began to tremble.

Thomas stepped quietly forward and lifted the baby from her arms, careful not to touch her – he had a feeling that might break her completely.

Tucking Samuel into the crook of one elbow, he reached into his pocket with his other hand to retrieve a handkerchief and held it up to her.

She shook her head.

"That trick always works for your father," he said to Samuel. "I think I'm maybe not actually as charming as everyone claims I am."

That worked, though. Mia let out a quiet chuckle. "No, you're not," she said.

He grinned. "Remember that, Samuel. When you find someone who understands the truth about you, you need to try to keep them around." He looked over at Mia. "What do you think?"

She sighed loudly, shaking her head at him. "I might as well. We're all going to be dead or in prison soon enough anyway."

"That's the other thing I like about you. You get right in there and challenge my optimism. Every time."

"At least I know I'm good at something."

He'd thought it would be hard, this – or at least he'd made it hard over the last several moons. It sounded hard, anyway, essentially baring his soul to another person. He'd expected the fear and the uncertainty, had even expected to maybe regret doing it, depending on her reaction – but what he hadn't anticipated was the *relief*. Now he understood that the freedom of sharing his feelings was worth whatever risk he was taking.

Smiling, he reached into his pocket again, this time to drop the coin and retrieve the bracelet. He took a step toward her. "Would you consider wearing this again?"

For a long moment she was quiet, looking at the bracelet and then at him. "Are you sure this is a good idea?" she finally asked.

"I don't know. It's what I want, but I understand if you're not sure right now – or if you've moved on."

She raised an eyebrow. "Moved on?"

"Well, James is a pretty great guy, and Kian – I think he could lift a horse over his head without breaking a sweat."

Mia giggled. "I don't know... I think if I *had* to choose, I might go for Ethan."

"He's a little old for you, isn't he?"

"Are you jealous?"

"Uh… yeah, actually a little. Or worried – you know, since I'm younger than you. I didn't know you had a thing for older men."

"He's just nice, Thomas. He helped me get all of the diapers out of the wash tub last night, you know – and even rigged up a line so I could hang them to dry."

Thomas closed his eyes. "I deserved that. I'm sorry."

She shrugged. "You meant it when you said you'd do it, but it wasn't your job, and other things came up."

He nodded, thinking for a moment about other things his sister had said. "Is it hard for you to talk to me sometimes – because I'm a prince and you're a baby nurse?"

Her gaze dropped to the floor. "I don't know the right way to answer that question."

Swallowing hard, he reached over to her, using one finger to lift her chin until she was looking at him again. "However you actually feel would be easiest."

She didn't speak, but she nodded.

"I'm sorry," he whispered. "I don't mean for it to be that way."

"You don't have to *mean* for it to be, Thomas, it just is."

"I know. Sometimes I wish I wasn't a prince, you know… then I'd be free to have my spoiled temper tantrum and put equal responsibility on you when things get tough, but I get it. You're in a much harder place than I am when we argue. I have to remember that and take care of you."

"It wasn't all your fault. I did want to ask for this job, and I didn't tell you."

He reached for her hand, matching the tip of each of her fingers with his fingertips.

"I'm sorry," she said.

He nodded and leaned in closer, taking her whole hand in his, tucking the bracelet between their palms, and bending his face down until his lips just touched hers, brushing them gently. Then he leaned his forehead against hers. "Let's just don't do that again, okay? Talk to me, please?"

She nodded gently against his forehead, biting her lip and exhaling as she accepted the bracelet, holding it tight in her curled fist. "Can I ask the same of you?"

"Yes."

Just as he went to kiss her again, Samuel squirmed in his arms and let out a squeal.

Thomas and Mia both laughed.

"Did you think I forgot about you, Little Man?" Thomas asked, pulling back and bouncing him gently, kissing his soft black hair instead.

"Actually," Mia said, "I suspect he's having a different issue." She pointed to Thomas' shirt; a dark, wet circle had appeared in the place where he'd been cradling Samuel close to his chest.

He sighed. "I love you, too, Samuel. Goodness."

"Could be worse," Mia said, smiling and holding her arms out for the baby.

"Things could always be worse," Thomas agreed. "I think I'll go and find another shirt."

"Good idea."

Just as he opened the door, though, he heard voices in the hallway – William and Quinn were returning, and Linnea was with them. He pulled the door open wide for them.

William looked surprised to see Thomas there. "We're not interrupting anything, are we?" he whispered, casting a glance at Mia.

Thomas shook his head, mouthing, "We're good."

"Uh-oh, Samuel," William cooed, walking quickly toward Mia – hiding his quick interaction with Thomas – "did you make a mess for Mia?"

"It's no problem," Mia said. "We have a whole stack of fresh diapers now. Thomas is the one who got hit."

Samuel let out a loud gurgle as Mia laid him on the bed – Thomas was certain his nephew was enjoying the joke. "Can I borrow one of your shirts, Will?" he asked, already walking toward the dresser. Now that both William and Quinn were here, he didn't want to miss any of the conversation they were about to have.

"It's still snowing hard outside," William said, ignoring Thomas' digging in his drawers. "There are no signs of it letting up anytime soon – not today for sure."

Thomas looked out the window as he unbuttoned the wet shirt. The snowdrifts were impossibly high already, and William was right – the thick white flakes continued to fill so much of the sky it was hard to see even the other buildings on Tobias' property. "So what does it mean?"

"It means we're stuck here," Quinn said. "As long as that's going on, Tobias' house might as well be an entirely different world by itself. We can't send the birds out in this, we can't get messages – we have no way to find out what's going on at the castle."

He felt it coming again – the agitation that built up inside him every time he thought about Tolliver. It tightened every muscle in his body and he had to work to draw enough air into his lungs.

Although she still held Samuel, Mia took several unobtrusive steps toward Thomas, stopping short of touching him, and looking at him in the way that reminded him just *why* it had been worth it to swallow his pride and apologize first. He needed to find much more alone time with her again – soon.

Thinking about Mia, and how grateful he was for her right then, allowed him to calm enough to refocus his thoughts a bit.

William folded his hands in front of him. "Our main concern, of course, is the servants and guards we left behind at the castle. We're also worried about the safety of Charles and Ellen – but unfortunately there's nothing we can do from here right now."

"So, basically, you're outlining all of the things we should worry about that we can't do anything about?" Thomas asked. Attempting to insert some levity was the only way he was going to keep any semblance of serenity right now.

"Yes, basically. Welcome to being the brother of the king and queen."

At least William was making it easy. "I've been your brother since I was born, Will. Worrying is not a new habit for you."

"But now I have an official excuse for it."

"Then I have an official excuse to knock some sense into you."

William grinned. "You can't. I'm the king. It would be treason."

"Whatever." Thomas punched William playfully on the arm. "I think you have bigger fish to fry on the whole treason thing, don't you?"

Quinn ignored their banter, taking Samuel from Mia and settling down against the pillows at the head of the bed to feed him. "Marcus and Nathaniel believe that Friends inside the castle have plans in place for emergency situations like this and are hopeful that many of them were able to make it to safety."

"Provided they didn't stay and try to fight," William said.

"Many of the troops and castle guards were already preparing for the possibility that things would take a hostile turn," Quinn said. "We can hope they were prepared enough to at least keep themselves safe, and if they were lucky, they might have inflicted some damage on the invaders."

"Can I hope they *inflicted damage* on Tolliver already?" Thomas asked. This time, Mia moved all the way next to him, carefully touching the side of her hand to his. He grabbed onto it.

Linnea sneezed loudly, causing them all to turn and look. "Are you all right, Nay?" William asked.

"I'm fine."

William frowned and walked toward her – now that Thomas was paying attention, she did look a little pale.

"Back off," she said. "I sneezed." She backed up from William, moving closer to Quinn, though Thomas noticed she kept her distance from the baby. "What are you going to do about Sophia?"

Quinn rubbed at her temple with one hand. "I don't know. If she's responsible for all of this – or even if she's played a large part in it, I don't think I have any choice but to arrest her, and possibly execute her alongside Tolliver. That is, of course, if we win this war."

"That is not an *if*," Thomas said. "We're not going to lose – the crown is yours, not Tolliver's, not Ivan's, not anyone's. Losing is not a possibility."

For a second, he thought Quinn was going to argue with him, but she didn't. "You're right. I've given up way too much already to lose it all like this. If Tolliver wants that throne, he's going to have to come through me – and my four guards."

"And me." Thomas put his leg up on the bench at the end of the bed and pulled the small dagger from the sheath under his pants leg.

"I don't think that's going to do much against the snow," Quinn said.

Linnea's chortle turned into a cough, but Thomas only got out the words, "Are you…," before she shot him down with a death glare.

"Zander wants to join the Friends of Philip," she said, deftly shifting the focus off herself.

He decided to let her get away with it – for now.

# SICK

DESPITE HAVING BEEN TOLD several times that he didn't have to, Zander dragged himself out of bed when the first hints of light appeared at the bottom of the curtain. His shoulder screeched in protest when he pushed himself up, forcing him to re-think the idea of using his left arm at all.

Until last night, he'd sort of believed that all the stories about the pain of the tattoo were exaggerations – that the ominous warnings had been just a form of hazing. He should have realized that while Thomas or Linnea might engage in that sort of teasing, William wouldn't have. Quinn probably wouldn't, either.

Nobody had been kidding in the least.

For a moment, he eyed the little bottle of pain pills sitting on his bedside table – but the medicine was growing scarce now that the gate was closed, and he could handle it. Sort of.

James and Dorian were already gone, their beds neatly made. He must have been sleeping harder than he'd thought.

They probably hadn't gone out to the barn yet. Zander opened the curtain – and immediately regretted it. The sunlight reflecting off the snow blinded him momentarily, making his eyes water. He had to blink several times just to be able to see the inside of the bedroom again.

Well, the storm was over. The dawn sky was bright blue over the waist-high blanket of snow on the ground. He didn't know whether the sunshine was cause for joy or dread. It didn't matter, he supposed. There was no changing the weather.

Ignoring the searing sensation across his chest and down his arm, he dressed for the snow.

Even walking was painful as he made his way down the hall; each time his boots hit the wooden floor, the vibration traveled up his body and reverberated in the tattoo. He wished he could blame Linnea for talking him into this, but it had truthfully been his decision.

Just the difference in how the other guards had treated him last night told him it was worth it, but it was more than that. Although he knew very little about the politics in Philotheum, he knew as much as he needed to about Queen Quinn and those on her side.

Quinn and William could have treated him so much differently when he'd come so unexpectedly to their world – especially when he, himself had been so angry. William could have kept his wife's ex-boyfriend away from them – could have had guards with swords lock him in a dungeon until it was time to send him back to his own world. Given the way Zander had spoken to Quinn in front of William the last time he'd seen them in Bristlecone, William might have even been justified in protecting Quinn from him.

Really, from a practical standpoint, the leaders of both kingdoms had taken an enormous chance in allowing Zander to move freely about at all. His knowledge of the secret gate was a phenomenal risk to this world – from both sides of that gate. It wouldn't have been entirely unreasonable for either Quinn or Stephen to order him locked up here permanently.

But they hadn't. From the moment he'd arrived, they'd – all of them – treated him as a welcome guest. They'd put him in a nice room, provided clothes, and tried to help him navigate the unfamiliar food … the unfamiliar *world*. William, who could have seen Zander's obvious jealousy as a threat, chose to be gracious and kind.

Even Quinn's personal guard, whose very *job* it was to be implicitly on her side and shield her from even the kind of rude remarks Zander made at first, chose to overlook his anger and confusion and treat him as a friend.

Linnea was right. He knew which side he was on already. They'd staked their lives and their kingdoms on trusting him – even when he'd done nothing to deserve it. Even if he *did* return to his own world, he couldn't erase what had happened here. The tattoo wasn't a commitment he wasn't ready for; it was only a symbol that marked him for who he'd already become.

But it freaking hurt.

When he reached the kitchen, his heart sank. Tobias stood at the counter, stirring something in a metal cup that had a suspiciously familiar smell – he hadn't smelled that since he'd been in this world.

"Did they already go out to the barn?" Zander asked.

Tobias nodded without looking up at him; he removed the spoon from his cup and set it on the counter, then lifted the drink to his mouth, taking a long sip before finally setting it down and turning his attention to Zander.

"Where are you all dressed and ready to go?"

"I was going to go out and help with the horses."

Tobias frowned. "I remember you being told to stay in and rest and take care of that shoulder."

"I can keep up. There's too much to do for one person to be down."

"Save that attitude for in case you get to see an actual battle. No need to create fights where there are none. You've done enough proving yourself to last at least a day."

"There are a lot of horses to take care of."

"Sit, Zander. Thomas, Nathaniel, Dorian, and Marcus all went out to help. Now that the snow and the wind have quieted, they wanted to get the horses some exercise, keep them ready for travel. I mean it. Sit. You're not going out there."

Zander slumped onto one of the stools, forgetting and putting his elbows on the counter, which sent another electric shock through his shoulder.

"Mmm-hmm… doesn't a nice bumpy ride through the snow on your horse sound perfect right about now?"

Zander scowled at him, which only made Tobias chuckle.

"Would you like me to make you some tea – or can I offer you a cup of this mud?" He held up his mug.

"Is that *coffee*?"

Tobias raised an eyebrow. "You have this in your world?"

"Yes, but I've never seen it here. Where did you get it?"

"They grow it in another kingdom across the sea to the south. I have a friend who sends me some from time to time. Not many people bother importing it here – most don't like the taste. They save their coins for cocoa instead. Would you like a cup?"

"I don't want to deplete your supply."

"Nonsense. I never have someone to share it with these days."

"Do you have cream and sugar?"

"Is that what they do in your world? Same as some people do with tea?"

"Some people. Me."

"Help yourself."


After eating breakfast with Tobias, Zander was in a better mood – drinking coffee again after so long without it probably had something to do with it. Even the pain in his shoulder was easier to deal with; he'd have to be careful not to get used to this.

He'd taken a few steps down the hall when he noticed something lying on the floor outside Linnea's door – a tray. He didn't remember seeing it there before, but then again, he'd sort of been concentrating on staring straight ahead. The fruit, sweet rolls, and juice looked untouched.

There was a piece of paper there, too, tucked under a white napkin.

It wasn't any of his business, really, how it had gotten there. None of his concern at all. He'd already taken a step away from Linnea's door when he heard her cough loudly inside – a horrible, lingering sound that alarmed him. Without stopping to think, he knocked on the door. "Princess Linnea?"

For a moment, there was silence. He almost knocked again, but then she croaked out a muffled, "I'm fine."

He turned the knob and pushed the door open just enough to peer inside and see that the room was still dim. "No you're not."

"Zander…" her hoarse protest was drowned out in another fit of coughing.

He picked up the tray and carried it into her room, setting it down on the table next to her bed.

She was still buried under the covers. "You brought me breakfast?"

He only considered fibbing for a second before he shook his head and reached for the note, holding it just far enough out that she had to reach for it – allowing him a surreptitious brush against her wrist. "Linnea! You're burning up."

"Really? Because I'm freezing." She pulled the note inside her quilted cocoon.

Zander took a match from the little carved box on the bedside table and used it to light the oil lamp, then adjusted the lamp so the light from it shone close to her face.

"Thanks," she whispered.

As she read the note, he went over to the fireplace, pulled open the screen and set another log on the grate. He stoked the embers for a minute until the flames caught, sending a blast of welcome warmth into the room. It *was* chilly in here, but he suspected that wasn't Linnea's biggest problem.

He stood and turned to face the bed again, just in time to see her fold the note and shove it under her blankets as another coughing spell overtook her. In the dim light, her face was sallow and pale, except the flaring red circles on her cheeks.

This time the coughing lasted longer and she sounded like she was having trouble catching her breath.

"I'm going to go get someone," he said.

"Don't, Zander. It's just a cold. Don't wake William or Nathaniel up."

"What makes you think they're sleeping?"

"You're the only one in here."

He chuckled. "I think Nathaniel actually is awake – Tobias said he went out to the barn. Is that who wrote the note?"

"Nathaniel? No."

He'd meant Tobias – but it didn't matter. He shouldn't have asked. If anything had been drilled into him in guard training it was that absolutely *nothing* was his business unless he was invited.

Her silence reaffirmed that notion – right up until she pulled the covers tighter around her and said, "It's from James."

*From James?* Oh… so very, very not his concern, and yet… "Well, that was nice of him." It *was* a nice thing… so why on Earth – on Deusterros – did he feel a flash of annoyance?

Linnea nodded.

"Are you hungry? The rolls are fresh."

"Uh-uh."

"Then you at least need to drink some juice."

She started to shake her head, but he picked up the glass from the tray and held it out to her.

"I'm not kidding. You drink, or I go pound on William's door."

"You shouldn't even be in here," she said. "You don't want to catch whatever this is."

"Mmm… I'm only allowed to put myself in danger for the royal family if it involves swords now? Sit up. Drink. Or I go get William."

"Not necessary," said a voice from the doorway that led to the washroom. "I'm here." William had obviously just woken up, but he was fully alert when he reached Linnea's bedside a second later. "What's going on?"

"Nothing. It's just a…" Another long coughing fit interrupted Linnea's protest.

William's hand flew to her forehead, his eyes widening in concern as he registered the heat. He sat down next to her on the mattress, rubbing her back until she was finished, and then he took the glass from Zander and helped her take several small sips.

She didn't fight William. He made her finish about half the juice before setting the glass back on the tray. "Can you stay with her for a minute?" he asked Zander. "I need to go get my bag."

"Sure."

Once William was gone, Zander held up his hands. "I didn't do it."

"You were talking loud enough for him to hear you."

"You were coughing loud enough for people at the castle to hear you. We'll have soldiers at the door any minute."

She ignored that. "How's your shoulder today?"

He shrugged. "Can't be much worse than your throat, from the sound of it."

"I'm impressed. I didn't think you'd actually take the pain medicine."

For no apparent reason, his cheeks warmed. "I didn't."

"There's a difference between brave and just ridiculous, Zander."

"Ridiculous? You mean like not wanting help from a qualified person when you're practically on your deathbed?" As soon as that word was out, he regretted it. The flash of pain in her eyes matched the one in his chest, only hers was amplified at least a thousand times. "Sorry," he whispered.

She scrunched her nose and shook her head once. "It's just a hazard of speaking at all now. You can't guard everything that comes out of your mouth forever."

Another coughing spell interrupted her; this one was worse than the last few had been; Zander felt like he should do something, but he didn't know what. Just as the coughing finally tapered off, he heard what he thought was William returning, but it was Quinn.

"Not another step," Linnea said as soon as she saw her. "You're not getting sick. And you're especially not taking any germs in to Samuel."

"Nay…"

"I mean it, Quinn."

Quinn stood in the doorway for several seconds; Zander had no idea if she was going to listen or not. Finally, she sighed. "You'll have someone get me if you need anything?"

"No. If it's taking William this long to gather supplies, he's clearly freaked out. Get out of here. Zander can relay messages, since he's clearly sticking around like an idiot already." Linnea was so hoarse now her voice barely carried across the room, but Quinn got the message anyway – she sighed and left.

Zander picked up the glass of juice again and handed it to her.

"Do you want me to leave?"

"If you were smart, you would."

"Yeah, I caught your opinion of my intelligence, but that's not what I asked."

She closed her eyes and took a sip of the juice, then handed it back to him. He set the glass back down on the tray and stayed where he was.

William came back in a minute later through the hallway door – Zander guessed he'd retrieved things from Nathaniel's room as well.

While William sat down next to Linnea, Zander turned his attention to the fire again. A little teakettle sat on the side of the hearth – it couldn't hurt to boil some water for tea.

"You don't think this is just a cold, do you?" Linnea was asking as Zander returned from the washroom with the filled kettle.

"Not with this fever," William said. "I don't like how high it is, and your lungs don't sound good, either."

"Then what is it?" Her teeth chattered.

"I don't know for sure. You're cold, aren't you? Get back under the covers. I'm going to take a little blood in a minute, but I only need your arm for that."

Knowing it was safe to look again, Zander turned back at the sound of her little grumble.

"You ever had him draw your blood before?" he asked as she watched William's every move.

She shook her head.

"I have. It hurts about as much as being licked by a puppy."

Her eyes narrowed, but she gave a raspy chuckle. "What is it with you and dogs, anyway?"

"I like them."

"Did you have one in your world?"

"No. My mom used to say maybe when I was old enough to take care of one myself — but when I finally was, they had two more kids. My dad said one creature pooping in the house at a time was enough."

That made her giggle — and kept her eyes off the objects William was pulling out of his bag.

"If we ever make it back to the castle, we should get a dog," he said.

"Two creatures pooping in the castle at a time will be enough," William said — though he was barely concealing a chortle, and Linnea laughed hard enough to make herself cough again. William could joke — who knew?

"We should have gotten one before."

She scoffed. "I'm sure that would have gone over well with Sophia."

"I don't know. I think we could have had fun with Sophia and a puppy."

"Define *fun*," she said, giving him half a grin.

"Okay. Back in my world, we have people like her, too, you know. Several of my mom's relatives – but the worst was always my Great-Aunt Charlene. Every summer, my family has these horrible reunions – three days at some ridiculous campground in the middle of nowhere…"

"You must *really* be enjoying it here."

"Imagine if Sophia was here with us. Then imagine you were fourteen, and Sophia reported every move you made that annoyed her to your parents, who had to yell at you and punish you for it, just to keep peace with her."

"I can imagine," she said. "I have an aunt like that, actually – only my mother is the queen, and, well, you've met her."

"Spoiled princess."

She stuck her tongue out at him.

"Anyway, like I said, it was three days of misery, every year until the summer my cousin Ty brought his new puppy."

Linnea's eyes were locked on to him now, and he was surprised to realize he was kind of enjoying himself – it had been awhile since he'd allowed himself to think of normal things from home.

"The puppy was a black lab; he was fluffy with ears and feet far too big for his little body, and he hopped around everywhere, licking everyone he came across and trying to steal scraps of food from everyone's plates."

"I'm sure Great-Aunt Charlene loved *that*."

"Adored it. The other thing about my lovely Great-Aunt Charlene is that she's deaf. Well, mostly deaf. So she wears hearing aids."

"Is that like an ear trumpet?"

"Kind of," William said. "But fancier. They use battery power, and people wear them all the time."

"Oh that's neat," she said.

"Yeah. When they work." Zander grinned. "But sometimes they don't work. Or at least *hers* didn't. My Uncle Bob never had the same problem – but Aunt Charlene would just sit there fiddling with hers all day long and complaining about them."

Linnea smiled. "I'm beginning to see the connection to Sophia."

"Exactly. Anyway, this one day, she had just been driving us crazy. She yelled at me and Ty *all* morning. We were too loud, we were running too much, we knocked over her drink with a football…"

"Totally innocent, were you?"

"Completely. Both of our moms finally got so frustrated they told us not to talk around her at all if we could help it – which gave Ty his idea."

"Your poor mothers…." Linnea shook her head.

"Hey, they were the ones who made us go. Anyway, we started walking past her moving our lips like we were talking, but never making any actual sound. We got really into it – fake laughing, Ty mouthed a few swear words... She would glare at us, and then the second we were past her, she'd start playing with her hearing aid.

"We walked by her like fifty times, getting more and more ridiculous. I almost laughed out loud and gave us away so many times. She just kept playing with her hearing aid and glaring at us, her face getting redder and redder."

Linnea shook her head again, but her laughing made the criticism weightless. Even William was chuckling – he'd already finished and put his supplies away without Linnea ever noticing.

"So, where does the dog fit into this story?" she asked.

"Oh, the dog was the finale. After about the fiftieth time we passed her, she gave us this look, like she'd figured out that she could hear everything except us – and she was *mad*. Ty and I were about to high-tail it back into one of the cabins and hide. But then, the dog came up to us with half a hot dog in its mouth that one of the little kids dropped – and I had the best idea *ever*."

"Not all your definitions match other people's you know. Particularly when it comes to the phrase *'best idea'*."

"Oh, this one was totally the best. She hated the dog – who hates a puppy? But she said it barked too much. Puppies bark. We were outside in the mountains with half a billion chipmunks and birds – what else is it going to do? But my aunt would just *not* stop complaining about it. I think Ty's mom about murdered Charlene that weekend. After the first day, she did tell her that if it bothered her so much, she should turn off her hearing aid, but of course, she didn't. She just spent the entire weekend chasing that dog around whenever it barked and yelling at everyone else.

"Anyway, we took the dog over to one of the picnic tables and gave him an *enormous* spoonful of peanut butter. He loved it, spent the next ten minutes licking every corner of his mouth trying to get every last bit of it. And … to a mean, old, half-deaf lady, he looked exactly like he was barking without making a noise."

Linnea and William were both laughing.

"Yep, she chased that dog all over the camp screaming at it to shut up, when all it was doing was licking peanut butter."

When she finished laughing – and made it through the coughing spell after – she finally looked over at William, and then down at the neat white bandage on her arm.

"See? You didn't even feel it."

"Yeah, yeah. You're right about everything." She sounded tired, and she sneezed for emphasis.

William handed her a clean handkerchief and tucked her arm back under the covers.

"Do you think the baby's okay?" she asked quietly.

"I'm sure everything's fine," William said. "The biggest problem is it limits what I can give you to make you more comfortable. I want to get your fever down, but we need to be careful. We'll start with cold compresses, and then I'll see what else I have that's safe I can try and listen to the baby if you want me to."

Her eyes grew big. "Will you be able to hear her?"

"I think I might. You're over four moons now, I think, so it's a good possibility. It would be easier if I had a Doppler, but I can try anyway."

Zander went to pull the now-boiling kettle from the fire, setting it back down on the brick surface of the hearth before going into the washroom to look for the stack of cloths he'd seen in there the day before.

"Everything okay?" he asked as he carried a damp cloth over to the bed.

"Yes. We found the baby's heartbeat – it's quiet, but it sounds great." William took the compress from him, laid it gently across Linnea's forehead, and then tucked the covers tightly around her.

"I want an answer, Will," she said through chattering teeth. "What do you *think* it is?"

"Whatever it is, you need to rest. Try to fall asleep."

Zander couldn't help the small chuckle under his breath as he went to pour Linnea a cup of tea. Surely William didn't think she'd let him get away with that.

She didn't. Rather than closing her eyes the way William clearly wished she would, she sat up and stared at him.

William sighed. "I'm worried it's pimaeum, Nay. But I don't know for sure."

"Okay." She laid back against the pillows and pulled the quilt around her, lasting only a second before she started coughing again and had to sit up to catch her breath.

"What does *that* mean?" Zander asked.

"It means I'm sick," Linnea said. "Oh, and contagious. But don't worry. It's only deadly sometimes."

"Can't you give her an antibiotic or something?" Exasperation crept into his voice. He didn't like how sick she was – he wanted to help, but didn't know what he could do.

"I don't know." William's composure wasn't holding out very well, either. "I don't have everything I need here – we left most of the supplies back in the carriage. I only have the one emergency dose I keep in my bag. I wouldn't even be able to do this blood test if..." he broke off because Linnea's eyes were wide. "Sorry, Nay. It's going to be fine, but I need to figure some things out, okay? I need to talk to Nathaniel."

She nodded, accepting the mug of tea from Zander.

The sips of hot liquid seemed to help. Her voice sounded better, and when she lay back down, the coughing didn't start again. William and Zander both watched for several minutes until her eyelids stayed closed.

"It's not that serious, is it?" Zander asked when they were out in the hall, though why he was asking for reassurance when William was in this kind of mood, he didn't know. He'd been in this world for long enough now to know that wasn't a good idea.

William probably wouldn't have glorified the question with a response even if Quinn hadn't stepped into the hallway right then.

"What's going on?" she demanded.

"Linnea's pretty sick. I think it might be pimaeum." William didn't look at her as he said it.

Quinn looked as confused as Zander felt. "I won't try to pronounce that – just tell me how bad it is."

William shrugged. "It can vary, depending on how susceptible you are. Linnea's pregnant so that's probably why she got it first. We need to keep Samuel away from her completely. And we need to boil any clothes or fabric she might have breathed on or touched."

"Okay." Quinn's calm voice belied the quick panic that flashed across her eyes. "What else do you need? Can you treat it?"

"Yes. I need to confirm that's what it is first, but it's actually treatable with antibiotics. And if we're quick enough, we can usually keep it from spreading by dosing everyone she's been in contact with, too. I just don't have enough here at the house."

"Is there enough in the carriage?" Zander asked.

"Yes."

Quinn covered her face with her hands. "In those crates you guys grabbed before we left, right?"

"Over a hundred doses."

Before coming to this world, Zander had really believed that physical touch was the most intense kind of intimacy, but he'd been wrong. The look that Quinn and William shared now proved that.

# TRUST

THE DOOR TO LINNEA'S room was open slightly; Zander could hear William and Nathaniel speaking in quiet tones inside. He hesitated for a moment, almost turning and going the other direction, but then decided at the last minute to just go inside.

"Hey, Zander," Linnea said in her rough voice. She sounded even worse than she had yesterday, despite the dose of antibiotic Nathaniel had given her last night.

"Hey. I thought I'd come and see if there was anything you wanted me to get for you from the carriage."

She rolled her eyes, even though at this point the motion looked painful. "I think you're going to have enough to worry about with the snow and the cold."

"It's not so cold," he told her. "I was just out there. It's sunny and the snow is melting fast. Looks like it will warm up even more."

"Melting snow… wonderful. Stay away from the rivers, then," she said.

"We'll be fine, Linnea," Nathaniel said. "We'll stay away from rivers; we'll be back in a few hours. Take a long enough nap, and we'll be back before you wake up."

"I'm not sure I should be looking forward to that," she said. "Then you'll give me more medicine." A new coughing fit overtook her at the end of her sentence, invalidating her complaint.

When she was breathing again, Nathaniel leaned down and kissed her on the forehead. "Sleep. I'll be back soon."

She nodded.

Nathaniel patted Zander on the shoulder as he walked toward the door. "I'll see you outside."

"You're sure you're up for this?" William asked. "How's your shoulder?"

"Entirely better than Linnea's cough."

"Still, it's going to be a difficult ride in the snow."

Behind him, the door opened again. All three of them looked to see James entering. He was already in a long cloak and his leather boots. "Sorry if I'm interrupting, milady," he said. "I just thought I'd check to see how you're feeling today."

She sighed. "Not well enough to tell you not to go, I'm afraid. You really shouldn't be in here." Since confirming the diagnosis, everyone had been told to stay away from Linnea's room. Nathaniel and William went in anyway, of course – and Zander figured he'd already missed that boat. But they were all doing their best to stay away from the other people in the house, too.

James only shrugged. "Then we will hurry back as soon as possible … here, I thought you might like something to entertain you and to brighten your room." His voice wobbled slightly as he stepped toward her, pulling something out of his cloak and holding it out to her.

Zander didn't know which way to look.

"The book is Tobias'," James said. "I just thought it was one you might enjoy. The other is yours to keep."

"Thank you, James."

"You're welcome, milady." Was it possible to *hear* someone's cheeks turning red, or was Zander imagining it?

He didn't look at Linnea again until James was halfway across the room and she started coughing again. William whisked the book and the other object out of her hand and set them on the night table.

It was a small piece of wood, carved into the shape of a delicate flower – what kind, Zander didn't know, but it was beautiful.

Linnea hadn't thought James needed a warning to keep the horses away from the river in weather like this.

He cleared his throat. "I should get going."

"I really don't think you *have* to, Zander," Linnea said. "I heard Kian offered to go if you weren't up to it yet."

"You know, either I'm capable of this whole guard and Friends of Philip thing, or I'm not. Two days ago, you acted like I wasn't stepping up enough, but now that I'm trying, you're telling me I can't handle it."

She stared at him, a whole story in her eyes that he didn't know how to read. "Fine, Zander. I'll see you later."

"Do you think it's a mistake to send them?" Quinn asked Marcus as she stared out the window, watching Nathaniel, Zander, James, and Ethan ride toward the gate.

"I hope not. As I said before, if we're going to send them at all – and I think we *should* – soonest is best, before the snow melts enough to encourage Ivan's soldiers to spread out from the castle. As far as we know, there's no reason to suspect they'd look for us in this direction."

"No." She held up the folded paper in her still-shaking hand. "They think we've gone toward Eirentheos."

"Stephen's army is well prepared, Your Majesty."

"They shouldn't have to be. We're supposed to be at peace – that was the whole point of all this."

"*We* still are at peace. Stephen's army won't be fighting against Philotheum, but against those attacking us. This is an invasion."

"It doesn't seem right to ask them to risk their lives."

Marcus cocked his head to the side. "No? What would you expect them to do – what would you ask your army to do if Eirentheos was in trouble?"

She pressed her fingertips to her temples.

"*That* is the whole point."

"I know. Thank you for reminding me." She took a deep breath. "Is there any way Stephen could suspect where we are?" They'd made certain that none of the messages sent to Eirentheos – or anywhere else – contained any evidence of their location, not even whether they were still inside Philotheum. She would have shared the information with Stephen, of course, if there was no chance it could be intercepted, but she worried that he might take it upon himself to try to come.

"I don't know. He knows Tobias exists, but I don't know if he knows exactly where he lives – and I don't know if he'd guess we might come here. I don't think we can worry about it right now."

She looked out the window again. "We've still heard nothing back from Jonathan, Ellen, or Charles."

"No. But until we know otherwise, I think we should take it as a sign they've made it to safety somewhere our birds can't find them. Ellen and Charles, anyway. I don't think we can expect a response from Jonathan even if he does receive our message."

Nodding, she paced the floor of Tobias' sitting room, which had become her temporary office.

Marcus sat perched on the edge of one of the leather armchairs, his chin propped on his folded hands. His eyes followed Quinn's path from one window to the other, but he didn't speak, allowing her to process her thoughts.

"Do you think I made a mistake trusting Jonathan?" she asked.

He didn't answer for several seconds; finally, he met her gaze. "I think you need to quit worrying about whether you made a mistake or not. It doesn't matter now."

"It doesn't?"

"No, it doesn't. You made a decision that night, and it's over now. You can't go back and make a different one, can you?"

"No. But what if I messed up and made everything worse?"

"What if you did?"

She blinked. "Then that would be bad."

"Yes. But bad things happen. Bad decisions happen. If you knocked a vase off a counter, and it smashed all over the floor, that would be bad. But would you stand there and stare at it for the next several moons thinking about how bad it was?"

"No."

"Exactly. So, however this mess got here, all we can do is clean it up – see if we can fix it, or if we're going to have to replace it."

"All right." She sighed.

"For the record, I don't believe that choosing to trust is ever the wrong choice. It might not work out well; the person you trusted might betray you – but that's not on you. I think it's much worse to deny trust to someone who deserves it than to give it to someone who doesn't. You might lose the outside battle by trusting them, but if you don't trust when you should, you lose yourself."

She took a deep breath. "Thank you, Marcus, for your good advice, and also for the 'we' in all the clean-up talk."

"I thought that part was understood, Quinn."

"It is, Marcus – but that doesn't mean I can't remind you from time to time of how much I appreciate it."

# CAMP

"ARE YOU DOING all right?"

If it had been anyone other than Nathaniel asking that right now, Zander might have lost it. But it was Nathaniel; he'd ridden up close beside him, out of earshot of the two guards ahead of them. So he nodded. "I'm fine. It's actually nice to be out riding instead of stuck in Tobias' house – it feels like I'm doing something."

To his relief, Nathaniel didn't press the point about his shoulder; he only nodded. "I know what you mean."

"Are we getting close to where we left the carriage, do you think?" In truth, the ride had been long and far more challenging than anything he was used to. His shoulder was killing him, but he was proud of the way he'd been able to handle Ember in the deep snow.

"Shouldn't be far." Nathaniel reached behind him into the saddlebag and pulled out a silver compass and the leather-bound map he'd been using all morning. His stride was perfect, even though the map appeared to consume all of his attention. "Maybe fifteen more minutes, though going into the trees might slow us down."

Unlike when they'd traveled to Tobias' house, today they'd stayed mostly on what they could see of roads, trying to keep the horses away from hidden dangers under the layers of snow.

The road they were on now cut directly through a forest; trees loomed on either side of the narrow, snow-packed thoroughfare – really more a path than a road. Zander kept careful watch of the trees, and ahead of them, James and Ethan did the same; nobody wanted a small avalanche of snow dropping from a branch onto one of the horses.

"Do you think Linnea will be okay?" he asked.

Nathaniel looked over at him, warmth and kindness in his gray eyes. "I think so. I want to get this medicine back to her, and I want to make sure everyone else gets a dose so this thing doesn't spread, but I think everything will be all right."

"What would happen if someone got sick like that and you didn't have medicine from my world?"

"There is medicine in this world as well, Zander – what we're retrieving from the carriage was made here; it's not exactly the same as the kind in your world."

"Well, I know that."

"Yes, it's not what you were asking. An illness like Linnea's can be treated here by healers trained in the arts of this world with some success – but no, her chances wouldn't be as good as they are with the knowledge we attained in your world. And neither would ours. An epidemic of pimaeum could be a serious problem without the right medicine. I truly was interested in the science of Earth, and I'm grateful for what I learned there."

"So you don't regret leaving your kingdom and going to live there?"

"I can't go back and change it, so no; I don't see the point in regretting it."

"What about not telling Quinn who she really is?"

Nathaniel sighed. "I regret lying to her, and not pushing harder to have the kind of relationship I wanted to have with her as she was growing up. I regret the way she found out and the hardships that has caused for her. I'm sorry I hurt her, and I will spend the rest of my life trying to make those things up to her, and restore things between us."

He paused, looking ahead at the other two guards – they were still too far away to hear the conversation. "I'm also sorry for the way it affected you, Zander. My choices – and Samuel's – put Quinn in a position that caused her to hurt other people, and you were one of them. I hope you can forgive me for my part in that."

"It's not your fault I'm stuck here."

"No." Nathaniel chuckled. "When you voluntarily walk off a broken bridge in the middle of an icy river, you have to take some responsibility for the consequences."

"Owen could have been a little more upfront."

"*Owen* is eight, and you were responsible for taking care of *him*."

"Minor details."

Nathaniel laughed. "Yes, well. I have to say I am grateful you listened to him. You saved William's life, and possibly many others'."

At that moment, Zander caught a glimpse of something that made him freeze, bringing Ember to a halt right there in the middle of the path. Nathaniel had to circle back around to meet him, letting out a loud whistle as he did that made James and Ethan turn around immediately.

Up in the trees to the left of them, maybe fifty yards ahead, there was a flash of green in the trees – the color worn by Philothean guards.

Nobody spoke at first. Zander nodded toward the trees and the other men followed his gaze. James and Ethan both already had their hands on their hilts, and Ethan's eyes swept the entire area – searching for more hidden threats, Zander realized.

He looked around, too, while he thought about the best response. "We've already called attention to ourselves," he said quietly.

James shrugged with one shoulder. "Better than being ambushed."

"So do we confront them, wait for them to confront us, or keep traveling and pretend we didn't see them?" Zander asked.

"We don't know how many of them there are," Ethan said. "We don't stand much chance with four. Perhaps if we appear to be commoners..." He pulled the hood of his plain brown cloak over his head.

Zander didn't know if that was a good idea or not, but he followed suit. A moment later, though, it didn't matter. The single flutter of green suddenly turned into a wave as three fully uniformed men rode down out of the trees and began heading toward them.

He didn't need to watch what James and Ethan were doing; his sword was out and ready.

The three guards approached more slowly than he would have expected for a confrontation. Zander had plenty of time to continue searching the surrounding forest for anything else out of place, but he didn't see anything.

When they were finally close enough to really get a good look, James let out a surprised breath. All three men appeared disheveled, their uniforms wrinkled and smudges of dirt on their hands and faces. One, the youngest-looking, had a large bloodstain on the side of his cloak.

Zander's concern changed to a different kind; the tight grip he had on his sword loosened a little.

"Do you live near here?" one of the guards called. He was the oldest of the three, perhaps in his late-twenties. Though it didn't mean anything, Zander had never seen him before – he would have remembered the man's shoulder-length light, wavy hair.

"Why?" Ethan asked.

The man's blue eyes narrowed. "I'm just trying to understand why you'd brave this weather to travel in such dangerous times. The next village is quite far – and we haven't come across any homes in this area."

Ethan coaxed his horse a couple of steps to the side, concealing his sword arm behind both his cloak and the animal. "What's so dangerous about traveling right now?"

"Have you not heard? King Ivan's army has invaded the capital city. They've taken over the castle."

Zander had to give Ethan credit for his ability to feign surprise. He had just the right amount of surprised panic in his voice when he asked, "The queen?"

The guard shook his head. "We don't know. There are rumors…"

"What rumors?" James asked.

This time, the younger guard – the one with the bloodstain – spoke. "We have a friend who was in the battle at the castle… he says the queen and the royal family weren't there, and he believes they may have escaped to safety. Others are afraid…"

"What are you doing out here so far, then?" Ethan asked.

The three guards exchanged wary glances.

Zander frowned, returning to his search of the trees – these guards had revealed too much to a group of unknown men traveling through the snow. That could only mean that, despite their bedraggled appearance, they weren't afraid. There had to be more soldiers nearby, ready to defend them. He could feel Nathaniel doing the same thing next to him.

Nathaniel's search lasted only a minute, though. When the guards hesitated a little too long in answering, he asked, "How many of you are there? Soldiers in these woods?"

The guard who hadn't yet spoken closed his eyes as the oldest of the three sighed and said, "A fair few. Are you hiding a battalion as well?"

The middle guard now had an expression that matched the one Zander knew he'd been wearing a few minutes ago – a "so-this-is-how-we-die" look.

"No," Nathaniel said, drawing back his hood and allowing them to see him for the first time.

The youngest guard recognized him first; he gasped, dismounting his horse in one fluid motion, and dropping to one knee in the snow. "Your Highness! It's Prince Nathaniel," he hissed to the others.

The other two guards were halfway to the ground before Nathaniel could object. "That's not necessary," he said. "Please don't get wet."

Following James' lead, Zander re-sheathed his sword, though he kept his hand close to the hilt.

"Please, come out of the snow," Nathaniel said again. "You look cold already. Are you all right?" The question was directed at all three of them, but his eyes were on the blood on the youngest one's cloak.

"It's not mine," the man said. "I'm not hurt – I've just been helping tend the injured."

"The injured?"

"Yes." The middle one finally spoke. "Since yesterday, we've been searching for those who were able to escape the castle during or after the battle. Many are injured and in need of assistance."

"I see." Nathaniel sighed. "What is your name?"

"I'm Ellis Kirk; this is my brother Rhys," he nodded to the younger one, "and this is Isaac Pearce."

"Kirk?" Nathaniel asked. "Is your father Spencer?"

"Yes."

"Spencer Kirk?" Ethan asked. He looked at Zander and James. "He was on duty the night of the invasion."

Ellis nodded.

"Is he here as well?"

"No," Rhys said. The underlying tone of his words made Zander's stomach twist uncomfortably.

"He's missing," Ellis clarified. "We don't know if he survived, but nobody has seen or heard from him yet."

"We had to stop traveling back toward the castle yesterday afternoon," Isaac said. "More troops started moving into the city after the snow stopped. They've occupied nearly the whole city now. We don't know how to get more people safely out."

"Do you know whether the queen is still alive?" Ellis asked. "We've been trying everything to get information, but nobody knows anything."

"The queen is safe," Nathaniel said. "So are the king and the prince. That is all I can tell you right now."

When all three men practically melted in relief, Zander finally let go of his sword. "Where are the injured men?" he asked. "Do you need assistance?"

"We need all the help we can get," Rhys said. "We need healers, supplies, shelter. That storm couldn't have hit at a worse time."

"All right." Nathaniel nodded. "Can you give me a minute to discuss things with my men, and then you can show us where you're set up?"

As soon as the three guards were out of earshot, Ethan rounded on Nathaniel. "This could be a trap!"

"It could," Nathaniel agreed.

"We're going to do it anyway, aren't we?"

"*I* am, Ethan. Whether you stay and help, or return to Tobias' is up to you."

"You'd risk everything we're doing on this?"

Nathaniel took a deep breath. "What is *everything we're doing* if it involves – even possibly – leaving our own men to die?"

Ethan's mouth fell open. He looked back and forth between James and Zander for support.

"I'm living a borrowed life already, thanks to Queen Quinn," James said. "I won't leave others to suffer at Tolliver's hands."

Zander cleared his throat and met Ethan's glare with a steady, calculated calm. "I'm with Nathaniel in any case – but if it's a trap, it's a trap. We're already in it. We don't have an army waiting somewhere to protect us. I'd rather walk in and understand what we're up against than accidentally lead someone back to Tobias' place."

The cold logic registered with Ethan, and he nodded. "All right. I'm sure we'll need the supplies from the carriage for the soldiers. Since we're close already, should we go there first, or try to keep that location hidden?"

"The location of the carriage doesn't tell them anything they don't already know from finding us here," Zander said, shrugging.

"What about getting the medicine to the princess?" James asked.

Nathaniel whistled long and low. His seeker bird, Aidel, responded immediately, fluttering down from the treetops and landing right on his outstretched arm. "I'll send a message back to everyone letting them know what's going on. Once we've been to the carriage, I can send a vial of the powder back to William. He'll be able to handle the rest there. We'll make sure to save enough for any more emergencies back at Tobias'."

# NOVICE

"CAN I HELP YOU with that?" It was becoming Thomas' go-to entry line – she'd already teased him about it – but he figured there were worse ways to start a conversation.

Mia looked away from the clothesline she'd rigged up in front of the fireplace in her room and raised an eyebrow. "You really want to tackle *that?*" She tilted her head toward a large bucket of wet clothes.

He hadn't known he was holding his breath for her reaction until it came out, leaving a flood of relief in its place. Despite everything, things were still okay between them today. He grinned. "Does anyone *want* to? I'm sure you don't either, but we all need clean clothes."

She stepped aside. "How is Linnea?"

"She's asleep, finally. I think I was keeping her awake being in there, so I left for a bit. William is down in the basement trying to figure out how to grow mold to make antibiotics or something I don't understand. I don't know that we'll be here for long enough for him to accomplish anything."

"He probably just needs to feel like he's doing something."

"That's Will, for sure." Thomas pulled a shirt out of the bucket and shook it in front of the fire, frowning at the color of the fabric. "Is this Tobias'?"

She nodded. "He insisted I didn't need to do his, but…"

He hung the shirt carefully over an empty section of the line and then turned and reached for her, taking her into his arms and pressing his lips against hers.

It was several minutes before she finally pulled away. "What was that for?"

"Do I have to have a reason other than you're adorable *and* amazing?"

"And here I actually believed for a minute that you came in here to help with the laundry."

"I've never been satisfied doing only one thing at a time," he said, shrugging and planting another kiss on the top of her head as he reached into the bucket again.

Just as he finished hanging another shirt, there was a wiggling motion in the center of the bed and then a loud screech.

Mia sighed. "This is why I never get more than three things hung up at a time. He's been much more restless than usual."

"You can't really blame him." Thomas walked over and scooped his nephew from the little nest Mia had made with pillows. "We keep taking him to new places and disrupting his schedule, and everyone's stressed out around him." He rocked Samuel gently back and forth in his arms. The baby's cries grew quieter, but didn't stop completely.

"He's probably wet and hungry by now," Mia said.

"I can fix one of those things at least." Thomas reached for the diaper bag. "And then I'll take him to Quinn. She and Marcus should be ready for a break."

"I should make a comment about you skipping out on the laundry," she said, this time approaching him, "but instead I think I'll just do this."

He grinned as he leaned down to meet her lips. "Samuel's going to think this is all we ever do."

"I'm all right with that," she said when they were finished.

Catching her hand with his free one, he looked deep into her green eyes. "Me too, Mia."

Thomas paused outside the door to Tobias' sitting room, debating whether it was safe to interrupt – he couldn't hear any voices.

After only a few seconds, Samuel settled the question by letting out an ear-splitting wail, bringing Quinn to the door immediately.

"I think he can *smell* you," he said as she took the baby. Samuel quieted immediately once he was in her arms.

"Yeah, I think so." She smiled, though underneath that he could see how worried she was. "You can come in, Thomas. I was actually alone for a minute."

"Where's Marcus?" he asked, following her as she carried Samuel over to a couch.

"He went to go see if any more birds have returned with messages."

"Do you need me to do anything?"

"You're keeping an eye on Linnea, right? She won't let me anywhere near her."

"I know. She and Will both made me promise to wash my hands and face before so much as talking to you or Samuel – don't worry, I did. Changed my shirt, too."

"Thanks."

He nodded, looking around the room at the maps and books laid out on every flat surface. "Finally learning the geography of your kingdom?"

"I had to start sometime, right?"

He chuckled. Back at the castle, an entire wall of Quinn and William's sitting room was covered with enormous canvas maps of both Eirentheos and Philotheum. She'd asked for them even before her coronation.

"This area was actually quite interesting," she said, pointing to a space on a map stretched over a low table.

Thomas leaned down to look, mentally calculating directions. He glanced out the window, then back at the map, and then up at Quinn. "That's where we are, right?"

She nodded. "Kind of close to this little village here." She pointed to a spot that showed a small body of water, and bore a name he couldn't quite read. A huge chunk of the map surrounding it was blank. "That's all forest," she said.

"Tobias likes his privacy, huh?"

She nodded. "The map I have at the castle shows nothing in this region at all."

"That isn't actually all that surprising. There are probably a few villages like that in Eirentheos, too."

"Marcus said that, too. It's still hard for me to wrap my brain around a world without satellite imaging."

"I didn't spend enough time in your world for that to even sound like real words, Quinn."

She chuckled.

"I don't know if you're worried about *why* Tobias would be out here like this ... I see why you're concerned, but ... he hasn't killed us yet."

"It's not that. Not that I don't still have questions about him, but they're not my most pressing ones. It's this village – Valderwood. Marcus said that some of the people there aren't overly friendly toward the royal family. Many of them moved out here to get away from the authority of the capital – they even have their own soldiers."

"In all fairness, if I was living under Hector's reign, I might have joined them. I'm not bad with a sword either, you know."

"I know." She sighed. "I don't even know how they feel about my taking over the crown, if anyone trusts me, or if it's more people who want me arrested or dead. It's just another complication."

"Well, at least you have something new to add to your map. Geography is good."

"Yeah... now if I could just get a handle on the history... Everything I learn leads me to ten other pieces of information that might have been helpful."

"You're doing great you know."

"Uh-huh... Running away from the castle and allowing a usurper to take control of my kingdom is *fantastic* leadership. Someday, Nathaniel's going to finally slip with the secret that I was actually my father's second-born child."

"Hmmm... How much older than you is Zander *exactly*?"

"*Not funny*, Thomas!"

"Yes, it kind of is." He laughed at the face she was making. "Okay, so maybe it isn't – but the only *reason* it isn't is because at this point I don't think it would shock me."

She shook her head like she was trying to send that thought flying across the room. "Maybe I am following my father's example anyway – running away from the fight just to save my own skin."

"Yeah?" He perched on the arm of an overstuffed chair. "Now that you're out of imminent danger and can think, are you planning on taking yourself and the true heir to another world and forgetting all of this ever happened?"

"No."

"See? Totally different. Relax. Even if you did give up your castle for a bit, you can still die for your kingdom."

"Especially now that I gave up my castle and came to the middle of nowhere next to a town with a militia that might hate me."

"Exactly."

She chuckled as she ran her fingers through Samuel's downy black hair. "You always know what to say to make me feel better, Thomas."

"It's my job. Besides, you're not dying for this kingdom without taking me with you."

"Unless pimaeum gets to all of us first."

"And there's my sister – full of optimism, as usual."

"Your Majesty?" Marcus' voice called from the doorway.

"It's fine, Marcus. Thomas and I were just chatting. Is there any news?"

"Yes. Another message from Stephen … and one from Nathaniel."

Thomas knew his own expression must match the alarm in hers. "Is everything all right?"

"Nathaniel is fine – and so are the guards with him. They've come across a whole encampment of soldiers." He held a folded piece of paper out to her.

Thomas had to sit on his hands to keep from snatching the paper or reading over her shoulder. "Do you want me to leave?" he forced himself to ask.

She shook her head, looking up from the paper with an awed expression. "Nearly fifty guards, from both the castle and the city."

"Where?" Thomas asked.

"It doesn't say." She held up the note. "I think Nathaniel is being extra safe not sending that information. A number of the men were injured in the battle."

Thomas closed his eyes. "So there was a battle, then?"

"That's what all of this is sounding like. Something happened. This says he'll try to get more details and send them later, but he's doing what he can for the men now. Did he send something as well?"

"Yes." Marcus pulled a vial from his pocket; Thomas could see some kind of powder through the brown glass – one of William's medicines, no doubt.

"He says that should be enough for everyone here – they might not attempt coming back and giving away our position." She looked at Marcus. "Did they have enough supplies with them to be safe in this weather?"

"They made it to the carriage, Quinn," Thomas said. "There was plenty there, and Nathaniel knows what he's doing." He squeezed her shoulder.

"Okay, then we'd better get this to William."

# ALLOWED

"DO YOU KNOW HOW to start a fire?" Nathaniel asked.

Zander nodded. "I"m getting better."

"Good. I'm going to need a fire over here for boiling water." He pointed at a clear spot on the ground, close to the tent the guards had set up as a makeshift hospital. "Maybe after, you can check to make sure all the medical supplies are unloaded?"

"Sure."

"Thank you."

Having a task he could handle felt better than watching the flurry of activity around him and trying to jump in. Finding a pile of rocks to build a fire circle was harder than he expected. The soldiers working tirelessly to build a safe haven here had cleared rocks along with the snow between shelters.

The campsite was impressive for having been set up so hastily in the wake of a blizzard – and with so few necessities.

On their way here with the carriage, Rhys had told them about the scarcity here. Most of the men, fleeing from the confusion of the castle and the city, had brought only what they could grab in haste.

The medical tent was the only real shelter – the uninjured men had spent the stormy nights huddled around fires in caves dug from the snow banks and under whatever blankets and extra coats they could find.

He looked around in amazement as he worked to coax a flame from the damp wood, wondering what he'd gotten himself into agreeing to be a guard. Surely, he'd have been the first to die out here in a situation like this one. Or two months – moons, whatever – ago, he would have. Now… well, he'd probably still have been one of the guards being carried into the medical tent with frostbite.

Even for the experienced soldiers here, though, the conditions were dire. Ethan and James had already pulled every bit of fabric they could from the carriage and were helping to set up more shelters and fires.

As soon as Zander had a bucket of fresh snow sitting in the crackling flames, he went to find Nathaniel.

"Did you send a message to Quinn?" he asked, as soon as he managed to corner Nathaniel in a quiet spot.

"Yes."

"Did you tell her what it's like here?"

"I told her we'd come across these soldiers, yes, but it isn't safe to exchange a lot of information right now."

The words sounded logical; he couldn't argue with the idea. They didn't know many of these guards, and protecting Quinn and Samuel was the most important thing – but there was something he didn't like about it. He couldn't put the feeling into words, though, so he started trying to unpack and organize supplies.

"Sir Zander?" The voice was familiar, but he couldn't place it until he turned around to see the man standing there. He was a guard in the castle – Kenneth? He thought that was right. Zander had talked to him a few times during his training, and once Kenneth had invited him to a crumple game among the guards, though Zander hadn't gone. "Is that you?"

"Yes, it's me."

"Oh, thank the Maker! I was looking for you – are you all right?"

"Me?" He looked at the ragged bandage wound around Kenneth's left arm. It might have once been white, but was now brown and gray, the fraying edges revealing dark shades of purple and red underneath. "I'm fine. What happened to you?"

"It's not too serious, just a cut."

That wasn't the whole story; Zander could tell by the way he moved that there were other injuries hidden by his shirt and green cloak – a cloak he'd been wearing even as he laid on one of the pallets in the tent. All of his clothes were disheveled, and his face was flushed and shining. "From what?"

"A sword. I'll be all right."

"I hope the other guy looks worse."

"He does. Much."

"Were you in the battle?"

"I suppose you could call it that. I was on duty the night of the invasion, patrolling in the front hall when I heard the shouting. Someone at the northern gate had let them in – at least sixty men. My father ran past me, yelling at me to help stop them as they came in, but I was so worried about the queen and her family, I went upstairs instead. I didn't know they were already gone."

Raw, hot shame flooded through Zander, curling in sick waves through his chest and into his limbs. He'd been far away and safe by then. "And then what happened?"

Kenneth shook his head. "I don't know how they did it, exactly, but they must have sent someone in first to take the king and queen. Three soldiers, actually. Some of their best ones, I'm sure, but they were anticipating a sleeping family trying to protect an infant – not trained guards willing to take chances."

"What kind of chances?" The longer he talked to Kenneth, the more Zander noticed the way he held himself a little too stiffly, how sometimes just talking made him almost wince.

"After I was certain the family wasn't in the room, I put the end of a broom into the embers of the fire and used it as a weapon to disarm the soldier who seemed the strongest – and then I used my sword."

"Did you kill him?"

"Yes. Another was badly injured, and his friend took him and fled the fire once I lit the bedding and the rugs."

By this point, their conversation had drawn Nathaniel's attention.

"Who was with you?"

"Felix Bosch."

"And he…?"

Kenneth shook his head; the slow motion back and forth pulled Zander's stomach right along with it. "I tried to get him out of there, but he was already… It was a bad idea staying in the room as long as I did." He glanced down toward the right side of his body. "I was just lucky the intruders don't know all the exits from that wing of the castle."

"Has anyone looked at *your* injuries?" Nathaniel asked.

"Just my friend Ellis. I don't think he appreciated the view, though. We haven't had any healers here – some of the men know a little, but not enough to do anything."

Nathaniel flew into action immediately, his hand stretching toward Kenneth's forehead immediately – Zander could tell by the hard set of Nathaniel's jaw that he didn't like his findings. Somehow, in the next instant, Kenneth lay on the pallet again as Nathaniel pulled back his cloak and began unbuttoning his shirt.

Zander retrieved Nathaniel's bag from the other side of the tent without being asked. "What else do you need?"

"Everything." Nathaniel didn't take his eyes from what he was doing for even a second as he lifted Kenneth's shirt, revealing hot, red blisters underneath. Zander was grateful for a strong stomach. "Did you bring all the supplies out of the carriage?"

"Yes."

"Okay, I'm going to need some of that water you boiled, as much pain medicine as you can find, valoris seed…"

Zander stared at him. "You need more help than me. I don't even know what valoris seed looks like!"

"We have to make do with what we have here, *Sir* Zander. I can tell you what I need; it's easy enough."

The veiled reminder of his duty to Quinn was meant to keep him quiet, to stop even considering divulging the fact he knew the location of the royal family – but Nathaniel's words had the opposite effect. What he felt instead was a surge of defiant indignation – at least as much on Quinn's behalf as his own.

In any other situation, Nathaniel would have had his priorities in order; his actions when they'd first met the soldiers on the trail told Zander that much. Right now, though, he wasn't acting as a prince of his kingdom, or even as a healer who would do everything in his power to provide the best help for these men. Right now, his actions spoke only "overprotective uncle."

But however noble that might be – however much Zander understood the instinct to protect Quinn – the decision didn't belong to Nathaniel.

For the next fifteen minutes, he hauled over every supply Nathaniel asked for. He dug through crates and boxes, asked questions, and learned vocabulary he'd never intended to need. And the whole time, he thought about what to do.

Once Zander had finally given Nathaniel everything he needed, he mumbled an – honest – excuse about not wanting to watch whatever was about to happen and he escaped the tent.

He didn't stop to second guess himself, or to chance an encounter that might compel him to explain.

The horses were all tied up close together in a small clearing near the icy stream. In the hurry to investigate the encampment and provide assistance to the wounded soldiers, nobody had bothered to unsaddle them. Zander paused for only a moment to check Ember's saddlebags for anything that might be of use at the camp, but the only thing left in them was a half-full canteen and, in a special pocket where he always kept it, one of the notebooks Quinn had given him once when he'd mentioned missing having a place to write down his thoughts.

For only a second, the notebook gave him pause as he remembered the story of Quinn being kidnapped from an emergency encampment. Although his heart pounded in his hurry to leave, he was rational enough to realize the danger it might cause to have people worrying about him. At least paper was the solution to one of his problems.

His breath felt heavy and tight in his chest as he rode around the outside of the camp, tracing the route they'd traveled coming here from the trail, only this time in reverse. With every step he expected someone to appear through the trees to stop him – though he didn't even know what he would do if someone did. *Could* they stop him? He wasn't afraid of any of the guards here; if he had been, he wouldn't be on his horse right now.

It didn't happen anyway. He stayed just far enough away from the shelters and activity to avoid notice, and after a few minutes, the road that had brought them here stretched before him. Without another second of hesitation, he headed back in the direction of Tobias' house.

He'd been riding for over an hour and could tell he was getting closer to Tobias' when he heard it – the heavy pounding of a horse's hooves behind him on the snowy trail. Maybe more than one horse. There was only one way to find out.

Bringing Ember to a halt, he pulled his sword all the way out of its sheath, holding it ready as he brought his horse slowly around.

What he saw nearly made him drop the weapon into the snow.

He didn't know much about horses, even after all the time he'd spent around them here, but he knew he'd never seen that breed in

Deusterros. He knew because he would have recognized the massive beast – not from a personal encounter, but from beer commercials back in his world.

The rider he had seen here. Now that he thought about it, the man would have been a nice touch in one of those commercials. One of the holiday ones, maybe.

"You might want to get a better grip on that thing, Zander. You don't want to scratch it up before you've ever had a chance to use it."

After the initial shock of *that horse* – Ember wasn't a small horse in any estimation, but that animal dwarfed him – Zander couldn't even muster up surprise at this encounter. "I've got it," he said, sliding it back in place.

"I must say, you've gained some excellent control of both the weapon and your horse since the last time I saw you," Alvin said, with a note of approval in his voice that did little for Zander except annoy him.

He shrugged. "I figure if I can't *watch* reality television, I might as well play and see how long it takes me to get voted off."

Alvin's laugh was bright and sincere. "I hear you were audience favorite last week. Although your social media scores might be higher if you played up the romance angle just a bit."

"What are you doing here, Alvin?"

"I would have thought that was obvious. Traveling to have a chat with the queen, much the same as you, I expect. Of course, at this pace we'll never get there. Let's pick it up a bit, shall we?"

And with those words he was moving again, leaving Zander with little choice but to turn and try to catch up.

"Did Nathaniel send you after me when he realized I wasn't back at the camp?" he asked when he finally brought Ember alongside the other horse.

It was a stupid question, and Alvin didn't bother acknowledging it with a real response. "You were awfully confident you'd be able to find your way back to Tobias'."

"Was I wrong?"

"No. You do realize, of course, that the birds can travel much faster than you can, and that we'll be encountering a search party from Tobias' in rather short order?"

"Well, I don't have a bird."

"What would you have done if you did?"

He bit his upper lip. "If I had a bird, I'd have just sent a message to Quinn. I didn't *want* to run away from there when they needed so much help. But Nathaniel wasn't going to listen to me, and having an argument with him in front of all those guards would have been more obvious than leaving. Who knows what kind of information might have leaked if things got heated. Quinn can send him a message when I get there – but she needs to know."

"I agree."

Those words brought him up short, leaving the taste of a bitter retort frozen on his tongue. "You do?"

"Yes, Zander, I do." He paused, his eyes on the road ahead of them for a moment before he spoke again. "Can I ask why you didn't inform James or Ethan about what you were doing?"

"I did. I left a note on James' saddle where he'd see it before they came looking for me, so they wouldn't worry I'd been taken or something."

"You could have asked one of them to come with you. It would have been safer."

Zander's whole forehead scrunched in irritation. "Neither one of them would do anything like that without orders. They'd have gone straight to Nathaniel, and this whole thing would have blown up. He's a prince, and – apparently – somewhere near the top of the Friends of Philip. They'd have followed anything he said."

Alvin nodded silently.

"So are you going to give me the lecture about how I made all the wrong choices in this now, or can it wait until there are more people to join in?"

Alvin chuckled as he pulled his horse just in front of Ember and brought it to a stop, blocking Zander's path. "Why do you think I would chastise you about your decisions here?"

"Why wouldn't you? You've never been shy about commenting before."

"I don't think you're being quite fair, Zander. I've let you know once or twice when you were making a choice that might make things difficult for you – but last we talked I told you how much I think you've grown."

"And you still think that after what I'm doing now?"

"More so." He smiled, absently pulling his long fingers through the horse's mane. "I'd apologize for the appearance of lecturing today, except that I'm rather certain the fault there lay in your perception rather than my delivery. On my end, I was only enjoying hearing the details of your consciously making the best decision you could and then acting on it, even though it was difficult."

This warm glow in his neck was different than the kind he was used to. He brushed at his collarbone with his fingertips. "I don't know if it was the right decision, though. There's a good chance this could lead to Quinn and Samuel…" He couldn't finish the sentence the way he'd started it. "I might be putting everyone in danger."

"It could," Alvin agreed, dashing any secret hopes Zander might have had about getting reassurance from him. "You don't have any control over the decisions other people make – but would that make what you're doing wrong?"

"No. Quinn needs to know. They're her men, this is her call. And those men deserve to have a queen who is actually informed about what's going on in her kingdom. Some of them have already died for her. If Nathaniel and everyone else want the 'rightful' queen to fulfill their prophecy or whatever, then they need to accept it when they get her. *Nathaniel* is wrong."

"He just loves her, Zander."

For the first time ever, he met Alvin's gaze straight-on, with no defiance or sarcasm. "Does that change the fact?"

# UNCHARTED TERRITORY

"CAN I SPEAK TO Zander alone for a few minutes, please?"

His heart thudded in his throat and a slick feeling coated his palms as everyone followed Quinn's request. Even William disappeared after lingering in the doorway for a moment before allowing Marcus to pull it tightly closed.

She was quiet for what felt like a very long time, studying him, her eyes a piercing shade of gray inside an expression that transformed her into someone he'd never seen before. A teasing quip bubbled on his tongue, but couldn't come out.

"That was pretty dangerous," she finally said. "You worried everyone. You could have gotten lost or something else could have happened. Did you even think about that?"

"I did think about worrying people. I left a note."

"And the other part?"

His gaze fell to his feet; the leather of his boots no longer shouted untried and new. "I wasn't really thinking about the danger to myself, no."

She crossed her arms across her chest, quiet again for a moment before shaking her head. "Almost getting yourself killed once was enough, you know. You don't have to put that endeavor on repeat."

"I'm not suicidal, Quinn. I wasn't trying to do anything dangerous. But my life is not worth more than those soldiers'."

"Don't I get to make *that* decision, too? How much your safety matters?" There was an edge to her voice that belied more than just the sarcasm over the reason he'd come.

"I think you have enough on your plate with the things you're supposed to control," he said, purposefully keeping his tone light to soften the mood.

"Especially since it's starting to look like I haven't even *seen* most of my plate."

He didn't know how to respond other than giving her a little nod of solidarity.

"Yeah, so anyway…" She chuckled under her breath.

"So how much trouble am I in, exactly? Should I hand over my sword now?"

Her entire forehead crinkled with the effort of her frown. "In trouble? For what? Being the only guard – the only person – to tell me what's really going on? For taking charge in the best way you knew how and doing what you thought was right?"

"Sure. That too." He sank into a chair as some of the tension he'd been feeling finally drained. At least he wasn't going to be trapped in a house with everyone mad at him.

She watched him for a moment and then sat down on one of the couches herself, tucking her knees up under her chin – suddenly a completely different creature than the queen she'd been only moments ago. This girl was familiar.

After a few minutes of silence between them, she cleared her throat. "Do you know what Jonathan said to me the night we left the castle?"

He raised an eyebrow.

"He said it was an interesting time for me to start acting like a queen."

Zander scoffed. "Let's see… you left your world and your family, sacrificed your link to them, married into the family they wanted you to, had the baby they wanted you to have, moved away from the *other* family you've grown close to, lost a good friend… What more does Jonathan want, do you think?"

She buried her forehead in her knees. "I don't know. Maybe he wants an actual queen – one who makes decisions and protects her kingdom against a foreign invasion."

"That's kind of hard to do when nobody will *let* you. They're all so busy worrying about you and shuttling you around, and only telling you half of what's going on…"

She looked up now, her eyes meeting his again. "Who *let* you come back from that camp to tell me what's going on right now?"

His mouth opened to eject a quick retort, but he had to close it again when the right one eluded him.

"It is the same, Zan. In the ways that matter, it is the same. You've been here for, what, about three moons? And none of this was your choice, really – you had no idea what you were getting into, you haven't had as much time to learn about things here, to even understand what's going on… But yet, when it came time to make a decision, to take the lead and do the right thing, you just did it. Then there's me – I have the crown and the castle, and I *chose* this. But I'm hiding behind other people, and making excuses instead of difficult decisions. Instead of leading."

"It's a lot more complicated for you, Quinn. I mostly only have to worry about you beheading me or something – and I'm probably safe on that account. You have to worry about what *everyone* thinks and wants. I don't think you're *hiding* behind those people or making excuses. I think they're standing in front of you."

"Maybe. But some of this could be simpler, don't you think? Someone can only stand in front of you if you stay behind them. I mean, I love Nathaniel. He's my only tie between all the different parts of my family – all the parts of *me*. But I am the queen. If he

thinks it's okay to withhold critical information about the kingdom…
I'm not sure I've done my job. And if my own guards are following
him instead of me… Somewhere in here, I am not leading them."

He wanted to reassure her – tell her she was being too hard on
herself, this was too much for a seventeen-year-old girl, but he
couldn't. There was too much truth in what she was saying. And even
if it was more responsibility than he thought she should have, that
didn't matter. She needed someone in her corner who would push
her, not make more excuses. Instead he asked, "What does William
say about it?"

Her cheeks puckered like she was biting the insides of them as
she contemplated him. "William is… He's my husband, Zander. He's
the father of my son, and my best friend, and later today I will tell
him every word of this, and he'll tell me his thoughts about it. *But* I'm
having this conversation with you for a reason."

He propped his chin on his hands, his elbows on his knees,
waiting for the rest.

"He's a healer, you know. That is his passion, and what he
thinks about, and what he gets so lost in sometimes, even I can't find
him. It's who he *is*. And I love that about him, and I love listening to
every detail – even the ones I don't understand. Whenever I'm able, I
help him think through things and try to give suggestions and offer
solutions. I try to give him support and encourage him in what he
believes he should do…"

She paused, her eyes flicking away from Zander's and toward
where her fingers were picking at an invisible speck on her pants.
"But if he tried to talk to me about whether or not he should go and
help out with an infectious plague – I could not be held responsible
for giving him objective advice."

"You mean if he thought you were in danger, he would stand
in your way, too." He purposefully phrased it as a statement, but
the way her eyes crinkled made him wish he'd said it with less
certainty.

"No. I wouldn't stop him. If he told me that was what he needed to do, I would swallow back my terror, and tell him I was proud of him, and it would be true. But I'm very grateful he has people like Nathaniel and Jacob to help him make some of those decisions in the first place."

The full weight of what she was telling him hit slowly, like a slow tide rather than a freight train, but the impact was still the same.

They'd carefully avoided venturing anywhere close to this territory ever since he'd come here, but right now seemed like an appropriate time to broach it, at least a little. "*I'd* have stopped you."

She nodded, though there was no judgment or anger in the motion, just calm acceptance. "And yet, somehow you're now the person I can trust to push me to do what I need to do."

"I still don't want to see you get yourself killed."

Untucking herself, she set her feet on the floor and sat up straight; the transformation was small, gradual, but visible. The girl he'd known in Bristlecone still existed – she hadn't been erased, but reshaped. Her next words, sensitive as they might be, were spoken with quiet assurance, rather than doubt.

"I know I hurt you, Zander. If things had been different ... you and I would have been so different, too. As sorry as I am for how I made you feel, though – and as much as I wish this whole situation wasn't as hard for you as it is – I have to tell you that I'm glad you're here. Not just that it's good we're getting along since we're stuck together, but really and truly glad that even in all of this, I have your friendship. I don't deserve it probably, but I'm glad I didn't lose you."

He sighed. "You know, when I first came here and found out about ... everything ... I wasn't sure I could ever not be angry at you again."

"I know."

"Oh, let me finish before you keep beating yourself up over it, will you?"

"Fine." Her grudging acquiescence made him smile.

"What I was *going* to say, is that I'm *not* angry anymore, Quinn. I'm not even hurt anymore … most of the time, anyway. I like that you have William and Samuel. I'm *jealous* a lot, though mostly because I wish I had what you guys have with someone. But more than any of that… I'm really glad I still have you. And if what we have together turns out instead to be a really great friendship where we can support each other, and push each other, and say the hard stuff… I think in the end that will be something better than what we might have had back in Bristlecone."

He'd never articulated those thoughts before – not even to himself – but he knew what he was saying was true. This was different than having Quinn as his girlfriend, but it wasn't worse, and with a little more time, he could see that it could even be better.

She didn't answer out loud, but she extended her hand across the table to him, and he stretched his out, too, so he could squeeze hers gently.

"However," he said, standing now and walking toward the window. "If we're going to get to enjoy this friendship, we have to figure out how to save your kingdom."

She stood, too, placing her hands on the back of the couch, her eyebrows tightening in concentration. "You're right. So… these soldiers are camping in the woods, some of them are injured, and they don't have enough supplies?"

"Yes."

"And Nathaniel thinks it's too dangerous for me to reveal my location by getting involved."

He nodded. "Nathaniel thinks so."

"What do *you* think?"

Zander bit the side of his thumb – the persistent hangnail there was *never* going to heal. "I think he's right that it's dangerous for you. Even if – and that's a big *if* – every single one of those soldiers is

194

trustworthy and there are no spies among them, word will spread quickly that you and Samuel are alive and in the kingdom."

"But?"

"*But* they're your men. They've been out there fighting a battle at the castle you ran away from. They've already lost friends in the fight, and some of them are injured enough that cold and hunger like this… well, it's not good."

She inhaled deeply and blew the breath back out slowly. "Okay. I don't have any idea what I have to offer them, but let's start with help. I'll talk to Tobias and Will and Marcus."

"What do you need me to do?"

"I have no idea right this second, except brace yourself."

"For total chaos?" he asked, grinning because humor seemed easier than overwhelming dread.

"Well, that … and for the fallout that will surely come when I have to recognize you for your actions today."

"What else can you do to me?" he groaned. "You've already given a brand-new guard a medal and a freaking *title*."

"Oh… I have more where those came from."

# NIGHT DUTY

THE HOUSE WAS DARK as Linnea crept down the hallway, although it wasn't quiet. With so many people here now, it never was. Even now, as she passed William and Quinn's room, she could hear Samuel's soft cries and her brother's hum as he sang to his son.

She tried to smile through the prickling sensation in her eyes at the image, tried not to see the picture in her mind of Ben cradling their child in the night.

*I'll do it,* she promised him silently, curling her hands around the small, tight rounding of her belly. *I'll do it every night and tell her it's from you.*

Her thoughts were still far away when she stepped into the moonlit kitchen, so the glimpse of the shadowy figure on one of the stools by the counter startled her so badly she gasped out loud and reached instinctively for a weapon.

"It's just me, Linnea!" Zander's voice was low but quick, trying to reassure her. He stood, holding up empty hands. "I didn't mean to scare you."

"Oh," she heaved a sigh, trying to control her stuttering heartbeat, though the exertion triggered her lingering cough again.

"You okay?" he asked when she was finished. "Can I get you something to drink? I have a cup of tea; I could make you one."

"Sure. That sounds good. Thank you." She settled on one of the stools as he worked in the dark, pouring a mug of tea and passing it across the counter to her. She liked the atmosphere of the kitchen at this hour, lit half by a wide swath of moonlight across the counter and floor, and half by the dancing orange glow of the dampened fire. Warm orange and white shapes danced on every surface, reflecting on the metal of the mugs in intricate patterns.

"What are you doing up in the middle of the night, anyway?" she asked. A leather-bound journal lay on the oiled wood of the counter next to Zander's mug, and a discarded pencil wobbled half off the edge a few inches away.

"I'm on duty." He saw the pencil, too; he picked it up and tucked it under the cover of the notebook. "I tend not to wake people up with the creaky floorboards or scare people as much if I stay in here to listen."

She chuckled. "No, you just wait and pounce when they come in here."

"I am sorry. I heard you coming, but I didn't think calling out to you or towering over you in the hallway were much better options than sitting here trying to be small and unthreatening."

"Probably not," she laughed. "If you'd blocked my path in the hallway you might have needed that sword."

His broad shoulders relaxed and he grinned. "You're ready to knock me flat again? Sounds like you're feeling better."

"Finally." She took a sip of the tea; the warm liquid soothed her still-scratchy throat. "It only took me a week. I slept through everything."

"Oh, I think there will be plenty more to be awake through. Things are just getting interesting."

"Yeah." She shivered, pulling her dressing gown closed more tightly around her shoulders. Zander must have noticed; he went immediately to the low fire and stoked it a little before laying down another log to coax more heat into the room. When he reached for another, she said, "That's perfect right there. Any more and you'll remind me of being stuck in bed with a fever."

"Got it." He set the wood back in the pile and poked at the embers again.

"So, how did you know it was me, anyway – and not one of the soldiers creeping into the house to kill us all?"

He straightened and turned around. In the dim light, she could see just the shadow of one of his eyebrows lifting, changing the shape of his expression. "Well, you came out of one of the bedrooms, and nobody else has gone *in* there. Besides, if a soldier wanted to come in here and kill us, he'd probably wear boots and carry a sword. You're in socks and walking much too softly to be carrying anything more than a small knife."

She coughed again, but this time it had nothing to do with the protracted effects of pimaeum.

"What? You didn't think I'd ever catch on to any of this guard stuff?"

"Someday, *Sir* Zander, you might learn to accept a compliment without leaping to the conclusion that someone doesn't think you actually deserve it."

"Mmm… Someday, *Princess* Linnea, you might learn to give an actual compliment."

She regretted having taken a drink of her tea right then, as she nearly spit the entire mouthful across the counter. "All right. I'll give you the checkmate on that one."

"Just don't choke, too."

"Fine, then." She rolled her eyes and wiped her mouth on her sleeve as he returned to the counter. "I'm impressed at the job you've done since you've begun training as a guard. You've earned the accolades you've received."

He took a sip, too, avoiding answering her – making her smile as he proved her point that even if she could give a compliment, he couldn't take it. "So why are *you* up at this hour?"

She chuckled softly, deciding she'd tortured him enough for the moment. She closed her hands over the bump again. "Someone decided I need practice not sleeping through the night."

"Can you feel the baby moving already?" he asked, leaning in close, his tone a little awed – which made her smile.

"Yes, just in the last week or so. It's not so obnoxious it wakes me up, though. Right now, it's the trips to the washroom. And after the most recent one, I'm wide awake. I think I've been sleeping so much while I've been sick that I just can't stay in bed anymore."

"Sometimes I really can't complain about the fact that I'm a guy." Zander laughed.

She shrugged. "I don't really mind. I like knowing she's here."

"Yeah…" Even from across the counter, she could hear him swallow. "Do you think it's really a girl?"

"I don't know. It's not like he could have really known that. It's a fifty-fifty chance, though, right? I figure I'll humor him until I know for sure." She heard the little catch in her voice, but that was as bad as it got this time.

"I'm sorry," he whispered. "I shouldn't have…"

"Stop apologizing, Zander."

"I just – I…"

"You just. I know. But it's going to come up. He was my husband. I'm having his child. And he was your friend. We can't never talk about that. Yes, it still hurts – but it's worse when everyone avoids mentioning him like they think I might *forget* or something. Or like they've forgotten."

This time he masked whatever his reaction was by pouring more water into his mug and setting the kettle back down with a muted *clunk*. After a moment, he leaned his elbows on the counter, his face closer to her, the firelight flickering across his features. "I haven't forgotten."

"I know."

She stirred at her own tea with the chain of the tea ball for over a minute, wondering if he was actually going to talk to her about this. So far, Ben had been a verboten topic between them, though she'd wished for a while now that he wasn't. Zander had been there with Ben when it happened; he'd sacrificed everything to try to save him. She wanted to be able to tell him how much that meant to her – to share that with him, but she didn't want to push him on it – she probably wouldn't have been able to even if she did.

"I remember every detail of that night," he finally muttered. "Every tree, the way the river looked… even what everything smelled like."

She sighed, reaching across the counter toward him, unsure of what she was doing, really. It startled her when he actually took her hand – for a second anyway. As soon as they touched – his hands were warm from being wrapped around his steaming mug – they both jumped and pulled them back.

Immediately, she picked up her own mug and held it to her lips, pretending to take a much longer drink than she actually did.

"Don't think I don't know how this is hard on you, too, Zander," she said once she'd finally set it down again. "I know everyone's worried about me, including you, but I think in some ways you lost more that night than I did."

"He wasn't my husband."

"And that's the only kind of relationship that matters?"

"I'd only just met him. It's not the same."

"Of course it's not the same, but so what? The first time Quinn came through the gate, I'd just met her, but if something had happened to her – even then, it wouldn't have been okay. We were friends. It didn't take cycles for that to happen, but it was very real – still *is* real. That's how it was for you and Ben, too. I know it was for him – he told me. And you can't pretend to me that it wasn't that way for you, too. You never would have given up your way home for him if it wasn't."

"He told you that he considered me a friend?"

She took a deep breath and another sip of tea. "Yes, Zander, he did. He liked you right away, even that first night you came to the castle."

"Really? I kind of thought he hated me."

She scoffed. "Yeah, he spent time with you instead of his new bride because he loathed you. That would make perfect sense."

He was quiet, processing that for a minute. "I'm sorry I took that time from you."

The exasperation that bubbled up in her then caused her to make a sound she'd never made before. "Don't be stupid, Zander. What I wanted you to understand was that he wanted to spend the time he did with you. If I'm mad at you it's because you're drowning in all this weird guilt from stuff that's not your fault. I don't know if you think Ben would be mad at you for surviving that fight, or what, but if you think so, you're wrong. He'd be glad that you're okay, and even that you're *here*. It made him sad, actually, that you were leaving and going back to your own world. He thought you fit in here; he wished you were coming to Philotheum with us. He wanted to get to know you better. *I* still do."

She hadn't meant for that last sentence to slip out, but she was too worked up to stop it.

"Well, I'm stuck here now, right?" he said quietly. "I couldn't go back to my world if I wanted to."

"Yeah." She stared at the fire again for a minute before turning back to him. He still hunched over the counter, swirling his finger in his tea. "What would you do if we found a gate back to Bristlecone tomorrow?"

"You ask that like it's a simple question."

"On a purely hypothetical level – let's say there was nothing dangerous about using the gate, and you knew exactly where it would take you and when."

"I wasn't even thinking about that part."

"Oh?" That surprised her – and so did the other feeling that sprang up at the idea that he might not flee Deusterros at the first opportunity. She ignored that feeling, though. It didn't make any sense.

"There's also the part where I'm really not sure what it would be like to go home. I've been missing for a while now; things have got to be pretty crazy."

She shrugged. "With the time difference it's not *that* long."

"Even a day is a long time to go missing when you have no explanation about where you went. And it's been a lot longer than that."

"I suppose that's true." It still seemed like a flimsy excuse, although that probably wasn't a good thing to say. "It's your family, though."

"You're that desperate to get rid of me, huh? You're probably right. I might just be overthinking it so I don't have to... *Hang on.*" He held his hand up, palm toward her, as he cocked his ear toward the door.

Linnea went silent immediately, reaching down toward the dagger concealed in a sheath strapped to her calf. She heard it too, now – footsteps in the hallway, approaching the kitchen. Whoever was coming was wearing boots.

Zander shook his head once. "It's okay," he mouthed, impressing her yet again with his ability to pay attention to two things at once. Despite his reassurance to her, his right hand hovered near his sword until James appeared in the doorway.

"Princess Linnea!" James hurried across the kitchen to her. "Is everything all right? How are you feeling?"

The flare of annoyance that made her fists clench involuntarily surprised her. She liked James, and his concern was sweet. It shouldn't bother her. "I'm all right," she said with a forced chuckle. "I'm feeling much better. I was just pestering poor Sir Zander here to fill me in on what I missed while I was sick."

Zander raised an eyebrow at her – her purposeful use of his title might have been a bit too obvious.

"It's chilly in here," James continued, heading over to the fire.

Zander's eyebrow crooked up even further when she didn't say a word as James set two more logs in the flames, flooding the kitchen with bright orange heat.

"Are you hungry?" James asked. He didn't wait for her answer before he pulled a plate down from one of the shelves and began digging around in the breadbox.

She wasn't, but she accepted the snack with a quiet, "Thank you."

"Some milk? For the baby?"

The look on Zander's face as James disappeared into the cold cellar made her want to smack him. "What?" she snapped, in a half-whisper that wasn't as quiet as it should have been.

Zander pursed his lips and blinked. "Nothing. Nothing at all. What were you wondering about what's been going on? I thought Thomas had been filling you in."

"He has. Mostly anyway. So how many injured soldiers are here?"

"Fifteen."

"Sixteen now," James said, returning with a bucket of milk in one hand and a crate of vegetables cradled against his chest with the other. "They brought another one over from the camp yesterday evening when you were asleep. Not an injury, though. This one had a high fever."

"That's two of those then," Zander sighed.

"Yes," James said. "Don't worry, though, milady, the ill soldiers are staying in one of Tobias' smaller barns. They're warm and have what they need, but Prince Nathaniel hopes to keep the infection away from the house and the other soldiers."

"Which has been interesting, because some of the soldiers have never heard of germs before," Zander said. "Apparently Nathaniel and William's *strange ideas* about healing haven't made it to all the areas of Philotheum."

Linnea had to bite her lip to keep from snickering. Not over what Zander was telling her – she didn't find that amusing at all – but over the not-accidental way he dropped William's and Nathaniel's first names without their titles in front of James. She contained her amusement when he glanced her way, though, and shot him a severe look.

"The good news is that there are now over a hundred soldiers at the camp," James said, oblivious to their exchange. "And yesterday, they brought in a group from one of the Dovelnian border stations who managed to acquire a good number of supplies from somewhere – tents, extra cloaks, and even some food."

"And how many here at Tobias'?" Linnea asked.

"Thirty-six, counting the injured ones, plus those of us who traveled here with you, milady."

She nodded, taking a bite of the roll he'd put in front of her. "Have we heard anything from my father about how things are going on the Eirenthean front?"

"There have been some minor skirmishes along the border because King Stephen has closed it to travel while things are so unstable," Zander said. "But Her Majesty has actually been worried about how little communication she's received from Eirentheos in the last couple of days."

"My father may just be worried about messages being intercepted." She directed a surreptitious nod of approval at him while she had his attention.

"Probably," Zander agreed, although he didn't sound convinced.

"Is it true that Alvin was here?" she asked. She'd heard something about him days ago, but she'd been in the depths of her illness then.

"Yes, but he was weird as usual," Zander said. "He was here the whole time I was telling Quinn about the camp of soldiers, but then he left without another word to anyone, and as far as I know, nobody's heard from him since."

"I would be lying if I said that surprised me."

Zander chuckled.

"So what is the plan now?"

"Well, the plan for *today* is to take a group of men out to scout around the villages north of the capital city, searching for some known Friends of Philip safe houses," James said. "We still haven't had any word on the whereabouts of Princess Ellen or Prince Charles."

Linnea wasn't sure she liked the sound of that. "Who is going?"

"I am," James said. "I'll be leading the group, since I know where two of the houses are."

She looked at Zander, wondering if her eyes were as wide as they felt. "I have to stay here," he said. "Occupational hazard of night duty – I lose out on the next day's adventure."

Though she didn't understand why – and she never would have admitted it – she was relieved.

# A Letter

"YOUR MAJESTY?"

Quinn looked up from watching Samuel's eyelashes flutter against his tiny cheeks to see Tobias standing in the doorway. "Come in."

When he came in he stood over her for a minute, peeking down at Samuel, then he sighed and sat down on the other end of the couch from where Linnea was sitting. "He's always sleeping when I come around."

"I could come find you when he wakes."

"Actually, I'm not sure I'll be around this afternoon — that was what I came in here to talk to you about."

Even a moon ago, a statement like that would have set her heart racing, but after many days of constantly being bombarded with dramatic decisions, she was becoming accustomed to remaining calm. She ran her fingers through Samuel's hair as she waited for whatever Tobias was going to tell her.

"Every moon around this time, I go into the village to trade supplies and take care of some business matters."

"And if you don't appear, you'll be missed, I assume?"

"Yes. I can't promise nobody will ever come looking for me even if I do go, but surely someone will check in on an old man if I don't. It wouldn't have been such an issue when there were only a few of you, but with the soldiers here now…"

"There's no hiding it."

"Correct."

"Then of course you'll have to go."

"My crates are packed and ready to go already. But while we're on the topic, I was wondering if you had a plan as regards your relationship with Valderwood?"

She frowned. "I thought the people who lived there were suspicious of any involvement with the capital and the royal family."

"Yes. Most of them are."

"Exactly. So my current *plan* as regards my relationship with them was to do my best to avoid making more enemies who want to kill me. I was going to leave them alone."

"All right." Tobias nodded and started to stand.

"Do you think I should have a *different* plan?"

"Can *I* answer that?" Linnea interrupted. "Because I think ignoring them is more than a little dangerous."

"More dangerous than making them mad?"

"Yes, actually. At least if you go out and make an enemy, you know you have one. Haven't you learned by now that what you don't know is more dangerous than what you do?"

Quinn sighed. "By that argument, *I'm* more dangerous to Valderwood if they don't know about me."

"Is that what you want to be?" Tobias asked. "Dangerous to your people? You're building an army close to their village. With any luck, we'll be able to grow this army considerably before we try to take on the castle. Do you want the people of Valderwood to discover a massive army by accident?"

"Of course not. What I really want is for them not to be wary and fearful of me. I want them to trust me."

"It's far from my concern, but that sounds like a far better plan than conducting a war in their kingdom without telling them."

"That's not a plan, Tobias. It's wishful thinking. I can't just tell them to trust me and call it good."

"Of course not. You can't tell anyone to trust you. Trust isn't something communicated with words."

"Then how do I get them to trust me?"

Tobias leaned forward, rubbing at his chin as he contemplated her. "When you first arrived here, Your Majesty, you had no reason to trust me – in fact, with the information you had at hand, and the danger you were in, you were justified in being very suspicious of me. After all, you didn't know me, and you'd been lied to about me, even by someone you did trust."

"Keep talking, Tobias, and I might be calling for one of my guards."

He chuckled. "Exactly. If you had to rely on my *words* you wouldn't be in the same room with me without a guard between us. Why is your guard in the hallway?"

That was easy. "Because we've been here for over a week and you haven't done anything except provide help and support and share food and supplies you can't possibly afford to be sharing with us."

"To be fair, your guards have done their share of hunting and cultivating in the winter garden. And the barn they finished restoring yesterday will be a tremendous boon to me in the coming cycle."

"Even all those things together wouldn't add up to what you've contributed to us, Tobias."

"Perhaps. But when you add in the other currency used to pay me, I would argue that I'm still in your debt."

"And what currency is that?"

"Your trust."

She smiled. "You're right. You have earned that." As much of it as she was willing to give *anyone* right now, anyway. "So what do I have to offer the people of Valderwood without expecting anything in return?"

"I can't promise anything will work with some of them, Your Majesty – but several families in the village are experiencing the same fever illness we've been dealing with here."

"All right," she sighed. "Before you leave, why don't you talk to Nathaniel about going along?"

"That opens up the risk of people in the village realizing he's not missing, and that you might not be far away."

"I know. I can't ask for trust without giving up something real in return. I think Nathaniel is in the barn."

Once Tobias was gone, Linnea looked at her. "He could have just asked to take Nathaniel in the first place."

Quinn nodded. "Is it terrible if I just choose to not even think about why he didn't right now?"

"Only if thinking about it would help you make a better decision about it sometime in the next fifteen minutes."

"Does fifteen cycles count?"

Linnea snorted. "Okay, my turn to hold the baby for a bit."

Not five minutes after Tobias left, Marcus entered the room holding a folded piece of paper. He didn't speak as he handed it to Quinn, but Linnea didn't like the hard set of his shoulders or the too-heavy sound of his footfalls.

"What's wrong?" Linnea asked before she even got the note open, but Quinn ignored her, reading the note more than once before she finally looked up at Marcus.

"Who sent this?"

"I'm not certain. It's not signed, and I believe that was intentional."

"Well, it's not *addressed* either, but it's definitely for me."

"Yes."

"Do you have a guess as to who might have sent it? What bird brought it?"

"It was one of Tobias' birds we've been using to send messages to Eirentheos."

Linnea knew better, but the sudden ice in her chest at the mention of Eirentheos made her not care. A second later she was across the room, snatching the note from Quinn's hands.

What she saw when she scanned it didn't help, though, instead the burning cold raced outward from her center, down her arms and legs. "I know who wrote this. What I don't know is what he's doing in Philotheum."

"Engaging in some kind of battle," Quinn said, standing and walking over to one of her maps. Her voice shook. "It's not your father – that's not his writing."

"No, it isn't. It's my brother's. It's from Maxwell."

"What is he doing here?"

Linnea's mouth fell open – she had *no* idea, but Quinn was speaking to Marcus.

"I don't know. Let's find this location." Marcus followed her to the map, tracing his finger down the blue line of a river until it intersected with another one. "Here."

"I'm still bad with scale here," Quinn said. "How long would it take to travel there from here?"

"Probably under two hours, depending on the terrain. I don't know this area well, and there aren't many roads. The mountains in this area isolate it well, but still – they're close."

"Mountains?" Quinn sounded confused.

Linnea frowned. "You know, the big hills out there. Lots of trees. What did you think they were?"

"She thought they were big hills." William's voice made Linnea turn around; she hadn't heard him come into the room. "Mountains are a little bigger where she's from." He smiled, taking Samuel from Linnea's arms before going to stand next to Quinn. "We're in the mountains here, though, love, at least the Philothean version of them."

"I'll take your word for it," she said, pressing her fingers to her forehead as she handed the note to William.

The smile he'd been wearing faded into something dark and bleak as his eyes scanned Max's words. "Well, that explains the relative lack of communication from Eirentheos the last couple of days."

"Explains it *how*? Why wouldn't Stephen have told me Max was coming? *Why* is Max here?"

"Those two questions are undoubtedly related," Marcus said. "Stephen would have wanted to make sure no information about Maxwell's location was compromised until he reached safety."

"So he wouldn't tell *me*?"

"Remember that he doesn't know exactly who's with us here. All he knows is that this whole situation started because there were untrustworthy people around you – and around him. Our messages to him haven't been overly informative, either, in case someone in the castle who can't be trusted reads one. You haven't even told him exactly where we are, although he must have guessed. From this note, I don't think Maxwell knows how to get any closer than where he is."

"So we need to send a brigade to find him," Quinn said.

"That's dangerous. They could be followed, either on the way there, or on the way back," Marcus said. "I don't know what the situation is, exactly, but it sounds as though Max and whoever he's with may have run into some of Tolliver's troops."

"Yes, it's dangerous," Quinn agreed. "I suppose that's why they call it war. Can you please find me several men who are trustworthy and willing to go?"

# VALDERWOOD

"YOU'VE NEVER BEEN TO Valderwood, have you?" Tobias asked. "Not in all the times you visited me."

"No." Nathaniel rubbed at a spot on the horn of his saddle. "I would have liked to – I'm always interested in new places, but you always talked me out of revealing you had strange visitors. I wonder how they'll receive me now." After everything Tobias had told them about the village, he had to admit he was nervous about going – unsure what to expect. Contrary to Quinn's wishes, they hadn't even brought along a guard; Tobias didn't want to make the villagers defensive.

"It's perhaps not as bad there as I led Her Majesty to believe at first. Most of the people there are kind and trustworthy. They wish to be left alone more than anything. Only a few take a hard line in enforcing that."

"So why didn't you tell her the truth?"

"For some of the same reasons you have trouble being honest with her about certain things, Nathaniel. She showed up here with almost nothing in the way of an army, when she needs one badly. I

213

wasn't sure how she'd react to the idea of fifty armed and trained men only half an hour away. She could have caused a lot of trouble if she'd demanded their help immediately. If she handles it right, though, I think at least some of them could be an asset to her."

Nathaniel tipped his head sideways at his uncle. "You underestimate her."

"Yes. At first I did. I realize now I could have given her more credit."

"So why didn't you tell her the truth before we left today?"

Tobias scoffed. "You of all people should understand how much more difficult it is to change your story in the middle than just tell it straight the first time."

"Indeed." He rubbed at the back of his neck. "At this point I feel like everything I ever tell her is a contradiction to what she believed. I never meant to lie to her – only to keep her safe."

"I know. And it's that much harder when you're not entirely sure which part is the truth, and which part is just something you were wrong about anyway." Tobias' voice had taken on a tone thick with an underlying meaning that made Nathaniel follow his gaze. What he saw made his palms sweat and he wondered if Tobias hadn't told Quinn the full truth the first time.

They had nearly reached Valderwood – or what Nathaniel assumed was the village, anyway. The stone wall surrounding it was too high to make out even the rooftops of whatever buildings were inside.

He couldn't tell whether the heavy iron gate was all the way closed or just mostly – the view was too obstructed by the armed men on horseback in front of it.

"Do you always get this kind of warm reception when you come here?"

Tobias didn't answer, but it didn't matter – there wouldn't have been time for a conversation. Two of the men were already riding toward them.

Nathaniel could hear Tobias' breath coming in too-fast gulps, but the older man looked composed as the two soldiers came right up to them.

His heart pounded, and his hand hovered halfway to his sword as he fought between the competing urges to both be prepared to defend himself and to not appear as a threat.

"Hello Tobias," said the first man who reached them.

"It's good to see you, Joel. How's your leg?"

Nathaniel couldn't stop himself from looking down to see what Tobias was talking about, but if there was anything to see it was hidden by the man's long pants and boots, and he didn't give up any information, either.

"Who's your companion?" Joel asked. "We were expecting you to come alone."

Tobias coughed. "I'd have thought you'd be happy to see me with some company – now nobody will have to make the trek out to check up on me for a while."

"We might feel that way, Tobias, if Queen Quinn hadn't gone and gotten herself involved in a war that's brought troops into the area. Makes it a strange time for you to show up with an unannounced stranger – especially one with a sword."

Nathaniel's fist closed tightly around the reins as he forced himself not to clutch at his sword instead. The horse snorted, warning him to be careful of his grip.

"Perhaps you'd like to tell us why you have a guest at such a time," a second man said. "And what you might know about the armies nearby."

Tobias looked at Nathaniel, and it was clear from the deep creases in his forehead that whatever he'd expected in coming here, this wasn't it. He didn't have an answer ready for these men. "Victor…"

Nathaniel cleared his throat, interrupting Tobias. "How close have the troops gotten to your village?"

The man called Joel scowled. "Too close. They haven't found us, we don't think. And we don't plan on allowing that to change."

Though the statement was obviously a threat, Nathaniel was bolstered by the fact he'd gotten an answer at all – and that all of the men's swords were still sheathed. For a long moment, he pondered how to respond. He wasn't sure what kind of information was most likely to get him killed, but in the end he decided that this time the truth was safer than a lie. Hopefully.

"Her Majesty would also prefer to keep any fighting far from your village."

Now all of the men found the hilts of their swords.

"Are you with Queen Quinn's army?" Joel demanded.

"Calling it an army at this point would be generous." It wasn't entirely a lie. Quinn was in desperate need of more men if she was to have any chance against the army King Ivan had surely provided for Tolliver.

His response only agitated the men more.

"You still haven't told us how you know so much about the queen's army." The second man had his sword partway out.

"Yes, well, that's because I haven't introduced myself properly. I am Nathaniel Rose."

"*Prince* Nathaniel Rose?" The sword came all the way out.

"Yes, Victor," Tobias said, his voice calm. "Prince Nathaniel – the fourth-born *healer*. I brought him here to help."

"Help what? Help occupy our town with soldiers? Force us to participate in a fight that isn't ours?"

Victor was angry. Nathaniel didn't think there was anything he might say that would allay his fear and suspicion. But Joel's initial reaction to Nathaniel's identity was different – for just a moment he'd regarded him with curiosity rather than anger. And one of the younger guards behind the two obvious leaders had an even stronger response. His eyes were unable to hide a flicker of hope.

When he answered, he directed his response to Joel, but also glanced carefully toward the hopeful young man, including him in the conversation as much as he could. "I speak with authority when I tell you that Queen Quinn has no intention of interfering with your village. Tobias and I have brought no soldiers with us to visit you today. If you sweep the area, you'll find none of her army waiting to attack you. The only thing we have brought is medicine to help with your fever outbreak – medicine the troops themselves could use, but that the queen has chosen to share instead."

"Why would she do that?" Dark suspicion colored Joel's voice, but his knuckles were no longer white on the hilt of his sword.

"Because you are her people, and she is able to."

"What if we don't *want* to be 'her people'?" Victor spat. "We've done well enough on our own under Hector's reign."

"She doesn't intend to force you to accept her help. Or my help, as the case is today. But you and I both know that Hector wasn't even aware that Valderwood exists. And even if he had, Hector wouldn't likely have found it worthwhile to risk stirring dissent in an area with so little to offer him."

If he'd been out here alone with Victor, the man would have planted the sword in his chest by now. But the other men were listening. Only one more was holding a knife and sweeping his gaze over the surrounding woods.

"I know Tolliver. I don't expect him to be nearly as tolerant of those unwilling to declare allegiance to him. There are already stories coming in of entire villages destroyed except for those willing to join Tolliver's army."

Victor's eyes were so narrow at this point that Nathaniel wondered if he could even see. "How many of those villages were harboring the queen when they were attacked?"

"None of them. The queen is safe and slowly amassing an army, and today she is offering whatever assistance you need, even while she can ill afford to do so."

"In exchange for what?"

"If she were here in front of you now, she would ask for nothing in return, Victor. As her ambassador and prince, though, I might be bold enough to ask for your soldiers here to not move against her or her army."

There was a long, weighted silence as Victor didn't respond at all. Finally, Joel sighed. "Can you really help us with the fever illness?"

"Yes. I'll need to see the people who are sick first before I know how much I can do and what promises I can make, but I'm here to do what I can. And I can also take a look at whatever is going on with your leg."

"Come on then."

# BIRD

"WE SHOULD BE GETTING close," Dorian said, bringing his horse to a stop as he reached to pull a map out of his saddle bag.

"How do you think we should do this?" Zander asked. "We don't know what we're going to find when we get there. I don't know if it's a good idea to burst into the middle of the situation with twenty soldiers." He looked around at the men behind them.

Dorian nodded.

"Can I see that map?" He wasn't certain he'd be able to make sense of it, but he wanted to understand more about the world he was living in now. Over the last couple of weeks his map skills, at least, had improved considerably.

Dorian handed over the map without hesitation, although at the moment he did, something came zooming toward them from the sky.

For a second, the motion startled Zander too much to understand what it was. One hand flew up to protect his face while his other fist clenched around Ember's reins to keep him from spooking, but the horse didn't react at all. When he finally focused on the flying object, he understood why.

It was a large, charcoal gray seeker – he thought it might be the same bird he'd noticed in the barn the day of his incident in the barn with Raeyan. It rested on the ground for a minute, its shiny black eyes shifting back and forth between Dorian and Zander. Dorian held out his arm to invite the creature on, but when the bird stretched its wings to fly up, it landed carefully on Ember's neck. Though the bird was enormous, Ember remained calm and still.

Zander had never been this close to one of the birds. He stretched his hand tentatively toward it, more than a little nervous about its razor-sharp beak at as he reached for the little metal cylinder attached to its leg.

The bird tipped its head sideways so far it nearly went upside down, and if Zander hadn't known better, he would have sworn it sighed. Then, while his hand was still several inches away, the animal picked up its leg and set it down right in the middle of his palm.

"All right," he said, chuckling and reaching for the lid to the container.

The bird looked up at him – not making eye contact, but staring at the top of his head. Now he knew it was the bird from the barn.

"I'm sorry! Give me a chance to learn here, would you?"

When he finally had the folded piece of paper in his hand, he held it out to Dorian.

The older guard shook his head. "I would say the bird knew who she was aiming for, Sir Zander."

He wasn't sure he agreed, but he unfolded the note anyway.

*The situation is mostly contained. Instruct your troops to come in together and finish securing the area. Search for any stragglers. We'll need transport for prisoners and our wounded if possible. Please respond with ETA for your troops.*

The note ended with numbers and letters he couldn't decode, though he knew they were coordinates – yet another thing he needed to learn. "I think this message may have been intended for Her Majesty," he told Dorian, handing it over.

The bird pecked at his hand.

"Hey!"

Dorian chuckled. "She's offended that you'd doubt her intentions – and she'd like a treat."

"Really?" Zander said as he dug around inside his saddle bag until he found a sandwich. He ripped off the corner so he could offer her the bread and the meat. "You take a message to the wrong person, and you *still* expect a tip?"

Stopping in the middle of a bite, the bird looked right at him and bobbed her head once.

"Did she just nod at me?"

"Yes. I think she likes you."

"Guess I won't complain about that. So what do we do with this?" He gestured toward the note.

"It sounds like we take all of our men into the scene. We should be running into them just over that next hill there." Dorian pointed. "I think Prince Maxwell sent this bird within the last half hour – probably even sooner – and she spotted us on her way to the queen."

The bird chirped.

"Okay then," Zander said. He reached into his bag again and pulled out another piece of meat for the bird. When he held it out, she blinked at him, took a small hop toward him and rubbed her head right against the underside of his hand. A little thrill of surprise raced up his arm at her touch, making him smile. Then she yanked the meat from between his fingers.

He cleared his throat, concentrating on the bird in front of him. "Do you think we should send this note to Her Majesty, along with our own note about our plans?"

"Yes. You can go ahead and write it as soon as we decide exactly how to go about this."

"We?" He'd been expecting Dorian to give him orders, not to include him in the process.

"What do you think is the best process for securing the area, in case there are any stragglers?" Dorian didn't even seem to notice the doubt in his voice.

Zander's hands suddenly felt unsteady, like he might lose his grip on Ember's reins. The bird took another step toward him, the ends of her folded wings resting right against the inside of his leg. He took a deep breath. "If we're dealing with an army under Tolliver's control, we should be worrying about any kind of second wave in the trees," he said. "I think we should send some men wide around the perimeter to search – and then I think we need to get in and out quickly in case anyone managed to communicate to reinforcements anywhere."

Dorian nodded. "I think that's a good plan. The prisoners and wounded?"

"We assess the situation when we get there, and then do what we can with what we have at the site, and we hope to hear back from Qu – from Her Majesty with further instructions."

"All right." Dorian already had a pencil and paper in his hand.

"Not that I have any idea what I'm talking about, you know. I'm making this up as I go along."

Dorian shrugged with one shoulder as he wrote; a slight grin lifting the corner of his mouth. "So are the rest of us, if you hadn't noticed."

"I think you might be a bit more qualified than I am."

"Well, I might ask you to refrain from swinging your sword anywhere near me when we get in there, Sir Zander, and I'm rather grateful you're riding a horse that knows how to control *you*, but when it comes to the rest of it, I'm honored to be doing this beside you."

Warmth pooled in his chest, and for a minute he couldn't look at Dorian. This time the ridiculous bird climbed all the way onto his leg and made a soft warbling sound deep in her throat.

"Just don't get killed in there, okay?" Dorian said, before making a clicking sound that called the bird over to him so he could put the rolled-up notes in her carrier.

"Don't you, either."

"I'll do my best not to, Sir Zander."

Dorian's map skills were thankfully much stronger than Zander's. After a short ride to the top of the next hill, Zander could see the smoke and movement between the trees down in the valley below them. He didn't like how easy it was to see from here, actually, and he and Dorian stopped earlier than they'd planned to send ten of the men in a wide loop around the whole gully.

"Are you ready?" Dorian asked him once the guards had left.

"No."

"Good. Let's go."

For all of his preparation to be shocked and terrified, actually riding into the clearing felt far too mundane. The only thing that surprised him was the sheer number of guards in purple waiting there. Though Max's note had indicated fatalities and injuries, there was no immediate indication of any of that. In fact, the first thing he saw was guards gathered around two campfires, cooking something that smelled a lot better than the sandwiches tucked in his saddlebags.

Max saw them coming long before they made it to the site, and he was ready when they arrived, standing next to a fully uniformed guard Zander recognized from Eirentheos, but didn't know well, Davis Jones.

"That was faster than we expected you," Max said as Dorian and Zander dismounted.

"Your last message came to us before continuing on to Queen Quinn," Dorian said. "What happened here?"

"We arrived early this morning," Max said. "We were intending to stop here and wait while I sent communication to Quinn about our arrival and to ask her where would be the best place to concentrate our efforts. Before I got a message to her, though, we were attacked by a small patrol. We thought we were isolated here, but they must have seen the smoke from our cook fires."

"How many men?" Dorian asked.

"They had twenty."

"And now?"

"Three are still alive. We're holding them for now. As far as we can tell, none escaped. We've swept the area several times for more men, and we haven't found any so far, but there's no way to be sure; it's too wooded here."

"Who was leading them?"

"A castle guard." Davis' voice was filled with bitter contempt. "He's alive if you'd like to speak with him."

A large part of Zander hoped desperately that the responsibility of speaking to that guard wouldn't fall on him, but a small – and vicious – part of him hoped that it would.

"What information are you hoping to get out of him?" he asked Max.

Max gave him a sideways look. "Are you asking why we didn't just kill him?"

"Yes." Zander wondered if he should feel remorse for that, but right now he couldn't feel anything except anger that a guard Quinn had trusted – probably one *Ben* had trusted – was helping Tolliver.

Max's eyes slid between Zander and Dorian, and then out toward the other guards who'd come with them.

Zander felt his own eyes narrow. "There's nobody higher-ranking than me and Dorian here, *Prince* Maxwell. You can keep hold of whatever it is until we get all the way back to Quinn, or you can tell us what's going on so we can actually secure this area."

"All right, *Sir* Zander. I didn't kill the baseborn myself because I'm hoping he'll be persuaded to tell me how he found us – and how many are backing him up."

"What makes you think it wasn't just your fires, and that they're not alone?"

Max looked down. "This wasn't our first incident since entering Philotheum." Taking his arm out of his cloak, he pulled back the sleeve of his sweater, revealing a nasty cut that was still red and raw, but too scabbed over to have happened today. "The border was better guarded than we anticipated."

Zander whistled. "Tolliver has already managed to secure the borders?"

"Not quite. These were regular border guards, still stationed there under Quinn's rule. Several of them were — are — even Friends of Philip. They'd heard rumors of the coup, but hadn't received new orders. So they just continued patrolling the area around their station. Only some of them were apparently awaiting new orders from someone other than Quinn."

"How many casualties there?"

"Eight. And we acquired eight more soldiers for our side there. As far as I can determine, nobody got away from that battle, they all either died or came with us. And it's a long ride from here."

"But you think someone might have followed you?"

"I don't know. I'm almost certain someone sent the soldiers who attacked us today. But we can't get anything out of these men, not even under threat of death."

"It's pretty stupid to send twenty men into battle against — what? A hundred? More?"

"One fifty-eight, counting those who joined us yesterday. And, yes, that bothers me, too. It means there could be a strong second wave, but we can't find any evidence of one. We searched for hours before even sending the message to Quinn."

"Then I say we get out of here as quickly as possible."

Max nodded. "And where are we going?"

Zander considered the question. They couldn't risk traveling with this large a group all the way back to Tobias', especially if there were more troops ready to follow them. He wasn't sure how much longer they could keep Quinn's location secret, but it was still a bad idea to lead someone right to her.

"We have a base camp established about an hour away from the queen," Dorian said. "The captains there are well prepared to defend, and they're in desperate need of supplies."

Zander looked around at the trees again. "This patrol that attacked you – what direction did they come from?"

"Same direction as you." Davis nodded over Zander's shoulder.

Suddenly, he felt ice-cold and a little sick to his stomach. "What can we do to help you and your troops prepare to travel?"

# WAR

ZANDER HAD HAD A bad feeling about this trek with Maxwell's army from the get-go. He'd known the peace felt suspicious and that there was something strange about twenty soldiers attacking a battalion the size of the one Max was leading. The whole time they rode he was on edge, his back straight, his eyes constantly combing the trees on either side of the path they were forging.

For a long time, the only threat was the fact that the weather was cooling again; it had dropped a good ten degrees from the time they left Maxwell's camp, and a thick line of bluish-gray clouds was building on the far northern horizon, but Zander knew that wasn't why he was so sensitive, why even the hair on the back of his neck stood at constant attention.

He was beyond prepared for an encounter with something bad. So it shouldn't have been a surprise to him when he one of his sweeps caught a glimpse of unfamiliar crimson buried deep in the woods, tucked so far behind a hill that he was lucky to have seen it at all, before whoever it was saw him.

He whistled in two short, low notes – the signal for danger. Nobody stopped; everyone here was too well trained to even appear as if they'd heard. But a dark shape swooped down from the trees, coming to rest on Ember's mane again. That bird.

"That wasn't for you," he whispered so quietly that he couldn't even hear himself over the noise of the horses.

If birds could shrug, this one would have. She took two steps closer to Zander and then sat down, settling in for the ride.

Not that they rode far. Dorian and Davis moved to the head of the line and turned as quickly as they could, leading the whole group steeply uphill. Zander followed them as far up as they went, and so did Max, but he noticed that the rest of the line broke off and went in front of and behind them, forming a tight circle of protection. As soon as they stopped, every soldier drew his sword. He wondered what the other guards would think of him – if he'd made another huge mistake putting himself in the middle like this.

Max pulled out a set of binoculars so high-tech that Zander wondered how he managed to explain them to his soldiers – there was only one place he could have gotten them.

Zander tried to make himself as unobtrusive as possible as he waited impatiently for Max to finish looking and report his findings to Dorian and Davis.

So when Max pulled the binoculars away from his eyes and held them out to Zander, he was so startled it took him a minute to reach for them.

That was when he remembered that he, too, was an officer now.

His hands were a little shaky as he held them up to his eyes; he took deep breaths as he prepared himself to see just how much trouble they were actually in.

When he finally looked, it wasn't as bad as he'd been worried about – he'd feared a massive number, but there were only maybe thirty or so, some in green, some in that strange red, all circling a man with long, graying brown hair under whose red cloak Zander could see the tell-tale sash of a high-level officer.

Still, at the first sight of them, his legs grew weak and he had trouble catching his breath as he passed the glasses to Davis. The sensations only grew worse when Davis took one look before he pushed quickly past him, hissing, "Callum Haddon!" to Max.

He might not have recognized the man, but the name he placed immediately. Callum Haddon, the man they'd been searching for, who'd been involved in Thomas' torture, who'd been bold enough to show up at Samuel's Naming Ceremony before betraying them all, was an *officer* in King Ivan's army.

He grabbed the binoculars from Dorian to get a better look.

"Twenty-seven," he said to Max, after counting twice. "I don't see signs of any more anywhere."

"I'll bet their numbers are why they didn't ambush," Max said. "They probably hid back there hoping we wouldn't notice them."

"They could be waiting for more to back them up."

"Possibly," Davis said. "It's more likely they intended to see where we lead them – and then they'll bring the numbers."

"Well, we have the numbers to take care of the threat." Zander wasn't sure where his words were coming from. They poured out on their own as he stared through the binoculars at Callum Haddon.

"We need to do it quickly, in case more are coming." There wasn't even a note of dissent in Dorian's voice.

"And we need to push them off our course, move in the opposite direction of the queen and the rest of the soldiers," Zander said.

"All right," Max agreed. "Let's do it. But I think we need to send a message to Quinn and to our other troops. Give them our location, but tell them to come the long way around so they don't tip off what direction they're coming from. Can you do that, Zander?"

"Me? I don't have a bird."

Max raised an eyebrow at the creature still nestled tightly in Ember's mane. As soon as Zander looked down at her, she stood, turning the leg with her cylinder toward him. "Looks like one has you."

He shook his head a little, to clear it. "Um, how do these things work, anyway?"

"Write a note and tell her you want her to take it to Quinn."

"But how does she know who Quinn is and how to get it to her?"

"How? It's hard to say. They seem to track people they know and other birds they know. They're almost always in range of "their" person, unless they're carrying a message or otherwise separated, so they work it out somehow."

There was no paper inside the bird's cylinder, so Zander dug through his saddle bag for his notebook. "You mean I could just send this bird to find Quinn anywhere, as long as she knows her?"

Max grimaced. "Not exactly. They can track people to a certain extent, but they won't usually go somewhere they've never been, especially if there's not a bird they know to guide them, and if they perceive any danger at all, it's hard to convince them to land for anyone except their own companion."

"What is our location, by the way?" he asked, pulling two pieces of paper out of his notebook and ripping each of them into quarters before scribbling a note on one of the smaller scraps as Max read numbers to him from a map. "They can find someone en route though, right? They've been finding you."

"The ones who have a good idea of where I might be can track me, sure. They're ridiculously intelligent. And I have a bird they can search out. It's a little harder to find people who don't have seekers, though they manage a lot of the time."

"Can you give this to Quinn for me?" Zander asked the bird as he tucked the note and the extra sheets into the canister.

The bird chirped once, pressing her head against his hand.

"All right." He reached into his bag again, this time pulling out a piece of dried fruit and holding it out to her. "Please will you take this to Quinn?"

She pushed against his hand again, this time rubbing her wing back and forth on his wrist before pulling away, bobbing her head once, and then taking off with a silent flutter. He tried to watch where she went, but as soon as she reached the first tree, she disappeared, her flight invisible, not disturbing even a single branch.

"That was good if that's your first time. Whose bird is she?"

"Tobias' I think. He has several of them."

"Several? That's very unusual."

"That's what I hear. None of them have been able to find Ellen or Charles, though. Nor have any of the birds who should know them."

Max nodded. "They must not be in any of their usual places – or if they are, the birds can't reach them for some reason. Have the birds you've been sending to them been returning?"

"Yes, just empty handed, except for the notes Quinn has sent with them."

"Well, at least they're not being captured. It sounds like there's a lot to catch me up on when we make it back to where Quinn is." Max was looking through the binoculars again, but after a moment he handed them to Zander.

"What's going on over there?" Zander asked.

"Nothing so far. Surely someone had to have seen us come through, and they must have realized we saw them when we stopped, but they don't seem to be responding at all. How do you think we should approach this?"

"Me?" Zander looked around, but both Davis and Dorian seemed to be waiting to hear what he had to say, too.

"I'm guessing you didn't earn that sash with your horsemanship or your swordplay, so, yes, I want to hear your thoughts."

He tried to hide his reddening cheeks behind the binoculars. "Maybe she gave me this because she feels sorry for me."

"She's not stupid, and neither am I. She wouldn't undermine herself by giving you that without a reason – and you wouldn't wear it if she did. So what do you think?"

"I think we have a problem. Look around, quick."

The response to his command was instantaneous, but still not fast enough – or maybe it was just in time. Max was turned halfway when the first arrow came, so it caught him in the elbow rather than his middle.

Two more arrows sailed into their formation in the time it took Zander and Davis to dismount and pull Max down behind his horse. One drifted into a bank of melting snow, but the other struck Max's horse in the neck.

Two lines of guards behind them moved immediately, rushing at the archers. Three more arrows flew, but then stopped.

"Get Callum!" Zander yelled to Dorian, who was already leading several lines of soldiers at the front in a charge down toward the soldiers in the trees.

"How many are up that way?" Max's face contorted in pain. The arrow had gone entirely through his upper arm and was lodged there now.

Zander's head spun and blood pounded in every part of his body, even his toes pulsed with every beat of his heart. "I can't see, but there were two missing from the group down there – I saw twenty-five and there should have been twenty-seven. I think there were three shooters."

He was glad that Davis seemed to have some idea of what he was doing; he stopped Max from pulling on the arrow and instead took off his sash and wrapped it around Max's arm, stabilizing the wood.

Though he was barely able to make his legs move at all, he pushed himself to his feet wanting to see what was going on, but before he was halfway up, an Eirenthean guard he didn't recognize caught his shoulder and shoved him back toward the ground. "Stay down!"

So many things were going on at once that it was hard to focus on anything, even if his brain had been functioning properly.

Davis and several other guards were busy attending to Max, and more guards surrounded them completely, blocking his view of everything, and it was *loud*. There was commotion everywhere – the swing of swords, shouting, the frenetic neighing of the wounded horse – Zander couldn't make sense of most of it.

Suddenly, in the middle of everything, a now-familiar swoop of feathers landed right by his boots.

The bird regarded him for a minute, apparently aware how disoriented he was, but once she was sure he recognized her, she stepped right up onto his leg.

For just a second, he stared at her, wondering if she was real.

Then she butted her head into his chest.

He put one finger against her and edged her back. "You couldn't possibly have made it to Quinn and back already."

Even as he said it, he understood. Even if he couldn't figure out the scene around him, he knew why the bird was here. She'd seen, and she'd come back – knowing he'd want to add to his message.

His fingers were so clumsy it took three tries to get the canister open, and once he did, he was only capable of scribbling a single line before shoving the paper back in.

The bird didn't ask for a treat or affection this time. As soon as the cylinder snapped closed, she was gone.

# CONTROL

THE FOOTSTEPS BEHIND her were soft, but the sound still made Quinn jump, startling the baby in her arms and making him fuss.

"Sorry, sorry." Thomas hurried around the couch so she could see him. He leaned down to take Samuel from her. "I didn't mean to wake him. I'll get him back to sleep."

"It's not your fault I'm so jumpy." She allowed him to take the baby, though. Thomas seemed a bit steadier than she was right now; he rocked Samuel in his arms and cooed quietly. After only a moment, the infant was out cold again.

"You still haven't heard anything from anyone?"

"No. Not from James or Dorian or even from Nathaniel going to Valderwood with Tobias. I feel so useless just sitting here when I've sent people to three different dangerous places."

"You're not just sitting here, Quinn. You're coordinating everything and making decisions."

"It just seems like I should be out there with them."

"With who? If you'd have gone with James' group this morning, you'd have missed the communication with Max, and then what?

Abandon them and take some of their men to change missions? Or maybe you should be in the village with Tobias and Nathaniel?"

She stood and walked over to one of the maps on the wall again, studying the three different places she'd sent people today, running her finger along the lines of the rivers and the shaded area that marked the spot most of her troops were currently stationed. "I know you're right. I even know why it would be the definition of insanity to put a king or a queen anywhere near conflict if it can be helped. I just hate waiting."

"Patience has never been one of your greatest virtues, milady. Especially when it comes to not knowing things you'd like to know."

She whirled around at the voice that didn't belong to Thomas.

"Alvin! How did you get in here?"

"The door's open."

She wondered why she'd even bothered asking the question. "Is that what this is, then, Alvin? Some grand lesson to teach me patience?"

His thick white eyebrows knitted together, though the rest of his face remained serene. "A lesson, Your Majesty? No, I don't think it's a lesson. I think it's a war."

"And what happens if I don't learn to be more patient?"

"I really don't know. It was only an observation, milady. If my memory serves, your impatience has, on occasion, served you quite well."

"It hasn't always."

"Everyone has traits that are assets in some situations and challenges in others. I've always seen your impatience as part of you, and since I'm fond of you, I tend to like that trait of yours. I think what you choose to *do* with your traits is a much better way to determine whether they're good or bad, anyway. Look at Thomas and Tolliver. Both are charismatic, and capable of inducing loyalty in others in a matter of minutes. The trait is the same, their hearts are not."

"I'm afraid you lost me when you put Tolliver in the same sentence as Thomas."

Thomas coughed. "And I think I'd better go and give this child to Mia for a while."

Quinn and Alvin both watched Thomas carry Samuel out of the room, closing the door behind him, even though she hadn't asked him to.

"So, why are you here then?"

"Do I have to have a reason?"

"No. You're welcome with us at any time, Alvin." She went to the window now, scanning the gray sky for any sign of birds returning with messages. "If you're only here for a visit, I might still impose and ask for advice."

"What sort of advice can I offer?"

She kept her eyes on the sky outside. "For starters, did I do the right thing sending James and Nathaniel and Dorian and Zander to all those different places today?"

He was quiet for so long that she finally turned around to face him. When she did, he met her gaze. "What's the 'right thing', Quinn?"

She sighed, looking down at the floor. "Did I just send any of them off to get killed?"

"I don't know. Did you?"

Her eyes snapped back up. "I'm being serious, Alvin."

"As am I. When you strategized your responses to the situations, did you look at the risks and the people you were sending, and decide which ones would be more useful to you dead than alive?"

Her mouth fell open so far she had trouble getting her answer out. "Of course not!"

"Some people do, you know. But if you didn't, then I think you have the answer to your question."

She had no control over the exasperated huff that escaped from her lips. "Just because I didn't send them off for the purpose of getting killed doesn't mean they won't!"

"No, you're right. It doesn't." Alvin laid his hand on her arm, just below her elbow. But *if* that happened today, if one of them was killed, would that automatically mean your decisions were poor ones?"

"Kind of. I mean, it is my job to keep them safe."

"Yes, to an extent it is. But I don't think you're the one endangering them."

"But I'm not protecting them."

Alvin's voice was quiet and gentle. "What *would* protect them?"

She knew the answer, and the look in his eyes told her that he knew she did.

"You can't control what other people do, Quinn. Even as queen, there are things you will never be able to dictate. When you decided this morning to send those men out, you were deciding there was something more important than their safety. What was so important?"

"Finding Ellen and Charles and other Friends of Philip to bring them to safety, getting medical care to Valderwood, and getting assistance to Max and his troops."

"Do you think any of those are poor decisions?"

Turning to the window again, she shook her head.

"What if the people of Valderwood took Nathaniel's help and used it against him? What if he went into the home of a sick man, healed him, and then the man turned around and used his healed body to murder Nathaniel and then went to fight in Tolliver's army?"

She folded her arms across her chest. "Is that what I just sent him into?"

"I truly have no idea, Your Majesty. But if you thought it was, would you send a bird right now telling him to deny help to a sick man?"

After taking a very long deep breath she faced him again. "Do you want my first instinct, or what I'd probably do after thinking about it for a minute?"

He just nodded. "That's who you are, Quinn. Given the real choice, you'd rather take a risk than be the one who denied help to someone who needed it."

"I don't know if that makes me a very effective commander of an army, though."

Alvin shrugged, chuckling softly. "I think the real trouble starts when people start imagining that good and evil are different at the top of the chain. Helping those who need help is always good – even if they make a choice to do evil with it."

"So it's intentions that matter?"

"No, not really, Quinn. Tolliver could convince himself – and plenty of other people – that his intentions are good. He had 'intentions' to unite the kingdoms by forcing Linnea to marry him. He has 'intentions' now of upholding values in Philotheum that are important to many of his supporters. In the end, *intentions* don't mean much of anything at all."

"But what if I sent Nathaniel to Valderwood today just to gain whatever support I can from those people and keep them from attacking me and messing up whatever small advantages I have in this war?"

He shrugged again. "You could have accomplished those goals – those intentions – in many ways. You could have attacked them first, or had the leaders of their village arrested, or loosed rabid animals in their streets. But you didn't. You sent your own supplies, and risked someone you love to offer them help, without even asking anything in return."

"If I'm honest, I'm *hoping* for something in return."

"Completely unselfish doesn't exist. It's not how the Maker built humans. It's not a question of whether you're selfish. It's a question of whether you use your selfishness to build or to destroy; of whether you care for the sick and feed the hungry, or take advantage of them."

"And if they take the help I give them and use it to destroy me?"

"Then that's on them, not you. You asked for my advice, and this is the only bit I know to give you. If you want to know that your decisions are good ones – both as a *person* and as a queen – then choose to do good things. Act on your own choices and beliefs, without regard for what others choose to do. Even if their choices are to use what you do against you."

She pressed her fingertips to her face, trying to make some of this conversation sink into her brain, to make sense of what any of it meant. When she couldn't, she looked up at him again. "It's not a coincidence that you're here right now, is it?"

"I don't believe in coincidences Your Majesty. And, in any case, I'm here because I came here, on purpose, to visit with you. I am glad we were able to have this conversation."

"Any particular reason?" She knew there was. At this point, she was ready for him to just tell her.

"Yes. In a minute, Sir Marcus is going to come in here with the messages you've been waiting for. Your time of making decisions for your troops and for the people of your kingdom is only just beginning."

"And I don't suppose you're going to help me *make* those decisions, right?"

Alvin smiled. "I'm not the queen. I can only advise."

"And the only advice you have for me is to choose to do good things."

"I have faith in you, Quinn."

# CALLUM

*COME ON, ZANDER. Hold it together.* He'd been chanting that mantra inside his head for the last hour, and it was working – mostly.

The twenty-six men under Callum Haddon's command hadn't been much of a match for the much-larger battalions led by Maxwell and Dorian. The battle had been over almost before it really got going. Zander hadn't even fought.

All that was left was waiting for the help Quinn had promised in a message while keeping watch over the captured officer, Callum Haddon, and two other guards who'd surrendered.

"Still not a word from Callum," Dorian said, coming up the hill to where Zander was sitting with Max. "Not even a threat that we'll be discovered by other troops in the area."

"Are all of the men prepared for another encounter?" Max asked. He was still in obvious pain, but one of the army healers had given him something to make him more comfortable. The healer had decided Max's injury could wait for Nathaniel or William to do the more delicate work. Removing the whole arrow was a risky procedure that could cause damage, so he'd just broken off the ends and stabilized Max's arm.

Max was ridiculously calm and focused for someone with part of a weapon embedded in him. Zander, on the other hand, couldn't say that he was handling the situation well at all. It reminded him too much of going through this with Ben, even if Max's injury wasn't as severe.

There was another soldier from Eirentheos who had been shot in the back. The healer was attending him now, and Zander couldn't bring himself to go anywhere near them.

This whole becoming-a-guard thing was starting to seem like a terrible idea, at least at the moment. Having a few good thoughts about strategy in no way qualified him for combat.

Of course, so long as he was here there was nothing stopping him from trying to get answers out of Callum Haddon … yes, that thought was better. Anger was much easier than – whatever it was he'd been feeling. In fact, he was going to go and have a chat with Callum right now.

He heard the commotion just as he walked down the hill toward where the prisoners were being held – the beating of hooves against the ground and the shouts of new voices. His sword was out before he looked up, but when he saw who it was, he turned and continued down the hill.

The newcomers were more of Quinn's soldiers, led by Kian. He shook his head. Unless something had changed at Tobias', sending Kian here left only Marcus and Ethan back guarding Quinn and Samuel. There were other soldiers, too now, of course, but none they could trust as implicitly as those who'd escaped from the castle with them.

Thinking about *that* kindled his anger into something closer to rage. Linnea was there too – her safety compromised along with Ben's unborn child's.

He didn't bother putting his sword away before he strode through the circle of guards surrounding the spot where Callum Haddon was tied to a tree.

It wasn't until he was inside the circle that he realized he'd been half-expecting resistance from those guards, to be denied access to the prisoner. But, of course, none of them had the authority to challenge him.

What had Quinn been thinking promoting him to an officer?

"She really is just a delusional child, isn't she?"

The greasy sound of Callum's voice caught him off-guard; from all accounts the man hadn't spoken the entire time he'd been in custody.

"Excuse me?"

"The little girl who thinks she can run a kingdom, but promotes an ignorant apprentice to third rank." He scoffed. "It's a terrible waste of lives to stage this useless..." The man didn't get to finish his sentence before the flat edge of Zander's sword met his jaw.

Zander wasn't fazed by the insults directed at him; those weren't the problem. "In Philotheum, you'll speak respectfully when you refer to the queen."

Callum snorted, giving a sideways glance to the sword. "At least I'm giving you a chance to play with your new toy before a proper king comes to take it away."

"Oh?" He raised an eyebrow. "Are you expecting to watch that happen today?"

The small falter in the man's expression lasted only half a second, but it was long enough to tell Zander what he wanted to know. There were no more troops lurking nearby – Callum was on his own.

"Tell me why I shouldn't kill you right now," Zander said.

"If you were capable of guarding a true ruler, you'd have done it by now. Instead, you're playacting like the rest of them. Your little princess doesn't have the stomach for executions, and she apparently selects guards too 'noble' to act in anything other than self-defense, so I've no doubt I'll be back at the castle in time to drink wine at Tolliver's coronation."

There was a rustling sound behind him – someone else had entered the circle, but Zander didn't take his eyes off Callum.

"I think you overestimate *my* desire to be noble, Mister Haddon."

"You're arrogant for such an inexperienced guard," Callum said. "Oh, yes – I know all about you. The child caused quite a stir among her guards when she brought in a ranked apprentice whose only claim to fame is the murder of a guard much more respected than you'll ever be. And it's *Sir* Haddon to you. My true second rank certainly outweighs your imaginary third. I will quite enjoy watching you get what's coming to you – you and the girl and Stephen's brats, including this one here I should have handled myself when I had the chance."

Now Zander knew it was Thomas who'd come to stand beside him.

"No matter," the man continued in his cringe-worthy drawl, "I'm sure he'd rather be a guest of *honor* when his sister marries a real man."

Zander laughed out loud, though the feeling in his stomach was as far from humor as anything could get. Though Thomas was at least three feet to the side of him, Zander could *feel* how rigid his body had gone. "If you think King Stephen would marry his daughter off to that man, you're the delusional one."

"Oh, I think Stephen will have to consider whether withholding a perfectly respectable marriage is worth hundreds of his people dying of water disease and shadeweed and … well, it's not really any of your concern. You won't be around to see it anyway. I'll take pleasure at making those arrangements myself." He looked at Thomas. "I wonder if Tolliver will give me a turn with his new bride in exchange for my little discovery today of your location here?"

In the next instant, Zander's sword saw its first real use. It wasn't a decision. Nothing went through his mind as the blade went through Callum's throat. Later, he would discover that he didn't even have a real memory of the event itself – only of the man's body slumping forward, shock frozen on his face.

It felt like a very long time – hours, maybe – before he was able to move his legs again, though he would be told that only seconds had passed. When he did finally turn toward Thomas, the only thing that registered in his frozen thoughts was that Thomas' sword was also drawn, the tip only inches away from where Callum's head had hit the ground.

Zander's sword fell right next to the body. He didn't retrieve it, he just walked away; the circle of guards parted to let him through without comment.

Dorian found him sometime later – possibly days later; he still had no concept of time. He was perched on a boulder in a darkened spot of the woods, his knees tucked up under his chin, his mind blank as he stared at the large gray bird sitting silently a short distance away.

The bird took flight when the older guard disturbed the silence of their space, though she flew only a few feet, landing again next to him on the rock.

Dorian cleared his throat. "Earlier today, Callum Haddon ordered an entire village destroyed because he believed they were concealing a safe house for the Friends of Philip. Over half the Philothean troops under his command turned against him or deserted him when he told the soldiers to round up the children of the village and put them all in the basement of the home he said he suspected."

"It wasn't a safe house, was it?" The voice coming from Zander's throat didn't even sound like his.

"I don't think so. My information is second-hand and incomplete right now. I heard all this from one of the Philothean soldiers we captured."

"One of the ones who *didn't* abandon him. Who stayed with him, even after he did that?"

"He's young, Zander."

"*I'm* young. What difference does that make?"

"He has a wife and a small daughter. Callum threatened them if he defected."

"You don't even know if that's true. Why wouldn't one of Quinn's soldiers *say something* to her about being threatened before joining the other side in a coup?"

Dorian's boot made a scraping sound against the ground, though he didn't take his eyes off Zander. "I don't know. It could be a lie. But he's not an active threat to us right now, so the most I'm willing to do is keep him under arrest. Decisions can be made later. We'll see what the other soldiers who were captured today have to say once we all get back to camp."

"Soldiers plural?" Zander frowned and climbed off the rock. "I thought only the two survived and surrendered."

"Here. There may be more. The other thing our prisoner told me is that the attack on the village was interrupted by more of our troops. There was some kind of conflict there – the reason Callum had so few men when we found him today was because he lost so many in the first battle."

This story finally brought Zander all the way back to reality and he realized he'd been more than a little selfish and useless walking off like this. He truly was failing at being a soldier. Now he noticed the hard line of Dorian's mouth, and the tense muscles up the sides of his neck.

"Were there … injuries on both sides?" He couldn't even bring himself to say the other word. He knew that he and Dorian were both thinking about who had been leading the other troop of soldiers today.

"From what little I understand, yes. I don't know any details. Thomas said William was waiting back at Tobias' to see what he could do, and Nathaniel hadn't returned, so we need to get Max there."

Zander swallowed back the taste of bile in his throat and took a deep breath. If Dorian could hear this news and still function – so could he. "Well, let's go then."

# MAX

BY THE TIME THEY were close to Tobias' house, Zander had discovered another difference between driving his truck and riding Ember. At home, when he was upset, he'd often taken off in his truck, cruising through the mountains with the radio blasting, but it had never calmed him as much as the reliable rhythm of the horse underneath him.

Even the sharp chill of the air that had descended on them felt cleansing, clearing his mind and steadying his nerves.

Okay, so maybe he wasn't exactly calm. He was composed; all traces of the emotions that had led him to walk out of the situation before were gone, replaced with determination to get to more help. Killing Callum had been somewhat impulsive, and there might be consequences for it later, but the man would never have given them useful information, and he was too dangerous to take chances with.

The biggest concern right now was that Max's condition was deteriorating rapidly – the hard motion of hooves on ground that brought relief to Zander's nerves brought only pain to Max.

Max was riding with Thomas, doing his best to stay balanced despite the grievous injury to his arm. For the first part of the trip, they'd tried to go slow and prevent jostling him, but when slow didn't seem to help, anyway, they'd decided to just get him back to Tobias' as quickly as possible.

Max's own horse wasn't making the journey.

They'd messaged for more help again – hoping that William or Nathaniel would be able to get to them sooner rather than later – but so far those requests had gone unanswered. For the moment, Zander preferred not to wonder why. He was sure he would find out as soon as they reached Tobias'.

The weather wasn't helping. The dark gray line of clouds that had looked so ominous on the horizon earlier were much more threatening piled over their heads. Only a light layer of snow coated the ground right now, but if the rapidly decreasing temperature of the wind was any indication, things were about to get much worse.

The first signs of chaos appeared even before Tobias' massive property came into view.

No snow stuck to the ground on this path – it was too beaten down with tracks from people and horses.

At first, the return of their group seemed to go unnoticed by the guards hurrying on horseback back and forth between Tobias' home and the camp of soldiers a short distance away. Zander didn't like it; how could they keep Quinn safe with lax security?

But before he could get really annoyed, a whole group of guards appeared suddenly from the trees, riding down and blocking their path. Even the soldiers who'd appeared to be ignoring them stopped and turned around to scrutinize.

He nodded in approval. That wasn't a bad plan at all – a quick glance behind him revealed that his entire traveling party was surrounded.

"Sir Dorian! Sir Zander!" The guard who spoke was one Zander recognized.

"What's going on here, Rhys?" Zander asked.

Rhys shook his head. "I don't know everything. There was a battle with some of Tolliver's troops at Dorvale Village earlier. Many injuries – villagers and guards, too. Most of our healers went out to Dorvale to help, but the worst injuries were brought back here. Last I heard, William was working to save one guard."

"And Nathaniel?"

"Hasn't returned from Valderwood."

"Do you know who the guard is that William is treating?"

The quick flick of Rhys' eyes to Dorian and then back to Zander told him everything he needed to know, and it was all he could do not to lose his composure and be sick right there.

Dorian saw it, too. His body grew so stiff he could have been a statue on horseback.

"Go, Dorian," Zander said. "Take a few men with you." He waved at four guards behind them, indicating they should follow, which they did, all of them disappearing over the crest of a hill seconds later.

Rhys' eyes had landed on Thomas and Maxwell. "What happened?" he gasped.

"We're two for two on battles today. Prince Maxwell took an arrow to the arm. We messaged for help, but I guess now we know why that didn't happen."

"Any lost?"

Zander shook his head. "Not on our side."

"And you have prisoners?" Rhys frowned toward the back of their line.

"Yes. And soldiers still back at the battle site with the casualties – including a high-ranking officer."

"Who?"

His heart pounded even at the thought of admitting what he'd done. Just *thinking* the name made his hands feel sweaty and weak, but he managed to choke out the name anyway. "Callum Haddon."

Rhys' reaction was far more normal than Zander expected. "Well that's more good news than bad, I suppose. I'll gather some men to go down and meet them. Will you tell Her Majesty?"

"Yes."

Despite the fact that she'd been wearing a path between the windows all afternoon, Quinn heard the commotion outside before she saw it. It figured someone would arrive as soon as she stepped away for a moment to see if Will had any updates on James.

When she heard the horses and the shouting, she ran back to the front room.

"It's Dorian," Linnea said, without taking her eyes off the scene outside the window. "How is James?"

Quinn didn't get the chance to answer before she heard the door burst open. A second later, Dorian was standing in front of her, his face ashen underneath a layer of sweat.

"What's going on? I heard…"

"He's alive, Dorian. But it isn't good. William is doing everything he can. He said to tell you that you can go in, if you want to, but to prepare yourself first."

"Thank you, Your Majesty."

She nodded and pointed down the hall, biting back her questions about whether the rest of the group was close behind and how badly Max was injured.

Linnea tapped her fingers on the windowsill and continued staring, but she didn't say anything. Quinn went to stand next to her, taking her hand and squeezing it.

As soon as Tobias' gate swung open out in the yard again, though, Linnea dropped her hand and bolted for the door.

Part of Quinn wanted to follow her, but the other part knew that it was best not to add to the confusion, not to turn herself into something the guards outside had to be mindful of as so many men poured in through the gate behind Thomas and Zander.

She was too worried about Max at the moment to care that it wasn't fully safe to be seen by all of the arriving soldiers, but she knew that doing so would expose her men, too.

The first thing Zander saw when he rode through the gate and into Tobias' property was Linnea, running across the porch toward them at breakneck speed. The look on her face was something he wasn't going to be able to get out of his mind for a while – maybe ever. He steered Ember to the side and dismounted before hurrying to meet her halfway.

"He's all right, Linnea," he called just before he reached her.

Though she acknowledged his words with a quick nod, she didn't stop running, and he didn't try to interfere, he just turned to follow.

Several guards ran up to assist them as he and Linnea reached to help Max down from Thomas' horse. One of them tried to step in front of Linnea, but Zander shook his head harshly. Her obvious need to be part of this was more important than shielding her; he could see that. "We've got it. Tend to the horses and the men with minor injuries, and get the prisoners secured, please," he said to them.

Maxwell didn't entirely agree. "You shouldn't be lifting me, Linnea. I'm all right."

"Keep insisting on babying me, Max, and you won't be."

He chuckled, though it was a weak, raspy sound that belied his insistence. So did the way he leaned shakily against Zander's shoulder. It was obvious that he would fall over without the support.

By this time, Thomas had dismounted. "Move, short one," he said, nudging Linnea out of the way. His height alone was probably the only reason she allowed him to slip into her place to help hold up their older brother.

Now she faced him. "You're still a terrible liar, anyway. What happened?"

"You want to see?" He lifted the side of his purple cloak, revealing the bloodied bandages wrapped around the piece of arrow in his arm.

Zander had to give her credit; her cheeks and temples went green, but only for about ten seconds before she got herself back under control. She looked at Thomas, the question clear in her eyes.

Thomas lifted one shoulder briefly but gave one shake of his head.

Zander agreed. He didn't know how bad Max's injury was, but it wasn't good. And judging from both the way Linnea had looked coming out here, and the fact that she was alone, neither William nor Nathaniel was available to help right now.

"So what happened to James?" Max asked as they started helping him walk toward the house.

"He was targeted," Linnea said. "As soon as they realized who he was, four – I won't call them guards or men – went at him at once. One changed his mind at the last minute, which gave James at least the chance to fight back and gave some of our guys enough time to get in there and help. James and Decker Josephson were both injured – but James is much worse. They thought he'd be okay to travel all the way back here, but William said there's internal bleeding."

Her voice was strong and certain, but Zander saw the small tremble of her lip when she took a breath and the way her fists were locked tight. She remained steady, though, helping him and Thomas as they carried Max up the steps of the porch.

The door swung open before they reached it; Quinn stood inside ready to help as well. She'd carefully hidden any display of shock over Max's condition. "Doesn't your father know I could use help that *isn't* covered in blood?" she asked once they were inside.

"Demanding today, aren't you?" Max was so shaky and weak that Zander wasn't sure how he could manage to affect a teasing tone with Quinn, but he did.

"What good is it to have older brothers if I can't be demanding of them?"

"I did my best to spoil you. It just didn't work out quite as well as I expected. But I did bring another hundred or so guards who are relatively unscathed."

"I suppose that will have to do – so long as you promise me you'll let William and Nathaniel patch you up."

"I'm not going anywhere, Quinn. You look like you could use a lot more military help."

"More than you could possibly realize. Although I was kind of serious about the covered-in-blood thing," she said as they helped him onto a bed in Thomas' room.

"My first piece of military advice, sweetheart? You're in a war. Get used to the blood."

"I'll work on it. You try and rest. Hopefully William will be able to look at this soon or Nathaniel will come back. I could have one of the other healers come in, too?"

"No, Quinn. I think this is okay for now. James needs William more than I do."

He wasn't convincing, though. As Zander helped him out of his cloak, he could feel how hot Max was. Sweat pooled in the dark hair at his neck, soaking the collar of his shirt. Once the cloak was off, he didn't lie down so much as fall back when Thomas tried to lower him gently. Landing on the mattress made him groan in pain.

"Would it be better on his side?" Linnea asked through clenched teeth.

Then there was a sound of footsteps at the door.

"Max!"

"Hey, Will."

Zander didn't think William even noticed there were other people in the room besides his older brother. He pushed through Zander and Thomas without a word. But then, when he grabbed a pair of scissors from his bag and began cutting up the side of Max's shirt, he looked at Thomas. "Take the girls out of here, please."

"I'll do it," Zander said, holding his hand up at Thomas. "Do you need me to bring you back anything?"

It took William a minute to respond. He already had Max's shirt off and he was pulling out a leather-wrapped tool kit. "No."

Zander waited until he'd closed the door behind him before looking at Quinn and Linnea. "I have to say I'm surprised neither one of you argued about that." And that neither of them had objected to being 'taken out' instead of being asked to leave for themselves. "You've both seen worse."

"William doesn't need the distraction of the two of us making him nervous when he's like that," Quinn said. "He's upset, then he gets worried that we're upset. It's just better to let him work."

"And it got you out of there, too," Linnea said.

He frowned. "Am I not supposed to be in there?"

"You're not *unwelcome* in there, but don't you think you could use a few minutes to decompress after the day you've had?" Quinn asked.

His stomach felt like it was collapsing in on itself as his gaze met hers.

"Well don't look at me like you did something wrong," she said.

"You mean something wrong like killing someone?"

She was silent for a minute, studying him as emotions he couldn't read swirled in her eyes. "At this point, the only thing I see wrong with you killing Callum Haddon is that it wasn't Tolliver."

"Yeah, well…" he glanced away, but "away" turned out to be right at Linnea. A violent shudder ripped through him as he thought of what Callum had said. He looked back at Quinn before just thinking about it made him murder someone else. "Trust me. He deserved it at least as much."

"Oh, I trust you Zander. I'm sure in the next few hours and days we'll have a lot to discuss about what happened today, but honestly, right now the only question I have for you is whether you would prefer to eat first or bathe."

# AFTERMATH

"WOULD YOU LIKE ANOTHER bowl?" Linnea asked, reaching for the empty dish in front of Zander.

He picked it up before she could. "You don't have to serve me. I can get it."

A second later, the bowl was out of his hand again.

Quinn shot him a teasing look as she handed it to Linnea.

He slumped back down on the stool. "Fine. Thank you." Truthfully, though, his motivation for getting it himself had little to do with saving Linnea the work. He needed the distraction. He didn't even notice picking up his spoon and attempting to spin it like a top until it flew across the counter, knocking into a metal mixing bowl.

Quinn retrieved it and set it back in front of him without comment.

He held the spoon between his fingers. "So no word from Nathaniel and Tobias yet?"

"No. I'm hoping they return soon, though. It sounds like it's getting nasty out there again."

He could hear the wind blowing against the house from where he was; now and then a strong gust would even make the flames in the fireplace flicker higher for a minute.

"It's starting to snow," Linnea said, stretching up on her toes to get a good look out the window over the sink. "Just a little bit so far."

Although the front door was two rooms away from them, they all looked in that direction as it opened unexpectedly. Zander swore he could feel the cooler air from his seat.

Quinn was on her feet immediately, and Zander leaped up, too, grabbing his sword from the counter and rushing to get in front of her.

Marcus was already in the entryway, looking on as two guards closed the door behind another man who was brushing flakes of snow off the shoulders of his cloak. Zander recognized him as one of the healers who'd been helping out at the camp, Nicholas-something.

"I heard you needed help," he said. "I came to do what I can."


Zander didn't really understand what happened in the next few minutes, but somehow he ended up back in the kitchen with Linnea. The new healer, Nicholas was with Max, and William had gone back to James who needed him more, and Quinn had disappeared with Marcus.

"You should finish that before it gets cold," Linnea said, nodding toward the full bowl of stew that had been left on the counter.

He looked at it and shook his head. "I'm not really so hungry anymore."

She nodded without answering and went over to the end of the room, settling into one of the more comfortable chairs by the fireplace.

Though he wasn't sure if it was a good idea, he followed her, sitting down on the chair across from her. "Are you doing okay?"

She pressed her fingers against the side of her forehead. "I was starting to think I could count on you to not ask stupid questions, Zander."

He snorted. "How is it my fault if you're not as smart about me as you thought you were?"

"All right, maybe that isn't your fault, though I think I can hold you accountable for trying to talk about me instead of you."

For half a second, he bought it, and the familiar weight of guilt settled in his chest, but then he narrowed his eyes. "Not so fast, Linnea ... Westbrook. Having the most tragic backstory is not an indefinite 'get out of humanity free card'... What's your middle name, anyway?"

"Why? So you can call me by it?"

"When you deserve it. Yes."

"It's still a stupid question, Zander-Whatever-Cunningham. Just as stupid as if I asked you if you're doing okay after you slit someone's throat today. Obviously I'm not. My brother's injured, my uncle's out in the snowstorm, we're at *war*, and James, who has been pursuing me mercilessly despite getting nothing in return, might die – and then where will I be? The question is so ridiculous it needs its own category of stupid."

He stared at the floor, though her tirade didn't embarrass him the way it would have if almost anyone else spoke to him that way. "You're right," he said when she was finished.

After several minutes of silence, her voice was low when she spoke again. "If there's one of those topics you're in need of discussing in detail, I can do that. But I can't deal with the polite lying or trying to cheer each other up right now, okay?"

He chuckled. "You mean, let's just hang out and be wrecks together?"

"Complete wrecks."

"I can handle that. As much as I can handle anything right now, anyway," he said, smiling at her.

"So, obviously he deserved it for just daring to come back inside this kingdom, but what made you decide to solve the Callum Haddon problem today?"

His gaze flicked back to the fire immediately; he couldn't look at her and think about that… not man. He wasn't – hadn't been – any kind of a man.

"Never mind," she said. "I guess I'm not immune to asking stupid questions today, either. Do you want to help me get dinner started? Everyone is going to be hungry, and there's not enough stew for another whole meal."

"Sure." He wondered if she'd seen the way his right hand had clenched the hilt of his sword when she'd mentioned Callum. Even once he managed to pry his fingers loose, they were sore.

For a long while, he and Linnea peeled and chopped vegetables in silence, but it was comfortable. Having something to do with his hands felt good, and despite the fact that everything Linnea had said was true, and that neither of them was functioning well emotionally, just being in the room with her, working together, had a steadying, calming effect.

Until a heartrending scream filled the house.

Zander's knife clattered to the wooden counter.

Linnea uttered a word he wouldn't have guessed she knew, which turned his attention to her instead of to the shouts and slamming doors in the back of the house.

What he saw nearly made the same word come out of *his* mouth, and he raced to get a towel.

He knew exactly what had happened, of course. The noise had startled her, too, only her knife hadn't dropped harmlessly.

By the time he reached her with the towel, there was already a puddle of blood on the counter, and her cheeks were an odd dusky color.

"It's all right," he said, taking her hand and wrapping the towel tightly around it. "It's just a little blood."

She nodded, but the gray in her features turned slowly green.

He grabbed her around the waist and moved her to the large sink just in time, pulling her long hair out of the way.

"Ugh, sorry," she said afterwards as he reached for a cup while still trying to hold the towel tightly against her hand. "I don't know why that happened."

He filled the cup with water and handed it to her. "Well, you are pregnant. Maybe the baby doesn't like her mom getting hurt." He bent his head toward her stomach. "I have to say I agree with you there, kiddo."

When he straightened back up, Linnea was giving him a strange look – one that made his neck feel warm, though he wasn't sure exactly why.

He cleared his throat and turned his attention back to her hand. "Let's wash it off and see how bad it is, okay?"

She nodded tentatively; her face turned pale and sweaty again, but he didn't think she'd be sick this time.

He held tightly to the makeshift bandage while he lifted the pump handle over the sink and got the water flowing again. Then he unwrapped her hand and carefully helped her slide it under the stream. "You're doing good," he said, rubbing gently at her wrist when she winced.

Her sigh made him chuckle. "I know. You'd rather knock my teeth out than let me think you can't take care of this yourself. But I think I should get a pass tonight since I'm the only reason there's no puke in your hair right now."

She looked at him. "Actually, I was thinking that I'm probably the only one in this house who can't be trusted to cut vegetables without causing more drama that we don't need."

"Hey," he looked away, concentrating on rinsing the blood between her fingers and trying to look at the cut – cuts. The knife had left deep red streaks across three of her fingers. "What's a war without a couple of war wounds? At least you sliced your own hand instead of getting mad and taking it out on someone else's throat."

"That's only because I wasn't there."

"Weren't where?" Thomas' voice startled them. Although it wasn't nearly the same shock as the earlier scream had been; they were both still jumpy. He could feel Linnea's accelerated heartbeat in her wrist as he turned off the water and reached for the towel.

As soon as they turned to face Thomas, he started running across the room. "Whoa, Nay! What happened?"

Zander looked down – he hadn't thought the cuts were that bad. Then he saw the blood all down the front of her white apron. "Minor cooking incident," he said quickly. "It looks worse than it is. She's okay."

Thomas grabbed a clean towel before he approached her and took her hand in his. "We'll have Will take a look at it."

Although there was no good reason for anything to be funny right now, the little sound Linnea made when she was exasperated amused him, and he couldn't help smiling. "I think Will has enough to deal with right now. How is Max?"

"Nicholas was working on his arm until just a few minutes ago, but then Will came and asked him to go and tend to James instead."

She looked at Thomas with wide eyes.

"William says that James is stable for right now. I don't know exactly what that means, because it still doesn't sound good, but it's better than nothing. Dorian is staying right by his side."

"What happened a couple of minutes ago?"

Thomas shook his head, and the meaning was clear: they didn't want to know the answer to that question. "You can go see both of them now if you'd like," Thomas said. "Max is awake, although I don't know for how much longer. I was going to go check on James in a couple of minutes. You need to show William your hand, anyway. I'll clean this up."

Linnea raised an eyebrow. She left the room – but not headed in William's direction.

For a tense moment, Zander wasn't sure if Thomas was going to challenge her, but he didn't. Apparently even Thomas knew the outer limits of Linnea's patience.

He headed to the basket where Tobias kept stacks of clean towels. By the time he returned to the counter with it, Thomas was already there with the bottle full of bleaching solution they used for the laundry.

He carefully salvaged all of the uncontaminated vegetables and put them in a bowl before Thomas poured the sharp-smelling liquid.

"You don't get to feel bad about what happened today," Thomas said as they worked.

"I'm not sure I can just *not feel bad* about killing someone."

"You killed Rahas. Do you feel bad about that?"

He sighed. "Not really, but then, he was trying to kill me."

"So was Callum Haddon. Just because he didn't have a sword right then doesn't mean anything. What he was saying about Quinn? That was treason – and in a way that wouldn't have given her any other choice but to have him executed, because all he was trying to do was prove that she was too weak to do it."

His eyes flicked to Thomas'. He hated the question he was about to ask, but he did it anyway. "Do you think she would have been?"

Thomas' gaze was sharp and clear as he looked back. "I think there's a reason she has you."

Zander swallowed, concentrating very hard on scrubbing an invisible drop of blood from the counter.

"We didn't start this war, Zander. We didn't invade their kingdom, we didn't try to usurp their throne, or kidnap any of their royal children, or poison their people. And Callum Haddon was *not* an innocent bystander. I'm honored to know that someone like you – who could still feel bad about killing him – is on our side, but, you did us all a favor today. It wasn't wrong."

"My senior year was not supposed to be this complicated, you know."

"Yeah, well, neither was my sister's pregnancy. But life doesn't end just because something happened that we didn't originally plan for."

He nodded.

Thomas reached for the rag Zander had finished using. "Speaking of my sister, I don't plan to *ever* tell her what Callum said about her today. I don't know if it's something she should hear or not. Whether the topic ever has reason to come up between the two of you, I'll leave it there."

His mouth dropped open; he wasn't sure what Thomas was implying – or at least, he didn't want to think about it.

"I'll go put these in the laundry."

# LARYA

"SO WHEN WERE YOU planning on showing me your hand, Linnea?" William's voice was unexpected, interrupting her half-asleep daze as she stared into the fire in the sitting room.

Across from her, Zander raised his head – and an eyebrow. "You still didn't tell him?"

"I'm fine. I didn't cut my hand *off*."

She regretted it as soon as the words were out of her mouth. Everyone in the room was silent, looking anywhere but at her or at each other.

An hour ago, when he'd stepped out of Max's room for long enough to accept a plate of dinner, William had broken the news that he wasn't sure Max's arm could be saved – at least not all of it. Max didn't know yet; they'd all been sort of in shock since then.

Only William didn't seem to acknowledge the awkwardness of her comment. "It still needs to be treated, Linnea," he said, though he walked toward the window instead of her, setting his bag on a low table as he went.

They still hadn't heard anything from Nathaniel. Thomas and Zander kept taking turns pacing to the window and back, looking for any sign of him, or for a message from a bird.

Quinn had already had to talk Marcus out of going out into the snow searching for him – it wasn't worth it to risk Marcus' life, since there was a good chance Nathaniel was safe in the village, and not out in the weather.

Thomas cleared his throat. "At this point, I'm just praying he's not out there. Even Aidel would have a challenge getting us a message through *that*."

Sometime since dinner, the weather had turned from an ordinary snowstorm to a blizzard. The wind shook the windows every couple of minutes, and the air outside was blindingly white. As William looked out, something – a stick maybe – flew up and smacked the glass, making all of them jump.

After a tense few seconds, William confirmed that it hadn't caused any damage.

"We should go out and close the shutters," Thomas said. "It'll help it warm up in here anyway."

"Depends on your definition of *warm*," Zander grumbled, though he got up and followed Thomas without hesitation.

William continued staring out the window as long as he could, until the heavy wooden shutters clattered shut, blocking his view – or most of it. Someone opened the slats a little, but William still turned away and came to sit on the table across from her. "Okay Nay, let's have a look." He grabbed a pillow and set it on her lap before taking hold of her towel-wrapped hand and laying it on the cushion.

*"It's not still bleeding,"* she said. At least not enough to seep through the towel.

He nodded, though she could tell he wasn't really focused on what she was saying; his mind was somewhere else.

When Quinn appeared in the doorway a second later, Linnea was relieved.

"Hey," Quinn said, walking over and laying a hand on William's shoulder.

She would probably never cease to be amazed at the way Quinn's touch could literally turn the light back on in her brother's eyes. His whole body grew visibly less stiff as he lifted his hand to his shoulder to place over hers.

Quinn leaned down and kissed the top of his head, pausing to comb his hair back off his forehead with her fingers before she came and sat down on the couch beside Linnea.

"Samuel's fed and back with Mia," she said. "He should be good for a little while."

"Is he asleep?" William asked.

"Not for the night."

"Good. I miss him."

Linnea sometimes wondered if Quinn had any idea just how much she meant to William, but then she was pretty sure that Quinn was just as affected by him.

She winced and sucked in a breath as William pried the towel from the spots where the blood had begun to dry. A fresh trickle started flowing from her pointer finger. She knew she sounded dramatic when she mumbled, "What are you going to do to me this time?"

Quinn chuckled and gently rubbed Linnea's back, but William only shrugged. "It's up to you, Nay. It's not that bad. The bleeding will stop. Two of the cuts are fine. This one," he pointed to the fresh blood, "will probably leave a scar if I don't put a stitch in it, but it will be small. So you can choose."

"Will it heal faster if I let you do it?"

"Yes. Faster and better. It'll stop hurting sooner, too – though it'll hurt worse tonight and tomorrow once the numbing stuff wears off."

She sighed. She didn't care about the scar, really, but she didn't want to be any more useless to everyone than being nearly five moons pregnant already made her. They'd already had to help her so much when she'd been sick; she needed her hands. "Do you have time to be worrying about me?"

"I wish that wasn't a valid question right now, but yes, I can give you a few minutes. Max is asleep, and James… I've done everything I can. Now I can only keep him comfortable and wait to see what happens."

She nodded. She'd been in to see James earlier. After seeing that, she wasn't sure what to wish for.

"Do you think Nathaniel would be able to do anything else if he was here?"

"No. Although I wouldn't have had to allow that Nicholas guy to mangle Max's arm getting the arrow out."

"Will…" Quinn's voice was low; she leaned all the way forward until her forehead was nearly touching William's and squeezed his knee with her hand.

He closed his eyes, inhaling and exhaling deeply several times before he opened them again. "I know," he whispered.

"Ugh. All right, enough," Linnea said. "There's still a chance James will make it, right?"

"Yes."

"And still a chance that Max's arm will be okay?"

William grimaced. "A chance, yes."

"And Callum Haddon is dead, along with nearly all of the troops that didn't desert him. Things could be worse. I think it's time to celebrate instead of moping."

Quinn gave her half a smile. "You're right. Things could be a lot worse tonight."

"Especially for you," William teased, as she felt a sudden stinging sensation in her finger.

"Ow, William!" She gritted her teeth. "You are not my favorite brother right now."

Though his head stayed down, concentrating on her hand, she could see his forehead crinkle in amusement. "Am I ever?"

"No."

That was a lie – mostly. She did actually appreciate his skilled, steady hand, especially a moment later when the door in the entryway burst open with a blast of frigid air, and he didn't flinch. He didn't even look up as a snow-covered object flew into the room, flapping ice crystals everywhere. He did use his thumb to brush away the freezing drop that landed on Linnea's palm.

He was a lot less annoying now that her finger was going numb, too.

"It's just us," Thomas called.

"And a *bird*," Linnea said.

As if she'd called it, the creature circled over her head and then landed on the table next to William, blinking right at her.

"Who are you?" she asked. She'd never seen this bird before.

"He's one of Tobias'," Zander said from the doorway. His hat was so crusted with white, it might have been made from snow.

At the sound of his voice, the bird perked up, nodding once at Linnea before flying right over William's head and across the room, landing on Zander's shoulder.

"All day, he's been saying that the bird belongs to Tobias," Thomas said, "but all day the bird has been disagreeing with him. Not always politely, either."

Quinn stood and walked halfway across the room, making the clicking sound that ordinarily summoned a bird, but this one didn't budge. Instead it tapped one foot on Zander's shoulder.

Zander flinched. "I don't think I like having those talons quite so close to my neck, Miss Bird."

The chirruping sound the creature made sounded exactly like a chuckle, and she launched herself down, swooping neatly to land again on Zander's outstretched arm.

"That's better. Thank you," he said, reaching with his other hand to pop open the clasp on the bird's canister. "Do you have anything in here?"

She did. Several small sheets were rolled together inside the container. One fell as Zander pulled them out. Thomas retrieved it and then took the whole roll of papers and handed them to Quinn.

Linnea was frustrated at being pinned down by her hand as she watched Quinn frown, flipping to the last paper first and then try to organize the notes again.

"It's from Nathaniel," Quinn said after a minute. "He's safe – he never left Valderwood. He was in the middle of some kind of surgery when he and Tobias decided the storm looked too threatening to chance it."

"Is there a place he's welcome to stay there?" William asked.

"I can only guess they have some kind of option. He didn't say who they were with, just not to expect him until the weather's clear for travel." She looked at Zander. "And Tobias sides with the bird in the argument you're having. Apparently he recognizes her from his barn, but she's never been willing to carry messages for him before."

"Looks like you found yourself a bird," Thomas said.

Zander's eyes widened. "Can I just *do* that – just find a bird and take it?"

"No," Linnea said, chuckling, "you can't. The proper way to phrase it is that she's found a human. If you're nice enough to her, she might keep you."

"I don't think I've been very *nice* to her so far."

"She gets to decide that, too."

"And if I don't *want* a bird?"

As soon as he said it, the bird flew from his arm to his shoulder again; Linnea laughed as her talons made indents in his sweater.

Zander heaved a heavy sigh. "All right already! I'm sorry!"

Everyone in the room was laughing by the time the bird landed on the back of an armchair.

"Well, you are good for entertainment value, anyway," Zander said. "Since we don't have the internet."

Linnea could see it, though – he already liked the bird at least as much as it liked him. She wasn't going to be surprised if the thing flew out of his room in the morning.

"Okay, Nay, I'm all finished here." William's words startled her; she'd almost forgotten he was right there, working on her hand.

"Thanks," she said, after the second it took her concentration to return. "That was fast."

"Not really," William said, glancing back at Zander and the bird. "But I think we were both a little distracted."

She didn't know what he meant by that, but whatever it was, if he didn't stop looking at her that way, she was going to kick him. Lucky for him, he packed up and left the room – probably to go check on Max and James again.

"So what are you going to name her?" she asked, walking over to Zander and the bird.

The terror in Zander's eyes nearly made her laugh again. "I have to come up with some kind of bird name now?"

"Apparently she doesn't have one," Quinn said, flipping through the pages of Nathaniel's note again.

"I don't know anything about bird names."

"There aren't rules. You can just pick something you like."

He frowned. "Your birds all have some kind of strange bird names. She's already going to be odd for hanging around me."

This was *so* the wrong time for her to be finding anyone adorable. "Fine. How about Larya?"

"That's a bird name?"

"Sure."

He narrowed his eyes. "You're not just telling me that so that my bird will be the strange one and I won't even know?"

"Meech, Zander! Have I really been that awful to you before?"

He might have tried to answer the question – if his face hadn't been turning purple. The laugh that spilled out of him filled the entire room. "*Meech?*" he spluttered when he managed to catch a breath. "I'm asking an honest question here, and you come out with *meech?*"

She looked at Quinn. "Not a word in your world?"

"No." Quinn glanced up from her letter only long enough to give Linnea the same kind of look William had. *Stupid married people.*

"All right then. Yes, Zander, *meech*. Now you have a new bird and a new word."

"And it's not even my birthday," he muttered.

# NIGHT DUTY AGAIN

LINNEA HAD NO IDEA what time it was when she came out of Max and Thomas' room and pulled the door silently closed, but she knew it was late, so the sight of the figure in the hallway surprised her.

"What are you doing out here?"

"Second night of duty," Zander said. "I didn't realize you were still up."

She looked down the hall. The door to the bedroom she'd been using was standing wide open.

When she looked back at him, she thought maybe his cheeks had gone a little red, but she couldn't tell for sure.

There was no reason to say anything.

"Is William still with James?"

He shook his head. "I promised to wake him if Dorian came out and said they needed him so he'd listen to Quinn and try to get a couple hours of sleep."

"He'll be back in an hour, tops."

"He already poked his head out ten minutes after he went in there."

"Sounds about right." She frowned at him. "You're not supposed to still take a night shift when you end up working the entire day, you know."

"And you're not supposed to still be wandering around the house at midnight checking on everyone when there are other people to do it. I don't seem to remember you getting enough sleep last night, either."

"*I* wasn't riding around the kingdom and fighting in battles all day. I took a *nap* earlier, before everything got so crazy. You can't go days on end without any sleep…" She paused as she thought of something. "You were sleeping in there, with Dorian and James." In the room where James was now fighting for his life.

He pressed his lips together so tightly they nearly disappeared.

"Zander!"

His eyes dropped to the floor, and something at the bottom of her rib cage went right along with them.

She took a deep breath. Was he planning on sleeping on the floor in the hallway? "Nathaniel isn't here tonight. His bed is empty."

Zander grimaced. "He's sharing a room with Marcus."

"Is Marcus in bed?"

"No."

"Come on."

When he didn't follow her immediately, she grabbed his hand.

His whole body stiffened before he yanked it back.

"Sorry," she whispered. Though she didn't know if she was.

"No, I'm sorry. You just surprised me."

He was a terrible liar. "Come on then."

Fifteen minutes later, Zander had a bed to sleep in and a change of clothes, though she wasn't entirely convinced he would use either. At least she'd tried.

She was halfway down the hall contemplating actually going into her own room when a door opened and Dorian stepped into the hallway. She hurried over to him.

"Is everything all right?"

He nodded. "James is awake. He must be feeling a little better because he insisted I get out for a little while and make myself a fresh cup of tea."

"I can get one for you."

"He was fairly insistent that I be gone for at least ten minutes."

She smiled – or tried to.

He turned to look at the door. "I don't like leaving him for that long, though."

"Would you like me to stay with him for a little bit?"

His hesitation was clear, but eventually he disappeared down the hall while she knocked softly and then opened the door.

"James?" she whispered.

"Princess Linnea?" His voice was weak, but he definitely looked better than when she'd come in here earlier. Or more conscious, at least. The cut by his left eye didn't look too terrible, but she knew the more egregious injuries were hidden underneath the piles of quilts.

"Yes, it's me."

"What time is it?"

"I don't know. Late. How are you? Are you in pain?"

"It's all right for now." He was lying, but she decided to let it go. "I'm sorry you have to see me like this, though."

"You're sorry for me to see you like what? A hero?"

"Not quite, milady. But thank you."

She swallowed hard. "Can I get you anything?"

He shook his head, then lifted his hand a little, jiggling the rubber tube that ran from his hand to a glass bottle hanging from the bedpost. "I can't have anything else."

"Right, sorry."

"Don't be sorry, Princess. Actually, it is I who need to apologize to you."

"You're a guard, James. You did what you were supposed to do. I heard you saved the lives of those children."

"I don't mean that. Given the chance to do today all over, there's nothing I would change. If I could have saved any more of those people, I'd have gladly laid down my life right then to do so."

"And that's what makes you one of Quinn's very best guards – it's what makes all of us, myself included, so incredibly grateful to have your service."

"But it's also why I must apologize for my recent attempts to pursue your affections."

Her stomach twisted into unnatural shapes and she could feel her pulse everywhere. "I don't think that's something you should have to be sorry for, either, James."

"Yes it is. After what you've been through, after losing Ben the way you did, it was horribly unfair of me to even consider asking you to put yourself in that position again. You've already made the ultimate sacrifice in marriage to a soldier."

"*I* didn't get into a swordfight. You're being too hard on yourself."

"No, I'm not. My sacrifice might be large, but it's easy. I knew my life might be forfeit when I made the choice to join. I've been living on borrowed time as it is ever since I was arrested by Tolliver. And now that it's time to pay that debt, it will be simple."

"It's not time to pay that debt yet. You're going to be fine."

He closed his eyes for several seconds, which was good because it meant he couldn't see her trembling lip.

His eyelids were a deep bluish-gray color that suggested a little too strongly that he might not be wrong, but she wasn't going to think that way right now. He seemed to have trouble lifting them back open. "Either way, no one will ever ask me to do it twice. It would be wrong of me – was wrong of me – to even consider asking you to risk a price you've already paid."

"Don't I get to decide what price I'm willing to pay?"

"Certainly you do, milady. But we both know you weren't attempting to pursue me."

"Only because I'm not pursuing anyone right now, James. If I was in a different place…"

"Then I would have considered the return of your attentions the highest honor, milady. But it still wouldn't make it right for me to ask for them. My greatest fear now, whatever happens, is that you might feel obligated to me in some way, and I never want that."

"Well, I do owe you my sincere gratitude for your excellent service."

"I'll accept that." His lips curled into the smallest semblance of a smile.

If they hadn't lapsed into silence then, she would never have heard the tiny knock on the door, but she did, and turned around in time to see William enter.

He only managed to get his mouth halfway open before she stopped him with her most threatening glare. "You don't get to comment on my bedtime unless I'm allowed to comment on yours."

William sighed, but didn't respond. "Are you ready for some more pain medicine, James?"

The way James looked now made it hard to believe she'd been having a full conversation with him only moments ago. His breathing was labored, and he barely managed to give William a nod of assent — though Will was already at his bedside with a glass syringe full of pale yellow liquid.

Once the medicine was in the tube, the harsh movements of James' chest calmed, and his eyes closed. Within seconds, Linnea knew he was asleep. She stood and leaned over him, brushing his hair back from his hot, dry forehead before planting a kiss there. "Rest well, James," she whispered.

# BATTLES

THE STORM RAGED FOR over three days. Sometimes the snow would stop, but the wind would howl, slamming piles of white crystals against the sides of the house until the drifts towered over everyone's heads. Sometimes it was so quiet outside that William swore he could hear the fluffy flakes drifting down and landing on each other.

Sometimes, the storm was inside.

The first day felt almost like a reprieve from the pressures they'd been facing. All was calm; nobody even had to go out and tend to the animals because so many guards were camped in every barn and building on Tobias' property. No birds could travel in the weather, either.

On what was probably his fiftieth trip back and forth between Max's room and James', Quinn stepped in front of him in the hallway, grabbing hold of his elbow. "They're both asleep," she said.

He nodded.

"Thomas is with Max. He knows when to get you."

"But James…" he whispered.

She laid her hand on his chest, and for a moment it calmed the frantic beating there. "Is there anything you can do for him right now that you haven't done already?"

He didn't answer; he knew she wasn't expecting him to.

"Love, you barely slept all night. You need some rest."

"Look who's talking." He ran his thumb over the shadows on her cheekbones.

Laying her hand over his, she pressed her soft cheek against his palm and then turned her lips in to plant a kiss in it. "I know. That's why I've fed Samuel and given him to Mia; I've talked to Thomas about keeping an eye on Max and to Kian about looking in regularly on Dorian and James. Everyone who should be is under orders to wake us if we're needed for *anything*, but right this moment, we aren't."

"Quinn, I can't. What if…?"

"Come on." She closed her hand around his and pulled him toward their bedroom. He didn't manage to finish his protest before she got the door closed behind them.

Once he was alone with her, his objections didn't seem so important. He looked down into her deep gray eyes, and she nodded.

"See? It will be okay."

The fire had been stoked high enough that the room was warm, despite the howling outside the shuttered window. The bed was turned down and the pillows fluffed; the blankets looked soft and inviting.

He took a deep breath, letting the tension slip away. The all-consuming urge to *do something*, to fix everything, to help everyone didn't fade completely, but it subsided, the way it only ever did when he was with her.

She must have felt it; she wrapped her arms around his waist and relaxed into him.

He ran one finger along the soft line of her chin, turning up her face and bringing his lips down to hers, suddenly very aware that the two of them hadn't been alone together like this for a long time.

It wasn't long enough – could never *be* enough, but for a little while he allowed himself to get lost in her, to slip away and not be anything but hers – the king to her queen.

And then they slept, wrapped in each other's arms, buried in the blankets and their love.

The only interruption came late in the afternoon when Mia knocked so softly she didn't even wake Quinn.

"Everyone is fine," she whispered as she handed Samuel to William. "Thomas said if you don't trust him to handle a few doses of meds by this point, he'll disown you, and that if he needs to ask a guard to stand outside the door to keep you in here, he will."

Although he could have come up with any number of them, he decided not to offer a retort. Instead he smiled. "Tell him I'm lucky to have him, Mia – and you as well. Thank you."

When Mia was gone, he carried his cooing son over to the bed.

"Oh no. I thought we were quiet," he said when he saw Quinn's open eyes.

"You were." She sat up, propping herself against the pillows. "*He* wasn't." She reached for the baby.

William sat down on the bed and snuggled over to her before setting Samuel in her arms and kissing her hair. The tiniest noise Samuel made when he was awake could rouse her – it was like she had an extra sense that alerted her. He loved it though, loved everything about cuddling like this with his beautiful little family, rubbing his thumb over his baby's chubby, silky foot while he nursed, his wife resting her head against his shoulder.

It was these moments in the midst of chaos around them that reminded him what they were all fighting so hard for.

By lunchtime on the second day, though, he was he was grateful he'd been able to get any rest at all.

James, who had been doing better the day before – awake and responsive, at least – spiked a fever shortly after breakfast. Nothing William did could make it come down, and James stopped waking for more than a few minutes at a time.

He'd known from the beginning that Max was in serious trouble with his arm. He spent the morning performing another surgery, trying everything he knew – and even experimenting with things he'd never tried before – to fix it.

But after lunch he had to have the worst kind of conversation with Max he could imagine.

"Almost the worst," Max corrected when he used those words.

William raised an eyebrow.

"Actually…" Max looked around the room, at Thomas and Linnea and Quinn and Samuel who were gathered near the bed. "I can think of many worse conversations than this one. It's just an arm, right?"

"It won't grow back, you know," Thomas said.

"Neither, apparently, will your sense of humor, little brother."

Thomas looked at William. "Did you give him the good drugs already?"

William couldn't bring himself to smile. "Not good enough. I'm sorry," he said.

"For what, William? Not letting my arm rot off and take me with it? I suppose I could beg you to change your mind, but it seems counter-productive."

"Nothing about this has anything to do with my *mind*, Max."

"I've no doubt. I know you're waiting for me to fight you on this, Will, but… well, it would be a lot easier for me to be angry at you if I didn't know that you'd rather rip off your own arm and give it to me than do this."

"Well, I don't know if I'd go that far."

Max smiled. At least the pain medication – which Max and his men had mercifully brought plenty of – was working. "Either way, the only thing I can feel about you being here is grateful. If this had happened anywhere else, I know I'd likely be losing more than my arm. The person I'm angry with about it is dead, and I won't be, so I've got my revenge, right?"

"Let's not forget about all the lives you saved by bringing those soldiers here and being in the right place at the right time," Quinn said. "Who knows how many more villages Callum's men would have attacked if you hadn't stopped them."

"Speaking of Callum – did you find out anything else from those guards we captured?"

She nodded. "Now's not the time for you to worry about it, but just know that you really are a hero, okay? Heal quickly, though, because I'll need your help deciding how to handle some of what we learned."

"So, see, I'll be a one-armed war hero. I'll be the most eligible bachelor in Eirentheos."

Thomas lightly punched Max's good arm. "Yeah, now that I've moved to Philotheum, you might actually have a chance with the ladies."

"You're not going to let him anywhere near the saw, are you?" Max asked William.

"No. I was thinking Linnea."

Max chuckled. "You be careful. She punches harder than Thomas."

Although he knew that not all of Max's optimism was real, that Max was mostly being an amazing brother while trying to keep his own spirits up, the encouragement did help William get through the surgery.

Thomas assisted him, as he'd done more than a few times before, but his usual running banter was absent, traded for meticulously following William's every direction and occasionally leaning down to whisper reassurances into Max's ear.

"He can hear me," Thomas insisted once, when William looked over at him.

"Well, I sincerely hope he *can't*, but I know he feels your support, T."

Quinn was waiting for him when he finally emerged.

So was Mia – though she ducked immediately into the room with towels and a steaming bucket of bleach-smelling water.

He laid his forehead on Quinn's shoulder.

She wrapped her arms around his waist without even checking to see if he was covered in blood. "Thomas said it went well."

"Better than I thought I could do. He's going to be fine – all things considered, anyway."

Quinn's news wasn't nearly as good. Sometime in the middle of Max's surgery, James had taken a decided turn for the worse. The other healer had tried what he knew – even some traditional things William wouldn't have used, but at this point, every effort was worth making.

In the still-dark morning hours of the third day of the storm, with everyone in the house awake and gathered together, James lost his final battle.

# ALLIES

ALTHOUGH THE NEWEST STORM had dumped more snow on them than the previous one, this time there were so many people around to help that they dug out much more quickly.

Not as fast as some, though. On the second day after the snow stopped, Zander was outside when he heard shouts. He stopped clearing the ice over the well in the pump house and ran into the yard. By the time he got there, several guards were working to pull open the gate to let Nathaniel and Tobias in.

Curious as he often was, his interest was not enough to make him want to be in the house when they heard the news. Quinn and William hadn't even sent a message to Stephen until this morning.

He was freezing, even more so when he finally got the water running again and it sprayed his clothes, but he still stayed out and shoveled snow. It took an icy wind blowing snow up under his frozen cape before he finally trudged through the back door.

"The water's been working in the kitchen for a long time," Kian said when he opened the door for him.

Zander busied himself shaking the snow out of his cloak and boots and setting them up to try. "That was the idea."

He was expecting that everyone would be buried deep in meeting together in the front room and that he could slip by to go sit in front of a fire somewhere, but when he walked by, the door was open.

"Zander!" Linnea called.

He closed his eyes and sighed, but he went into the room, surprised to discover that only Quinn, Linnea, and Thomas were inside.

"Nathaniel and William went to see Max. William wants him to check Max's arm." Quinn must have read the confusion in his expression.

"Oh. And Tobias?"

"Talking with Dorian, I think," Linnea said.

Thomas took one look at him and walked over to the fireplace to lay another log on the grate, and that was when Zander realized he'd done it again – avoided the one thing that would have made him feel better. He went and sat down on the tall brick hearth. "So how is Nathaniel?"

Quinn looked over at him. "His stay in Valderwood gained us the support of their head councilman and most of their militia. They're willing to help us secure three other villages in the river valley as well as provide our troops with supplies."

"Wow." Zander rubbed his hands together, trying to warm them faster. Thomas handed him a steaming mug of tea. "Thanks."

"Sure." Thomas perched on the brick seat next to him.

"So…" He took a careful sip of the hot drink. "If Nathaniel and Tobias can travel through the mess out there then so can others."

"Yes," Quinn agreed.

For a moment, he stared into his tea, mulling over the right way to phrase his next thoughts, but then decided it was time to stop hesitating over things. Max had lost an arm, James and Ben had lost their lives – the least Zander could do was lose his shell. It wasn't doing him any good, anyway. "We have to get ahead of them, Quinn. You've been reacting defensively to them forever. They're always a step ahead of you. We have to make the first moves for a change."

"Do you have any ideas for accomplishing that?" she asked. "I don't think we'd be successful storming the castle like they did."

"No. Not yet, anyway. I think that should be the ultimate goal. But right now they're probably expecting that."

"Expecting what?"

They all turned to see Marcus standing in the doorway.

"Sorry," he said. "You were just having the conversation with the door open."

"Come in," Quinn said. She explained what they'd been talking about as Marcus closed the door and came in to sit down in an armchair.

Between the fire and the hot tea, Zander was finally thawing out, so he stood and walked over to sit on the couch across from Quinn and Linnea. Thomas joined him.

"I agree with you, Zander," Marcus said. "They're probably expecting us to storm the castle. I actually got the impression from one of the prisoners we captured that they're surprised we haven't already."

"We had to have surprised Tolliver and Ivan just by not being in the castle when they attacked," Thomas said. "Their whole original plan would have depended on that."

Zander nodded. "But taking all this time to act on anything has disrupted any advantage we might have had on that angle – not that we've had the manpower to act. Now that we have the soldiers from Eirentheos and the support of the Valderwood militia, though, I think we need to move as quickly as we can. Luckily, the weather has to have impacted them as much as it has us." He looked at Marcus. "Did any of the prisoners give you any hints of what Callum's goal was in attacking that village?"

"You mean, besides destroying a village because people in it were supporting Quinn?"

Zander bit his lip, thinking. "They were also looking to draft more soldiers. Was there something special about that village – was it a stronghold of the Friends of Philip or anything?"

"No. It was just a village. I've spoken extensively to the men who came from there. I can't figure out why it was targeted."

"Then it probably *wasn't*."

Quinn stood and started pacing between the maps. He recognized her rigid posture – she'd figured out the same thing he had.

"So what village is next?" she asked after several minutes. "If they're going to destroy my whole kingdom, piece by piece, where do they start?"

Marcus was on his feet in the next instant, poring over the large map spread on a table. "Hopefully the loss of Callum and his men was enough to at least buy us some time," he said.

Zander pressed his fingers against his temples. "I think *that*, right there, is what we have to stop doing. We have to stop just responding to them."

Marcus turned and raised an eyebrow. "I agree."

"But… You do?"

"I do, Zander. I've been thinking about it, trying to decide how to approach this. We need to figure out how to get ahead of them, but also establish Quinn as a strong ruler."

"Exactly. So what do you think we should do?"

"Well, I have some ideas, Zander, but I would love to hear yours. If you were in charge, what would you suggest?"

Zander stared at him for several seconds, still unsure, but Marcus looked sincere – truly interested in what he had to say. So he took a deep breath. "I think we should make our own moves first. Look what just happened when we – when Quinn and Nathaniel – made the first move with Valderwood. They didn't wait until the village was in danger, they didn't go in an emergency, they went in and made allies."

"Making allies wasn't my purpose." Quinn was staring at the map, but Zander knew her thoughts were somewhere else. "I sent Tobias and Nathaniel there to help, that's all."

"You don't think the people in any other villages in your kingdom need help, Quinn?" He knew the answer. They'd had this conversation over the past days. He knew she didn't want battles and war – and suddenly he saw a way she might be able to regain her kingdom by doing exactly what she would have wanted to do in the first place.

"So you think I should just go help them?"

"Yeah. I mean, I don't think every situation will look like Valderwood, and I think sometimes you're going to flat out have to ask for their support and for volunteer soldiers – but I think you should be the opposite of Tolliver. You don't need a castle to be their queen. The prophecy wasn't a building. They don't need you to be in the capital city, they just need their true heir. All you have to do is be her."

Zander didn't know how long they stayed in the room planning and strategizing their first moves. He only knew that it had been long enough that he should have been exhausted and hungry, but he wasn't. He was energized. Here, finally, was something he felt like he could do – a problem that he could solve.

Nathaniel and William both joined them, and the discussion was lively, overshadowing the grief they'd all been dealing with for the past couple of days.

Eventually, sometime late in the afternoon, they were interrupted by Mia, who had clearly been trying to keep Samuel happy for just a little too long, and they all decided to break until after dinner.

Zander wasn't ready to stop; he was so engrossed in making notes and studying maps that he didn't notice for a long time that he wasn't alone in the room. When he glanced toward the window and caught a motion out of the corner of his eye, his heart nearly stopped.

"Sorry," Linnea said.

"It's okay. It's my fault for not paying attention to the world around me." He didn't ask the stupid question this time. The skin under her eyes was puffy and pink – but all of them looked like that right now, probably himself included, though he couldn't remember the last time he'd seen a mirror. "What are you doing, anyway?"

She shrugged. "I don't really know. Just watching."

"Watching me make an idiot out of myself?"

Her eyebrows knitted together. "Don't do that, Zander – you were just finally getting confident with something. It was … nice to see. Don't spoil it."

He stared at her for several long seconds. "I don't know how to respond when you say things like that," he finally said.

"Join the club," she said, chuckling. "I hear it's a large one."

Perhaps laughing should have felt wrong right now, but it didn't. Instead, it was… cathartic. He'd never understood the meaning of that word until now. Once they started, neither of them could stop. He was afraid the noise they were making would disrupt everyone and bring them back into the room, but even though the door was open, nobody came.

He wasn't sure when Linnea's laughter turned to tears; he only knew that when he looked at her and saw the glistening drops running down her cheeks, he wanted to cry, too.

Maybe he did – he couldn't really tell, and Linnea never said anything. All he knew was that he pulled her into his arms and held her there for a very long time, until her shoulders finally stopped heaving, and the front of his shirt was soaked.

"Sorry," she whispered when she finally pulled away.

*That* word broke something so deep inside of him that he couldn't even get out a response before she turned and exited the room.

He stood there staring at the door she'd gone through, struggling to remember how to breathe.

The room was dark except for the flickering light of the dying fire when he finally registered Marcus' silhouette in the doorway. The way Marcus was looking at him gave him the impression that he'd been standing there for at least a little while.

"Come on, Zander," Marcus said quietly. "Dinner is ready."

# REIGNING

FOR THE FIRST TIME since leaving the castle – probably for the first time since her coronation, really – Quinn felt like she actually sort of knew what she was doing.

Zander's strategy worked. They started by sending troops to some of the more isolated villages, spreading the news that Quinn was alive and fighting for her kingdom, and offering whatever help they could provide to the people there.

Not everyone was immediately receptive. In at least one village, Kian reported seeing men leave, headed for the direction of the capital.

She surprised everyone when she told him to let them go – her fight was with Tolliver, not her people.

That worked, too. As she slowly gained the trust of the people, the number of her supporters swelled, and even some of her most hostile detractors became at least neutral.

Her army grew so rapidly it became hard to contain. At this rate, she was going to have to give Tobias an entirely new property after all the damage they'd done to this one, constructing shelters and supply buildings to create a strong base for the army and house guards. Of course, he insisted he didn't mind, but they did what they could to establish bases in other areas to minimize the impact on one place and to spread out her troops.

Despite the harsh winter that kept disrupting their movements, often keeping everyone locked inside for days, within less than three moons, Quinn's troops had the entire region secured. The Friends of Philip was no longer a clandestine resistance, but a powerful force.

So far, they'd had two run-ins with Tolliver's army, but her troops had won both battles easily, causing severe damage to the other side while sustaining few casualties themselves.

Zander, of course, was the one who noted exactly what was keeping Tolliver's troops mostly at bay – any time he used forces containing Philothean soldiers, many of them would defect to Quinn's side during a battle.

Tolliver and the army captains he'd chosen were apparently relying on force and threats – often against wives and children – to draft men into his army.

In the second battle – a particularly victorious one in the valley between Milldale and Greybell – twenty of Tolliver's Philothean soldiers turned on their captains during the initial assault, beheading two high-level officers from Dovelnia.

The initial soldiers who'd banded together and come to find Quinn on their own were mostly young men without wives or children – men who weren't as easy to threaten, because they had so much less to lose.

It wasn't until they dug deeper, and had the chance to talk to some of those who defected during battles – or who were taken prisoner – that they'd discovered the real depths of Dovelnia's reach.

She had to admit that Tolliver's plans had been well-laid and careful, built over a long time. Much of the groundwork had probably been done by Hector, long before he'd even made public his plans to put Tolliver on the throne. Quinn wondered how much of the initial stages had happened even when her father was alive.

Hector had been nothing if not patient.

For many cycles, the officers and leaders among the Philothean guards had been carefully chosen – those with strong family ties in important cities and villages.

Those families had been lavished, with property, food, gifts. They'd spent time in the royal court of Dovelnia. They'd been promised much more. If Tolliver were to become king, they'd have power, too.

The only mistake Hector had made – and Tolliver had certainly not bothered to correct – was in ignoring those people and places they didn't feel were helpful to them. They'd concentrated all their efforts on the capital and other stronghold cities in the middle of the kingdom and on the borders, but they'd ignored the smaller ones in rural areas. The entire mountainous western region of Philotheum – where Tobias lived – was open to Quinn.

Once she understood what had been done to her guards – and what her people so desperately needed – she concentrated her efforts on meeting their needs. Whenever guards defected from Tolliver's army, she dispatched troops to do whatever they could to get the man's family to safety.

In every town they contacted, the first priority was securing the town against invasion, getting food and supplies into protected places, and always leaving enough guards to mount an adequate defense.

News of the safe havens spread through the kingdom surprisingly quickly, and soon many of the villages were overwhelmed with refugees – most of them willing to defend and fight, too.

At the beginning of the war, Tolliver's troops had controlled the borders successfully. Quinn didn't dare send her troops anywhere near the major towns there. Now, though, the situation in the border towns was slowly improving – at least along the Eirenthean border.

It had taken both Quinn and Max arguing with everything they had to keep Stephen from traveling to Philotheum himself after Max's injury. The letters had flown back and forth between the two kingdoms for days. After the second day, Stephen's response time had improved so dramatically that Quinn had been terrified – she knew he was traveling, and she also knew that the border was then a place Tolliver was enjoying a much greater advantage.

After an impassioned – angry – letter from Max, Stephen had finally listened and gone back to his own castle, but after that, he'd dedicated so many troops to the effort at the border they were finally starting to make some headway. Two weeks ago, Stephen's troops had successfully taken the border crossing at Estora and now occupied the town.

Quinn had worried about that occupation at first, but Stephen gave the same instructions to his troops that she'd been giving to hers – they housed themselves and provided whatever supplies and help they could to the townspeople. Stephen's troops had the added advantage of more healers trained in Nathaniel and William's medical knowledge. Within days, the entire town of Estora was solidly united against Tolliver.

The castle and capital city, however, were untouchable. They were still unable to even get communication in or out of there. Two of Tobias' birds never returned after attempts to get messages to a Friends of Philip safe house northeast of the capital.

All of this was why, on the day that Marcus handed a letter to Quinn and she flipped it over to see the royal seal of Philotheum, her heart nearly stopped.

She must have made a noise, too, although she didn't notice, because Linnea pushed herself off the couch and came over to see.

"What bird brought this?"

"Larya."

She frowned so hard that a sudden pain rushed from the back of her head to her temples. "How is that possible?" Zander's bird had just carried a message to the military base outside Lincliff this morning.

As if just the name of his bird summoned him, Zander knocked once and then opened the door and poked his head inside. "Can I come in?"

"Isn't it a little late to ask?" Linnea gave him a sideways glance as she stepped back to make room for him.

Quinn narrowed her eyes at Linnea's tone – she needed to have a conversation with her sister *today*, but first she looked at Zander. "Do you know anything about Larya bringing this?"

He shook his head. "I didn't even see her. I was helping put a temporary roof on the new barracks. It looks like another bad storm is getting ready to roll in."

"Do you want me to open it?" Linnea asked. "If it's from Tolliver and he's already taken over the base at Lincliff we might want to know."

"I can handle it." She slipped her finger under the flap and broke the green wax seal. As she read, her mouth fell open, and by the time she finished, she didn't know whether to cheer or throw the letter across the room. Instead of doing either, she shoved it into Marcus' hand. "It's from Jonathan."

"From *Jonathan?*" Zander spluttered. "At this point, he'd better be writing from beyond the grave."

"You'd think, but no. It's intelligence. Apparently several castle guards disappeared two days ago along with a massive stockpile of weapons and food meant for a mission."

Zander frowned. "I don't know if that's good news for us or bad news."

"The way Jonathan writes, it sounds like he thinks it's good news."

"Yeah, well, Jonathan hasn't bothered to contact us in the entire three and a half moons since we left the castle, so I don't know how I feel about his opinions."

Quinn sighed. "Neither do I."

"I don't suppose he at least knows what happened to Ellen and Charles?"

"He does. They're in a town called Wellham."

The name was barely out of her mouth before Zander was over at the map on the wall. She knew he'd find it.

Marcus looked up from the letter, finished reading. "And Tolliver is planning to send troops to attack Wellham and arrest them."

"Or he was," Quinn agreed.

"Until his weapons disappeared?" Linnea said.

"That I don't actually know. It sounds like he may still be planning on it, but now Jonathan doesn't know how or when."

Zander turned around, though he kept his finger on a spot on the map. "But why now? Why wait all this time and then contact you out of the blue to tell you something like this? Let me guess. He heard you have troops and supplies?"

"Well, that's my guess, too, but he didn't say why he's contacting me now."

"He said he would be in touch again soon," Marcus said, folding the letter and setting it on a table.

"How did he get *in touch* this time?" Linnea asked. "How did he get ahold of Zander's bird? Where is he?"

Quinn scoffed. "It's Jonathan. He didn't disclose any of that – I don't think I'd put money on *ever* getting answers to all of those questions."

She looked down at the floor, rubbing the back of her neck – until the sound of the windows suddenly rattling distracted her.

Wind. Again. And already the sky was spitting tiny frozen drops against the windowpanes, crackling like gravel as they hit.

"Apparently we won't get any more answers at all today. Can you two go and make sure everything is closed down for the storm? In a little while we'll get Max, Nathaniel, and Tobias all in here and we can discuss this news."

Linnea started to follow Nathaniel and Zander out of the room, but Quinn dashed in front of her and closed the door.

"Is everything okay?" Linnea asked, frowning.

"It is with me." She didn't add the obligatory, "except for what we just found out about the war," statement – after this long, they were all too used to that to bother complaining.

The expression on Linnea's face changed from concern to suspicion. "And what do you think is wrong with me?"

"I don't have any idea. That's why I'm asking."

"I'm fine."

"Really? Then what was that with the being rude to Zander back there?"

"He was rude just sticking his head in!"

"As he's been doing when he knows I'm discussing something with Marcus every day for moons now, Nay. I don't have a secretary, and Zander outranks any guards who might be out there. He's not the problem. Or, at least, his part of *this* problem is not the one I'm discussing right now."

Linnea's cheeks went through three colors as she collapsed sideways onto a loveseat.

Quinn closed her eyes and took a deep breath, consciously checking herself to make sure she wasn't talking like a queen. She took off her shoes and climbed up on the arm of the loveseat, tucking her feet under a cushion near Linnea's legs.

"You know, back when we first got here, I thought you and Zander were getting along pretty well – it seemed like the two of you were talking a lot and… I don't know. It was nice. But ever since James died… it's been different. You're snappy and edgy with him all the time."

"I'm almost eight moons pregnant, Quinn, and we're in the middle of a *war*. My stomach is so huge I'm surprised I fit through doorways. I'm snappy and edgy at *spoons*."

Quinn set her elbows on her knees and her chin on her hands and stared, waiting.

"What?"

"Linnea, I've been *your* sister for entirely too long now to fall for that kind of nonsense."

Linnea huffed. "I liked you better when you were all shy and nervous and new."

"Yeah, well, I liked you better when… Okay, never, actually. I thought you were pretty awesome the first time I met you, and now that you're my sister I think I must be the luckiest person in the world and I love you to pieces. So I'm not going to leave you alone until you tell me what's going on."

"You're insufferable."

"I learned from the best."

Linnea sighed, picking at a loose piece of cream-colored yarn on the blanket that hung over the back of the seat. "I don't know. Everything you just said is true. I know I've been horrible the whole last couple of moons, but I don't know *why.*"

"You haven't been horrible to everyone, Nay. Just to Zander."

Linnea's eyes widened. "Did he say something?"

"No. Honestly, I think he either doesn't notice that you're only doing it to him, or else… I don't know. It's kind of like he thinks he deserves it or something. He's been different around you, too."

"Did you jump down his throat about it, too?"

"Never mind. You are cranky to everyone."

"See?" Linnea kicked playfully at Quinn's foot.

Quinn rolled her eyes. "But no, I didn't talk to him because he hasn't been *mean* to you, just more distant than he was. And besides, while Zander and I can talk about a lot of things together now, I have a feeling *this* topic might never be an appropriate one for him and me."

Linnea was giving her a death glare now, but Quinn decided she didn't care. Whatever was going on was making Linnea more miserable than she needed to be already.

"Did you two kiss or something, Nay?"

"No!" Linnea's response was so emphatic and immediate that Quinn knew she wasn't lying, but the brilliant magenta that lit up her cheeks and forehead gave away the rest of the story.

"Oh, Nay." She slid down onto the cushion beside Linnea, scooting as close to her as she could get. "You like him."

"No I don't."

She raised an eyebrow.

"I have a dead husband and I'm about to have a baby. We're in the middle of a *war*. I can't go liking a man from another world that my sister used to court. So no, I don't."

Quinn reached for Linnea's hand and squeezed it. "I don't think it works that way. All of those things might be true, but none of them have anything to do with how you feel."

Linnea made a noise in the back of her throat. "I don't know how I feel."

"That's probably because you've loaded it all up with all of this other stuff about what you should and shouldn't be allowed to feel. I'm not going to tell you what I think you should do, because I know I can't anyway."

"There's nothing for me to do, Quinn. It's just how things are."

"No. You still have choices. For starters, it doesn't matter even a little bit that Zander and I once dated. In case you haven't noticed, I'm married now, and he doesn't have feelings for me anymore. So as far as this little list you're keeping in your head of why it's impossible – you can cross that one off. You've got enough real issues without inventing ridiculous ones."

She chuckled, which made Quinn smile – and her heart ache. None of these things felt like excuses to Linnea. Everything just hurt.

"Nay..." Her voice was nearly a whisper. "The last thing Ben would ever have wanted is for you to hold yourself back from something good for his sake."

The entire piece of yarn was going to come loose from that blanket – Linnea already had it halfway unraveled. "I know that. He was a guard – we had that conversation before he ever proposed. I think he'd come back and yell at me if he found out I wasn't happy."

"Ben yelling at you for any reason is not something I can picture."

"Okay, maybe I meant I'd have done that to him if the situation was reversed."

Quinn smiled. "That sounds more accurate."

"That's why you love me."

"It is one of the reasons, yes…. So, if it's not actually about me and Zander, and it's not really about Ben… what is it?"

"You already said it, Quinn. When you said I shouldn't hold myself back from something good. You might be right about that – but how do I know what's good? Even if I did like him, I don't know how he feels about me."

Quinn knew. Although she wasn't sure Zander was aware of the answer.

"And even if he liked me, so what? I'm still about to have another man's child, and it's not fair to ask anyone else to take that on, least of all a guy who might want to go back to his own world someday if that's ever possible."

Quinn closed her eyes. She couldn't argue with that.

"And if that wouldn't be enough on its own – we're still in the middle of the war here, and he's a guard."

He was a guard Quinn hadn't been sending to battles, who'd been "safely" ensconced with them at Tobias' house ever since the incident that had cost Max his arm. She told herself it was all because Zander was much more valuable to her in the command room, planning and strategizing – and that was true – but she couldn't deny that part of it was how much killing Callum and seeing what happened to Max had affected Zander. He might have been a born planner, but he wasn't a fighter.

And she knew there was also at least a small part of keeping him here that was because of the same thing Linnea was saying.

It wasn't safe to be anyone right now – least of all a guard.

And Linnea had already been through too much of that.

So instead of launching any more of the arguments that had seemed so well-planned when she'd first thought of them, Quinn held out her arms toward Linnea for a hug.

"I'll try to be nicer to him, okay?" Linnea said, after a few minutes.

"Okay."

"Ooh, feel that."

Quinn laid her hand over the place Linnea pointed to on her belly. Underneath, the baby pushed and twisted, maybe snuggling up to the warmth and pressure. "Well, at least something good is coming soon," she cooed to Linnea's stomach.

# PIMAEUM

ONCE UPON A TIME, William had told her that winters in this world were milder than the ones in the mountains of Colorado where she'd grown up.

She no longer believed him.

The newest storm brought raging wind and pounding snow for the better part of a week.

When the sun finally appeared after six days, it took eight men three solid hours to dig open Tobias' large barn.

Of course they'd heard nothing from Jonathan during the snow. Travel would have been impossible for even the most adventurous bird. But once the storm ended, the weather turned clear and bright. Quinn found herself watching the sky much too frequently, waiting for more answers, wanting some kind of a plan – or at least to know what Jonathan really wanted from her.

But no message came.

They sent birds out looking for him, too. Larya, of course, but Aelwyn and Raeyan also spent hours searching.

All of them returned with empty canisters.

By the third day, when the snow had melted enough to contemplate traveling again, Quinn and her advisors resumed their plans for slowly pushing their occupation east, into the more central regions of Philotheum.

After a full day of planning, Kian and thirty other guards left Tobias' to meet up with a larger regiment at the Lincliff base before they made a move on a new village.

They returned two hours later escorting Jonathan.

Forewarned by a message, Quinn, Marcus, Maxwell, Zander, and Ethan were waiting on the porch when Kian led Jonathan through the gate.

Kian clearly trusted Jonathan less than Quinn did. He'd forced him to dismount before Tobias' property came into view, and had escorted him personally. Jonathan's hands were tied behind his back, and Kian's sword was drawn.

Quinn wasn't convinced that was necessary, but if she was being honest it sort of amused her, so she didn't say anything. She wondered if having a prince brought before her in shackles was "queenly" enough for her uncle.

Jonathan, for his part, didn't seem disturbed at all. In fact, when they stopped at the bottom of the stairs, the way he smirked up at her answered her question.

"Nice place you have here, Your Majesty."

She shrugged, watching his expression. "I suppose it's not as impressive as a castle, but it will do."

"Yes, I'm sure it's been a lovely temporary dwelling – but don't you think it's about time to get your castle back?"

This time, his tone made her chuckle. "You say that like it's just a matter of walking in the door."

He grimaced. "It may be just a tad more complicated than *that*."

"And what do you suggest?"

He twisted his head from side to side, looking at the guards who held him. "Any chance you might untie me and then we could discuss it somewhere other than knee-deep in the snow?"

Quinn glanced down at the clean, shoveled steps under her feet and then at her unbound wrists.

Jonathan laughed out loud. "My darling niece has indeed learned something about being a queen."

She looked at Kian. "You've got his weapons, right?"

"Yes, Your Majesty."

"You can untie him. Marcus and Zander, please take him to the sitting room for me."

Although Kian was clearly on edge about leaving her with minimal security, Quinn invited only Max, Zander, and Marcus into the room with her and Jonathan.

Jonathan stared at Max. "I guess I've missed quite a bit."

"Only everything," Quinn agreed.

"Who was responsible for that?" He nodded to Max's arm.

Max cleared his throat. "I don't know whose arrow it was — some poor drafted kid who's dead now. But I hold Callum Haddon responsible."

"And Callum — where is he?"

"He's no longer a problem," Quinn said.

"Impressive." Jonathan walked toward the map on the desk, but Zander stepped in front of him.

"There's another map on the wall if you need one," Zander said.

Quinn nodded at him — the one on the desk showed all of the information about where her troops were stationed and their movements.

"You don't trust me at all, do you Quinn?"

"Should I, Jonathan? I haven't heard from you in moons, and then you just show up here out of the blue, alone — why would you be alone? And how did you find me anyway?"

"Really, Your Majesty? Did you think you could keep your location secret forever when you're establishing a formidable army in one section of the kingdom? It took a while, I'll admit, but you can hardly expect it's still a secret at this point. And speaking of your army – do you think I'd be standing here to talk to you if I'd tried to get through to you with guards of my own?"

She glanced at Marcus. He didn't say anything, but at this point she could read his face so well she didn't need him to. They could buy Jonathan's explanation – for now.

"So what made you decide to show up here now?"

Jonathan laced his fingers together, staring at his hands for a minute before looking back up at her. "You've done well, Quinn. Better than I would have expected. You have the support you need to do this thing. Word has spread – even to the parts of the kingdom you haven't been able to reach. And Stephen's troops are making major headway up through the border. But you're out of time. You need to get your kingdom back under your control before the tide turns."

A cold chill crept from her neck to her knees. "Out of time *how?*"

"You have, I imagine, begun to get reports from your easternmost bases about increased cases of pimaeum?"

Zander let out a dark oath.

Her knees went so weak she had to lean against the back of an armchair. They'd been battling the illness sporadically all winter. William and Nathaniel couldn't figure out where it was coming from, but treating everyone around each case of infection had been helping, and they'd been able to find a way to make more medicine. Lately, though, it had been getting harder to keep up.

"You have to realize there are no depths to which Tolliver will not sink," Jonathan said. "They tried it at the castle before the invasion, with infected blankets and curtains, but it didn't work like they'd intended."

*She closed her eyes.* Except on Linnea, who'd been susceptible because of her pregnancy.

"But those bases of yours – guards huddled together in hastily built shelters and tents? And once they figured out how much more effective it is to plant an infected *person* than an object…"

Now Quinn had to sit down.

Zander looked like steam might begin pouring out of his ears.

They'd missed it. Again. Even after Zander had pointed out that Dovelnia and Tolliver had been using "biological warfare" since before Quinn had even come to Deusterros.

"He has guards willing to risk *death* to carry this disease into my bases?"

"I don't know how much the guards are being told about what they've been exposed to. I only know that a lot of them who are sneezing are being assigned as spies. Some of them may know – he's found ones willing to work with rabid animals if you'll remember. But it's not just your bases, Quinn."

She closed her eyes. Her façade of standing up and looking like a powerful queen fell to pieces as she curled her legs against her chest.

Zander and Marcus covered her immediately, coming to stand to either side of her protectively.

"The villages…" she squeaked out.

"They've figured out what you're doing, Your Majesty. It was brilliant, and it worked. But the places you've not yet occupied are in imminent danger of destruction, and the towns where your soldiers are… many of them are already under silent attack. Well, silent aside from the coughing in marketplaces, inns, and churches."

Quinn was silent for several minutes, trying to process everything he'd just told her. It didn't work. She was going to need more time, and to talk with people besides Jonathan.

"Tell me about the situation in Wellham."

He nodded, sitting down in a chair across from her. "For obvious reasons, I wasn't forthcoming with all of the information about the situation in Wellham. The city is secure at present, and has been for a considerable amount of time. Both Ellen and Charles are there, and they've established a strong army of Philothean soldiers themselves."

Max whistled. "Wellham is awfully close to the castle to accomplish a feat like that."

"It was very risky," Jonathan agreed. "It's possible you underestimate what some people are willing to do for you."

"Willing to do for the history of the kingdom and the prophecy, anyway."

"And you, Quinn. Although I admit to seeing where you might have trouble believing that."

"*Might have trouble?* Where's your mother these days, Jonathan?"

"My mother – your father's mother – *Tolliver's* mother – is in the castle, Your Majesty. Despairing over the level of fire damage to the building, no doubt."

"And yet I only *might* have trouble trusting that my own family supports me?"

"Touché. Regardless, Wellham is a secure city with its own army ready to join yours in an assault on the castle. Tolliver had plans of sending poisoned food and supplies there, but we've stopped it. If we move fast, we can strike before he can recoup and cause more damage."

# WELLHAM

DECIDING TO TRUST JONATHAN wasn't easy. Quinn stalled for two days of intense debate and discussion. Now that she finally had a location, she was able to send messages directly to Charles, and he mostly confirmed what Jonathan was telling her, but something still didn't feel right. In the end, though, two events made the decision for her.

The first was the worst outbreak of pimaeum they'd had yet – exactly where Jonathan had told her it would happen – the easternmost town they'd occupied. The second was when her guards caught two different groups of spies much too close to Tobias' house for comfort.

Whether Jonathan was being fully truthful didn't matter. They weren't safe any longer – and neither were her people.

She'd known it all along, really. Even during the days she insisted she hadn't made up her mind, they'd planned for traveling, for troop movement, and for battle.

The hardest conversation was with Tobias.

"You're sure you want to stay here? I'm sure Tolliver knows this location now."

"Plenty of the militiamen from Valderwood will be here, Your Majesty."

"I worry that it won't be enough."

"Nothing has been 'enough' for a generation now. There's no such place as safe until we make it that way for everyone."

"I know that, but I can't help feeling that I want to protect you especially, *Uncle* Tobias."

He smiled. "You have the weight of an entire kingdom on your shoulders, my sweet niece. The least I can do is provide you with an elder who worries with the task of taking care of *you*. You can't worry about me. Whatever happens, I'll be all right."

She swallowed hard, daring to reveal one of her worst fears. "But what if you're not?"

Though he never had before, Tobias put his hands on her shoulders and leaned forward to kiss her forehead. "I'll be all right. Either in the way you define it, or in the way the Maker does. Just remember that I love you and you'll always have this place to call home. You might like Wellham, anyway. I lived there once."

In some ways, the actual travel away from Tobias' house didn't seem all that different than traveling to it had been.

They traveled in the dark again, though this time they left closer to dusk than dawn. The people in the carriage were nearly the same, only this time Max was with them as well.

Outside the carriage was different – they felt the absence of James profoundly, but they were surrounded by so many more guards this time that Marcus commented they might be safer now than they'd ever be again.

William wrapped his arms around both her and Samuel and held them tight.

Although Linnea didn't say anything, Quinn knew she had to be uncomfortable. Her pregnancy was close to full term, and in the last weeks, it had been difficult for her to get around sometimes. Watching her now in the carriage brought back unpleasant memories for Quinn, and she stretched her hand to take hold of Linnea's.

Light snow fell as they traveled, but it was nothing like the many violent storms they'd had. It didn't make their trip any more difficult. Part of her believed it was the reason their trip seemed to go quickly and smoothly; despite all of the tension and weaponry around her, the watchful guards encountered no soldiers hiding in the trees. She didn't know if the snow was a hidden blessing, but she decided to be grateful anyway.

Between her own nerves and Samuel's understandable restlessness, she didn't think any kind of rest was possible in the carriage, but she must have dozed off at some point, because she was startled awake when they came to an abrupt halt.

Across from her, Zander and Marcus stood immediately. William moved when she did, whisking Samuel from her arms so she could investigate.

Thomas and Max were alert and watching, too.

So many guards on horseback surrounded the carriage that she couldn't really see anything out the windows except capes and a streak of pinkish light in the sky, but she heard the rumble of conversation. Her traveling party was no longer alone.

She found herself moved to the back of the carriage next to Linnea and William as the rest of the men blocked them and readied their weapons.

They made nearly no noise. Even the movement hadn't woken Samuel, and Linnea slept on, curled up on Nathaniel's coat all the way at the end of one of the benches. Someone had covered her with another heavy cloak – it looked suspiciously like Zander's.

Though she was fully prepared, her hand curled around the hilt of her own dagger and an awareness of everything and everyone inside the carriage, her whole body still jolted off the bench when the carriage door swung open.

Even when she saw who it was – maybe even *because* of who it was – her heart pounded so heavily it was hard to hear.

"Charles!"

"Your Majesty!"

The greeting was less formal than it sounded, because a second later he was through her extensive guardians (after being divested of his weapons, she noticed; Marcus didn't trust *anyone*) and he had his arms around her in a tight embrace.

"You're all right?" he asked, when he pulled away.

"I told you I was."

"You'll forgive me for needing to see it myself? And the prince?" He looked around until his eyes landed on Samuel, who was awake now, sitting up on William's lap and blinking at his great uncle with enormous gray eyes. "Thank goodness you're all safe."

"Safe enough, anyway," Max said, causing Charles to turn and look at him.

"As if we didn't owe your kingdom enough already." Charles sighed.

"We've never made a great distinction between the two, and we've no plans to start now."

"Yes." Charles nodded. "I wish I'd taken that more seriously in the past and avoided some of the situation we have now."

"Well, I'm for working on solutions now, Charles, not regrets," Quinn said. "How did you find us here?"

"Because you've arrived at Wellham."


That the town of Wellham was "secured" was an understatement. A massive wooden fence surrounded the entire town, and in many places the wood had already been reinforced by walls of stone.

There were guards everywhere, lining the streets as the carriage passed through, all of them with their swords drawn, especially until the gate was securely closed behind all of her guards.

The soldiers who would continue to arrive in Wellham from their respective bases would be joining the soldiers already established in the massive camp that encircled the town.

When the carriage came to a stop again, they were in the yard of a house that was likely large by Wellham standards, but much more modest than Tobias'.

Ellen was waiting on the porch. "Interesting ruling, running away from the castle in the middle of the night," she said after she'd hugged Quinn.

"Did anyone ever tell you that you take after your mother sometimes?"

William coughed once, close to her ear, and tightened his hand around her waist.

"I've been told." Ellen cleared her throat, unfazed. "I wasn't sure *you'd* ever pick up on some of the family traits, though. I'm pleased to see I was wrong."

Behind her, she could practically hear both William's and Zander's faces turning shades of red and purple at the remark – though for entirely different reasons, she knew.

Not for the first time, something inside of her swelled in gratefulness that she was going through this with both of them.

The house where Charles and Ellen were staying had long been an important location for the Friends of Philip, Nathaniel had told her. It had once been owned by an original member of the Friends, but nobody had lived there for a long time. Instead, it had been maintained as a safe house by various Friends.

Both Marcus and Nathaniel admitted to having thoughts that they should have checked into Wellham as a possible location for Ellen and Charles, but it was so close to the capital city that they'd thought it too dangerous for anyone to attempt.

Despite the massive security of the town, they were far from safe here. Once word reached Tolliver that Quinn and Samuel were here, they would be inviting all-out attack. And it was surely only a matter of time until word reached the castle.

# SECRET PASSAGE

FROM THE FIRST DISCUSSIONS of this plan, Zander hadn't liked it any more than Quinn had.

This was too close to the castle. Although the last couple of moons at Tobias' had yielded Quinn a significant army, he just couldn't help believing that risking putting the queen herself this close to the center of the inevitable battle was a bad idea.

But there wasn't a better one.

He didn't trust any of these people as much as he wanted to. He didn't trust this house, this town, or Charles – or especially Jonathan.

Though it surprised him, he did sort of trust Ellen. She was brash and fierce, but honest. Sometimes brutally so, which he couldn't help respecting.

If William had been the punching type, he might have taken Ellen out for the comment she'd made to Quinn about her grandmother. Zander, though, was grateful when he didn't spew snot everywhere from trying to hold in his laughter.

Quinn had picked up a thicker skin over the past few moons, and a much stronger ability to delegate responsibility to those who served her.

And she'd needed those. Desperately.

He wished it relieved him that they'd made it to Wellham – all the way to this "safe house" without incident – but it didn't. Every minute they spent pretending things were normal, that they were just setting up living quarters in a new, temporary location, that Quinn engaged in idle, catching-up chitchat with her aunt and uncles in the front room of the house made his stomach churn and his hands twitch.

He tried to ignore it as he helped unload the last of the supplies from the carriage and carried them to the back bedrooms of the house.

There would be no private rooms here.

Mia was working diligently to set up a pallet on the floor of one of the rooms for Linnea, though right now Linnea was curled up on the bed that would be Quinn's and William's. She wasn't feeling well after the long carriage ride, and Zander couldn't blame her.

Samuel was asleep next to her, despite the noise of things being carried in and out and William and Nathaniel loading supplies into a large closet as Zander hovered nearby wearing his sword.

The closet surprised Zander – there weren't many of those in this world. Even in the castle belongings were stored in armoires and dressers rather than the separate little built-in rooms familiar on Earth.

He'd actually been investigating whether it would be big enough to use as a little room for himself, even with all of William and Nathaniel's medical supplies inside.

He thought it would. The storage space seemed to take up the entire wall between two rooms. Of course, Linnea might appreciate a small room to herself even more. Maybe he'd talk to Mia about moving the pallet in here in a few minutes.

The whole process of moving in to the new house should have been a rare moment of peace, but Zander just couldn't convince himself that it was.

Sometimes he hated being right.

He didn't know what the shouts and stomping and pounding coming from the front of the house meant. He only knew that it wasn't good and that the baby was back here and so he scooped the infant into his arms.

Samuel was surprised, and Zander was instantly terrified that he might cry, but apparently he was now familiar enough with Zander to be easily soothed by him.

He felt someone grab his arm by the elbow and he whirled around to face Nathaniel, who was frantically waving with his other hand for Zander – and everyone else – to follow him.

The next few seconds made no sense to him, as Nathaniel shooed everyone into the closet. Mia was helping a disoriented Linnea.

William didn't freak out until Nathaniel closed the closet door with all of them inside.

"Quinn!" he whispered frantically, and Zander heard William's hand on the inside doorknob.

"No." Nathaniel's voice wasn't loud, but it was far more commanding than Zander had ever guessed him capable of. "The baby is in here."

Knowing that even Nathaniel's words wouldn't be enough for William, whose body was nearly shaking the whole enclosed space, Zander carefully fitted Samuel into his father's arms.

The shaking stopped.

Zander strained to hear whatever was going on in the rest of the house – he thought he could hear the distant clang of metal, but the sounds were drowned out by whatever Nathaniel was doing, moving objects around in the small room.

No part of Zander could even begin to understand why Nathaniel would be worried about those things right now, let alone to risk making noise to move them, until the soft scraping and footstep noises began moving farther away – like they were falling.

Then there was the distinct sound of something small scraping against stone, and a tiny light flickered to life.

Zander put his hand over his mouth to keep from gasping out loud.

Nathaniel's face was below them, looking up from a dark, black hole, illuminated now by the tiny flickering light of a white candle. "Come on," he whispered.

William balked again, backing up toward the closet door. "Not without Quinn."

Zander would never be able to express how much he agreed with William, but he was possessed of a slightly larger piece of sanity, bolstered by his moons of guard training and war planning.

So he moved behind William and literally pushed him toward the hole.

Mia, who was perhaps the sanest of all of them, reached for the baby, but Zander blocked her hand. He needed William to need to keep Samuel safe himself.

The opening in the floor turned out to be a set of stone stairs, making him wonder just how elaborate this whole Friends of Philip safe house was. A part in the back of his mind wondered who else knew about this little hiding spot, but he couldn't worry about it.

Once they were all on the stairs, below the level of the floor, Nathaniel lowered the trap door over them.

"We can't do this. I need to know what's happening," William whispered.

The stress in his voice made Samuel whine, which, thank the Maker, or whoever it was they thanked here, got William to shut up and follow Nathaniel.

Zander grabbed one of the crates that Nathaniel had set on the steps and followed behind everyone, making sure William couldn't turn around and make a run for it.

William started shaking again when they reached the bottom of the stairs and the black space widened out into a larger area.

Now Zander moved the baby from his arms to Mia's and grabbed William's wrist, dragging him away from everyone, but especially from the stairs.

"You have to get it together, Will," he whispered.

William looked up, twisting his ear toward the ceiling as if he was trying to listen.

Zander sighed. He now remembered the story of Quinn and William under the floorboards in someone's – Ellen's? – house. "This isn't the basement," he said. "The stairs took us in the direction of the outside wall." He wasn't sure how he'd had the presence of mind to notice that, but he knew it was true. He reached up, easily pressing his hand against the low ceiling. "Yep. That's dirt. We're not under the house."

It probably wasn't a helpful thing to say. He was risking spooking William even more, but everyone needed to be on the same page with the truth. "We can't *leave* her! Or Thomas…"

Yeah. Freaking out.

"They have guards, William. They might be fine. What we *cannot* do is run into the middle of a bad situation with this child. *If* there even is a bad situation. Keep it together for a little while."

He looked over at Nathaniel, who was reaching the bottom of the stairs for a second time with another crate. "Will they be able to find us if everything is okay?"

"Marcus will. I don't know about anyone else." He walked over to William. "Marcus will take care of her."

"If he can."

Nathaniel put his hand on William's shoulder. Linnea came up on the other side of him and wrapped her arms around one of his. "If something is so wrong up there that Marcus can't take care of her, then it's even more important you're not there. She can't keep herself safe if she's worrying about you. The Maker forbid someone uses you against her to get what they want. And Samuel needs one of you. I'd sacrifice myself this instant to go help her if I thought it would,

William, but we need to find out what's going on before we take any risks with her at all."

William nodded. Even in the dim light Zander could see the flash of understanding form. "She's the one who can keep me calm in a dark basement, you know."

"Yeah, well, just remember not to kiss anybody this time, o...kay?"

The remark would probably have had them all laughing, if Linnea's voice hadn't sounded so ... *not right* on the last word. Now Zander noticed she was breathing a little heavily, too.

"Ow, Nay!" William's voice was a bit louder than the whisper they'd all been using. "You're about to take my arm off. Are you okay?"

"I'm fine."

"You'd better be. I am not replaying the whole dark-basement scenario again, with or without kissing."

*Good.* William was sane again.

"Well," Nathaniel whispered, "as Zander figured out, we're not in a basement. We should be under the barn in the back of the house. But we're not staying here." "We're going back up now?" Zander asked. He didn't think that was a good idea at all.

"No. Mia has Samuel, so can the rest of you grab crates?"

"Okay," Linnea said. Her voice still didn't sound normal, "I don't think I can do a crate, but give me the baby."

Zander hoped they weren't going far. He didn't know where to find one of the long cloths they often used to tie Samuel to someone so he wouldn't fall. Of course, he couldn't understand how they could be going anywhere at all.

Crates in hand, they all followed Nathaniel across the space, which was larger than Zander would have expected. When they finally reached the farthest wall, the candle's light no longer stretched far enough to illuminate the stairs they'd come down.

There was nothing here, though, nowhere else to go.

Or perhaps he was wrong. He heard a faint rustle of something soft, and then the distinct click of a door. *A door?*

Yes, there was a door here. It had been hidden behind a black cloth, undetectable in the dark underground room unless you knew where it was or brought a *lot* of light with you.

"Are you ever going to tell Quinn everything you know?" he asked Nathaniel once they were through the door and inside what looked like another black passageway.

"Do you wish anyone up there right now knew about this? Perhaps it would have been great if Thomas had come running back and followed us with someone on his tail?"

He closed his eyes. "I guess I just don't know how you managed it."

"Oh, you could become an expert at revealing limited information from people in two different worlds without too much trouble, I think, Zander."

"I couldn't," Linnea said, her voice sort of normal again.

"No." Nathaniel chuckled as he led them down the – long – whatever it was. "You couldn't. It's yet another reason I might not have told everything to *Quinn*. And anyway, I'd never anticipated having to use this place as a safe house ever again. I'd rather had hopes of using the property for a clinic in Wellham – all of this might have been turned into excellent laboratory and storage space."

William's shoulders were beginning to tense up again, so Zander decided to interrupt. "Wellham is going to need a clinic after we finish killing Tolliver. That bedroom is the perfect size for an operating room."

# CAUGHT

IT HAD TO HAVE been planned, Quinn knew. That much was obvious. There was no other explanation for how perfectly it had gone.

Sure, her soldiers outside had put up a decent fight once they'd realized what was going on – but it had happened too quickly and unobtrusively for them to understand in time.

One minute she'd been standing in the front room of the safe house with Marcus, Ellen, Charles, Dorian, and Thomas, and in the next instant everything had dissolved into pure chaos. There were swords and yelling and green cloaks everywhere, but she couldn't figure out which were her friends and which were her foes.

She still couldn't explain exactly what had happened herself. All she knew now was that she was in a moving wagon, alone. Her dagger was gone. She'd planted it in the side of the first man who'd put his arms around her. The shock of seeing him drop to the ground had distracted her for too long to grab it back before someone else had tied her arms behind her back.

At that point, panic had overtaken her. Her only thoughts had been of being pulled away from Samuel and Will as two men took hold of her and carried her outside. Oh, she'd tried to fight back. She'd kicked and yelled, but without her hands, and without her dagger, she'd been completely ineffective.

And she regretted it now. If only she'd been calm – or calm*er* – she might have been able to take note of faces, to see the horses, to understand something more than the inside of this small carriage.

She had no doubt about where she was being taken, nor about who – ultimately – was behind this. Her mind was filled with the choice words she would say to Tolliver when she saw him.

If she wasn't killed first.

No – thinking about what she was going to say to Tolliver was much better than allowing bleak thoughts. Her body already ached for Samuel, but she wasn't going to make the mistake of freaking out again. Samuel had been in the back of the house with William and Linnea. Wherever they were right now – even if it was in another carriage – William would be freaking out, she knew. And they had an agreement. She would stay calm.

The tunnel went on for much longer than Zander expected it to. This was elaborate. "How long has this safe house been here?" he asked Nathaniel. It was getting easier to talk in a normal voice. They were now too far from the house to possibly be heard, and there had been no signs of anyone following them. Perhaps nobody else had known about the tunnel.

"A very long time."

"Who does the house belong to, anyway?" As far as he knew, Ellen and Charles had been staying there on their own, along with Ellen's husband and some guards. He didn't have any idea where

Charles' family was, but then Charles had always been careful and secretive about them.

"It belongs to the Friends of Philip. Nobody lives there anymore."

"But who used to?" This time it was William who asked the question – Zander already knew the answer.

"It was Tobias' wasn't it?" he asked.

"Yes."

"Then surely some other people knew about this place and this tunnel from the beginning of the Friends of Philip, right?"

Nathaniel stopped walking and turned around to face him. Even in the dim candlelight, the sadness in his eyes was unmistakable. Again, Zander knew the answer before it was spoken. "Other people did, yes. Once."

Several minutes of silence followed that statement, broken only by a small gasp from Linnea. He looked at her in concern, but the venomous glare he got back in exchange made him look away immediately. Maybe her arms were only getting tired like his were. The crate he was holding seemed to get heavier with every step. Samuel looked fine, so he could leave it be for now.

He didn't know how far they'd gone when the tunnel changed noticeably. What had been packed dirt under their feet, and dirt walls supported every few feet by wooden beams changed to hard, solid stone all around them.

The temperature dropped, too, and unless he was mistaken, it was getting lighter.

He was about to say something when Nathaniel stopped and set his crate on the ground. "This should be good for now."

"A *cave?*" William asked.

"Yes. Where do you think Tobias got the idea of tunneling back to the house? He found this first."

"Where does it come out at?"

"Go and see for yourself." Nathaniel pointed to a curve in the wall around which there was now a distinct line of light. "Take the baby with you. I'd like to have a chat with Linnea anyway."

"Here," Mia said, setting down her crate, then taking the strap of the diaper bag off her shoulder and holding it out to Zander.

Of course she'd had it the whole time. He hadn't even noticed her handling the weight of the full bag along with the crate. "You're kind of amazing," he said as he accepted the bag from her.

She shrugged. "I don't have a sword."

Even in the dim light, Zander could see that her eyes didn't have their usual sparkle. Not that she let him see that for more than a second before she turned and started investigating the supplies, no doubt making a mental inventory and deciding how to organize them better.

"We'll find them, Mia. He's all right," he said.

"You're a terrible liar, Sir Zander, but I'll pretend to believe you."

"Mia?"

"Yes?"

"If you ever again refer to me in a way that sounds like you think I outrank you, or that implies I've made a greater contribution to *any* of this than you have, I will put spiders in your bed."

She didn't look at him, but her shoulders shook for a second, and there was laughter in her voice when she answered. "No spider would dare to stay in my bed."

"She's got a point," Nathaniel said.

"Maybe so – but it's one that only proves mine."

Mia was so absorbed in her task that she wasn't even listening to him anymore. A few feet away, though, Samuel was beginning to whine.

"Come on Will, let's go explore."

The straight, narrow tunnel they'd followed here was no more, he discovered as they walked. This was a larger cavern that seemed to branch out in more than one direction. Zander headed toward the light.

After they twisted through a narrow, curved passageway, the light suddenly got much brighter, flooding the floor. Wherever they were, they'd nearly reached the outside again. He didn't think they could be far enough away from the house to be out of danger. He looked at William. "Stay here for a minute."

William bounced the baby, who was beginning to fuss again. A new smell alerted Zander to the reason. "You shouldn't go any farther, either. We don't know who's out there."

"I'll be careful," he said, pulling the strap of the diaper bag up over his neck and extending it toward William. "Here, you need this."

Anyone else would have argued with him. Quinn or Linnea would have had his head, but William just sighed and dug in the bag for a blanket to lay Samuel on. Zander was actually sort of glad he was alone with William – he would have gone anyway, and the arguing might have gotten loud.

He was cautious, of course, drawing his sword well before he reached the last corner, and he stopped to listen before he dared even peek around the edge of the exit. He didn't hear anything except a light trickling sound, like running water. When he was absolutely certain there were no voices or footsteps he stepped into the patch of sunshine. The full light of day was nearly blinding, so much so that he stepped back into the cave for a moment, afraid he wouldn't be able to see danger.

Once his eyes were adjusted, he took the plunge and stepped outside for real.

The scene outside was unexpected enough that it took him a minute to understand where they must be.

He stood on a rocky strip of land next to a mostly-frozen stream – maybe it was a river in the warmer months, but right now the water level was low. The trickling noise came from the very edges where moving water lapped against the frozen layer on top.

He hadn't even known he was holding his breath until he was able to exhale when he saw the rest of the landscape around him.

The entrance to the cave was at the bottom of a deep ravine; the walls of earth on both sides of the stream towered well over his head, and trees lined both sides of the ravine all the way to the edge, their roots protruding everywhere, forming a web that could obscure anyone's view.

Nobody would be able to see them down here – nobody would even *try* to look, unless they knew about the entrance to the cave already. And since they'd pretty much be toast anyway if someone did, it wasn't worth worrying about.

Out here, he could hear more noises, but they were distant, muffled by the trees and the sounds of the stream. There were definitely voices, possibly even horses, but none of them sounded like any kind of imminent threat. The town was surrounded by soldiers, after all – ones who were theoretically on the same side he was.

He was much more concerned about the smell.

There was most definitely a fire somewhere nearby; the crisp, acrid smell was much too strong and foul to be an ordinary campfire. He squinted up into the bright gray sky, searching until he found it – a thin line of black smoke.

He had a sinking feeling he knew exactly what was burning.

He ducked back into the cave.

"I don't think they're still searching for us in the house," he told William, who was just picking Samuel up off the blanket on the ground.

William sighed when Zander told him his suspicions. "I wouldn't expect anything less. I think we're probably far enough away here to be safe."

Zander nodded. They hadn't smelled any smoke in the tunnels.

Now that they thought it would be safe, William followed Zander outside for a while. The fresh air calmed Samuel a little, who was still fussy despite the clean diaper.

"He's getting hungry," William said, his voice catching a little.

"Haven't you been giving him a little bit of food lately?"

"A very little. It's not enough for him still."

Zander still didn't understand how babies worked here. In his world, Samuel would have been getting close to a year old. Aging was different here, where they lived ten times longer, but learning wasn't any slower, and William had explained to him that the newborn stage of infancy wasn't much longer in Deusterros than it was on Earth.

There was some long-winded thing about brain development that Quinn probably ate up, but Zander didn't care. All he knew was that Samuel was about as developed as a five-month-old baby in his world.

Not that he knew all that much about five-month-old babies on Earth, either. His sisters had mostly seemed like drooling blobs until they started crawling. He liked Samuel, but he really wasn't much more than a drooling blob who smiled and laughed – and fussed. A lot.

"Well, let's do what we can to keep him happy for now, Will. I'm sure between you and Nathaniel and Mia, we'll figure out a solution."

They settled for getting all three of them a drink from the stream before heading back into the cave to find everyone again.

There must have been a good supply of candles in one of the crates, because Nathaniel and Mia had lit enough of them to illuminate the whole circular cavern they occupied. It was light enough for him to read Nathaniel's expression immediately.

William clearly read it as well. "What's wrong, Nathaniel?"

"Linnea is in labor."

# UNDERGROUND

QUINN HAD NEVER ACTUALLY seen this part of the castle. It was probably ridiculous, considering it was *her* castle, the home of her ancestors, and the place she was determined would be the home of her descendants. But she'd never seen the need to visit the cells where prisoners were held before their trials.

She'd made a lot of mistakes.

Although they wore green uniforms, she'd also never seen the four guards who removed her from the carriage and held her arms tightly as they escorted her under the portcullis and into the deepest, darkest part of the castle.

She knew she should have been terrified as the men shoved her into one of the barred cells, unceremoniously slamming the iron gate closed behind her. Or at least she *once* would have been scared. Now, though, the only emotion she could summon was anger.

Once she managed to take a few deep breaths and get her bearings – small cell, one window, wooden cot with a straw mattress, one barred window, more cells circling the large room around her – her anger turned to fury.

Though all of the guards except one had retreated after locking her door, she was far from alone. Few of the cells were empty, and she recognized the faces of nearly all the prisoners who were standing by their doors, watching her.

One by one, as her eyes landed on the familiar faces, – mostly guards she'd trusted, but a few servants, too – each person dropped to his or her knees, bowing their heads in respect.

She didn't deserve it.

Tears dripped down her cheeks as she looked in each cell – she'd left them here, to fend for themselves, these people who'd been loyal to her, who'd believed in her, who knelt before her still.

"Oh enough of that, Your Majesty," said a voice – the most familiar one of them all; this one turned her dribble of tears into a torrent. She turned to a cell quite near hers and looked into the too-kind eyes of her head housekeeper, Ruth.

"I'm so sorry," she choked out. "I didn't mean to…"

"Hush. We know you did what you had to do to protect Prince Samuel. And even in here, we've heard about what you've done out there."

"Nothing to help you."

"We've held our own, most of us, Your Majesty. We're only worried about you now."

Across the room, the lone guard cleared his throat, but he didn't approach.

Far from intimidating her, as she was sure his noise was intended to do, it stopped her tears and brought back her focus.

Yes, she was sorry she hadn't made every right decision as queen, ever. Yes, she wished she'd been able to protect every loyal person in the castle the night she fled.

But now wasn't the time to allow her past mistakes to dictate her future. She couldn't fix the things she hadn't done right before, but she didn't have to make the wrong decisions now.

"What do you think I need to know about right now?"

Ruth's gaze fell to the floor for a moment, but then she looked Quinn in the eye. "Tolliver has been certain of your capture for days, Your Majesty. I didn't believe it myself – until five minutes ago. I've been hoping he would publicly humiliate himself with the victory speech he has planned for this afternoon."

Quinn's heart sank into her stomach. "This afternoon?"

"Yes." Ruth nodded to one of the high windows. "They're already decorating for the public celebration."

She bit her lip and swallowed, trying to keep back the bile that wanted to rise in her throat.

"Do you know who is helping him?"

Ruth shook her head. "As I said, I really didn't believe the rumors. From everything we heard, you'd been doing so well – amassing an enormous army in the west. I wasn't sure those of us down here would survive, but I was certain you would."

The second part of Ruth's statement didn't need to be said out loud. The optimism was gone. Everyone in the dungeon was bowing before her not because they believed she would bring victory and salvation, but because they were paying their respects.

"How far apart are the contractions?" William asked.

"Getting a lot closer. She's been in labor most of the day, I think."

Both William's and Nathaniel's voices were calm and focused, the way they only reliably were in a medical situation.

Zander didn't know what to think. Most of the day? "How long has this been going on, Linnea?" he asked. It had been at least the whole time they'd been in the tunnel; he understood that now.

"Does it matter?" she spat. "At what point today would it have been convenient?"

Though the anger in her words might have been intended to rile him up, the tiny catch in her voice did exactly the opposite. It broke him into pieces.

This wasn't an added inconvenience in an already dire situation. This was the birth of her child. Of Ben's child.

This was supposed to have happened in a nice room in a castle with a midwife and Ben next to her, not in a cold, dingy cave with her brother and Zander while she worried for the safety of everyone else she loved.

If he were in that situation, he wouldn't have wanted to admit going into labor in a carriage or an unsafe "safe house", or a tunnel, either.

"I think we're safe here." He could barely force his throat to create more than a whisper. "Nobody will find us."

Nathaniel nodded.

What must have been a contraction hit her then, making her close her arms around her belly and her face scrunch as she worked hard to breathe.

"Do you need to sit down?" Zander asked, reaching toward her.

She shook her head, taking a small step back from him. "This is better."

"That was only three minutes," William said, when she'd finally relaxed and was breathing normally again.

Suddenly, Zander felt panic for a different reason. "She's not due yet, is she?"

If Linnea's eyes had been daggers, Zander would have been dead on the spot, but he was more worried about her safety than what she thought right now.

"It's a few weeks early," Nathaniel answered, "but late enough that I probably wouldn't be able to stop it even if I had a way to with the supplies we have here."

"What can I do?" He hoped desperately that whatever they needed from him, it wouldn't be delivering a baby.

"Well, I could really use a fire and some clean water. I don't know what's going on outside this cave, but I know we're not leaving it without another baby."

As if to punctuate Nathaniel's point, Samuel picked then to start crying in earnest.

Zander needed air. He didn't say anything as he headed back out of the cave to look for firewood. He needed to find a way *not* to think about what any of this meant, how dangerous it might be – and he definitely didn't need to have time to wonder about the rest of their friends who'd been in that house.

He needed a task.

His foot hadn't even hit the ground outside the cave when he heard a screeching sound that made him jerk back and hit his elbow on the rough stone surrounding the narrow opening.

"Seriously?" He muttered an expletive under his breath as he rubbed his elbow, grateful he was wearing his leather arm guards and cloak. It still hurt. "I would have seen you if you'd made a reasonable noise too, you know."

The bird didn't look remorseful in the least. If anything, it was regarding him reproachfully.

"What did I do wrong now?" he asked.

Larya made a clicking sound and looked up at something behind his head. He turned.

Zylia was up there, perched on one of the tangled roots sticking out of the dirt cliff.

He didn't know how a bird could look worried, but this one did. "She's in there, Zylia." He pointed. "She's fine." *Depending on your definition of fine, anyway.*

Zylia blinked at him, but stayed where she was. Larya squawked again.

Zander frowned and knelt down to open her canister. It was empty, but the bird was still tipping her head impatiently, even pecking his hand with her beak. He fished in the inside pocket of his cloak where he always kept something for her and pulled out a piece of dried meat, but when he held it out to her, she didn't take it.

"Who do you want me to send a message to?" he asked. He hadn't discussed the idea with William or Nathaniel, but trying to communicate with anyone right now seemed like a bad idea. He didn't know who'd betrayed them, but someone obviously had, and it could too easily have been one of the people he thought they could trust. Jonathan, Charles, and Ellen were all suspect right now.

Tobias was probably trustworthy – or he at least wanted to believe that he was. But what could Tobias do from where he was anyway?

Back inside the cave, Linnea made a noise that set his teeth on edge. Zylia disappeared into the cave with a quick flutter of her wings. He couldn't figure out whether his own urge to run to her or away from here was stronger, but he knew who he should send a message to.

He knelt down to dig for paper and a pencil.

Even if her supporters in the castle prison had resigned themselves to defeat, Quinn hadn't.

She'd worked too hard, earned the trust of too many people. She meant the promises she'd made to them about peace and safety, and she would fulfill them.

Everyone was watching her, she was aware of that, but she couldn't worry about what they were thinking – at this point she didn't even care about the guard in the corner who would barely take his eyes off her long enough to blink.

She paced back and forth in her cell trying to think. She needed more information, but didn't know how to get it.

Twice now, she'd climbed up on a wooden stool to get a look out the window high in the wall. The view confirmed what Ruth had told her. The whole courtyard in front of the castle was decked in gold and green, except for a few black and red banners that didn't belong at all. She wondered if she'd been put into this particular cell for the purpose of seeing this.

She could do this – whatever happened today, she could do this.

Or she would die. In front of her entire kingdom. What would William do if that happened? What about Samuel?

She was trying to push those thoughts away, physically *push* them into the stone of the back wall when the sound of a door slamming open interrupted her, making her spin around, trying to hide the damp front of her shirt by crossing her arms.

No amount of planning or self-talk or even flat-out *imagination* could have prepared her for who was coming across the center of the dungeon.

A second later, Sophia was standing in front of the door of her cell, ordering the guard to open the lock.

Quinn's entire body felt like it had turned to jelly. By the time Sophia stepped inside the bars and toward her, she had to look to see if she was even still standing, because she didn't understand how she could be.

"Where is Samuel?" Sophia demanded.

Those words were enough to do it – for the woman to *dare* mention her son's name like she had a right to know where he was. The jelly in her bones hardened right back up – into steel. The same steel hardened in her eyes and she turned them on Sophia, but she didn't answer.

Sophia reacted as if she hadn't expected an answer – she'd mastered this game long ago, unfortunately. Her eyes narrowed as they swept downward over Quinn, piercing deeply enough to make Quinn's arms clench tighter over her chest – but it didn't help. "Clearly you've been with him recently. You didn't bother to follow any of my advice even for your own purposes. He'll be discovered, you know. Wherever it is you've hidden him, it can't be far. And how long can he go without you, anyway?"

She didn't know how, but she managed to keep herself from flinching – or knocking the woman flat with her fist.

"And what is that you're wearing? *This* is how you present yourself in public?"

It was getting easier to just stare, to just ignore and tune out whatever Sophia was saying. Her grandmother – if she lived through today, that term would have an entirely different meaning to her than it did to most people – was, of course, dressed in a green velvet gown that swept the tops of her glistening black boots. Her gray curls were secured back with an elaborate green and gold barrette. The thing that drew Quinn's attention the most, though, was the red satin sash tied around Sophia's waist.

Quinn couldn't even remember what she was wearing, and she wasn't going to look down to check now. Although it wasn't a dress, it couldn't have been terrible – wrinkled, maybe, after being *captured and thrown in prison*, but she didn't need to look to know that the clothes themselves were worthy of her station. Even amidst war and traveling, she'd still had Mia to attend to her wardrobe.

Sophia finally got frustrated with her inability to get a reaction from Quinn – or else she'd never intended to do anything more than stand in the cell for a moment and hurl insults. "I guess you don't want my help or advice."

*What was your first clue?* Quinn wondered, though she didn't say anything. In truth, she was surprised at how little she cared about anything Sophia was saying – maybe being betrayed by her had its perks.

"Apparently we'll have to see how you handle yourself on your own in public in an hour. Although, if I were you, I would at *least* consider changing."

The statement didn't make any sense. The cell was empty except for a rough wool blanket on the cot – surely whatever she had on was better than *that*, even if it was wrinkled.

But then, Sophia held her hand out toward the guard who stood at the entrance of the cell. He handed her the strap of a simple, white canvas bag. Sophia dropped it unceremoniously on the cot before turning and exiting. She was all the way out of the dungeon by the time the guard had finished re-locking Quinn's door.

# SURPRISES

ZANDER HAD FINALLY MANAGED to get a small fire going just inside the first part of the entrance to the cave – it had taken him a while to figure out how to obscure any smoke without sending the fumes into the larger cavern – when a soft scuffle of talons on stone alerted him that Larya had returned.

He whirled around to face her. "Is it really too much to ask for you to follow *one* direction without just doing what you want to do anyway?"

She lifted the canister toward him.

"There'd better not be a new note in there, bird. You shouldn't have taken my note to anyone except Stephen, and an hour is *not* long enough to get to Eirentheos. You're going to get us killed!"

He had to fight to keep his hand steady and not be rough with the bird as he popped open the canister and reached inside.

Larya – as usual – was smug, already butting her head against his pants leg as if he'd be so happy when he saw the note that he'd give her *all* the treats in his pockets.

She'd been right about that before, but when Zander unrolled *this* note, he wasn't happy at all. Instead, he thought he was going to be sick.

He still reached into his cloak pocket and emptied it onto the ground in front of the bird, spilling both dried meat and some seeds he'd saved.

Because she'd done exactly what he'd asked her to.

The note in his hand was from Stephen.

And there was only one way the king of Eirentheos could have sent a response that quickly.

"What am I supposed to do about *this*?" he mumbled.

Larya looked up at him for a moment, but then returned to hunting the largest strips of meat from the cave floor.

"Zander! Can you bring some water, please?" Nathaniel yelled. The tone in his voice completely negated the "please", so Zander grabbed the bucket of water he'd meant to put on to boil and ran into the larger cavern.

He was just in time to be there for the part he'd been hoping to miss, but he really was needed.

Mia was entirely occupied with a crying Samuel; she carried him out outside just as Zander came in. William and Nathaniel both looked completely calm and were focused intently on their tasks – which he knew meant they were stressed past their ability to do *anything* except keep Linnea and the almost-arrived baby safe and alive.

So he ignored everything in the room except Linnea's face and he went and knelt next to her pile of blankets on the floor, facing her. He reached for her hand, grateful when she allowed him to take it, and he brushed her hair back from her sweaty forehead. "You've got this," he told her.

"I don't think I do." Her hand closed tightly around his, and he helped her pull herself up so she was sitting more than lying down.

"All right Linnea, one more time, I think." Nathaniel's voice was steady and soothing – but not all that helpful.

"You have it," Zander said. "Let's meet her."

She squeezed his hand so hard he wasn't sure he'd be able to use it again today, but he didn't care. He didn't say anything else – he knew she didn't need words – he just held her up, and squeezed her hand in return.

After a long, tense, loud moment, there was a tiny squeak, and Zander helped Linnea lie back onto the blankets.

"Beautiful, Linnea," Nathaniel said. "Here sh… Well, this is a surprise." A second later, he laid a tiny, still-slippery bundle on Linnea's chest. It wasn't nearly as disgusting as Zander would have imagined – well, maybe it was a little – but even so, it was so amazing that he couldn't stop staring.

Nathaniel laid another blanket over both of them. "It's a boy."

Zander's eyes darted to Linnea's face, worried she might be disappointed, but the light in her gray eyes told him the tears on her cheeks were anything but sad ones. She ran her fingers through the thin wisps of black hair on the baby's head.

"He's *so* little," she whispered.

It was true. The baby's head was barely bigger than Linnea's hand. Zander was used to Samuel, but even so, this one seemed miniature. "Maybe that explains the fast labor," he said.

"No. Being Charlotte's daughter explains that," Nathaniel said, smiling. "There's a reason she didn't make Stephen move into his own apartment after the first few babies."

Linnea still looked concerned. "Is he all right?" she asked.

Nathaniel nodded. "He's pink and he's breathing; he looks perfect, really – and he's already hungry."

That was also true. The baby was making grunting noises into his mother's neck.

"I think he's just small," William agreed. "We could definitely use some *warm* water in here now, though."

Zander had a hard time peeling himself up off the floor and away from them, but he did. "I'll be back in a few minutes."

Quinn approached the white bag on her cot as if it were a snake that might bite her. For all she knew, it contained one.

She looked over at Ruth's cell; the kind woman only shrugged before turning around and picking up a book.

At least the people in prison for their loyalty to her weren't being tortured.

None of the other prisoners were looking at her, out of respect, she supposed. The guard's eyes still flicked to her every few seconds, although less intently than before. Maybe he'd expected her to make a break for it when Sophia had come in. She wasn't that stupid.

There was no private way for her to change clothes. Not that she had any intention of wearing whatever Sophia had brought for her. But she was curious.

She lifted the bag before she opened it. The fact that it was heavier than it should have been for clothes made her even more wary.

For a minute, she really wasn't sure that she would open the bag at all. Whatever was inside could easily be infected with pimaeum or coated in shadeweed powder. Eventually, though, her curiosity won out. If they really wanted to poison her, they'd put it on her bed or in her food, anyway. She untied the heavy string.

The heavy green silk that poured from the bag was almost the richest material she'd ever seen. Even as queen, she'd only seen dresses this expensive and fancy twice before — at her wedding and at her coronation.

She thought she was going to be sick. Waves of nausea washed over her as she took in the beautiful details of the gold embroidery and lace.

*What kind of sick joke was this?* She'd known these people were manipulative and evil, but *this?* The nausea faded as quickly as it had come, replaced with a red, raw fury that was so consuming and distracting that she almost didn't see the heavy object that fell from the folds of the fabric and landed on the cot.

She had to throw the bag back on top of it to conceal it.

*What in the?* She looked around at the other prison cells and at the guard. Nobody seemed to be paying attention or like anything was out of the ordinary.

She reached into the bag again. There were other items inside, but they were innocuous – sort of. There was a hairbrush and a set of golden combs. All of this was a game for someone, but she had no idea what the rules might be.

Under the guise of smoothing out wrinkles, she carefully patted down the rest of the dress, checking for anything else hidden inside. When she didn't find anything, she sneaked another peek at the object now hidden under the dress and the bag.

Yes, it was exactly what she'd thought in that first glimpse. A dagger. A shiny, heavy, well-made dagger with a gold and green inlay in the hilt. It was even in a leather sheath that could be strapped to her ankle.

Or to her arm, if she was wearing that dress with its loose, flowing sleeves.

*It could be a trap. It's probably some kind of trap.* But she didn't know what kind. She went over and over it in her head as she shrugged out of her shirt and into the soft silk slip she'd also found in the bag. Her privacy now concerned her much less than keeping the weapon hidden. Everything she might need was here, except shoes – and the long dress would conceal her black boots, which weren't terrible in any case.

It probably was a trap – but as she stepped into the dress she could almost *see* Zander standing next to her shrugging. If it was a trap, she was screwed anyway – and having a weapon had to be better than walking into it unarmed.

"Do you have superpowers I don't know about?" Zander asked Mia when he got back to the small cavern near the entrance where he'd built the fire.

Samuel was perfectly calm – asleep, actually, against Mia's chest where she'd secured him using some kind of cloth – it might have been her own undershirt stretched over her clothes. He didn't care what it was; he was impressed.

Not only was Samuel fully tended to, but the fire was stoked nicely, and somehow making less smoke than the smaller one Zander had been working with, and a bucket of water was starting to bubble over the embers.

"That's something from your world again, right?" Mia asked, frowning.

"Superpowers?" He chuckled. "No. In *my* – in the world I came from – they're imaginary. Here they might be real, at least in this cave."

"How's Linnea?"

He smiled again. Mia didn't like compliments any more than he liked being called by his title. He could work with that. "She's good. It's a perfect little boy."

Mia's eyes lit up like Christmas morning, though she rolled them as she grinned. "Leave it to Ben to make sure this day would be as happy as possible even if he wasn't here."

He frowned. "How does Ben being wrong make it happier?"

Mia reached for the bucket as she spoke. "He knew she really wanted a son first – a boy who would carry his name. Besides, as much as she'd deny it most of the time, she loves having older brothers."

Zander moved her hand out of the way and put on one of his leather gloves before he retrieved the hot, heavy metal container. "Still…"

"So if he told her it was a girl, she'd have no choice but to celebrate – either she'd be happy that he was right, or she'd get her son."

His mouth fell open as he stared at her. "You think Ben was that…"

"Clever? Sweet? Maybe a bit conniving? Yes. I know he was."

He raised an eyebrow. He wasn't so sure.

"It's always the ones you think are quiet who can surprise you, Zander. You knew Ben a little, but think about it… he married Linnea."

"If you say so, Mia. You're tiny and quiet, and you surprise me almost all of the time, so…"

She laughed. "In any case, just wait until King Stephen hears the news. He might be the only disappointed one. Four grandsons and counting."

Ordinarily, Zander would have made a comment about how King Stephen still had plenty of baby girls at home. But he wasn't smiling now. *The note.* He looked around for Larya.

"You might murder me, Zander, but she's not here."

"What?"

"I read the note from Stephen – and I answered it. With our location."

"Why would you do that, Mia? He'll come here! There are soldiers out there. He could get killed!"

"Most of the soldiers out there are on our side, Zander. It's true we don't know which ones. There may still be some of those who betrayed Quinn's location. They may be searching for us. It's not safe for us to go out there with one guard, two healers, and women and babies. But *most* of them are not dangerous. If Stephen didn't come *here*, where do you think he would go?"

He closed his eyes, the horrible knowledge dawning on him. "The castle."

"Exactly. I have no idea what he was thinking coming as a king into this situation. I suspect his only thoughts were for his children – including Quinn, and probably the two of us – but would you rather have him and his troops come here, or go to the castle?"

He sighed. "Maybe that baby in there knew exactly what he was doing." If Linnea hadn't been in labor, he'd never have messaged Stephen right now.

Mia's green eyes pierced into him. "Thank the Maker."

Swallowing hard, he nodded. "I'd better get this in to them."

"Yes."

Even before he was inside the larger cavern with his bucket of water, he could tell something was wrong.

Linnea was making noises she shouldn't have been, and the baby was crying – in William's arms instead of his mother's.

Zander was lucky only a little bit of the scalding water splashed up on his leg as he set the bucket down hard.

"What's going on?" he asked, running up to William. His body was the one shaking now. "She's not supposed to still be in pain like that, is she?"

He didn't know if it was his special "healer" mindset, or what, but for once, William was a lot calmer than Zander. "She is if she's still in labor."

"What do you…?" he looked over at Linnea, then at the baby, then back up at Will, not understanding at all – until he did. "There's another baby?"

"Yep. Surprise."

Just then Linnea let out a scream much worse than any noise she'd made the first time.

"William! I need you!" Nathaniel called. "I think this one is breech."

Zander had only the vaguest idea of what that meant, but it didn't sound good, and his heart raced as William shoved the baby into his arms and ran over to Nathaniel and Linnea.

The baby was still crying and messy. Zander looked around helplessly. He saw Mia in the doorway – she must have come to investigate the yelling – but as soon as she took a step toward them, Samuel stirred, and then he started crying, too.

Mia carried him out again. Superpowers or no, nothing about this environment would calm Samuel down – and another crying baby would be the opposite of helpful in here.

He looked down at the new baby again. His face was turning red from the screaming, but his little foot had slipped out of the blanket and was starting to go blue. *Think, Zander.* He couldn't go over and help Linnea through her ordeal this time, but he could take care of her son.

"Okay, little one. You're precious, but you're disgusting. Let's get you cleaned up."

He carried the infant over to where he'd set the bucket of hot water.

Though he would never understand how, he managed to tune out all of the chaos and the noise as he tended to the newborn. There was probably more screaming, more worried shouts, more sounds that he had no desire to ever hear in his life, but for those moments, all that mattered was the child in front of him.

By the time the tiny boy was clean and wrapped in a new warm blanket, he was quiet, sucking on the side of his fist as Zander held him and swayed gently back and forth. Quiet enough for Zander to hear Nathaniel's tender voice say, "Ah. Here she is, Linnea. Your little girl."

# WAITING

IF THERE WAS ONE thing Quinn hated more than anything else, it was waiting – being forced to do nothing when all she wanted to do was take action.

When she'd first put on the dress and carefully hidden the dagger up her sleeve, she'd been terrified, her eyes darting from one person in the dungeon to another, trying to figure out if any of them had noticed.

But there was no quicker cure for her terror than boredom.

Now, after what had to have been at least an hour since Sophia had come, her emotions cycled rapid-fire, from fear, to anger, to rage, to apathy and back again.

She wasn't even afraid that the dagger was a trap anymore. It would at least provide her a way to never return to this cell again, to be stuck agonizing over where William and Samuel were, and Linnea, and Thomas, and… She reached up the sleeve of her dress to check the straps of the sheath again, making sure the weapon would be secure, but slide out easily the moment she needed it.

Her hand was still up her sleeve when the dungeon door clanged open again.

*Guess I deserved that for getting bored,* she thought, as she watched two new guards converse with the one who'd been watching her the whole time.

Blood pounded behind her ears and under her arms as the two guards approached her cell.

Only one of them came inside her cell. He had a rope in his hands. The other stood outside with his sword drawn.

It was *so hard* to fight the urge to pull her dagger out right then; she'd never before so fully understood how Zander had been able to kill Rahas and Callum. But it wouldn't accomplish anything right now – she had to repeat that like a mantra as the man moved behind her with the rope. She would only get herself killed for no purpose if she attacked him right now, so she didn't.

But then, as he pulled her wrists together to tie them, his fingers landed on the solid, heavy shape under her sleeve.

He pressed down, hard.

The whole world started spinning. Images flashed in front of her – her mother, Jeff, Annie, her birth father… and then Owen, and Will, and Samuel. Her coronation, her wedding… her wedding night… falling asleep in William's arms the other night. She squeezed her eyes closed and bit down on her tongue until she tasted blood.

The guard finished tying her wrists together and then pushed her forward, out of the cell.

Mia was right, – if Thomas was smart, he would just engrave that phrase on a stone wall somewhere, *Mia was right* – the soldiers surrounding the town of Wellham didn't pose much of a challenge to Stephen and his troops. In fact, their arrival helped weed out those soldiers who were loyal to Tolliver. The battle, if it could be called that, was over quickly and was almost bloodless.

The biggest challenge in the whole ordeal was getting Nathaniel, William, Mia, Zander, Linnea, and the three babies up and out of the ravine where the entrance to the cave was located.

Stephen dropped to his knees when he saw his daughter with his grandchildren for the first time. Tears streamed down his cheeks as he held the babies and kissed them tenderly everywhere – on the tops of their tiny heads, their miniature hands, and their feet.

As Zander had suspected, Stephen didn't have any favorites between the two. Although he practically burst with pride over the news of a long-awaited granddaughter, he spent just as long memorizing his new grandson's face and whispering blessings into his ear. When he'd finally handed one of the infants to Nathaniel and the other to Zander, he scooped Linnea into his arms, lifting her all the way off the ground and holding her for a long time.

Zander couldn't help comparing the scene to the one he imagined with his own father, which wouldn't have been much like this at all.

He didn't hate his father; he wasn't even angry at him anymore, at least not the way he'd been before he'd come to this world. The whole being an adult thing was so much different – harder – than he'd imagined it, and his dad had probably been doing the best he knew how. But after watching Stephen, and after seeing William emulate his own father with his son … Zander knew what kind of man, and perhaps father, he wanted to be someday.

Maybe the parents you learned the most important things from didn't always have to be your own.

Indeed, once Stephen had finished tucking Linnea and the babies under blankets inside a warm, guarded tent, and he'd embraced William long and hard, he turned to Zander.

"Would it be too much to ask?" he said, holding out his arms.

There was no part of Zander left that even wanted to try to object; he just accepted the hug.

"Thank you for taking such good care of my children."

*That* Zander could object to. "I think they took just as much care of me. Probably more."

"That's the way it's supposed to be. I'm still grateful for what you chose to do on your own. Also, don't backtalk when I'm thanking you and telling you that I'm proud of you."

Okay, so Stephen was *way* better at this father-thing than he could ever hope to be.

Zander decided it would be easiest just to change the subject. "So what have we missed being down in that cave?"

"I'm still trying to figure that out myself," Stephen said. "We just heard on the way here to you that Quinn was captured?"

"Yes. Along with Thomas, Max, Dorian and Marcus at least. I assume Ellen and Charles are gone as well?"

Luke had been standing nearby, ignoring their conversation while it was personal – he'd spent some time reuniting with Mia, himself – but Zander knew he'd been listening to the last part. "As far as I've been able to glean, everyone from your main traveling party was taken, except for some of the guards who escorted you. Percy Kilpatrick was killed in the attempt to stop the soldiers who took them. Nobody knew where the five – now seven – of you were. Ethan Power was afraid you'd been killed when the house burned. We had to stop him trying to go into the mess and search. Now he's in a healing tent having his burns looked after."

William got the words out just barely before Zander. "What? Is he hurt badly?"

"I don't know," Luke answered. "He was still walking, so I don't think it's too serious. I think he's more upset about not being able to defend Quinn and Thomas and Marcus and Dorian than anything."

"So we know they were all taken to the castle?" Zander asked.

Stephen nodded. "That's the best we can assume. We heard a rumor that Tolliver is planning something big at the castle today – some are speculating that it's his coronation."

Zander closed his eyes. "You wouldn't think hearing something like that would surprise me at this point.'"

"Does it actually?"

He looked back up at Stephen. "No. It doesn't. What does surprise me is that you're here. What were you thinking?" It wasn't until the words were in the air with no hope of him retrieving them that he realized how inappropriate it was to speak that way to a king.

Nobody commented, though. Either they were too preoccupied, or they'd just accepted that Zander was never going to learn.

"My children are here, Zander. And I swore a long time ago to defend the alliance between Eirentheos and Philotheum. When I heard that Quinn was mounting an attack against the castle…"

"You thought you'd put yourself in danger, too?"

"How can I be trusted to rule a kingdom if I'm not even willing to fight for my family?"

Zander didn't have an answer for that one. "So what is your plan?"

"Our plan *was* to be a surprise second wave for Quinn's assault on the castle, but now that they have her, and we were detoured here, I really don't know. Protect my children – that's it. And kill Tolliver if we can manage it."

"Can you add Sophia to that list?"

"I haven't ruled it out."

"Let's do it then." Zander looked down, straightening his cloak and tightening his belt, but when Stephen didn't answer him after a minute, he looked back up, wary.

Stephen's eyes were a strange mixture of apology and… something else.

"What?"

"I have a favor to ask of you, Zander."

"I am *not* staying here while a king runs off to put himself in danger. It's not even up for discussion." He was beyond certain he was crossing a line now, but he didn't care.

Stephen took a step closer to him, but there was nothing threatening about the movement, if anything the king's eyes were only gentler and almost... pleading. "Zander... what I'm asking has nothing to do with keeping you away from the battle. It's a personal favor." His voice was low. Nobody else would have been able to hear him even if they hadn't all moved and intentionally begun another conversation.

"The first regiments of soldiers have already gone to the castle. I don't plan on being involved in a power move. I plan on being there to show my support if – no when – we declare victory. That's not the place to make your stand, Zander. We still don't know if there are more traitors here. I need a guard I can trust completely to stay with Linnea and Mia and my grandchildren. I'm not asking you to stay out of the most important place – I'm asking you to stay *in* it."

He didn't know how to argue with that. "All right," he agreed.

# DAGGER

QUINN DIDN'T UNDERSTAND WHY there wasn't a knife in her back right now. The guard knew about the dagger – knew she had something up her sleeve, anyway. Not that she had any idea how to get the dagger *out* of her sleeve with her hands tied, especially not with people watching.

Perhaps she'd been wrong – there were situations it could be more dangerous to walk into with a weapon up her sleeve. Especially in front of hundreds of people.

She was imagining several of those possible situations when the guard who held her elbow said in a low, gruff voice, "Watch your step."

She looked up at him so quickly that she almost didn't heed his instructions, but she caught herself in time to avoid tripping over a stone that had somehow fallen out of the wall in the hallway he was leading her down.

"Thank you," she said quietly.

They'd reached the end of the hall, stopping in front of a huge double set of wooden doors. She was familiar with this part of the castle. These doors led to the main courtyard in front of the castle; this entrance was often used for servants to travel to and from the kitchen during parties.

Today, she was apparently the main course.

There were other people coming up the hall behind them; there were no voices, but she could hear the heavy, steady, clatter of boots on stone.

She wanted desperately to turn and see who was coming, to know who was around her, to understand what Tolliver might be planning for her and the people she loved. But she'd never be able to conceal that peek from the guard, so she looked up at him instead.

She didn't recognize this guard, either. He hadn't worked in the castle when she'd lived here; he wasn't an officer she'd met with. He was just a young-ish man, maybe in his mid-twenties, with sandy brown hair and bright blue eyes.

Maybe he noticed her questioning look, or maybe he'd been somehow planning to tell her all along, but when he looked back at her, he muttered under his breath, "I'm from Dorvale. My wife and children were there."

*Dorvale.* The name of that village would be burned in her memory forever – the village where James had saved the children, exchanging their lives for his own. She'd spent the last moons directing her soldiers to find homes for the people displaced there. Many of them had come to live at the army bases themselves, where Quinn knew they'd be provided food, shelter, and safety. The harsh winter had probably made it impossible for many of them to communicate their new whereabouts to their families in other places, though. Especially to guards in the castle.

"All of the children were spared," she whispered. "And none were without at least one parent."

There was no time for any other words. The doors in front of them opened then and he moved forward with her, escorting her down the long stone walkway.

Long before they reached the center of the main courtyard, she knew she was in the middle of her worst nightmare.

The entire plaza was filled with people, all dressed in their celebratory best – furs and heavy velvet capes against the winter chill, even though the day was sunny. The light breeze blew straight through the silk fabric of her dress, although she was rather certain it wasn't the only cause of the goose bumps that erupted all over her body.

The guard held her elbow all the way across the courtyard, and up the carpeted wooden steps of a tall platform that had been erected in front of the audience.

Even before she reached the stairs, her appearance caused a reaction in the waiting people; a cacophony of boos, whistles, cheers, and applause grew from a small stirring to an enormous swell.

She nearly stumbled on the second step from the top – but this time it wasn't because of an obstacle in her path.

At least not of the physical kind. What she saw up on the platform made her whole body weak.

The guard caught and steadied her before walking her the rest of the way to the middle of the stage, stopping just before they reached Thomas, Max, Marcus, and Dorian. He positioned her just to the side of Thomas and then moved behind her; they were so close to the green velvet curtain hanging behind them that it moved when the guard did, so he pushed her a tiny bit forward.

Her heart was pounding so hard she almost didn't feel the tugging sensation at her wrists, and even when she did, she didn't understand what had happened for a minute.

The rope was still there, dangling from her wrists. At a casual glance, it probably even looked like her hands were still tied – but she could get them free.

In the next moment, the guard disappeared down the steps.

Once Stephen and Luke gave the orders for their troops to move out, they were gone so quickly Zander wasn't even sure how it had happened.

For all the talk of titles and war heroes, Zander knew he wasn't at that level of being a guard. He might never be. Hopefully keeping the people he cared about safe today would be enough.

William was just stepping out of the tent as he walked over to it.

"How are they?" Zander asked.

"Good, all things considered. Linnea is exhausted and sore; she'll need lots of help. I did get some food into her. The babies are small but healthy."

"How did you not know it was twins? Weren't there two heartbeats?"

"I'm sure there were, but I wasn't searching for them, and a stethoscope is pretty inaccurate. It's possible, in your world, for an ultrasound to miss a second baby if it's hiding behind the other one. In our world, though, the baby doesn't really even have to hide. Linnea was a surprise baby like that herself, from the stories I've heard."

"Does that kind of thing run in families?"

"Non-identical twins? Yes. My mother had two sets. My sisters all have a higher than normal chance of having them."

"Not Quinn, though?" He regretted the words as soon as they were out. This was not the time to be mentioning her.

William must have seen the panic in his eyes. "I'm holding it together for now, Zander. For her and for our son." Then he shrugged. "I don't know if twins run in her family or not. I guess I should ask. I'll do that later today when I see her."

He swallowed, deciding to follow William's example. Worrying wouldn't do any good while they were stuck here anyway. "I really can't decide if the whole thing is awesome or a nightmare."

"It's definitely awesome – but we're *all* going to have to help Linnea." He patted Zander on the shoulder. "I'm going to go over to the medical tent with Nathaniel and check on Ethan."

"Should I go in there, do you think?" He raised an eyebrow toward the tent.

"Just don't wake any baby who happens to be sleeping."

Only one of the three babies in the tent *was* sleeping when Zander stepped in. The baby boy was crashed out next to Linnea, swaddled tight in the top part of a much-too-large blanket meant for soldiers.

Samuel was wide awake — and not happy about being stuck inside a tent his father had left.

"Can you sit with them for a few minutes?" Mia asked, as she bounced Samuel on her hip near the door.

He looked outside to make sure the tent was heavily guarded with people he trusted. Kian was out there, so he nodded and held the flap open for her until the two of them were safely out.

"Hey," he whispered as he walked over to the large bed someone — okay, he knew who — had built on the ground for Linnea from piles of blankets. More blankets were rolled and stacked up behind her so she could be propped up, but still rest if she wanted.

"Hi." She looked up from where she'd been staring at the baby girl in her arms. Mia had even brushed out Linnea's hair and braided it back. She looked much more comfortable than she had earlier — and heartbreakingly beautiful. He knew he should know better than to think that, than to see her that way, but it was true. He'd felt it for a long time, although until right now he'd mostly been able to keep the feelings at bay.

He crouched down next to the side of the blanket-bed. "How are you feeling?"

"Don't sit on the ground, Zander. There's enough bed here for eight people."

"I'm all right."

"Let me rephrase. I'm not going to let you near my babies if you're covered with dirt."

"Now you're just avoiding my question." Still, he sat down on the blankets, keeping his distance the best he could.

"I'm not the one violating our agreement about stupid questions."

"Whether a question is actually stupid is sort of dependent on the context, Linnea. If we were in my world, you'd be in the hospital right now. I think 'How are you feeling?' is appropriate."

She smiled. "You're getting better at this."

"Yes, I am. So what about you? The truth, this time."

"I've never lied to you, Zander. Just left out details."

"Well, leave them *in* this time."

"I am…" She looked down at the baby in her arms and then at the one asleep beside her. "Amazing. I'm thrilled, and shocked, and ecstatic, and in love with these two already… and also incredibly scared, and sad, and angry."

He bit the inside of his cheek.

"I mean…" Linnea sighed. "What kind of jerk fathers twins and then goes off and *dies* without even meeting them?" She brushed angrily at a tear that had dripped down onto her cheek.

Zander reached into his pockets, searching for a handkerchief, but she shook her head at him. "Don't. I can't actually start crying, or I'll never be able to stop. And this is supposed to be a happy day."

It wasn't a conscious decision; he didn't even know he was going to do it until he already had, but he scooted up next to her against the pillows and put his arm around her shoulder. She nearly gave him a heart attack when she didn't push him away, but leaned against him, instead.

"That was a jerk thing for him to do," he agreed, pretending everything was normal, though inside he couldn't help but wonder what the heck he was thinking.

Despite their talking, the baby girl was getting sleepy. Her eyes, which were a shocking shade of blue, were closing for longer and longer blinks. Although the boy already had traces of Linnea's dark curls, the gorgeous little girl's lighter brown fluff was her father's in every way.

"Maybe not as bad as dying even after I got myself stuck in another universe to save him."

Linnea threw her head back against the pillows. "Meech! I did marry a total chok, didn't I?"

"You said it. Not me…. Of course, I have no idea what you just said."

"People don't get married in your world?"

"If you hadn't given birth *today*, I would jab you with my elbow for that."

She giggled; the sound did interesting things to his insides.

"Seriously, what is up with the weird words? I've never heard William talk like that."

"William is used to the differences between our worlds – also, he has a cleaner mouth than I do."

He dropped his jaw, feigning shock. "So I have a princess *cursing* at me?"

"Do you have a problem with that?"

"No. Actually, I'm kind of impressed."

Her laugh was more than a giggle now, it was strong and musical, and the baby girl fell asleep to the sound of it, looking comforted.

The boy, on the other hand, woke up, his eyes searching out the noise and locking in on his mother's face like he didn't want to miss a moment of it.

"And so it begins," Linnea sighed.

"Give her to me," he said, reaching for the girl, tucking her against his chest as Linnea picked up the boy.

This baby was just slightly sturdier than her brother, though she still was the second-tiniest human he'd ever held. As small as she was, though, she was perfect. He couldn't help thinking of how amazed Ben would have been at the intricately detailed little fingers, and the way her lips pursed into a rosebud shape after she sighed in her sleep.

*Ben.* He should not be here curled up next to Ben's wife and their babies.

Of course, Ben was the jerk who had told him to take care of Linnea before he went and died. What did he expect?

*Wherever I am, when I look at her, I want to see her smile.* The words came unbidden into his mind. Ben had spoken them to him that night, shortly before…

"What are you going to name them?" he asked.

"We don't do that yet in my world, remember?"

"Oh, whatever. You at least have some idea."

She chuckled again, running her finger over her son's eyebrows. "Benjamin, of course, for him. Benjamin Thomas, maybe."

"Yeah?"

"It's a good name for a twin older brother, I think."

*Did she even know how amazing she was?* "It's just right. What about this one? You've had longer to plan for a girl."

She nodded. "Ben's mother was named Adeline… Maybe Adeline Charlotte?"

It took everything he had not to lean over and kiss her. He'd never, ever, wanted anything more in his life.

But this was not the right time. He wasn't sure if there would ever *be* a right time, but he knew this was the wrong one. This day was confusing and emotional and life-changing for her as it was. Even if she returned the gesture now, she might pay the price of regretting it later, and he couldn't do that to her.

It was better that he didn't, anyway, because just at that moment, Mia came into the tent looking panic stricken.

He stood in one fluid motion, still cradling the baby. "Mia, what's wrong?"

"We've just heard a disturbing rumor from the castle. Tolliver is planning to publicly execute his captives."

# THOMAS

THOMAS HAD A BLACK eye. That was the first thing she'd noticed back on the stairs. Although the sight of it at first had made her a little dizzy and weak, now she was just angry.

"Tell me the other guy looks worse," she mumbled under her breath to him, hoping the words would carry over the noise of the crowd.

He gave a single nod.

At that moment, the noise grew louder, all of the jeers and hisses drowned out by applause. Tolliver was coming up on the stage from the other side, surrounded by four guards.

Now that she was looking in that direction, Quinn could see Sophia, on a separate platform just to the side – a platform which also contained a large, plush throne.

Suddenly, she understood exactly what Tolliver had planned.

It didn't matter now how she'd gotten the dagger, or why her hands were loose, she couldn't make this situation worse if she tried.

As the guards and Tolliver marched across the stage to stand in front of her, she slipped one hand out of the ropes and reached up her sleeve.

Tolliver was grinning and waving, exuding a kind of charm that might have made her understand how he managed to gain so many followers – if the mere sight of him hadn't made her skin crawl.

There was something wrong with his neck, though. He'd tried to disguise it with the high collar of his cloak, but the raw, red mark extended up close to his ear. And unless she was mistaken, the dark purple shadow across his cheek was the beginnings of a bruise.

She sneaked a look up at Thomas, trying to ask the question with her eyes.

He nodded once again.

She wished she could give him a high five for that right now; regardless of how it had happened.

All of her panic was gone, replaced by anger and concentration. The dagger was in her hand, and she watched for her move.

Tolliver stood in the middle of the stage, directly in front of Max, flanked by two guards on either side of him.

He'd put Quinn in an odd place, all the way at the end of the line, as if she was the smallest of his concerns as a political prisoner. She didn't know if that was because he was stupid, or if that was his game – but she did know she wouldn't be able to reach him from here without drawing the attention of his guards.

Tolliver began some grand speech – she was sure she'd figure out more about his exact plans if she listened to it, but she didn't care.

Once the dagger was out of her sleeve and hidden behind her in the folds of her dress, she scooted as close to Thomas as she could get, sidling up almost under his arm.

"It's okay," Thomas whispered without moving his mouth, clearly thinking she was seeking comfort – until she slipped the blade through the middle of the rope that bound his hands.

She saw his eyes widen, but he caught on immediately and didn't react otherwise.

Perhaps she should have been listening to Tolliver, though, because whatever he said at that moment made two of the guards turn to face her.

She slipped the weapon into Thomas' hand just before one of the guards grabbed her shoulder and jerked her forward, showing her to the crowd.

Even now, she didn't know what Tolliver was saying about her, she was too focused on the guards and the crowd.

The dagger wasn't any more helpful to Thomas than it would have been to her. It was the only weapon they had against four fully armed guards. He would be crazy to use it on one of them right now in front of the entire crowd.

Which is why she gasped out loud when the guard on the left side of her dropped to the ground.

Screams and utter chaos broke out before she could even look down at the guard. The one who'd been on the right grabbed her and pushed her body in front of his. That was when she saw the arrow protruding from the first man's chest.

Fighting the urge to look and see where it had come from, she focused on the fact that both the guard's arms were in front of her — which meant his sword was still in its sheath. She picked up her foot and stomped, hard, with her heel on his leather boot while at the same time jabbing both elbows and her head backwards into him.

It was enough; he loosened his grip just barely, but she let her whole body go limp and slid out from under him.

Unfortunately, then she was on the ground in front of him, and his hand went immediately to his side. She threw her arm in front of her face and chest, bracing herself, but the weapon never rose into the air.

The man's sheath was empty.

The next arrow came out of nowhere, hitting his shoulder. It wasn't enough to take him down, but he spun to the side, revealing the silhouette of another man behind him. This one had a raised sword. Her heart jumped into her throat until she realized the sword belonged to the guard, but the man holding it was Marcus. In one swift motion, Marcus separated the guard from his head.

More guards were rushing the stage now. Marcus stepped past the man and reached down, lifting Quinn up off the ground and tucking her behind his arm, still holding the guard's sword out.

Just as two more guards ran toward them, someone in the crowd screamed – and another one cheered. More cheers followed.

Both guards turned to see the source of the noise, and at that instant, Quinn saw it, too.

Thomas was at the other end of the stage, standing behind Tolliver. His hand was wrapped around the hilt of the dagger, and the blade was planted solidly through Tolliver's back, all the way so the tip protruded from his chest, a dark bloodstain spread down the front of his green silk shirt.

Nobody stopped him. All the guards were frozen, or at least it seemed that way. It took until Tolliver fell forward and Thomas pulled out the knife and then stabbed him again before the guards nearest Quinn even reacted.

For that long moment, they were just standing there. One held his sword down to his side with only a loose grip on the hilt as he watched Thomas stab Tolliver. She reached for it without even thinking. As soon as she touched it, the guard turned to look at her, raising the sword.

Marcus' arm closed tightly around her, pinning her against his chest. She couldn't move as he slashed at the man with the sword he was holding, getting in a good strike across the guard's arm and forcing him to drop his weapon.

The next second she felt like she was falling; she couldn't make sense of anything around her, the world spun, and her head tipped toward the sky as she felt the velvet of the green curtains twisting around her. The side of her head slammed against something, lighting painful sparks behind her eyelids. Then someone shoved her roughly, and everything went dark.

For a moment she was so disoriented nothing made sense at all. Briefly, she wondered if she was dead, but then she realized she could still hear loud voices and shouting, and the odd sound of feet pounding and metal clashing over her head.

Each loud metallic clang and heavy wooden thump resonated through her head, all the way to the back of her skull.

There was another sound, too. It was softer, and it took her awhile to force her brain to register it over the other noises and understand what it was.

"Your Majesty! Quinn! Quinn! Are you all right?"

It was Marcus' voice, moving closer and closer to her face.

By the time his eyes appeared in her line of vision, she understood where they were.

He'd pulled her off the stage and then pushed her under it. Now his body was between her and the gap, blocking the light, but also keeping her safe, though it didn't seem like anyone was after them right this second.

"I'm fine, Marcus. I think, anyway."

"You're bleeding." He touched the side of her forehead gently with his thumb, making her suck a breath between her teeth.

"Are you all right? And Thomas! Max!" She struggled to sit up, nearly managing to bump her head on the underside of the stage again before Marcus pushed her back down.

Nausea twisted her insides into a wicked swirl; she couldn't even move her head before she was sick right there on the ground between them.

Marcus' eyes went wide with alarm. He used his elbows to pull himself closer to her, ignoring the mess on the ground.

"Quinn…"

"I'm okay." It was mostly true. She was conscious, anyway, which had to be a good sign. Although she wasn't sure she *wanted* to be conscious right then.

Suddenly, Marcus rolled over and scooted back, blocking her body completely just as the noise of boots on concrete came close to their hiding spot.

She couldn't see it, but she could feel it – she knew that someone was crouching down, looking under the stage. She bit the insides of her cheeks and breathed through her nose, trying desperately not to throw up in Marcus' hair.

"Queen Quinn? Sir Marcus?"

Just enough of the heavy tension flowed out of the taut lines in Marcus' neck to ease her panic.

"They're from Eirentheos," he whispered.

The condition of the castle would have alarmed William if he'd been able to concentrate on anything except following Marcus through the corridors as quickly as possible.

Entire hallways had been burned out, stones were missing, and none of the carpets seemed to be left. They finally ended up in a guest wing that, to William's knowledge, hadn't seen much use in decades.

There were guards everywhere, most of them in the purple of his father's kingdom, but a few in green whom he knew and trusted.

Many more guards roamed the other parts of the castle, methodically arresting and removing every single person who'd been here when they entered. This section had already been thoroughly cleared.

Marcus stopped in front of the door to an apartment near the end of the hallway.

William gave him a last questioning look.

"Just go see her," his father said quietly in his ear. Then he handed Samuel to William as Marcus opened the door.

Maxwell stood up from one of the couches as William entered, and after a second, Thomas stood from the floor where he'd been sitting next to... "Quinn!" William couldn't keep himself from shouting and running over to her.

"Oh, Will..." she breathed, struggling to sit up at the end of the couch.

"Don't love," he said, pressing gently on her shoulder.

A second later, she couldn't have gotten up anyway, because Samuel screeched and launched himself toward her, nearly falling out of William's arms.

"Are you okay if he...?" William asked, over their son's insistent fussing.

"Yes. I *need* him." She held out her arms, starting to pull herself up again.

Quickly, before Samuel or Quinn took it upon themselves to hasten the reunion, he settled the baby in next to her, and then sat down right there on the floor where he could be with them both.

"Oh, that's better," she said, cradling her arms around Samuel. "Hi, baby." She kissed his head and his hands and his cheeks. "I missed you so much. Thank you for taking care of your daddy for me."

They were alone in the room. Everyone had apparently decided to give them time.

"Wish I'd been there to take care of *you*." He lifted his fingers carefully toward the bandage on the side of Quinn's forehead. Even at his light touch, her whole face tightened.

"It was an accident," she whispered. "Marcus was just trying to get me out of there."

"I know. He feels terrible. Has a healer looked at it yet?"

She shook her head. "Thomas cleaned it up a little and put the bandage on, but he wanted to leave it for you or Nathaniel. There are enough injured guards out there to keep all of our healers busy."

He kissed the back of her hand. "I was so worried."

"Me too. Where were you?"

He told her about the trap door in the back of the safe house, and about the tunnel and the cave.

"Wow. How many secret passages do you think there are in this kingdom?"

He rolled his eyes. "Probably a lot, but I would prefer to never go in one, ever again. Especially with a pregnant woman."

Her eyes widened and he realized she didn't know. "Linnea's in labor?"

"She was."

"What? How is she? Where is she? How's the baby?"

"Linnea is good. She wasn't up for racing here on horseback like me, but she's fine. She'll be here soon. Nathaniel and Mia and Zander stayed with her to bring her in a carriage – with the babies."

"Bab*ies*?"

"Twins. A little boy and a little girl. They're perfect. Well," he leaned forward and kissed Samuel's dirty, sweaty hair, "maybe not as perfect as him, but, I think we'll keep them here and love them anyway."

"I think we can manage that." Her grin was huge, despite the fact that it obviously hurt to move the muscles in her face.

He smiled and leaned forward to kiss her softly on the lips. When he was finished, he kept his face close to hers, tucking a loose strand of auburn hair back behind her ear, breathing her in.

"I'm a disaster," she whispered.

"Not to me."

"Even if I bleed all over you?"

He scoffed. "You wouldn't even be the first person today, love. Speaking of this, though," he ran his finger lightly over the edge of the bandage, lifting it to peek at the ugly, bruised cut underneath, "do you want me to patch it up, or wait for Nathaniel and I'll distract you while he works?"

"I can handle it. Right now, I just want you."

Before he stood, he kissed the uninjured part of her forehead. "You've got me."

He was afraid he'd have to leave her for a moment to go and find his bag, but before he was halfway to the door, he spotted his medical bag sitting on an end table. Seeing it made his eyes a little watery; they had so many people to be grateful for.

Samuel was nearly asleep, his whole little body curled into his mother's side as if he wanted to attach himself there, under her skin so she'd never be separated from him again. William didn't blame him. He grabbed another blanket and laid it over both of them, kissing the baby's head again before he looked back at Quinn.

"So tell me what happened. I know Thomas killed Tolliver – wish I'd been there to see that."

"I'm glad you weren't. I kept telling myself I was willing to fight however I needed to, but I really thought we were all going to die." Her lip trembled a little. He leaned forward and kissed it again before turning his attention to his bag.

"But you didn't. Everyone is safe. Where was Sophia in all of this?"

He nearly dropped and broke the syringe he was filling when she told him about Sophia giving her the dagger. "Where is she now?"

"She's in a cell. Hopefully the same one she stuck me in earlier. She'd better hope that if and when Jonathan ever decides to show up that he has a good explanation for that, or I'm going to leave her there."

"You don't think she meant to save your life when she gave you that dagger?"

"I don't know what she meant. I'm grateful she did it, but I don't trust her motivations… and even if I thought it was true, it's not an excuse. There are ways to do things, there are ways to treat people. She's my grandmother. If she can't support me as queen until after I win a public death match against her son, then she doesn't deserve… I don't know, Will. I'll see what she has to say once things calm down, but don't plan on seeing her at the dinner table on a regular basis."

"Now *that* I don't think I can argue with."

# THE WINDOW SEAT

*HE KNEW HE WAS dreaming, but he couldn't wake himself from it even so. Not that he was especially trying to; really he was so glad to see the little boy in front of him that he wasn't in any hurry to wake back to a different reality.*

"How is Quinn?" Owen asked.

"You haven't been visiting her in her dreams yourself?"

"Not lately. It makes me miss her too much if I do it all the time, and I think it makes it harder for her, too."

"But you don't think it's hard for me, to see you but not be able to touch you?"

Owen took three steps forward, closing the space between them and setting his warm little hand on Zander's face. "I think it's already harder for you, Zander. You don't own the choice the way she does. You're already still half here and half there."

He closed his eyes. "Just because she chose doesn't mean she doesn't miss you."

"I know. But it does mean she can let go of here enough to get both her arms around her life there – her family there. And being whole is always easier than being ripped in two, even if some of the pieces are held together with tape."

"How can I not be ripped in two when my family doesn't even know what happened to me? They must think... What did your mother tell them?"

"She didn't know what to tell them, Zander. She tried, but there wasn't a good answer. At first they thought you must have gotten on a plane and gone to where Quinn was, and they demanded to know where she was – they still kind of think that, but the police won't help them because you're eighteen, and there's no evidence anything bad happened. They were a little freaked out about the money, though."

"Do they think I'm dead?"

"I told them you're not. That you're okay, and that you love them, and that they'll hear from you sometime. I don't know if they believed me, but even your dad stopped being angry, eventually. He cried. Is there a message you want me to give them?"

"My dad cried?"

"Yes. He loves you Zander. He thought it was his fault for pushing you too hard, that you maybe ran away because you didn't want to go into business with him, but I told him that wasn't true."

"Do you still see my parents?"

"No. We moved to Georgia now. But I can call them."

He sighed. "You don't need to do that, but if you talk to them, tell them that I love them."

"I will."

"Do you... still have the magnet that opens the gate?"

"No. Alvin helped me smash it and then he took the pieces with him. It's broken."

"So what do I do, Owen?"

"Live, Zander. You tape the pieces together and live. And then if we ever do find another gate, you'll at least be able to make a choice as a whole person. Maybe you'll even know what you want."

"How do you know so much, Owen?" He reached over to tousle the boy's hair; it felt silky soft and oh-so-real.

"I don't know more than anyone else, I just see different things sometimes. I see you."

"I love you, you know."

"I know. I love you, too. Will you give Quinn a hug for me? And Samuel, and William – and everyone?"

"Sure."

"Seriously, Addie? Right now? You had to wait until your mother was in the bath?" Zander looked down at the baby girl nestled against his chest.

She looked back at him with her blue eyes and drooled.

He sighed. "I know, I know. It's better now than once you're in your dress for the party." Linnea would be happy to avoid a repeat of what had happened two days ago at the twins' Naming Ceremony.

Reaching inside the cloth wrap tied around him, he extricated the infant and set her on his bed next to a diaper bag.

Though that diaper bag had sat on the side of his bed for days now, it was filled with fresh diapers. Even with the entire Rose family here this week for her to look after, Mia managed to keep up with even those small things.

"Mia is magic," he told Adeline. "But I'm not sure why she thinks diapers *belong* in my room."

The baby gurgled.

"Oh be quiet," he said, negating his words by kissing her toes. "You might look like your father, but you have your mother's mouth already."

She pursed her tiny lips together for a second before poking her tongue out between them.

"*That's* the thanks I get for giving you a clean diaper?" He scooped her back into his arms. "Should we go and find your dress since you're already out of your pajamas now?"

His question was interrupted by a tapping on his open door, and he looked up to see Stephen standing there.

"Is my granddaughter giving you a hard time?"

Zander shrugged and grinned. "Isn't that what girls are supposed to do?"

Stephen laughed, stepping into the room and holding out his arms. "Give her to me. Charlotte has the dress for her. We'll finish getting her ready. Where's Ben?"

"Thomas took Ben and I took this one so Linnea could have a bath and a little time to herself to get ready."

"That was kind of you," Stephen said as he lifted the baby into his arms. "Thank you for taking such good care of her."

Something in Stephen's voice made Zander think he wasn't referring to Adeline. He decided to ignore that, though, and shrugged. "It's not a problem. I don't need as much time to get ready as Linnea does."

Stephen apparently decided to let him get away with it. He looked around the room. "How are you settling back in?"

Zander couldn't help chortling as he glanced around at the mess. They were all temporarily living in a mostly-unused guest wing of the castle while their old rooms underwent massive repairs from the damage of fire and battle. Zander's room had long been used for storage.

Although the area with his bed and a dresser and two small tables had been cleared for him to use, even Mia hadn't been able to make much headway with the old crates and trunks and furniture piled in the rest. Especially when she'd been dealing with three infants even before Stephen's family arrived less than a week after the battle with Tolliver.

There hadn't been much time for him to tackle the job, either. There had been the Naming Ceremony for the twins already, and today they were celebrating the rededication of Quinn as queen of Philotheum.

Mostly, though, he'd been helping with the repair work on the main living wing, and also just enjoying spending time with Stephen and Charlotte and their family.

It had taken him a full week after their arrival to understand why being with them felt *so different* now. For the first time since his arrival in this world, the kingdoms were at peace. There was no danger, no major medical emergencies, no looking over their shoulders at every noise.

In the absence of all these things – or maybe because he'd *gone* through those things with them and made it out on the other side – he realized he really did like these people, and even this place, burned-down walls, cold well water and all.

"I'm doing okay…" He paused, suddenly terrified to say the next part, although it had been on his mind for a while now. "I'm not sure I'll stick with the whole guard thing forever."

The terror was all for nothing. Stephen shrugged. "I don't think I ever thought you would. There are a lot of other ways I could see you finding your place here in Philotheum, now that you've gotten your footing. But I'll forever be grateful for your service to both kingdoms during the war."

"Do you think Quinn will be upset?"

"Not even a little. You'd still be Sir Zander, you know. With any luck she'll need more advisors for building her kingdom than battling with it."

"Advise her on what, exactly?"

"I don't know. You've had some excellent ideas lately during the renovations we've made to the castle, for example, though I think I've already used my quota for pushing you in a certain direction. You're a smart, resourceful, *good* young man. You've earned the right to make those choices for yourself. Maybe your friend over there has more ideas for you."

"What?" Zander turned to look where Stephen was pointing, and he had to laugh. Larya was perched on the wide sill outside his window, beak against the glass, though she didn't start tapping until Zander was looking at her. "She's spoiled."

"She deserves it… Speaking of ladies who deserve to be spoiled, though, I'm going to take this darling baby and get her ready for the party. I'll see you there?"

"Yes."

After Stephen left he climbed up on the window seat and opened the window to feed the bird treats and talk to her.

She was a good listener; he often found himself chatting with her as if she could give him real advice. Sometimes she came in, and he could sit down on the wooden seat with her in front of him. Today, though, she seemed to be enjoying the unusually sunny day and declined the invite, so after a few minutes of kneeling on the hard surface, his knees started hurting.

"All right, if you're not going to come in, you need to shoo," he said, though he didn't close the window and she didn't leave.

One of his legs had fallen asleep, and he had trouble dragging it off the window seat; he ended up kicking the wall hard enough to make a sound that startled Larya, and she finally flew off.

He stood there, stomping his foot for a minute trying to restore the blood flow until something dawned on him.

The seat under the window would have to be hollow to make a sound that loud.

William might have been entirely over secret passages and compartments, but Zander wasn't. He started running his fingers over the top and side of the built-in box.

Once he was looking, he found it quickly, a small, carved-out notch just big enough to put his finger against and pull.

The compartment clearly hadn't been opened in a long time; it was challenging, but it slid open without too much effort.

The biggest problem was the dust; Zander coughed as a cloud of it hit him in the face.

It wasn't as exciting as he might have hoped. The first thing he pulled out was a long cushion that once probably fit the window seat perfectly, but was now so disgusting that he had to stop himself from launching it out the window immediately. Of course, doing that would have likely covered him in dust.

The rest of the items in the cabinet weren't much different from the junk that filled half his room already. He threw them on the piles of stuff to be sorted later – the cupboard might at least be nice storage for his things while he was staying in this room.

He'd cleared nearly everything from the space and was reaching in to do a final check when his fingers brushed against the crinkle of what felt like paper. He didn't know why, but he held his breath as he carefully pulled it out.

It was paper, several sheets of it folded together, all of them with a tattered edge that suggested they'd been ripped out of a book or something.

He didn't know how old they were, so he was extra gentle as he unfolded them, trying not to rip or crumble the sheets.

The writing on the first two sheets was strange. He could read the words, but none of them made any sense to him; it was possibly a ledger book from some kind of goods trading.

The next paper, though, had a drawing – a remarkably detailed drawing of a grove of trees by a river, one of the low mountains of this world rising in the background. Above the drawing were numbers written out in a format he recognized – they were map coordinates, although not a complete set.

The rest of the papers made little sense to him either – he'd have to show them to William or Thomas later, maybe they'd have an idea.

He was just setting the papers down on the top of one of the storage crates on the other side of his room when he was interrupted by the sound of someone clearing her throat.

"Oh, hey, Linnea," he said, looking toward the door.

"Um, where's my daughter?"

"Oh… uh…" He affected a panicked expression and pretended to look all over the room. "She was just here."

"Zander!"

"Okay, sorry. Your father came and took her. She's fine."

"That's not funny."

*Oops.* "I know. I'm sorry. I hoped you knew by now that I would never put her at any kind of risk, though."

"Speaking as someone who's been kidnapped from my own home…" She wasn't joking. He'd crossed a line.

His whole body felt like it was folding in on itself. "Linnea…" He walked over to her. "I'm sorry. I didn't think about it."

She shook her head. "No, I'm sorry. I don't know why I'm so sensitive lately."

"Don't do that. Seriously. It was a stupid thing for me to say to a new mom who has a legitimate reason to worry. But in the future, just know that if you trust me to watch your child, and you come in here and I'm not dead on the floor – the baby is safe, okay?"

She nodded. "Thank you for watching her for me." Her voice was too small, betraying that she still felt bad for her reaction.

"Come here, Nay." He held out his arms to her and she obliged, whether because she really wanted to or because it would be easier to hide her emotions he didn't know, but he held her tight and let her pull herself back together. "I'll think before I speak next time, okay?"

Her head moved up and down against his shoulder. "It feels stupid that you have to," she mumbled.

"Some of the things you've been through change the ordinary definition of stupid, sweetheart. It's not like I never require patience from anyone." He wasn't as touchy about kidnappings as she was, but there had been meetings about executing war prisoners he'd had to step out of. And some of his dreams…

She reached for his hand and squeezed it.

He didn't mean to kiss her forehead; it just happened, like a reflex he had no control over.

There was no time to regret it, though. In the next instant she turned her face up to his and put her arms around his neck, pulling him down toward her until their lips touched.

It wasn't like fireworks – sparks that might brilliantly illuminate the sky for a moment, but then fizzle into darkness, needing a new flame to ignite them every time. This was like the tide – strong, powerful, and inevitable washing over them both; eroding some part of who he had been and exposing something new underneath.

A long time – possibly days – passed before either of them could finally pull away.

"Wow," he breathed.

# CELEBRATION

THOMAS SNEAKED UP BEHIND Mia and cleared his throat. She jumped, nearly dropping Sarah, and turned around to give him a death glare – and a nice left hook to his shoulder.

"Hey!" he said. "I'm not the one who's *working* when Quinn specifically gave you the rest of the day off."

"Who's working?" She kissed Sarah on the nose. "I'm just enjoying a party with one of my favorite people. "It's beautiful, isn't it?"

It was beautiful. The massive ballroom in the center of the castle was the one space Tolliver had managed to restore. Although Quinn had made a few choice comments about the obvious order of his priorities, she'd decided not to turn her nose up at the opportunity to use the room – with some quick alterations and new decorations, of course.

Thomas wasn't terribly interested in the beauty of the castle right now, though. "If you'd let her go play, I know someone else who wouldn't mind a few of your kisses."

"And who is that?" Mia teased, but she planted another kiss on the toddler's head and then set her down.

Grinning, he wrapped his arms around her waist and pulled her close, kissing each of her freckled cheeks and then her nose.

"You're in a good mood," she said, running her index finger through the hair just above his ear, sending shivers all the way down him. She giggled, and this time he kissed her on the mouth.

"What's not to be in a good mood about? The war is over, the kingdoms are safe, my family is here, there are new babies… you're here with me."

There it was – the warm spread of pink across her cheeks that always made his heart beat faster. "Did you see Zander over there, staying within six inches of your sister?" she asked.

"Yes, I did. It's another reason I'm happy. I also see you, changing the subject away from yourself as usual."

She rolled her eyes. "There's no interesting news about me tonight."

"You don't think so?"

"Do you know something I don't?"

"Yes, actually."

Both of her eyebrows went up, and the pink grew darker, which made it even more fun. "And what do you know, Thomas?"

"That I'm planning on proposing to you later tonight."

The pink flowed out, replaced with white for a full twenty seconds before color rushed in again – this time a deep, dark scarlet. "Excuse me?"

He grinned. "I thought I would warn you first, to give you time to decide how you're going to answer."

"You think I need time to decide?"

"Well, I hope not. I wouldn't ask if I wasn't *almost* sure, but it seemed only fair to prepare you."

"Thomas John Rose…"

"Yes, Amelia Louise Willoughby?"

"You're impossible."

"Yes, I am. So will you marry me … after I propose to you later?"

"I'll think about it – I'll get back to you then."

He laughed. "I love you, Mia." He kissed her again, first on the nose, and then long and slow on her lips.

They finished just as horns began to sound, announcing the impending entrance of Quinn, William and Samuel. He wrapped his arms around Mia's waist as they turned to watch.

"Sophia looks so pleased," Mia said, twisting up to give Thomas a sardonic look.

"Hard to say if that's because of Quinn, or because Tobias is a guest of honor. She should probably just be glad she's at the party."

"Yes, with Jonathan baby-sitting her."

"I think it's fair. If Sophia does whatever serves her own interests best, then there's no reason Quinn shouldn't do the same with her. Quinn could have done much worse than stripping her titles and keeping her under supervision away from the castle."

Mia chuckled. "I wasn't disagreeing. I'm happy she gave Quinn that dagger, but she did too much to cause the problem in the first place. It was Quinn's own forces who shot those arrows and charged the stage – not Sophia's. It's a little unfair to make Jonathan watch her, though."

He shrugged. "Jonathan does his own thing. She didn't make him – nobody can make him do anything, I don't think. He believes she wasn't involved in the attack and abduction at Wellham, and maybe she wasn't, so he's being gracious, I guess."

"She is his mother."

"Yes, she is."

"And she did just lose another one of her sons."

There wasn't time to respond before the main doors opened, revealing Quinn and William, so he just nodded into Mia's hair. He couldn't be sorry that Tolliver was gone, but he supposed he could muster some sympathy for the man's mother. A little, anyway. So long as he didn't have to deal with her much.

The crowd was quiet as Quinn and William walked down the green carpet in the center of the floor, all the way up the steps of a stage. She was resplendent in her green gown, her auburn curls flowing around the delicate gold and green crown on her head.

William held Samuel; he was a tiny, chubby clone of his father in his matching fur-trimmed green velvet cape. Both of them kept their eyes on Quinn as she stepped forward, the shining adoration from them shouting that no matter how much her people loved her, they could never match the devotion of her family.

Thomas pulled Mia closer.

"Amazing, isn't she?" A voice said, close to Thomas' ear.

He nearly let go of Mia as he spun to look.

Alvin grinned, and Thomas settled back in with Mia to watch.

At Quinn's coronation, she had seemed so young and nervous and unsure of herself. Actually – Thomas knew – it had been more than just "seemed". She'd been a newlywed and was pregnant, and had no idea what she was doing.

There was no trace of any of that now. The young woman who stepped to the front of the stage to address her people was smiling and confident, her voice strong and clear.

A few feet from where he and Mia stood, he could see his parents both grinning widely as they held each other close.

"Thank you all so much for coming," Quinn said. "Tonight we celebrate the end of the war with Dovelnia and the beginning of peace in our kingdom."

She waited for the cheers to die down before she continued. "We are also celebrating the reunification of our kingdom to our brothers and sisters of Eirentheos. As of today, nearly all of the borders are open and citizens of both kingdoms are free to travel, emigrate, and trade between the kingdoms however they wish."

This, too, drew much cheering.

"I personally would like to extend my deepest gratitude to the king of Eirentheos – my dear father-in-law, King Stephen, for his unending support and provision of troops to help Philotheum in our time of need."

Thomas' father blew a kiss toward her and then bowed his head.

Quinn cleared her throat. "I have learned many things in my short time as queen of Philotheum. While it would be my wish to share only happy news this evening, I feel it is important to be honest with you all about the more difficult realities that follow a war."

Thomas saw her chest rise and fall sharply. William took a small step closer to her, but he didn't interfere – letting her stand on her own. "I intend to see Philotheum fully rebuilt and rise to become the strong, powerful, and gracious kingdom it was always meant to be. All citizens of Philotheum who wish to share in that dream will be welcomed, and provided and cared for.

"However, I have outgrown any patience I once had for those who wish to undermine those goals, or would work to sabotage the prosperity and safety of the citizens of this kingdom or our alliance with Eirentheos."

This time, the crowd was quiet.

"I will extend a one-time offer to those here who disagree with me, or with those goals. You may, in the next ten days, cross the border into Dovelnia if their beliefs are more in line with yours. Be advised that it will be a one-way trip. For the indefinite future, no person may cross the Dovelnian border coming toward Philotheum for any reason without express consent from me personally.

"Over the coming moons, my advisors and the captains of my guard will be conducting a thorough investigation in every town and village to uncover every person who assisted the Dovelnian army, or who funded their efforts, or who has harmed any loyal citizen or their property in any way. Those who have committed crimes will be punished for them, and all titles and property will be stripped from anyone who is found to have committed treason. I don't expect for every citizen to agree with every decision I make, and I am open to cooperative discussion, but I will not tolerate any sort of abuse of my people any longer. The crown has been restored to its rightful place, and here it will stay, on my head until it is time for Prince Samuel to wear it. I intend to wear it well, and to defend it as necessary."

Now the cheering was so loud, and went on for so long, that Quinn had to wait for several minutes before she could speak again.

"Enough with the not-so-fun news. It's time to celebrate. Please enjoy the wonderful dinner and dance and play with your loved ones. I know I will be with mine." She reached behind her for William's hand, and he took it and stepped forward, planting a chaste kiss on her lips before the two of them held their hands in the air together.

Even Samuel lifted his arms up as the people cheered their queen.

# ACKNOWLEDGEMENTS

Writing this series has been an amazingly fun and heartening undertaking. The best part of it has been meeting all of the amazing readers who have shared the journey, and have sent me notes, and made me smile when opening my inbox. It means more than you could possibly know.

I also have to give some very sincere thanks to some of the special beta readers and others without whom these books would not be what they are. Thank you SO much for your willingness to question things and push the direction of the characters and the storyline. (These are in NO particular order!)

*Janene Silvers*
*Michelle Patrick*
*Kristy K. James*
*Mallory Rock*
*Jennifer Simmons*
*Lori Dees*
*Linda Jarrett*
*Kathie Juliano*
*Brett Jonas*
*Lisa Pottgen*
*Angie Taylor*
*Kathi McBride*
*Melissa Goodwin*
*Jennifer Severino*
*Alicia Cutler*
*Terri Nesvacil*
*Abigail Rose*

*And a special mention to my friend, Steve Brownlee, who added a fun touch to the voice of Zander by providing the scene with the dog and the peanut butter, and encouraged me the times I thought I was stuck (though most readers will be glad I didn't take any of his story suggestions at those times to heart.*

# OTHER BOOKS BY BREEANA PUTTROFF

*The Dusk Gate Chronicles*
*The continued adventures of the Rose family in*
*Eirentheos and Philotheum*

*Rumpelstiltskin's Daughter*
*A new take on an old fairy tale*

*COMING SOON*
*The Gatekeepers*
*An all-new adventure featuring some familiar characters*

*Visit www.BreeanaPuttroff.net to find out more!*